THE TRUTH KEEPS SILENT

THE TRUTH KEEPS SILENT

TRUTH & LIES DUET, BOOK ONE

A.V. ASHER

WINTER ZEPHYR PRESS

ISBN:
Paperback: 978-1-7365439-1-7
Ebook: 978-1-7365439-0-0

Cover design: Damonza.com
Editing: Salt and Sage Books

NOTE FROM THE AUTHOR

The Truth Keeps Silent is the first book in my Truth & Lies duet. There was just too much story to tell! Mercedes and Alec will return in *The Lies that Shatter*, which will be released in the Autumn of 2021.

Content warning: This book is intended for a mature audience and contains strong language, explicit sex and graphic descriptions of violence which some readers may find disturbing. Reader discretion is advised.

Domestic violence can affect anyone. People of all races, genders, economic status and education levels can be impacted.
If you or someone you love is a victim of abuse, please call the National Domestic Abuse Hotline.
You are not alone.

USA - 1.800.799.7233
Canada- 1.866.863.0511
UK- 0808 2000 247
Australia -1800 737 732

When money speaks, the truth keeps silent.

— RUSSIAN PROVERB

PART I

CHAPTER ONE

Working at a coffeehouse wasn't what Mercedes Elliott had in mind when she moved to the other side of the world. She could have gone her entire life without knowing how to decorate foamy drinks.

She feathered the last bit of steamed milk into an elaborate Rosetta design atop rich espresso.

The customer smiled. "Ooh, beautiful. Well done."

"Thanks." She slid the drink across the counter.

She had to admit, though, that Capulus & Vinum was a lovely place to work. Coffee shop by day, wine and music bar by night, it brought in tourists, college kids, and the booming artistic community. The steady pace kept her from dwelling on the train wreck that was her life, at least for a few hours a day.

She wished it paid more. London was expensive. Not that San Francisco was any better.

"Hey Sadie, are you able to pull a double?" her boss, Jackie, called. "The switch over this evening is shorthanded. You free?"

Mercedes hesitated. Jason didn't like her to work so late, but her dwindling bank account was screaming for some love.

"I can. Do you need me until closing?" She dumped out the used espresso grounds.

"That would be fantastic, Sadie. Thank you." Jackie rang up the customer in front of her "Coffee is slowing down. Why don't you finish up and take a break for a few hours? Come back at six?"

"Do you mind if I hang out upstairs in the office? I'd like to call my sister."

"Of course. See you later this afternoon."

MERCEDES CLIMBED THE NARROW STAIRS TO THE SMALL OFFICE. She sat in the swivel chair, sweeping aside a pile of receipts and papers. Using the office phone, she dialed Charlotte's number. Mercedes let it ring twice, then hung up.

She hated resorting to these tactics to speak with her own sister, but she didn't want to deal with a meltdown from Jason when he checked her phone.

The phone rang, and Mercedes picked up on the first ring.

"Cap and Vin, this is Mercedes. How may I help you?"

"Good morning, sunshine," Charlotte's voice chimed through the phone, her American accent making Mercedes ache for home.

"Hello, love. How ya doing this fine morn?"

"Amazing. I saw a guy in a thousand-dollar business suit leaving a hotel with no shoes on, clearly still drunk off his ass."

"Not bad. Did he at least have socks on?"

"Nope, bare feet, walking down Valencia Avenue." Charlotte laughed. "How is the job hunt going?"

Mercedes straightened a pile of receipts on the desk and sighed. "Eh. Nothing from the latest round of resumes. I've called on a few but got the runaround."

"I'm sorry."

Mercedes grunted a response and thrummed her fingers

along the edge of the desk. "Maybe I should look at smaller practices outside downtown London. I must be aiming too high if I can't even get a meeting."

"You could look outside London altogether? Maybe they need an experienced corporate attorney in Manchester or Birmingham. Or Edinburgh. You loved Scotland when we were there for my wedding."

The reminder of Scotland made Mercedes's heart skip. "What would I do with Jason if I moved to Scotland?"

"Leave him in London," Charlotte muttered.

"Be nice, Charlie," Mercedes said, massaging her brow.

"Hmm. You could try the Bay Area again. San Jose or Marin? Or even go as far as Monterey?"

"I already did. I don't think anyone in California will work with me." A familiar pang ran through her heart. "Besides, I moved here to start over. I feel like I need to give it more time."

"Have you called him?"

A stagnant pause held the question in the air.

"No."

Charlotte sighed. "Why not? You know he'd help you."

"But I don't know that. We haven't spoken in three years. He's made it clear we aren't friends."

"Did he say that to you?"

Mercedes raised her eyebrows. "He's said *nothing* to me. Besides, I don't love the idea of asking a man who ghosted me for help."

"It's called networking, Sadie," Charlotte quipped.

"It sucks, Charlie," Mercedes shot back.

"I know. But it's an avenue you haven't played. He asked Luke how you were doing. A year or so ago."

"Oh really? A whole year ago? What'd Luke tell him?"

"He told him you were doing well. At least we thought so at the time." The remark had an edge to it, which Mercedes ignored.

"He ever explain himself?"

"No. But you know how Luke is with details. He hates to pry, so he didn't ask questions."

"Mm-hmm."

"Look, I get it. It's shitty. But honestly, you kinda need to suck it up," Charlotte said. "Otherwise, you're gonna have to ask Jason for tampon money every damn month."

Apprehension ran through her.

"If Jason found out . . ."

Charlotte scoffed. "The fact you're worried is a problem." Mercedes closed her eyes against the truth in her sister's words. "Don't tell him. Make the call from the coffee shop. The same way you have to call me," Charlotte added, a bite in her words.

Mercedes flinched. Charlotte was never one to hold back truth bombs when she saw the need. But she also lived in a very different reality. Charlotte's husband Luke would never deny Charlotte the right to call whoever she wanted, whenever she wanted.

"What if he tells me to piss off?"

"What if he does?"

"Easy for you to say."

Charlotte sighed. "I'm just saying, you've had to run through a whirlpool of shit to get even a fraction of what you've accomplished. It's one phone call to someone you used to know. The worst thing that happens is he tells you no. The best outcome is he tries to help you make a connection that can truly help you start over."

Mercedes didn't answer, her mind working through the minefield her sister was asking her to maneuver.

"Damn it, Sadie! I'm the one who freaks out about shit like this, not you."

Mercedes sighed, pinching the bridge of her nose. "I'll think about it. I better go. Give Luke my love."

"Give Alec mine." Charlotte snickered.

Mercedes groaned. "I hate you."

"I love you too, sister. Let me know how it goes." Charlotte was giggling as she hung up the phone.

Charlotte was right. There wasn't a reason to keep delaying. If there was any hope of connecting with the legal world here in London, she'd have to do more than send resumes to dead emails. Mercedes needed someone who could make introductions and open doors.

She opened her phone and searched her contacts. Her heart gave a little jump as she read his name at the top of the list.

Alec McKinley.

Damn.

Would he answer a call from her?

Not likely.

What should she say to him?

Hey, I know you blew me off years ago, but I totally have enough self-respect to beg you to find me a job right now.

Ugh.

She dialed his number on the office phone. While it rang, Mercedes took a steadying breath, trying to slow her heart.

God, this is humiliating.

Then she heard Alec's voice for the first time in three years. His Scottish accent sent a hum of warmth through her as he welcomed the caller to leave a message. She had the absurd thought that she was glad he had gone back to this recording. For a while, he used one of those generic voicemail greetings that sounded like a robot. She hated those.

Her scattered brain was so busy thinking about the greeting that she was surprised when the tone sounded.

"Hi Alec, this is Sadie. Um, Mercedes Elliott? It's been a while, and I . . . well, I hope you're doing well. I was calling because I recently moved to London and was hoping you might know someone in the city that's looking for an American corporate attorney. I know it's out of the blue. I hope that's okay. If you would, please call me at this number. It's the number for the coffeehouse I'm working at, so you might have to leave a message. I'll get back to you as soon as I can. Thanks. I look forward to speaking with you."

She gave the number for Cap & Vin and hung the phone up with a huge exhale. Not too bad, really. No major fumbles. It could have been so much worse.

As she typed out a text to Jason, Mercedes told herself her fingers were trembling because she'd had to call Alec. She was grateful she didn't have to tell Jason about the extra shift over the phone. He wasn't likely to be happy about it.

Maybe she should stick around the office to see if Alec would call back. It only took her a beat to decide he wasn't likely to call at all, so she wasn't going to wait around for him. She'd made that mistake before.

She looked at her watch. She'd have plenty of time to snag something at the deli next door and head to a park to eat.

Mercedes was about to head downstairs when the ring of the phone on Jackie's desk stopped her.

CHAPTER TWO

Alec McKinley held back a gag as he took a gulp of the vile green mixture his assistant, Mrs. Downey, had given him. He couldn't stop his face from grimacing at the taste. And the texture.

Christ, why was it slimy and *chunky?*

"Alright, down the hatch it went. Can I have my file now?" He held his hand out, putting on a smile he hoped would charm her.

She narrowed her eyes.

Damn. "I drank your green . . . uh, drink. Time to hold up your end of the bargain."

"Oh, all right then. You'll feel so much better after drinking it. It has all sorts of nutrients your body needs." She handed Alec the file and followed him as he strode to his office. "It doesn't taste bad for something that's so good for you, right?"

"Aye, like lawn clippings in jelly." With his eyes on the file, he grabbed the water bottle off the desk, flipped open the lid, and took a mouthful to wash away the chunky wheatgrass. "Anyone else you can accost with the green slime, or am I your only victim?"

"I got Mariah too. She was the one who suggested I bring orange slices. She says it makes it go down better. I'll be bringing those with me tomorrow."

"Looking forward to it." His cell phone buzzed, and he glanced at it. It wasn't a number he knew, so he let it go to voicemail.

"Hmph." Eyeing him, she picked up both the empty shot glass and his water bottle from his desk. Alec smiled as she pattered down the hall.

Mrs. Downey was a treasure. Most of the time, he indulged her fussing. She reminded him of an Irish version of his mum.

He thumbed through the case file and began to read the report his cousin, Declan, had written up on his most recent case. The assignment had gone smoothly, and there was a good chance their client would refer his wealthy German friends.

Since starting McKinley Security and Risk Management with Declan four and half years ago, Alec had been proud of the company's reputation and growth. They'd started as a team of five. Now they had operatives throughout the UK and Ireland.

Mrs. Downey returned with his refreshed water bottle and a small plate with three shortbread biscuits on it.

He quirked an eyebrow at her. "I thought we were going for health food this week?"

"Oh, don't I know it. But I know you love shortbread, so I thought I'd bring a few before you leave."

He flashed an appreciative smile. "Thank you. It'll hold me over until I get home."

"Anytime, lad. Mariah already left, and I'm heading out to an appointment. I'll see you tomorrow?"

"Aye, tomorrow then."

Alec picked up his phone and opened his voice mailbox.

Selecting the unheard voicemail at the top, he put the call on speaker and sat back in his chair with a sigh.

He had just taken a bite when her voice came across the line. His heart stopped.

It was timid and strained, but he recognized it right away. *Sadie Elliott.*

He listened to the rest of the message, frozen in his seat. *Did she say she had moved to London?*

He played it again. He'd heard it right the first time. She needed a job? What the hell happened in San Francisco?

Alec jotted down the number and sat back in his chair. The Cap & Vin was only a few streets away. How long had she been this close? It had been almost three years since he had last spoken to her.

He dialed the number. He had only given brief thought to what he might say when a soft American voice answered, "Cap & Vin, this is Mercedes. How may I help you?"

Alec paused, his heart racing. He wasn't sure if it was from anticipation or nerves. "Hey Sadie, it's Alec McKinley, giving you a ring back."

MERCEDES BIT HER LIP AT THE SOUND OF HIS VOICE, TINGED with the light Scottish burr she'd always found so charming.

"Hi. Wow, thanks for calling me back so quickly. I know it's been a while." Mercedes winced. Maybe she shouldn't remind him of that.

"Oh aye, for sure," Alec said. "How have you been?"

Oh, well, my life's collapsed into an utter shitshow, and now I need to call up men who didn't want me and beg for help.

But she forced a smile into her voice. "I'm good. Had a few unexpected changes in the last few months, but, you know, I'm adjusting. How about you? How's your security company?"

"It's going well, actually. We're moving into Europe, which will bring a wider variety of clientele. I now have forty full-time security personnel." The pride in his voice was unmistakable.

"That's amazing. Congratulations."

"Thank you." He cleared his throat. "I have to admit, it surprised me when you said you're in London. What brings you here?"

"Oh, well, it's a long story." Mercedes laughed. "I've been here about six months, and I recently completed the requirements to practice here, so I'm ready to go. I've submitted my resume to every place I can think of, but I keep striking out. So, I thought I'd call you and see if you knew of businesses or practices that might be in the market for an American corporate attorney."

"It's possible, though I'm having a hard time thinking of any names off the top of my head. We've a lot of business associates who might be looking for someone. I can put a list together for you."

"Oh, that would be so helpful, Alec. Thank you." Her heart wouldn't stop hammering in her chest.

"Of course. Always happy to help a friend."

Was she a friend? There was a slight lull in the conversation, and she sensed he was searching for something to say.

"What are your plans tomorrow afternoon?" she blurted. When he didn't say anything, she rushed on. "I mean . . . maybe you can come by the coffee shop after I get off work, and we could catch up?"

Holy God, what are you doing?

No help for it though, he'd think her nuts if she rescinded the offer. Maybe he'd decline.

"I actually don't have any plans set for tomorrow. I mean, I have things to do, but I can do them anytime. I'm heading out of town for work, so I gave myself tomorrow off to take care of a few things."

"Perfect. I work at Cap & Vin. It's a little coffee and wine bar in Kensington."

"Oh aye, I know the place. It's close to my office."

"Really?" She hadn't known he had been so close.

"I'll bring the list with me."

"Thanks again. I really appreciate it." Her heart was lighter than it had been in months.

"It's no trouble. I look forward to seeing you again. It's been a long time."

Her breath caught. Did he ever think about her? "Me too. It's been much too long. Goodnight, Alec."

"Night."

The phone went silent. She sat there for a moment, her smile fading as the realization of what she had done hit her.

Jason will lose his mind if he finds out.

CHAPTER THREE

Alec sat with his phone in his hand, staring at the home screen, his thoughts all over the place. Had he actually accepted a coffee date with Mercedes Elliott?

Her voice had taken him back to nearly three years ago when they had been . . . Well, there wasn't a name for what they had been.

He couldn't shake the feeling something was wrong. Mercedes had seemed . . . nervous? Was that it? Perhaps. He had been too.

She seemed more timid than he remembered. The Mercedes he'd known had been confident and charming. She lit up the room wherever she went.

But Alec had to admit he was likely biased. She'd held his attention from the first moment they had met.

He also hadn't missed the lack of details regarding the loss of her job. She'd worked her ass off to get through law school, pass the bar, and find work in one of the most prestigious firms on the West Coast of the United States. She'd never have walked away without another position in line.

Christ, what the hell happened?

Looking at his watch, he calculated what time it was in

San Francisco. Luke would be on his way to work. He dialed his younger cousin's number as he locked the office door and headed for the lift.

"Oi, what's up, ya Scottish prick?" Luke answered.

"Aye, fuck off, ya wee Yankee bastard. Dinna forget yer a Scot too," Alec said, exaggerating his accent.

"Oh, I dinna be forgettin'. The folk around these parts think I'm posh. I canna imagine why, though."

"Me neither." Alec laughed, falling back into his normal speech pattern. "Do you have a minute?"

"Aye, just a few. I have a meeting soon. What's up?"

"I got a call today . . . from Mercedes."

"Ah."

"So you knew she'd call me?" The lift door opened, and he walked toward his car.

"Aye, we hoped she would," Luke said. "Charlie's been trying to get her to call you for weeks. She's so feckin' stubborn, though."

"She said she's been in London for about six months and hadn't yet found a job as an attorney. Did she just walk away from the firm she was at?"

"Nah, man. I don't have time to go through it all right now, but a big case she was working on went to hell, and she took the fall for it. Personally, I don't think it was all her doing, but what do I know. Anyway, she lost her position and couldn't find work. So she made a big change."

"But why here? Surely somewhere in the states would have been easier."

"I know I told you she was with that computer programmer, Jason Marsh?"

"You did." *Damn.* He'd hoped that had changed. They must have been together for nearly three years now.

"He convinced Sadie to come with him. Promised he'd introduce her around all over town to get her foot in the door.

As far as we can tell, he hasn't done shit to help her. If anything, he's tightened his hold on her."

"Sounds like a real winner." Alec was unable to keep an edge from his voice.

"Well, let's just say he and I don't get along. Bit of a fuck-wit," Luke said. "He took a dislikin' to Charlie a year ago, and after that, we saw less and less of Sadie."

"He doesn't like *Charlie?*" Charlotte Elliott McKinley was one of the sweetest women he'd ever met.

"Right? Look, I don't want to invade her privacy, mate. Sadie's a smart lass. We just both think she could have done better."

Alec let the implication in Luke's voice go unanswered. He and Luke had never gone into why he and Mercedes hadn't worked out. He saved those sorts of heart to hearts for their cousin, Declan.

It didn't matter anyway. She'd moved on.

"I'm seeing her tomorrow afternoon."

"Are you? That's good. Charlie'll be thrilled to hear you're helping. She's been so worried."

"I can imagine." Mercedes had practically raised her younger sister. It must be so hard to have her on another continent.

"Look, mate, I have to go, my meeting is here. Can we talk later this week? I'm swamped for a few days."

Alec said his goodbyes and hung up. The hollow feeling in his stomach had gotten stronger. Calling Luke had created more questions than it answered. Why was Mercedes with a man who kept her from her sister? Something felt off.

He had to admit some of this might come from his own desire to dislike the man without knowing a single thing about him. Yeah, there was a bit of envy there for sure.

Alec never had any sort of claim on Mercedes. He'd once hoped they would try to make a go of it. But the transcontinental relationship had been too much. Well, it was more abrupt than that, but it hardly mattered now. He had to put those thoughts aside and do everything in his power to help her as a friend should. There was no reason to make her already tough situation harder by being a prick.

Boyfriend or not, he was looking forward to seeing her.

CHAPTER FOUR

His phone lit up for the third time, but Jason Marsh only glared at it. He wasn't in the mood to speak to the boss again. He'd said all he needed to say to that asshole. Anything else could wait.

As Jason crossed the road outside of the Cap and Vin, he took a few deep breaths to calm his irritation. Work had been shit, and he wasn't thrilled about eating dinner alone again. This damn job of hers was pissing him off. She spent far too many late evenings tied up in it. And what did he get out of it? Lukewarm takeout from the curry place again?

But he'd made a promise. It was one of the conditions he had negotiated in order to keep her. She'd get to work, and he'd have her with him in London. She had no idea how many strings he had to pull to put it together. And she never would.

As Jason pulled open the door to the cafe, he breathed in and held it to the count of three, like that overpaid head doctor in California suggested. Sometimes it worked. Other times his temper was a ticking time bomb nothing could stop.

The music from the live band blared as he found a table as

far away from the trumpets as he could. Did it have to be fucking jazz?

Jason scanned the crowded room and couldn't find her. He turned in his chair, searching every corner of the compact lounge.

Where the hell is she? His blood was rising. She better be where she was supposed to be.

He breathed deeply again.

Just as he was pulling out his phone to track her, Mercedes appeared in the doorway behind the counter, two bottles of wine in her hands. She smiled at her customers as she worked on the cork of one bottle. The tightening in his chest released.

That smile. Jesus.

They were so rare these days. When he first met her, she had been nothing but laughter and energy. In recent months, she'd faded, grown quiet and reserved. Not that he could blame her. Things in San Francisco had taken a toll. Regardless, he wouldn't feel bad for the months of trauma she went through. Without them, she wouldn't be here.

Mercedes must have sensed him watching. Looking up from the bar, she searched the room until she saw him. Her mouth quirked up in a flirty smile, and the irritation of the day melted away.

Mercedes pushed through the crowd to his table, a single glass of white wine in her hand.

"Hi, babe," Jason said.

"Hey! Just got this Pinot Grigio from California today. I thought you'd like to try it out."

Jason smiled and took up the stem. He loved good white wine, and she knew it. Crisp and chilled perfectly, he savored the flavors.

"Mmm," he responded.

"It's good, right?" She asked with a tinge of hope in her eyes. He loved how hard she tried to please him.

"Very. Thanks."

Mercedes gave him a wide grin, her hazel eyes crinkling in the corners. God damn, she was as close to perfect as he could get. Desire for her pulsed through him. Wrapping his arm around her waist, he pulled her to him.

"You're so beautiful," he whispered against her ear. The feel of her body against his made him painfully hard. He pressed himself into her, trying to relieve the ache. "Come home with me. Right now."

"Jace," she murmured. "I wish I could, but I'm working till midnight."

Mercedes's palm settled on his shoulder, fingertips twitching against him.

Always fidgeting.

Jason captured her hand in his to stop the motion. "You don't *have* to work until midnight. It won't matter if you leave." He brought her fingers to his mouth, brushing his lips against her smooth skin.

"It'd matter a lot. We're short-staffed, and it's packed."

Damn the stupid ass job she insisted on having. Taking a few deep breaths, he worked to calm the storm. She was his, for God's sake. He should come first. Was she trying to set him off?

Jason's lips pursed together to keep from saying what was on his mind. Nothing good could come from losing his temper here. Too many people could interfere— too many who could try to take her away from him.

He forced himself to smile. "I know. I miss you, is all."

Mercedes let her breath out in a sigh. Had she worried what he'd do? Another spasm of desire ran through him. He adjusted his hard-on through his slacks.

"I'll see you in a few hours then?"

Mercedes leaned in to kiss him gently. Unsatisfied, he grabbed her hair and plunged his tongue into her mouth. She tensed against him. She always hated making a scene, but he didn't care. This was his to take. When he released her, her breaths were coming in shallow pants.

She could pretend she didn't enjoy it, but she did.

"I'll see you tonight." Mercedes gave him a tight smile and walked back to the bar.

He was looking forward to it.

———

Breathing in the crisp air of the sleepy streets, Mercedes stepped out of the shop and set out for home. Her throat ached from shouting to be heard over the thrumming instruments. It'd be a while before the pounding headache would taper off.

She didn't mind the five-block walk to the one-bedroom flat she shared with Jason. On a usual night, she'd enjoy the moment, reflect on the day and relax.

But tonight, she couldn't keep the unease away. Jason didn't like to be told no. The look that had passed behind his eyes set off alarm bells. Mercedes wasn't sure what she was going home to.

She walked up the narrow stairs to the flat and pulled her keys from her purse to unlock the door. Jason was stretched out on the loveseat, a glass of wine on the table in front of him. A British sitcom blared on the television. She laid her things on the small table next to the door.

"Hey," she said, her voice low. Which Jason would she get this time?

He looked up and smiled, unnerving her. It seemed genuine, not his usual sneer when he was irritated. His crystal blue eyes were relaxed and affectionate.

"Hi babe," he said. "How was the rest of your shift?"

"Good. Customers were happy." She paused to regard him.

"That's good. Did you eat?"

"A while ago." She shook off her jacket. "I'm not hungry, just tired. I'm going to shower and get to bed. Are you going to stay up?"

"For a while longer. Any news on the job hunt?"

"Not really. I might have a lead. I spoke with one of our regulars today who might know of an opportunity. It's a bit of a stretch, but he might have some news for me in the next week."

"A customer from the shop?"

"Yeah. Not holding my breath, though." She hoped he wouldn't hear the lie in her voice. "Hey, I'm wiped out, and I have an early shift. Night."

Mercedes went to their bedroom and closed the door, her heart racing. As she gathered her things and headed to the bathroom, a tremor of guilt washed over her. She hated lying.

She stepped into the shower, unsure what to make of his change in behavior. It wasn't the first time his mood swings had startled her. The catalysts for these changes were arbitrary, always keeping her guessing about how the evening would go.

It was exhausting to always be on alert.

She'd tried to leave a couple of times. Once, too humiliated to tell Charlotte and Luke, not wanting them to learn how fucked up her relationship was, she checked herself into a hotel while figuring out what to do.

Jason had found her within an hour, begging her to give him another chance. He'd been so broken when he came to her, his handsome face tracked with tears. He begged for forgiveness and agreed to couple's counseling. For months, he attended all the counseling sessions and took full responsibility for his behavior. The Jason she loved came back to her, and she fell for him again.

It was that change in him that got her through the roughest time of her life. She'd be forever grateful for his steady hand when she needed him most.

Mercedes finished her shower and dried her hair. By the time she left the small bathroom, Jason was in bed waiting for her. She held back a sigh.

It wasn't a surprise. He'd been worked up at the bar. No doubt the time he waited for her had only made him hornier. She wasn't in the mood but resisting him would be pointless. At best, he'd sulk for a few days, at worst… well.

Mercedes tossed her towel in the hamper and climbed into bed naked.

Jason was on her before she could pull the covers up, kissing her neck and stroking her breasts with his thumbs. His mouth moved up, a wet tongue snaking in her ear. She hated when he did that, but she didn't bother to tell him again. She turned her face and kissed him. Jason moaned as she ran her hand down his abs and feathered his hardness.

Jason was a gorgeous man. With his pale blue eyes and wavy ash-blond hair, he could have walked out of a magazine. He wasn't a towering figure, but what he lacked in height, he made up for in strength and athleticism.

Sometimes she wondered what was wrong with her. She should be eager to have a man like him in her bed.

Jason positioned himself atop her and pressed inside her tight walls. Mercedes winced at the initial dryness. It passed quickly, and she relaxed, letting him take his pleasure. She moaned for him, her fingers roaming his back.

But her mind wandered. She had a few things to do in the morning. Luke's birthday was coming up. She needed to get something in the post soon. Maybe she could pick up a nice whisky.

Jason's pace became fevered, and he pumped harder until he cried out, finishing in rhythmic spasms. Panting as he rolled off her, he murmured, "Fuck, you're beautiful."

Mercedes smiled as he pulled the sheet over himself, settling into the bed. It wasn't a surprise when he didn't make a move to reciprocate. She was good with it. Exhaustion had hit her hours ago. Sleep sounded better.

Heading into the bathroom, she hopped back into the shower for a quick cleanup. It would have saved a lot of time if he had made his move before she showered.

When Mercedes came out, he was already asleep. She turned off the bedside lamp and settled against her pillow. Her fingers stroked a delicate tune on the soft edge of the blanket. *Moonlight Sonata* was one of her favorites to help her sleep.

The meeting with Alec came to mind, and she tensed.

Maybe I should cancel.

She pushed the thought away. There was nothing wrong with meeting with an old friend for coffee.

Still, she'd need to be careful. Jason had eyes everywhere.

CHAPTER FIVE

Mercedes's nerves were on edge all morning. The clock had slowed to a turtle's pace. She knocked over the container filled with used espresso grounds, making a slippery mess all over the floor.

Her coworker, Corie, frowned at her. "You alright there, Sade?"

"Damn it," Mercedes grumped, reaching for the broom. "Yeah, I'm fine. Bit of a mess today. I'll get this out of the way, so we don't kill ourselves."

Corie shot her a grin. "I might do for a little slip and fall today. I've a chemistry test I'd love to get out of."

"Ha. Fat chance." Mercedes laughed, pushing the sandy grounds into a corner. "I thought you studied."

"I did. I mean, I meant to," Corie said with a coy smile. "I got a tad bit distracted when Lindsay came over." She wagged her brows.

"Well, if it was for a good reason."

Mercedes reached for a mug to make the next drink order and promptly knocked a bottle of hazelnut syrup off the counter. She gave a magnificent effort to recover it, batting it back into the air two or three times before it crashed to the floor with a crack. Thick syrup added to the sludge of wet coffee grounds.

Mercedes gritted her teeth and uttered a guttural noise.

What the hell?

She had to get it together. The customers at the counter were staring at her.

"You sure everything's okay?" Corie furrowed her brow. "You're a bloody wreck."

"Yeah, I'm good. It's . . . Well, I'm meeting someone after work, sort of an acquaintance." At Corie's look of interest, she continued, "I'm hoping he'll help me find a job. I haven't seen him in a few years."

"Oh. So, he's just a business acquaintance?" Corie's frown made it clear she wasn't buying it.

"Yeah, sort of. I mean no, not really. He's an old . . . friend? I guess? His cousin is married to my sister. I haven't seen him since the wedding in Scotland three years ago."

"So, you're all aflutter for your sister's husband's cousin, who's just a business acquaintance?"

"Yeah." Mercedes shrugged.

"Uh-huh."

Her face reddened. If she was this much of a disaster now, how would it be when he got there?

If he even shows.

Mercedes took a deep breath. "Hand me a towel, would you?"

———

Just before Alec was due to arrive, Mercedes took a quick bathroom break, looking herself over in the mirror. Like most days, she had her long hair tied in a bun. Today she had taken a little extra time to make it look intentionally messy, rather than her usual "just out of bed" bun. They were very different.

She fussed with the shadow and mascara around her eyes and finished with a touch of color to her lips. Standing back to take account, she was thankful the cream scarf she had on over a simple black tank top had survived the coffee-ground incident.

The shop was empty when she returned, so she joined Corie in prepping the evening's charcuterie boards. As usual, Corie talked non-stop while Mercedes made little sounds of agreement. Her eyes kept darting to the clock on the wall.

Suddenly, Corie stopped and inhaled sharply. "*Please* tell me that is your uncle's, cousin's, friend's, nephew or whatever?" she murmured.

Mercedes's gaze shot to the door, her heart bottoming out. He hadn't changed much. Tall and broad-shouldered, his wavy dark hair, slightly longer than she remembered, framed his fair, sculptured face. Jesus, he was amazing.

"Yeah, that's him," she choked.

"Well, damn," Corie said in a low voice. "No wonder you were dropping shit all day."

"Yeah," she agreed—no point in denying it.

Mercedes took a controlled breath and walked around the counter to greet the man she'd once wanted to change her entire life for.

"Alec." She had to fight to keep her voice steady. "It's so good to see you."

"Hey, you." Alec smiled and held his arms out to her. Without thinking, she moved into them. Alec held her tight, encompassing her in his warmth. She bit back a sigh. He'd always given the best hugs. He felt as good as he looked. Breathing in his woodsy scent, she savored the feel of him against her.

Alec pulled away and gave her a kiss on the cheek. A thrill of electricity shot up her spine.

"It's been way too long." She guided him to a table near

the window, which was the farthest from Corie's watchful eye. "Can I get you something to drink? I'm buying."

"Oh well, if you're buying . . ." Alec grinned, eyeing the menu boards.

"Take it easy there, McKinley. Kinda on a budget here," she shot back with a laugh.

He gave an exaggerated sigh. "Aye, very well. Triple espresso, just a wee bit of cream?"

"You got it."

Alec's deep blue eyes caught hers and held them. She tried to disguise the flush growing across her cheeks by grinning at him and headed behind the counter to make their drinks.

Damn. He hasn't even been here two minutes, and I'm drooling all over him.

Corie shot her a covert glance. "Seriously, you never mentioned your brother's, boyfriend's, neighbor's cousin was straight up lush," Corie whispered. "I thought we were mates?"

"Well yeah, he's . . . lush, I guess. And he'd like a triple with cream. Can you get it for me while I make mine?"

Corie opened her mouth, looking as though she might make a dirty quip about triple cream.

"Please?" Mercedes's nerves were already at their end.

Corie's mouth snapped shut, and she sighed. "I know what you like. I'll bring them out to you. Go."

Mercedes nodded her thanks and headed back to the table. She couldn't help but brush her hand on his shoulder as she sat across from him. "I'm so glad you were free to come by today. I hope it wasn't too much trouble."

Alec shook his head. "Not at all. I'm happy you called."

"How's your family?"

"Oh, the same. Numerous and loud."

Mercedes chuckled at the fitting description of the McKinley brood. Corie delivered the drinks to their table and stayed long enough to be quickly introduced to Alec before retreating to the counter.

Once she was gone, Alec turned to her. "So, a move to London? Bold choice."

"I know, right? Things got a little out of hand, so I needed to make a change."

"Well, moving a continent away will certainly do it."

Mercedes laughed. "It's been a culture shock, for sure, but it was better than sticking around the Bay."

Alec tilted his head. "You all right then?"

"Oh yeah, I'll be fine."

His brow furrowed, but he didn't respond.

Mercedes inhaled deeply, trying to think of what she should say. "I had a few rough months. If I'm being honest, it was probably the worst time of my life." His eyebrows went up. He knew her history. "I'm doing my best to bounce back if that counts for anything."

"It counts." Alec's gaze never wavered from hers.

He cleared his throat and pulled a neatly folded piece of paper from his inside jacket pocket. "It's not much, but I started a list of possibilities for you. Some of them do international business and might be looking to bring on a lawyer from the States."

He opened the paper and laid it on the table in front of them, revealing six different contacts written in his scratchy hand.

"The first one there." He pointed to the list. "He's probably my best lead. The company manufactures textiles in the Scottish Highlands. They've recently expanded into the American market, hoping to sell to some luxury brands there. He might need a corporate attorney who knows the law there, especially in California."

Mercedes read through the list. She hadn't applied to any of these yet.

"I hope you don't mind, but I've already taken the liberty

of calling George this morning. He's a good friend. I left a message giving you a glowing review."

She let out a breath. "I can't tell you how much I appreciate this, Alec. Thank you."

He shrugged as if he hadn't just thrown her a huge lifeline. How could he know how much she needed this?

"What piece are you playing?" He broke into her thoughts. His cobalt eyes moved from the table to meet hers. It was like the oxygen had been sucked from the room.

Alec had been watching her hand as it tapped across the smooth edge of the saucer. She flushed, pulling her hand to her lap.

His eyes twinkled with amusement. "You'd be rubbish at poker."

"Only with you." She laughed.

Alec raised his brow, clearly not letting it go.

Mercedes bit her lip and glanced up at him. "It was the . . . Downton Abbey theme song," she admitted with a grimace.

His face lit up as he laughed. "Brilliant."

"Shut up," she giggled.

Their laughter died, and she moved the conversation back to the business at hand. "So, I have a few copies of my CV if you wouldn't mind taking them? I don't know if you'll need it, but maybe if someone wants to look."

"Certainly. I'd be happy to pass them on."

"I'll go grab them. Can I get you something else while I'm up? Water? A bite to eat? We have a cheese plate that's good."

He declined the food but accepted the offered water, and she got up and headed around the counter.

Corie gave her a smirk.

"It's not like that, Corie."

Corie rolled her eyes. "Well, it should be. Clearly, he fancies you back."

"You're such an ass. Here." She pushed two waters at her.

"Would you take this over to him, please? I have to get something from upstairs."

Mercedes ran up the steps, her heart feeling lighter than it had in months. It was amazing to hope again.

ALEC WATCHED HER WALK TO THE BAR. JESUS, SHE WAS AS engaging as ever. From the moment he walked in, he was surrounded by her warmth.

Mercedes was doing her best to hide how nervous she was. He'd never needed to call on his training to read her tells. They screamed at him. Her delicate fingers tapping out a song when she was worried or deep in thought were among his favorite things about her.

Damn, if she wasn't as beautiful as ever. Her hazel-green eyes sparked with amber that danced when she teased. She had high cheekbones and a delicate jawline. The only change was a wariness on her face he hadn't seen before.

Corie interrupted his thoughts by placing two glasses of water on the table. She smiled. "Have you ever been into the shop before?"

"No, actually," he said. "Although I have an office up the street."

"Well, stop back by, maybe for a glass of wine. We have a nice happy hour selection."

"I might have to try that."

Corie grabbed a wet cloth and wiped down a neighboring chair.

"Have you known Sadie long?" he asked.

"A little over four months." She ran the rag over the back of the seat. "She's a treasure."

"That she is." He couldn't agree more.

"You ever met the boyfriend?"

"No, not yet anyway." And not likely to, if he had anything to say about it. "You?"

Corie shrugged. "Yeah, a few times. I don't think he likes me, though. I made the mistake of hitting on Sadie when I first met her. I mean, she's, you know . . . bloody gorgeous. Who wouldn't take a fancy to her?"

Alec smiled. Another statement he could get on board with.

"Anyway, he didn't like that too much. He comes every few nights, especially when we've had live music. Mostly sticks to himself when he's here."

"So, he comes to hear Sadie play?" Alec hoped to move the conversation away from talking about Mercedes's boyfriend.

"Play what?"

Alec frowned. "Anything really. She's an incredible musician."

"Really? Huh," Corie said. "No idea."

Mercedes came back through the shop with a manila envelope. "Here you go." She set the packet on the table in front of him.

"So, funny thing. Corie tells me she was unaware of your music?"

Mercedes flushed. "Oh. Uh, yeah, I play lots of different instruments. It's how I put myself through school." She sank into her chair.

Corie's brows went up. "What? That's crazy. You need to play for us on open mic night."

"Mm-hmm," Mercedes said. The bell at the door chimed. Corie turned her attention to the customer who had entered.

Mercedes was avoiding Alec's eyes, suddenly interested in her water glass.

"Sadie, are you not playing *at all* anymore?"

"No, not really. I . . . I sort of gave it up." She waved her hand.

Alec said nothing, only leaning toward her.

She gave a sigh. "Obviously, I couldn't bring my piano with me, so I left it with Charlie and Luke when they took over my house." Mercedes toyed with a napkin, crushing it into a ball. "Then I sold the guitars. I never played them much, anyway."

Alec frowned. That hadn't been true three years ago.

There was a lengthy pause. She took in a deep breath, staring at her glass. "And since I was selling those, I sold the violins too."

He tilted his head. "All of them?"

"Yeah," she murmured. "One less thing to bring, right?"

He winced. This made no sense. She'd never sell them, especially her oldest violin, the one she had gotten from a kind foster mom when she was a teenager. Music was one of the most important parts of her life. Just like that, she'd given it all away?

"A violin can be carried onto an airplane."

"I know."

"Then why?"

Now she looked directly at him, the flecks of amber in her hazel eyes brightened by unshed tears. Pain ran through his heart at the desolation in her eyes.

"I've had to make a lot of sacrifices over the last year, Alec. Some of them were harder than others."

Christ. What the hell happened?

Guilt wracked him. He should have pushed Luke for answers, but it'd been easier to move on thinking she was happy and doing well.

On impulse, he took her hand. A familiar shot of electricity coursed through him. The connection they'd always had was still there. She drew in her breath, and he knew she felt it too. Her fingers tightened on his as if welcoming the touch.

Alec swallowed hard. "I'm sorry. Do you want to talk about it?"

Mercedes shook her head. "I don't know if I'm up for it. It's a long story. I'm doing what I can to start over. Which is why this is so helpful." Her finger tapped the paper.

"I'm glad I could help. I only want to see you happy."

"Thank you." Those eyes held him again like she was trying to read him. His heart sped up a tick. Why was it like this with her?

She pulled her hand away and picked up the list. "Can you tell me a little about each company? I want to prepare for when I reach out."

"Of course."

Mercedes moved her chair around the table, so they were shoulder to shoulder and set to work on the list. They spent the next few minutes discussing the potential legal needs of Alec's contacts. She pulled a pen out of her apron pocket and made notes about each as he ran through what he knew. He kept getting sidetracked by the scent of her hair and had to ask her to repeat her questions to keep up.

Finally, she sat back, a look of determination on her face. She glanced around the cafe. The clientele had changed, and the after-work crowd had trickled in.

"Damn," she exclaimed. "I didn't realize it was so late. I better go."

Alec didn't want to end their meeting, but he didn't see how he could put it off any longer. He had a few errands of his own to take care of before he left town.

He slid his jacket onto his shoulders and picked up the envelope. "I'll walk you out."

"Okay, let me grab my things." Mercedes hurried off to the back room and came back with a black knee-length jacket and her purse. Waving to Corie, he held the door for her as they stepped into the brisk afternoon air. The late spring weather was unpredictable, and the temperature had dropped once the sun had moved behind the buildings.

"Brrr. I thought I'd eventually get used to the weather here. I can't ever seem to get warm."

I bet I could find a way to keep you warm. Shit, not a helpful thought. "You sound like a Londoner already, not two steps out the door, and you're already on about the weather. You fit in quite well, lass."

She scoffed. "Do I? Most of the time I feel like a fish out of water."

"You'll get the hang of it."

They walked on, chatting about the weather until he noticed where they were going.

Shit. Alec stopped walking, feeling ridiculous. She halted beside him, looking at him in question.

"Um, I'm actually that way." He pointed to the way they had come.

"Oh." She looked down the pavement, probably trying to figure out what kind of arse walked three streets away in the wrong direction.

"Sorry. Bit distracted, I guess." He ran his hand through his hair.

Mercedes bit her lip. "It's alright. I liked the company."

It was his turn to flush in pleasure. "Can I see you again sometime?"

She looked away, uncertainty in her eyes. "I don't know, I . . ."

"It wouldn't be like that. I know you're with someone. But we can be friends, can't we?"

Her face softened. "Yeah, we can be friends. I'd like that."

Lord, she's beautiful. "Great, can I call you next week? Maybe we can have a drink and talk about the job hunt?"

There it was again, the hesitation. Was she afraid of him?

"You could bring your bloke with you if you like." Yeah,

he'd put up with her wanker boyfriend if it meant he could see her again.

"Oh, I don't think Jason would be up for that. But yeah, give me a call. You have to call the shop. If you leave a message, they'll pass it on."

Alec frowned but let it go. "Sounds like a plan."

Mercedes reached out to give him a hug, and he gathered her against him. She felt so good in his arms; he held on longer than intended.

Being "just a friend" to Mercedes Elliott wasn't going to be easy, but it would be worth it.

As he walked away, Mercedes called out. "Hey, McKinley, make sure you're headed in the right direction this time. Wouldn't want you to get lost."

He looked back at her, her crooked grin making him laugh. "Not going to let me live it down, are ya?"

"Nope," she called. Her laughter carried to him, and he didn't think he'd heard such a lovely sound in a long time.

CHAPTER SIX

Jason Marsh sat at his desk programming a code for his current project. His boss was up his ass about finishing it today, and it was pissing him the fuck off. He could only type so fast. His cell phone rang, but he ignored it. He didn't have time for anyone's bullshit today.

As soon as it stopped buzzing, it immediately started again.

What the fuck? He pressed answer. "This is Jason," he barked.

"You have a problem," the familiar voice said with a sneer. *Fucking Adam.*

"Yeah, what's that?"

"Your girl had a meeting today."

Jason's hands paused on the keys. "The fuck you mean?"

"She had a cozy meet-up after work this afternoon."

Jason's heart raced. "With who?"

"Who do you think? McKinley."

He could feel the blood leave his face. "No way. She knows better."

"Apparently not. You want the photos? Got one with them holding hands." The bastard's voice was dripping with glee.

Rage built in him. "Fuck you, Adam. You better not be fucking with me."

"Why would I fuck with you? Check your phone, man."

Jason's phone buzzed again with a text message. Dizziness overtook him as he scrolled to his message app.

There she was.

There *he* fucking was.

"Tell me," he said through clenched teeth.

"I only heard part of what they said, something about a job and her music shit. He's agreed to help her find work with friends of his. He brought some kind of list with him, and they sat together and went over it."

Jason's fist gripped his phone, and he scrolled through Adam's snapshots as he listened to the details. Adam had gone inside and ordered a drink. He wasn't able to hear everything they spoke about, but the parts he did hear made Jason's blood boil.

His Sadie. *His.* In the arms of that fucker.

He struggled to think straight. "I'm gonna fucking kill her," Jason burst out.

"Whoa, man." Adam was no longer taunting. "Take it easy. You need to be careful and not fuck this up. I don't want to be cleaning up your shit again."

"You think I can let this go?" he growled, grabbing his jacket from his chair.

"Well, no. But for fuck's sake, get it together. They were talking. It wasn't like she was fucking him on the table. And you're on thin ice as it is with—"

Jason jabbed the end button and stared at his phone, his breath ragged.

How could she do this to him? After all they had been through together, how could she want anything but him? He strode to the elevator and jabbed the button. Tonight, she'd know who she belonged to. Tonight, she'd remember what he'd done for her.

CHAPTER SEVEN

After saying goodbye to Alec, Mercedes began walking toward her apartment above the yoga studio, smiling. A weight had been lifted from her shoulders. Every single one of the positions Alec suggested she'd be happy with. Perhaps she could earn a decent living here as a consultant rather than as part of a legal practice.

Mercedes took a detour to the neighborhood grocer and purchased everything she needed for a quick pasta dish. Her cooking talents were notoriously awful, but she hoped Jason would be happy to eat something besides curry takeout from down the street.

Jason wasn't home when she arrived. Relieved to have a moment to think about the day uninterrupted, she unloaded the groceries and set a pot of water to boil. There was plenty of time to do some research about some of the companies Alec had given her while she waited for Jason's text, letting her know he was on his way.

Ten minutes later, the salted water gently boiling the pasta, Mercedes was poised at her desk, engrossed in her research. She'd already started on a list for the first contact, the Scottish textile mill.

Mercedes was so caught up in her research she was startled when the key turned in the door. Her heart skipped at the thought of telling Jason. He'd prefer her to stay home, but she hoped her enthusiasm would win him over.

She left her laptop and strained the pasta in the sink. After dinner, she'd research the ins and outs of textiles in the American market.

"Hi," she said. "How was your day?"

"Alright. Busy." Jason's voice was strange, detached. His phone buzzed, but he declined the call.

Mercedes's eyebrows drew together. "You okay?"

"Yeah, I'm good." His phone buzzed again, and without even looking, he silenced it.

He stood over her computer, looking at her web search and notebook. "What's this? Why are you researching Scotland?"

A chill ran up her spine. She had to tread carefully here.

"Oh, remember when I said I had a potential job lead from a customer at the shop? Well, he gave me a few names of companies who might be looking for a corporate attorney to help them expand into America. That's the first one. He gave me a few companies to check out."

Jason's mouth turned up into a scowl. "That right? Why is this customer so interested in you?"

Her heart jumped. Turning back to the sink, she poured the strained pasta back into the pot. She couldn't look at him and lie.

"He's a regular who chats with us occasionally. I mentioned I was a lawyer looking for work. So, he offered to put my name out there. It's not a big deal, but I appreciated it." *Please let that be the last of it.*

Jason's arms wrapped around her waist, and he nuzzled her hair. The tension in her shoulders released, and she relaxed against him. Her secret was safe.

"Would you like some wine?" she murmured. "I can open a bottle."

When he didn't answer right away, she tried to turn toward him. But his fingers tightened, digging into her flesh.

"No, I don't want wine," he growled.

Holy shit, what's going on? "Okay, I—"

"What I want to know is," he snarled against her, "have you fucked Alec McKinley in our bed?"

Oh, god.

Fear rushed through her veins like icy water. Mercedes closed her eyes. It was pointless to contradict him with the details. He'd never believe it was an innocent business meeting.

Jason laid his phone on the counter next to the sink, clouds of steam billowing from the pasta in front of her. An image glowed up at her, captured from across the street of the shop. She and Alec sitting at the little bistro table, his hand stretched out to hold hers. It was nothing more than a moment of kindness, but there was no way she could deny the appearance of intimacy.

"Jace, it's not what yo—"

Jason grasped her hair and slammed her head into the cabinet. Her cheekbone seemed to crack apart. Shooting pain radiated through her forehead.

The world spun.

Jason let her go. She staggered backward, falling to the floor. He stood over her, breathing hard and glaring. Crawling to the door was impossible. Mercedes's legs weren't moving fast enough.

"Get the fuck up." Lunging at her, he grabbed her around the throat, forcing her to her feet. Scratching and kicking did nothing. Fingernails dug into her flesh. Mercedes wheezed, desperate to suck in what air she could get. Jason crashed her against the wall, her head cracking the plaster.

"Are you fucking him?" he demanded. Only strangled

sounds came out as she struggled for air. "Answer me! Are you fucking him?" The hold on her throat tightened.

"No," she mouthed, shaking her head and clawing at his hands, tears, and blood blinding her. The last bit of air left her, and spots formed around her blurred vision.

This seemed to enrage him more, and he threw her to the ground. Gasping for air, she crawled toward the door, her arms shaking. She knew she'd never make it.

She was right.

The impact of the kick to her abdomen stole what little breath she had regained. Blinding pain tore through her. Mercedes wrapped her arms around her ribs and curled up. She couldn't breathe, her vision shrinking.

"You fucking bitch," he raged. "You gonna act like you haven't been his whore?" He straddled her, forcing her hands away from her face. The full weight of the blow landed on the left side of her jaw. Blood was filling her mouth and nose, and she gagged as it trickled down the back of her throat.

She wanted to plead with him. But the deadness in his eyes told her he wasn't able to hear her.

"You didn't think I'd find out about your little fuck date with that piece of shit Scotsman? I know everything you do. I know you fixed yourself up for him like a slut. I know you flirted with him and how many times you let him touch you. I know all of it, you dumb cunt. Did you think I'd let you get away with that? Embarrassing me?"

Mercedes lost count of how many times he struck her face and arms. She bucked him and tried to twist away, but he thrust his weight down, trapping her. Managing to free her right wrist from his grasp, she punched him in the face.

It didn't register.

Again.

This time, her fist connected with the bottom of his chin. Nothing. Mercedes reared up and set her claws to him, raking her nails down the side of his neck, and he hissed. An open-handed slap stopped her efforts.

His weight shifted. Keeping his hold on her throat, he raised himself up, looking at the countertop.

Please, let him be cycling down.

Instead, he pulled the large kitchen knife from the counter as she shrieked. A slap to the face silenced her.

Jason used the knife to cut away her black tank top, nicking her stomach with the tip. He pulled her breasts free of her bra and twisted her left nipple brutally. Wincing, she breathed through the pain.

"Look at these tits," he growled and pressed the knife into the side of her breast, the tip cutting into her skin. Mercedes held back a sob, willing herself to be quiet.

Jason brought the knife to rest on her nipple. She closed her eyes and braced for agony. But instead, he replaced the knife with his mouth, gentle at first. Then his teeth tore into her flesh, circling the tender peak of her breast.

He rocked his hips, grinding his arousal into her. Bile churned in her stomach, but she knew better than to move. The tip of the blade dug into her ribcage.

The last thing she wanted was to have him inside her, but if it made him stop, she'd do what needed to be done.

"Jace," she rasped.

He tensed at the sound of her voice, and the tip of the knife dug in deeper.

"No." His voice caught. He was close to tears. She'd lost most of her vision to the blood and swelling, but his eyes were in her sight.

"Why are you like this?" His voice was thick with emotion. "Why did you have to call him?"

Mercedes didn't answer, and she wouldn't apologize for it. It was an act of defiance she couldn't afford.

The unadulterated hate returned to his eyes. He tightened his iron grip on her wrists. With exacting precision, he dragged the blade through the soft flesh of her side, opening a thin ribbon from her ribs to her waistline. Mercedes screamed, the agony of it like nothing she'd ever known. He wouldn't relent.

Jason brought the knife up to carve her flesh again, but her hands broke free of his grasp. She fought to protect her vulnerable abdomen, the blade making a deep tear through the inside of her forearm. Blood poured onto her exposed chest, dropping in thick splatters all around her.

Mercedes kept screaming until a fist pummeled her in the face again, and the world fell away. She wasn't sure if she'd wake up from this one. She wasn't sure she wanted to.

CHAPTER EIGHT

Jason's raging mind reconnected to reality. He was straddling Mercedes's limp body. His chest heaved like he'd run a mile, and his stomach turned at the wreckage. Her matted hair clung to her face. The shredded tank top exposed her bare breast, slick with blood. Crimson streams were seeping from the long wavering cut traveling from her breast to the top of her jeans. His hand clutched the kitchen knife, but he couldn't remember how he'd gotten it. He tossed it to the side as if it burned him.

"Sadie?" His voice shook. A trembling hand reached out to cup her ruined face. "Oh god. Oh my god. Fuck, what did I do? Sadie, wake up."

When she didn't move, he pressed his fingers against her throat, terrified he wouldn't find her pulse. He caught the slight thump of it. The breath he'd been holding rushed out in relief.

A sickening flow pulsed from a gash on her arm, matching the beat of her heart. Rushing to the counter, he grabbed a thin towel. Wrapping it around her slack arm, he did his best to tie off a tourniquet. His shaky hands struggled to pull the cloth tight, but it slowed the loss to an ooze.

He found his cell phone next to the sink. A wall of text messages and call notifications glared at him from the home screen. Both Adam and Patrick had been trying to reach him. They knew what he'd do. Jesus, why hadn't they done more to stop him?

Giving her one last look, he lunged for the door and stumbled down the narrow staircase. His heart raced, and he worked to catch his breath. He burst out onto the sidewalk, careening away from the scene, his mind screaming at him.

Why had she done this? How could she have been so stupid?

The rage returned, strangling him. She *knew* better. She knew he'd find out. They'd discussed it, and he'd been clear. No men from her past. They'd talked about *that* asshole in particular.

Jason paused his furious pace. Maybe she'd *wanted* him to catch her. That was it. She'd planned this all along. Why else would she do something like this?

His brain flipped between panic and fury. If he didn't act now, she'd die. He couldn't clean this up on his own. He'd have to make the call.

A metallic scent flooded his nose. Jesus, he was standing in the middle of the sidewalk, coated in blood. Lowering his head, he dashed into a narrow alleyway. He leaned against the wall to stop his legs from collapsing. Pulling out his phone, he found Adam's contact and hit call.

Adam answered on the first ring. "Where the hell have you been?"

"I fucked up," Jason choked out.

"I *knew* it. What have you done?"

"I . . . I think I hurt Sadie."

"You *think*?"

"Yeah."

"Is she alive?"

"I . . . I think so. She was a minute ago. I need help . . . with clean up. And I'll need cover."

"You're not even sure she's alive? *God damn it.* Where is she now?"

Jason had a hard time remembering. "She's uh . . . at our apartment. Call an ambulance."

Adam gave a command to someone to call the emergency number. When he came back, he said, "I can't believe you fucked this up again, man. How hard is it to control yourself?"

"It wasn't my fault. She fucking lied to me." It was a waste of time. Adam would never understand. "Just come and get me. I'm on the street and I . . . have a lot of blood on me."

"Jesus fucking Christ," Adam muttered. "Stay hidden. We're already on the way to you."

Sirens howled in the distance. He could only hope they would make it in time.

Adam's sardonic voice came through the line before he hung up. "I hope you understand what a mess you've made of everything. *Again.* You'd better pray to whatever god pricks like you pray to she lives."

CHAPTER NINE

Alec was more than satisfied with the outcome of his recent meetings. The project was ahead of schedule and on budget. Plus, they were ready to go home a day early. He could get his notes typed up on the road and have time to stop by Cap and Vin for a drink. Happy hour would be over, but he didn't care about paying full price if he got another chance to see Mercedes again. All through the trip, she'd been on his mind.

"Hey man, can you drive?" He tossed the keys to his partner, Mason Wright. Mason snagged them out of the air and grinned.

"Oh, yeah," Mason said. Driving meant control of the music. "I'll get you to admit Frank is the man."

Alec rolled his eyes. Halfway through the journey to Manchester, a heated discussion about which of the Rat Pack was a better singer began. Mason grinned at him and played *The Way You Look Tonight*. Alec sighed. That was a tough one to beat.

Alec and Mason had met while on a tour of Afghanistan. They had shot the shit a few times at the base, with the usual amount of boasting between the Brits and the Americans that always ensued. He and Mason, a tall Black man with a heavy Boston accent, hit it off right away.

Then a firefight had blown through their camp, and Alec had taken a slug in his chest, below his left collarbone. Mason, a US Naval Corpsman, had been the one to stabilize Alec and kept him safe until they could extract him.

That day changed Alec's life. After a couple of surgeries and some physical therapy, he was back to himself. But the realities of war hit, and active combat wasn't what he wanted.

Still, he had a desire to serve, so he joined the Secret Intelligence Service. It was there he'd developed his skill set.

Alec's phone buzzed. He'd missed a call from Luke, but he popped it back in the center console, making a note to ring him when he got home. He was still racking his brain to think of Dean Martin songs when it rang again.

He frowned. It wasn't like Luke to keep on ringing him. "Better take this."

Mason reached out and turned down the music.

"Hey, Luke. You're on speaker. You've interrupted an epic battle between Sinatra and Martin. Mason's having his arse handed to him."

Mason made a "humph" noise and shook his head.

"Alec." Luke's manner was subdued. Alec sat straighter in alarm. Mason frowned and turned the stereo off.

"What is it?"

"I have Charlotte on speaker with me."

"Hey, Alec," she said. There was a strain in her voice. A shot of nervous energy shivered up his spine.

"Is everything okay, love?" Alec said. "Has something happened?"

"We were hoping you've seen Sadie. Today, or maybe yesterday?"

"No, I've been in Manchester. I had coffee with her on Tuesday."

Charlotte sniffed, and Luke's gentle voice whispered to her. Alec's heart picked up its pace.

"Guys, what's going on? Is Sadie okay?"

"We aren't sure. Charlie got a message from Sadie's boss. She's missed work for the last two days. No call, no show, and she's not answering her cell phone."

Alec frowned. "Perhaps she and the boyfriend ran off for a holiday."

"No way," Charlotte said. "Sadie's a planner. She'd have asked for the time off weeks ago. And she'd have called in if she were sick."

"So, what is it you think happened?"

There was a stifled pause. "There's something I didn't want to mention," Luke sighed. "Honestly, we thought things had changed . . . but maybe not."

"Right, so tell me now." Alec's jaw clenched, unease curling in his gut.

"Her boyfriend . . . The bastard's sent her to hospital in the past. Twice, that we're aware of."

"What?" Alec's stomach lurched. "Christ, Luke. Why the hell didn't you mention this when we spoke?"

"It wasn't something Sadie wanted announced. Charlie found out by accident."

"What would you have done, Alec?" Charlotte asked.

"I don't know." He ran his hand through his hair. "Why does she stay with him?"

"She's tried to leave," Charlotte said. "He always finds her and convinces her he'll change."

"It's more than him just finding her," Luke added. "One time, he showed up about thirty minutes after she checked into a hotel. He has surveillance and hacking experience, and I know for a fact he's planted listening devices on her and has her followed by a few of his friends."

Christ, that's crazy. "I'll contact my team and set up a search. It's faster if I have them do it rather than you making calls to every police station and hospital in the city. If we can't locate her, someone will go to her flat and check on her."

"Thank you, Alec," Charlotte said. "And please be careful. He knows who you are and what you look like." The warning in her voice didn't go unnoticed.

Let the bastard try something. "Thanks, Charlie, but I'll be alright. Tell me everything you know about the boyfriend."

Alec gathered what information Luke and Charlotte had on Mercedes's boyfriend, Jason Marsh. He promised to ring them as soon as he heard anything. Hanging up, he took a breath, letting it out slowly.

His mind raced, prioritizing. He needed Declan on this. He slid over to his message app and punched out a text to his cousin:

Emergency call ASAP. I need you. Confirm.

Relief washed over him when the speech bubble popped up immediately.

Whenever you're ready

"You okay?" Mason asked. "What do you need, man? Should I pull over?"

"No, I have to get to London. I need to find her. I'm pulling Cress and Shake from their assignments. This'll take priority." He was already dialing Shake's number.

"Yo, what up, boss?" The ring of Shake's voice came across the line.

"Where are you?"

"Finishing up at the office. Me and Cress are headed out. Lost a bet, so I have to take her to the chippy."

"I need you to put off dinner for a tick. There's an emergency. Have her join, please."

"Oy, Cress. Alec has somethin'. Hand me a pen and get over here," Shake called.

Alec conferenced in Declan while he waited for them to settle. He took a deep breath to help focus his scattered mind.

"All right, go," Cressida said.

"About five minutes ago, I received a missing persons report. The victim is high risk for domestic battery. We're looking for a white female, 32 years old. American. Long dark brown hair, hazel eyes, approximately five feet, five inches tall, medium build. Name is . . . Mercedes Rose Elliott."

"Oh shit," Declan said. "Are you serious?"

"Aye," he confirmed. "Last known sighting was Tuesday afternoon at the Cap and Vin Coffee and Wine Bar. She didn't come in for her expected shifts on Wednesday and Thursday. No call, no show."

He gave the description of Jason Marsh to the team. "White male, blue eyes, blond hair. Medium height and athletic build. He has a significant background in surveillance and IT. The extent of this knowledge is unknown. This man may have access to equipment and have abilities to commandeer security footage. He's kept her under surveillance in the past."

"Got it. Where should we start?" Cressida asked.

"I need a run of all hospital and police records for the past three days in the greater London area." He swallowed hard. "Better check the morgues too."

"Alright, it shouldn't take long."

"I'll also want a complete work up on that piece of shit boyfriend if possible. But find her first," he stressed.

"No problem. Have we confirmed the authenticity of the last seen report?" Cressida said.

Alec let out his breath. "I should hope so. It's mine."

"You saw her?" Declan asked, surprised.

"I did." His heart ached to think of her sad smile. Now he knew why. He cleared his throat. "I know this isn't something we usually do, but this is an important exception. Relay any news immediately and keep this locked down to the five of us. All other projects are on hold. Dec can reassign anything immediate if needed. I think Mariah is finishing her last case and is free. Any questions?"

"Nope," Shake said. "Cress and I are already working on the run. If she's there, we should know in the next ten minutes."

Declan stayed on the line after the others hung up. Alec took the call off speaker and brought it to his ear.

"You okay?" Declan's voice was somber.

"I will be when I know she's okay. Christ, Dec. What will I do if she's . . ." Alec's throat clenched.

"She's not," Declan said. "We'll find her. If things get to be too much, I'm here. I'll run point if needed."

"Thanks, mate." Alec disconnected the call. He couldn't ask for better back up on this. Declan was the only one who knew what Mercedes meant to him.

The meeting at the coffee shop had only lasted a couple of hours, but it was enough time to remind him of what it was like to be near her. Her beautiful, amber-flecked eyes held such sadness in them. Alec had fought the urge to draw her in his arms and erase the pain. Thoughts of her occupied his mind often. What if, while he daydreamed about her, she'd been lying in a morgue?

Alec set his head against the seat, his nerves thrumming. He wasn't used to feeling like this. Most of his adult life had been spent hanging out of helicopters and working covert missions in foreign countries. He'd grown accustomed to stressors from that way of life. But this was different. This was a fear he didn't know what to do with.

It seemed a lifetime before his phone buzzed again, and a grinning picture of Shake came up on his screen. He answered it on speaker. Shake had already conferenced in Cressida and Declan.

"We found her," Cressida said.

Alec's heart thundered. He took in a deep breath, not wanting to ask but knowing he must. "Tell me," he choked out.

Please don't let her be dead.

"They admitted her to Chelsea and Westminster Tuesday night. She's alive and in stable condition. An anonymous caller alerted emergency. She lost a *lot* of blood. Multiple transfusions helped to stabilize her.

"Her chart notes a concussion and extensive contusions, most notably on her face, neck, and abdomen." She paused. "It gets worse, I'm afraid. She has a twelve-inch knife wound running along her midsection. Luckily it was shallow. He missed her vitals."

Bile rose in Alec's throat.

Luck had played no part. That kind of surgical wound served a purpose. Although torture wasn't something he'd ever personally administered, Alec was familiar with the various techniques available to those with the stomach for it.

He pressed his head into his hands as Cressida continued her report. "She has another gash across the inside of her right arm, which resulted in significant blood loss. There was a rudimentary tourniquet applied when they found her, but they came close to losing her. A few minutes longer, and they would have."

She'd been bleeding out. Holy god.

The ache that had formed since hanging up with Luke was becoming more and more unbearable.

"Is there more?"

"Yeah." Cressida hesitated. "There's evidence of sexual assault. Her shirt had been cut away, and there were bite marks. Some broke the skin. They performed a rape kit. The results have yet to come in."

Alec could no longer hear the sound of the road. The thundering in his ears drowned it out. Mercedes had been beaten, tortured, sexually assaulted, possibly raped and left to bleed to death. The image of her living through that agony and fear made his gut churn. How could anyone do such a thing?

"Jesus. Poor little Sadie lass," Declan murmured, cutting into the silence.

Alec blinked hard to keep his eyes from spilling unshed tears. He cleared his throat. "What are the visiting hours? I'll have Mason drop me off as soon as we get to the city."

"Hold up, Alec," Shake said. "You can't walk in there blind. The fuckwit might be there with her. Even if he isn't there himself, Luke said he's kept her under surveillance before."

"Which is fucking weird," Cressida chimed in.

"You might make things worse if you show up in her hospital room uninvited," Shake finished.

Shake had a point. If that bastard was there with her, Alec wouldn't be able to restrain himself.

But he wouldn't stay away either. Mercedes needed to know she wasn't alone. "Okay, what do you suggest?"

"Let me go in there and take a lil' peek. I'll clear the room and make sure she doesn't have company. I think I have a disguise that'll work brilliantly."

"I've already gained access to the hospital's security footage, so I'll do a review of anyone coming and going from her room. It won't be too long. If he's been there, we'll see him," Cressida said.

"Yeah, all right. Let's do it," Alec said. "While you're in there, I want a workup of an extraction plan. I'm not leaving her stranded, thinking she has no way out. Give me something to offer her."

"You got it, man," Shake said. The Bennetts were by far the best support staff he could have with him. Cressida was the strongest overwatch he had, and Shake could adapt to pretty much anything. He'd trusted them with his own life. He could trust them with Mercedes.

While the setup was taking place, Alec called Luke and Charlotte. He was honest but didn't go into the details. Charlotte's quiet sniffles pierced his soul. Luke asked him to stay on the line while he stepped outside, no doubt protecting Charlotte from what he wanted to ask.

"How bad is it? Truly?" Luke asked when Charlotte was out of earshot.

"He fucked her up. It's bad."

"Fuck. Any way you can take the bloody bastard out? It'd be like riding a bike for you." Luke seldom mentioned Alec's training or his time in the service.

"I'd love to, trust me," Alec said. Luke had no idea how much he wanted to put a bullet in the fucker's face. "But getting eyes on Sadie is our priority. I'll let you know when it's done."

He disconnected and sat back, his mind running through the outcomes of seeing her again. What would he say to her? What could he offer her to keep her safe? Would she even want his help? What if she refused?

Jesus, the thought of leaving her in the hands of that piece of shit turned his stomach. But it wasn't up to him. She had to choose. The only thing he could do was make the offer.

CHAPTER TEN

Exhaustion made Mercedes want to weep. She hadn't a moment of sleep since the night they admitted her. Every injury throbbed. Her muscles ached from the hospital bed. There was no way to get comfortable.

Constant noise kept her wrecked nerves fully activated. The staff came and went from her room at all hours. Nurses changing shifts came to poke at her stitches or check her heart monitor. A sweet-faced custodian named Sandy felt it necessary to empty her trash can in the middle of the night. He apologized profusely, and she found it hard to stay annoyed with his puppy-dog brown eyes and crooked smile.

Anxiety kept her head spinning. What was she going to do? Where could she go? She'd have to decide soon, and none of the options were ideal. Counting out her breaths to relax, she hoped for at least a few hours of sleep to think straight. She was drifting off when a soft rustling woke her.

Mercedes's heart skipped a beat. Jason never visited. Doctors asked too many questions, so he stayed away. His friends often stood vigil, but always from a distance.

She braced herself and turned toward the noise. A man was occupying the lounge chair next to her bed. His broad shoulders bent forward, and his head was down, resting on his clasped hands. A black baseball cap obscured his face.

Scrambling for the call button, Mercedes winced as pain shot through her side. But then he looked up, and her heart stopped altogether.

Alec.

Her hand hovered over the switch as she stared into Alec's vivid blue eyes. Mercedes cast her gaze away, afraid there would be a disappointment in their stormy depths. He was the last person who should see her like this.

Alec reached out, his hand gentle as he guided her chin to face him. Mercedes forced herself to breathe as she met his eyes again. He showed no hint of pity or disgust. She didn't think she could bear either.

Instead, his piercing gaze roamed, taking stock of her injuries. Alec's thumb grazed her jaw as he studied her, the emotions in his eyes saying what he had yet to voice.

Mercedes opened her mouth, but Alec held up a finger to his lips and shook his head. She frowned as he pulled a gadget from his pocket. A blinking light pulsed from the device. He flipped a switch, and the light went out.

In a low voice, he said, "Artemis, going dark. Check-in ten minutes. Copy." He must have seen her confusion because he smiled at her. "We can speak freely now. You have a listening device planted somewhere in that bag of your things. I've disabled it."

Of course, there was. Fucking Jason.

Alec leaned toward her and captured her hand between his. A bolt of electricity shot through her, his warm hands enveloping hers. She hadn't realized she'd been cold until he touched her.

"Are you okay? Can I get you anything?"

Mercedes shook her head and tried to compose herself. "How did you know?"

"Your manager called Charlie. She called me. And, when

they told me of your . . . *friend's* tendency to put you in places like this, it didn't take us long to track you down."

Damn it.

She'd kept a lot of things from Charlotte, thinking she was protecting her. Apparently, she failed at that too. A wave of guilt washed over her. Her sister would be sick with worry.

"The police are investigating this as a burglary and assault, but I think you and I both know they won't find anything. Especially since you don't seem be cooperating."

To anyone else, she could downplay what happened. But she couldn't lie to Alec. He knew the worst parts of it already. "They never believe me anyway."

"Can you tell me?" When she hesitated, Alec squeezed her hand. "I'll believe you," he whispered.

Tears filled her eyes. "He came home acting a little off. Suddenly, he became irate and he . . . he just lost it." She stared at their hands, a single tear traveling down her face. "It's been bad in the past, but I've never seen him like that."

"Why was he irate?"

Mercedes grimaced. "He found out I . . . met with you for coffee. He had pictures. He accused me of sleeping with you."

Rage crossed his face. "That son of a bitch," he hissed.

"I'm sorry," she choked.

Alec's head snapped up. "Why are you sorry?"

"Because I got you involved in this. That wasn't my intention when I called you."

"Stop. You didn't do anything wrong." His eyes were alight with emotion, but she didn't flinch from him. Instead, she found herself unable to look away. "Christ, you've nothing to apologize for. You understand *you're* the victim here, right?"

She nodded. Another tear escaped, creating a path down her cheek.

Alec's eyes softened, and he wiped it away with a lingering stroke of his thumb. Mercedes touched his hand, turning her cheek into his palm. The warmth of his hand soothed and seared her all at once.

Closing her eyes, she breathed him in. *Please don't let me go.*

"You have to leave him." Alec's voice was brimming with torment.

Mercedes's eyes snapped open, and she pulled away. Panic welled in her chest. "I can't."

"Yes, you can."

"He'll find me. It's embarrassing how fast he is at tracking me down. He knows everything I do. I mean, he plants listening devices in my hospital room, for God's sake."

"I can help you." Alec's fingers tightened on hers. "We can get you out of here. Give you a safe place to recover. When you're ready, we'll get you home. Declan and I already have people ready to go."

Her heart sank. "Dec knows too?"

"Aye, he does. You're pretty much family, you know? A McKinley twice removed, if you will." His mouth quirked in a smile, and she couldn't help smiling, which made her wince.

"Why would you do this?"

His amiable smile faded, and his jaw tightened. A sadness crossed behind his eyes as he looked at their intertwined hands. His thumb swept back and forth against her wrist, sending thrills of electricity through her with each stroke.

Alec swallowed. "I can't leave you here. At least not without giving you a choice."

"You don't know what you're asking. He's dangerous."

"I can handle him. But he's escalating, and next time he might kill you. Do you have any idea how close it was?" His fingers moved up to her bandaged forearm.

"They told me." Her voice was flat. "He didn't even mean to do that one. I was fighting him, and the knife hit me. He meant the others, though."

"Jesus, please let me help you." Alec's words were hitched.

"I can only offer you my help; I can't make you take it. You have to choose."

Mercedes gazed around her bleak, sterile surroundings, taking stock of her life. Frightened, alone, in pain, and struggling to keep her anxiety at bay, she was a shell of herself. Here was a lifeline—someone to give her a little cover while she put herself back together. Every ounce of sense told her she should grab onto it.

But she'd already been burned playing with the fire Alec ignited. He might be offering the help she desperately needed, but could she live with the cost?

"What if . . ." she choked. "What if you bail on me again? When he finds me, it'll be a thousand times worse."

Alec flinched as if she had slapped him. He opened his mouth to speak but was cut off. The person in his ear was back. He murmured to them, then looked at her. "Shit, I have to go."

Her heart sank, and she gave him a tight smile. They hadn't even been able to get through the conversation before he was ready to jump ship.

Alec took her hand again. "I'm *not* bailing on you. I'd stay here all night if I could. But the man watching you is coming this way. It won't do either of us any good if he finds me here." He cupped her cheek in his hand again. "You don't have a lot of time to decide. I'll send someone to you tomorrow. I'll need your answer then. Aye?"

"Okay."

"You have to decide if you can trust me." His eyes pleading with her.

At her nod, Alec leaned over and kissed her forehead. The scent of fresh air and earth filled her senses, and she inhaled. He made his way to the door, giving her one last encouraging smile, then disappeared as silently as he'd come. It was as if a vacuum pulled through the room, sucking out all the warmth and leaving her in loneliness. Mercedes ached to call out for him to come back and stay with her. That she didn't care who saw him . . . but she knew better.

Drained of her last bit of energy, she lay back against the stiff pillow and closed her eyes, her fingers searching for the rhythm that would calm her into sleep. The lingering woodsy scent of Alec dulled the medicinal smell.

And as she drifted off into a much-needed sleep, his words returned to her: *You have to decide if you can trust me.*

CHAPTER ELEVEN

Mercedes's eyes burned, and her temples ached. Morning had come much too quickly. An abandoned tray of breakfast sat on the swivel table untouched. Even thinking about food made her stomach twist.

She'd awoken with no clearer idea of what she should do. Alec's offer was more than generous, but she didn't see how she could accept. Putting others at risk terrified her. Given the jealous rage Jason had flown into over a simple coffee date, he might already have a target on Alec.

Not to mention her attraction to Alec hadn't diminished over the years. From the moment they met at the hotel bar in Edinburgh, the chemistry between them had been pure fire.

Her fingers played a cadence against her stiff plastic hospital bracelet as she thought back to that night so long ago.

It was only early evening when she'd arrived in Scotland, but Mercedes had been looking forward to a hot shower and bed. So, when Charlotte called her about the impromptu cocktail hour being arranged in the bar, she almost cried. Twenty hours of delayed flights and a heavy dose of jet lag had her dragging ass. Getting dressed up to chat with strangers didn't sound appealing at all.

But Charlotte was so insecure about the lack of support on their side of the aisle that Mercedes caved. Tossing aside her comfy pajamas, she put on a classic black cocktail dress and heels that went well with every occasion. With a touch-up to her hair and makeup, she hoped to make a decent impression on Charlotte's new family.

Mercedes had envisioned a sedate lounge filled with Luke's elderly relatives talking about the wedding over glasses of wine. She wasn't ready for the cacophony of unruly Scots gathered. Scouting the room, she spotted Luke waving to her at the bar and made her way toward him. She was nearly to him when a lanky man stepped in her path.

"Hello, you must be on the bride's side. You're too pretty to be from this family."

Mercedes cringed at the line but fixed a polite smile on her face. "That's correct. I'm Mercedes Elliott, Charlotte's sister." She held her hand to him. He took it and gripped it despite her tug to take it back.

"Lovely to meet you. I'm one of Luke's cousins."

"Oh, are you Declan or Alec?" She frowned, taking in the man's features. Luke told her he and his cousins were often mistaken for brothers.

The smile left his face. "I'm not a McKinley; I'm from his mother's side," he sneered, dropping her hand. "I guess you like your men pretty."

Mercedes raised her eyebrow. "Oh, okay then. Excuse me." She brushed past him, but his hand snaked around her waist and pulled her to him. His breath reeked of old booze and onions. "Maybe you'll save a dance at the wedding for me then, lass?"

She narrowed her eyes at him. "If you don't take your fucking hands off me, they'll need to recover your tiny balls out of your asshole." She said it loud enough for others to hear her. A few stopped their conversation and stared at them.

"Ha. Get tae fuck off, Georgie," a nearby man jeered. The

others joined in, hooting. Georgie's hand snapped back to his side, his ruddy face reddening. Mercedes held his eyes, giving him an icy glare as he slunk away.

"That was fucking brilliant," an unfamiliar voice called.

A tall man, who clearly *was* a McKinley, leaned against the bar next to Luke. Same stunning blue eyes, same dark hair, and solid frame. By the identical looks of amusement, they'd caught the show.

"Christ, Luke. What the hell's up with that guy?" she asked, giving her soon-to-be brother-in-law a hug.

Luke snorted. "That's Georgie. He's always been a wanker. Not a proper first impression of this clan, I'm afraid," he apologized.

The unnamed McKinley held his hand out to her. A spark of electricity shot through her when she took it.

"I'm Alec. One of the pretty ones," he added with a crooked grin. "I owe you a drink, 'cause that was the most entertaining thing I've seen all week. What can I get you, lass?"

The way the words rolled off his tongue sent warmth shivering through her. Her logical mind told her that Luke shared this Scottish cadence and dialect. But Luke was just Luke. Alec was something else altogether.

"Well, it's my first night in Scotland. I suppose I'll have a whisky." She let her eyes fall on the glass in his hand, her gaze lingering on its way up. She took a moment to appreciate the way his shoulders filled out his dress shirt. "What do you suggest?"

Flirting with strangers wasn't something she did often, but it was so easy with him. From the way he cocked his head and grinned, he didn't mind at all.

After that night, they went out of their way to see each other. He offered to drive her to the florist for a change in the floral arrangements and to the tailor's for a final fitting. She moved seats with her sister to sit next to him at family dinners. Whenever they were together, they got lost in conversation, often forgetting their surroundings. She wanted to believe he was as attracted to her as she was to him.

Mercedes should have known better. She'd spent her childhood wondering what it felt like to be treasured, to be someone's everything. But being someone's everything wasn't who she was. The people she cared for could walk away from her with little impact to their lives. Alec had been no exception.

She'd put the trip to Scotland and the resulting months out of her mind years ago. It was nothing but another bitter reminder of how disposable she was. None of it was relevant now. Her goal was to extricate herself from the worst relationship of her life, not rekindle a crush on an unattainable man.

Taking a breath to focus herself, she ran down the list of options. Perhaps she could run to the American Embassy. The nurses might help her get a cab. First, she'd have to figure out how to get rid of the listening device. Plus, there were Jason's watchdogs. The closer she got to being released, the tighter they'd circle her.

"Hello, love." The voice came out of nowhere. Mercedes jumped, a yelp escaping her.

She'd been so engrossed in hatching her escape plan that she hadn't heard the woman come into her room. She was rather pretty, with a smooth, olive complexion, wide brown eyes, and dark caramel hair pulled back in a curly bun, tendrils framing her face.

"Oh, I'm so sorry to startle you out of your daydream, lass. My name is Sarah." Her R's rolled gently. "I'm a victim advocate. They asked me to pop in, thought you might need a wee bit of support."

Mercedes, wary of the unsolicited help, shot a glance at the name badge swinging from a lanyard around the woman's neck. "That's okay. I was staring off into space."

"Oh, my. You're an American. Far from home, are ya,

lass? Me as well, but I'm only from Dublin, so nae so bad. Have you ever been?"

"Um, to Dublin? Unfortunately, no."

Sarah found no shortage of things to discuss. The rain in Ireland compared to England, and how it was likely to be a pisser out there today, but she loved the flowers in the spring. Mercedes smiled, all the while reminding herself to keep her guard. Sarah busied herself flitting around Mercedes's bed, adjusting this or fluffing that, talking the whole while about nothing at all.

When she drew a breath, she turned her warm gaze onto Mercedes. "How are you feeling, love? Are you tolerating your pain medication okay?"

"I'm not taking anything. They tried to give me Sutanyl. I won't put that in my body."

Sarah frowned. "What are your plans for your discharge? Can I help arrange something for you?"

A qualm of fear shivered up her spine. Was this a test? Had they sent this person to test her loyalty to Jason? Even if Sarah was nothing more than a kind advocate, Jason could hear everything.

"No, my boyfriend will come to get me." The words tasted bitter.

"You sure that's what you want, lass?" Sarah crinkled her brow. "There are other choices for you."

"I'm sure." Even to her own ears, her response came off as weak.

Sarah nodded, resigned. She looked at her watch. "Oh my dear, listen to me goin' on and on, and you absolutely wrecked. Just one thing more, and I'll leave you be. Do you like music?"

"Um, yeah."

"I thought as much. You've the look of a musical lass." Sarah rummaged in her pocket, eventually holding out a wireless earbud. Mercedes wanted to refuse, but Sarah insisted.

"Oh, please listen. It'll be just the thing."

Mercedes took the earbud and placed it in her ear. She noticed Sarah was already wearing one. For a moment, nothing happened. Mercedes jumped when, instead of music, a man spoke to her. "Sadie, it's Alec. Don't speak."

Mercedes's heart leapt at his voice. Her gaze darted to the woman in front of her, who batted her lashes and gave her a serene smile.

"I hope you'll forgive the deception," he said. "The person before you isn't called Sarah. She's my associate, Cressida Bennett. She's also not Irish, but her accent has improved." Cressida Bennett smiled and rolled her eyes. "It's time, Sadie. Do you want our help, or should we stand down? You can give a nod to Cress, and we'll get started."

Mercedes hesitated, turmoil burning through her. Cressida cocked her head to the side, her compassionate smile encouraging her to say yes. The agonizing "what if" game assailed her. Frozen in panic, she imagined all the terrifying things that could befall Alec or even this pretty, sweet-faced woman. She couldn't live with herself if Jason hurt them.

Alec must have sensed her distress. "I know you're frightened, and I don't blame you." His voice was calming, and she closed her eyes to listen. "This is what I do, and I'm damn good at it. In the last twelve hours, we've been to see you three times without them having the slightest clue." Mercedes's eyes shot open, and she frowned. Cressida gave a crooked smile. Who else had been here?

"Sadie, there's no amount of money I wouldn't pay, no time I wouldn't give or risk I wouldn't take to protect you from that man. I would, *quite literally*, do anything to keep you safe." Alec paused. "Can you trust me?"

Her breath caught in her throat.

She had to forgive him for what had happened between them years ago and acknowledge what he was ready to do for her now. Cressida, who had taken her hand, offered silent support.

The tears welled in Mercedes's eyes. Inhaling deeply, she nodded her head.

Cressida broke into a triumphant grin. "Isn't it *lovely*? One of my favorites."

Mercedes quirked an eyebrow until she heard Alec exhale, "Oh, thank god," the relief thick in his voice. "Alright, here's where we are. You're scheduled for release tomorrow morning. And if we know, then he knows. We'll have to move you today. Later this afternoon, someone will escort you to the radiology department. From then on, you only need to follow his lead. If all goes well, I'll see you in a few hours."

It was strange to not be able to respond, so she removed the piece and gave it back to Cressida.

"Wasn't that wonderful? I always thought music could calm the soul. Now have a bite, lass." Cressida glanced at her untouched tray, her meaning clear: *Eat that.* "Try to rest. Recovery takes a lot of energy, to be sure."

"Thank you, Sarah. I feel much better."

The petite brunette scrunched her nose at her on her way out. "You're quite welcome. We'll speak again soon."

Mercedes took a shaky breath and let it out, her heart racing. The next few nerve-wracking hours would take their toll. She only hoped her battered body would comply if she had to run.

CHAPTER TWELVE

Every little noise made Mercedes's heartbeat plunge. Her nerves were shot. When Alec's man arrived, she could only gape at him. It was the same boyishly charming custodian, Sandy, who had woken her last night. Only now, he'd dressed in scrubs.

His face broke into a crooked grin at her recognition. "Hello, Ms. Elliott, I understand you needed a ride to radiology for scans before your doctor releases you?"

Sandy set to work, helping her into the wheelchair, all the while chatting pleasantly. He poked around the nightstand and the pile of clothes on the top, producing her cellphone. Jason had installed tracking software on it months ago, so she rarely used it.

Sandy continued his aimless chatter as he steered the chair out of the room. Mercedes tried to respond to the small talk, but her mind raced. This was it, no turning back.

The hospital's atrium windows towered overhead as he pushed her across the sunlit walkway. She caught sight of Adam Wilson, one of Jason's friends, leaning against a wall near the bank of elevators. He was tall, handsome, and hard to miss. She despised him.

Adam held her gaze. Mercedes's stomach roiled, but she kept her face passive. Did he know their plan?

When the doors opened, Sandy spun her chair around and backed into the lift. To her surprise, Adam peeled himself from the wall and joined them, pushing the button for one floor below.

The elevator slid shut, and she couldn't contain the trembling of her hands. Her heart was thumping so loud in her chest she was certain they could hear it. When the back of her neck prickled, she looked beside her. Adam had his eyes fixed on her, a sneer playing on his lips.

Mercedes held his gaze. The more time he spent looking at her, the less he was taking in Alec's associate. The young man was humming to himself, oblivious to Adam. The door slid open, and Adam stepped past them.

"Ma'am." Adam shot a final smirk at her.

Mercedes let out a shaky sigh as the doors closed.

"Prick," her new friend muttered. So, he had known who Adam was.

They arrived in the lobby, and her heart sank. Perched on a bench in the corridor sat Patrick Moore, another of Jason's friends.

Oh, for God's sake, don't these guys have anything else to do?

At least Patrick had the courtesy to appear indifferent to her. He didn't look up from his book when she rolled past.

The radiology and imaging department was a maze of rooms and hallways. Her chair turned into an unlit room with an examination table and a collection of medical equipment on rolling carts. Sandy took a quick peek outside the room, flipped on the lights, and quietly shut the door.

"Hi, Sadie." He kneeled before her. "I'm Shake."

Mercedes laughed. "Shake? I thought it was Sandy?"

Shake grinned and picked up a black backpack hidden in the corner. "Well, you can call me Sandy if you like. It's kind of my name, I guess. But only my Nan calls me that."

He pulled several articles of clothing out of the bag, laying them on the exam table.

"Apollo to Artemis, do you copy? Confirmed. Symphony secured and in place. ETA for stage two"—he checked his watch—"eight minutes."

He turned to her. "Right, here are some clothes for you. Do you need help getting dressed?"

"If you'd untie my gown, I think I can do the rest."

He complied, discreetly turning away. After five days in the hospital, modesty wasn't a priority, but she appreciated the gesture. Back turned, Shake stripped off his scrubs, a light blue plaid button-up, and khakis on underneath. To Mercedes, he looked like a different person.

She dressed as quickly as she could. Beads of sweat gathered on her brow, and she was shaking again. It was the most physical activity she'd had in days, and her weakened body was revolting.

She looked down at her ensemble and frowned. "The shirt's huge. Is it supposed to be this way?" She was swimming in it.

"Oh. That's the best bit of the plan."

Returning to the black bag, Shake rummaged around until he pulled out an oval-shaped pillow with a long, thick strap dangling from one side. Mercedes tilted her head at the contraption.

"It's to, you know, make you look preggers."

She raised her eyebrows at him. The corner of his mouth turned up. "No one looks at a woman when she's in labor. Makes people uncomfortable. Especially those two tossers."

Shake examined her face. "We have to do something about these bruises, though." With that, he produced a small makeup bag filled with an assortment of tubes and brushes.

"I don't have time to do a perfect concealment, but it should make you less conspicuous. This stuff is thick, and when it dries, a bit like cement." He worked deftly, layering the heavy cream on her face in gentle strokes.

"You know a lot about concealers," she remarked.

"I do." He laughed, turning her face to get better coverage. "My mum's an actor. My sister and I grew up in and out of West End theaters. Spent all our school holidays working with costume changes and such. Even had a few minor roles here and there. That's why Alec likes us to do this work. We're good at playing a part."

"We? Your sister works with Alec too?"

He grinned. "Oh, for sure. You met her already."

"Cressida?"

"Yep, she's my twin."

The resemblance became so obvious, she didn't know how she'd missed it. They shared the same warm brown eyes and soft curly hair, though his was cut shorter.

She couldn't seem to harness the belly around her waist, so Shake moved to help. When she lifted her shirt, he sucked in his breath with a hiss.

"Sorry, love. Didn't think about this part. This'll probably hurt."

"It's okay, I can manage."

Shake tightened the strap around her waist. She winced when the rough trim rubbed against her stitches, pulling when she moved.

But the finished result made it worth it. She looked like a trendy, expectant mother.

"Apollo and Symphony are ready." Shake packed the makeup into the bag. So she was Symphony then. Alec must have played a part in giving her the name.

"Right then. When we walk out this door, another member will escort us."

"Wouldn't more people draw attention?"

"Quite the opposite. Those buggers will be looking for an

orderly and a woman in a wheelchair. They won't even see us." He zipped the bag and slung it over his shoulder. "Plus, we need one of the big guys to carry you if our cover is blown and we have to run for it."

The blood rushed away from her face, making her head spin. She hoped it wouldn't come to that.

"Alright." Shake looked her over one more time. "Do what you think a laboring mother would do. Breathe heavy, cry out, or swear at me if you like; that'd be fun. But don't do it in your own accent. If they hear an American, it'll catch their attention."

Mercedes took all this in, terrified she'd make a mistake.

As Shake reached for the doorknob, he stopped. "Oh, and make sure you waddle."

"Waddle?" It struck her as absurd.

"Yeah, like." He made a penguin-like motion with his hands. "You know, waddle."

Mercedes couldn't help but smile at him. He looked ridiculous.

"Oi, you know what I mean." His grin told her he didn't mind the ribbing.

Mercedes agreed to add a little extra waddle to her step. And with that, she followed him out. A doctor leaned against the wall, reading a clipboard. When he turned, it took a beat to recognize him. The dancing blue eyes, so like his cousins', were gone. In their place, a pair of coffee-brown eyes peered over wire-framed glasses. He wore scrubs and a white coat, a colorful surgical cap covering his dark hair.

"Declan?"

He pulled her into a gentle hug. "Hi, Sadie lass. How ya feeling?"

"Nervous, but I'll do. Ready to waddle out of here."

He flashed a grin at her, then spoke into his earpiece that they were ready to move. Shake intertwined his arm with hers, and she allowed herself to lean on him. With a deep breath, she took her first steps into the main corridor as a laboring woman, supported by her apprehensive sweetheart.

CHAPTER THIRTEEN

S hake set the pace toward the elevator. Mercedes kept her head down, grimacing. She wasn't faking her discomfort. The strap around her waist irritated the hell out of her side.

She stole a glance at Patrick. He had lifted his head toward the radiology entrance, observing anyone who came in and out. His gaze moved toward them. So she cried out, slowing Shake down. Patrick shifted his attention to his book.

Huh, how bout that.

For their parts, Declan and Shake played the part of doctor and overwrought father-to-be brilliantly.

"Um, yeah, like is this normal?" Shake squawked at Declan.

"Yes, this is par for the course at this stage. We'll check her progress when we get her settled into a room."

They hobbled through the waiting area and were feet from the main hall when Mercedes's weakened knee gave out, rolling her ankle outward. She lurched to the side. Shake caught her, but her elbow jammed into her damaged ribs. A flash of blinding white pain hit her.

Mercedes clutched onto consciousness, taking full, even

breaths through her nose. She couldn't pass out in the waiting room.

Shake's voice pierced through the veil, becoming clearer as the pain receded. "Babe, are you all right? Babe?"

Somewhere in the fog, she fought to keep it together. "I'll do. Can I get my bloody drugs now?" she snapped in an English accent.

Her side throbbed, but the bank of elevators were only steps away. Her grip was cutting into Shake's hand. When they reached the doors, Shake murmured in her ear. "Alec says, 'Hang on a little longer. It'll be over soon.'"

Mercedes stared at him in surprise. Alec could hear them?

Once inside, Declan turned to her. "Are you all right?"

"I think so." The pain had subsided to a dull ache. "Are we safe to talk now?"

"Aye, Cress is manipulating the live camera streams. Anyone monitoring the feed will see an empty lift until its next pickup."

"Damn it. She's bleeding," Shake interjected. "Is it your rib or your arm?"

A crimson blotch was spreading across the floral maternity shirt and smearing against her sleeve. The nurses had dressed the injury on her forearm with a gauze bandage, but they'd left the long ribbon winding down her abdomen uncovered.

"It's the ribs, but I don't think it's bad," she said.

Shake traded a smirk with Declan. They both must have heard the same thing in their earpieces.

Declan rolled his eyes. "Aye, reel it in, man. She'll be all right." He turned to Mercedes. "Keep your arm against your body to hide it. Hopefully, they won't want to look at you."

"What every girl wants to hear," Mercedes snarked. Declan gave her a crooked grin.

The elevator opened, and the bustle of people disoriented her. They had arrived in the hospital's basement, the main entrance from the parking garage. Shake, holding her hand, led her off the lift and into the busy hallway.

She was keeping pace until her eyes landed on a familiar face in the crowd, stopping her heart.

Letting go of Shake, she spun and prayed he hadn't seen her. She dashed into an adjoining hallway and leaned against the wall for support. Taken aback, Declan and Shake followed.

"Jason's here," she whispered. "I think he saw me."

"You're sure?" Declan asked.

"Yes. Black jacket, brown hat near the car park entrance."

Declan scanned the hall. His eyes landed on a single, unisex bathroom. He threw the door open, hustled her inside, and jerked it closed behind her. Mercedes sat on the edge of the toilet seat, giving her protesting legs a break.

It was several minutes before the door opened, and Declan slid inside, the backpack over his shoulder. He was in mid-argument with his earpiece about this unexpected development.

"I don't think he saw her, but the bastard's not leaving. And we can't stay in the loo all day." There was a long pause. "What do you want me to do, shoot him in the middle of a hospital? Aye, I bet you would." Another pause. "You can't be seen here, and you know it. We have to shift to Plan B."

Declan seemed to win the battle and knelt next to her.

"How you holding up, lass?"

"Eh, I've been better." Mercedes shot him a crooked smile. Her muscles refused to stop trembling.

"We're going a different way. Luckily, we already have someone in place at that exit; we just have to get there. Can you manage?"

"Yeah, I'll be alright."

Declan stood and stripped off the blue scrubs, revealing a Manchester United jersey and a pair of jeans underneath, and shoved everything into the bag. Keeping the glasses on, he added a ball cap to cover his dark hair.

He helped her to her feet, and they rejoined Shake in the hall. "Don't worry about the act." Declan took her hand.

They returned to the elevators and rode up on a packed lift. Mercedes's nerves were on edge. She expected Jason to appear at any moment. Declan squeezed her hand. She looked up at him, and he smiled like this was just another day. How could he be so calm?

Then they were on the move again, walking as fast as Mercedes could manage across a glass atrium walkway. About midway across, Declan paused, sharing an alarmed look with Shake.

"Shit," he muttered. He put his hand on her back and hustled her across the narrow bridge. Her head swam, but she did her best to keep up with Declan's long strides.

"I'm so sorry. Dickhead number one changed course."

Declan put his back to an adjoining wall, spun her to face, him and pulled her into his arms in an embrace. He held the back of her head against his shoulder, his head buried against hers. Much like his cousin, he had a powerful upper body and gave great hugs.

"How'd you know he was there?" she murmured.

"Cress. She sees everything."

Mercedes smiled against his shoulder, grateful for a moment to catch her breath. "Why do you think Jason was here? I've never seen him at the hospital before. Do you think he knows something is up?"

"Aye, maybe. These assholes are ridiculous. But as soon as this slow arse piece of shite gets past us, we will be out the door."

Declan ducked his head closer. Adam must be in the same room as them now. She peered beyond Declan's shirt and saw him. She pressed her face against Declan's chest again and waited for some sort of sign.

Shake moved first, and Declan followed. They led her through the grand foyer of the main entrance. The glass doors shushed open, and for the first time in days, she was outside.

The soft cool rain touched her face, and she inhaled, grateful for fresh air. Declan, his hand in hers, led her down the sidewalk toward a black van.

The door slid open, and Cressida popped her head out. "Hello, love."

A tall Black man jumped out of the van, holding his hand out to her. Mercedes took it and stepped up, her legs like rubber. Declan and Shake jumped into the front seat. The van pulled away from the curb before the door slid shut.

The Black man gave her a warm smile. "Hi Sadie, I'm Mason Wright. I'm the team medic. I'd like to have a quick look at that laceration that's giving you trouble." He nodded to the blood on her shirt. "I might have to stitch you up tonight."

Mercedes's heart was slowing to a normal pace. The muscle aches returned with a vengeance, and the violent trembling made it difficult to remove the baby bump. A sheen of sweat covered her forehead.

Mason donned surgical gloves from his bag and examined her injuries while she tried to keep her balance. After he finished probing her ribs, he took her blood pressure and temperature and clipped an oxygen monitor to her finger.

"That wound will need watching, and I'm a little concerned about your color. Once you get some rest, that should improve."

"I can't seem to make the shaking stop."

"It's alright," Mason soothed. "Your body is recovering from all the stress. Adrenaline hangovers are a bitch. You might feel terrible for the rest of the day."

"Eh, I wasn't planning on feeling good today anyway," she quipped, which made them chuckle.

Laying her head back, Mercedes took in her surroundings.

They didn't feel real. It was like any moment she'd wake up and still be in that shitty apartment.

As she glanced around the van at the near-strangers who were risking their own safety for her, her heart swelled in gratitude. She wasn't going back to him, she vowed. "Thank you. I don't know what I'd have done without your help."

"Of course, love," Shake called from the front seat. "It was either that or watch the boss go to prison for putting a bullet in an arsehole's head. We thought this was a better route."

"That was his plan A," Declan laughed. She tried not to read too much into that.

"Can I ask for a favor?" she asked Cressida. "I mean, another favor." She waved her hand around her getaway van.

"Of course."

"Can you help me make a call to Jason tonight? A safe one?" Cressida hesitated. "Please? I need some closure."

"Alright." Cressida's face broke into a wide grin. "I'll be there cheering you on while you tell that wanker to piss off."

The van slowed to a snail's pace, and she peered out the window to see if there was a problem. Shouldn't they be driving as fast as they could out of the area? No one else seemed concerned. They pulled into a parking space and stopped. Declan jumped out and opened the sliding door. The brown contacts were gone, and his cobalt blue eyes had returned. He looked like Dec again.

"Come on out," He offered his hand to her.

Mercedes's legs had become relatively useless, but she somehow made it to Declan. The drizzling had subsided, and the sun's afternoon rays peeked from behind the clouds. They had pulled into a wooded park. Beyond a walking trail and a concrete wall, the River Thames flowed by.

"We didn't go far." They couldn't have been traveling even ten minutes. She had hoped to get as far from Jason as possible.

"Oh, aye. This is just a brief stop. Someone was anxious."

Declan lifted his chin toward the walking path. She turned to see Alec striding toward her. An unexpected relief washed over her, and she took a step toward him. The sun cast a rich glow across his defined features, sparking fire and copper in his dark hair. His vivid blue eyes took her in as he approached.

Without a pause in his stride, he opened his arms and enveloped her, his warmth and security folding in around her. No longer holding back her need to touch him, she sighed and sank into him, savoring the feel of his body against hers.

CHAPTER FOURTEEN

Alec held her gently, not wanting to hurt her battered body. She trembled in his arms, and he rubbed her back to warm her. He didn't want to let her go, but he pulled away, taking her in. Her eyes were enormous, and the gray pallor of her lips made the thick concealer garish in the light. The blood on her shirt had dried, and there was no evidence of fresh bleeding.

"Are you all right then?"

Mercedes nodded, her teeth chattering.

It was Cressida who spoke from inside the van. "Holding up like a champ. She's had a hell of a go of it, and the poor thing's knackered."

Mercedes moved into his arms again, resting her head against his chest. The tension that had grown in him since he'd gotten the call finally released. She was safe and letting him hold her. It was more than he could have asked for.

He looked to Cressida. "They know she's gone yet?"

Cressida leaned back to the bank of monitors. "Nope. Jason met up with Dickhead One. They're hanging out by a coffee cart. Dickhead Two is still in the imaging waiting room. He's pacing, so it won't be long."

Feeling Mercedes's energy waning, Alec guided her toward his black SUV he had parked several spaces down. The team followed. "All right, Dec, you're with us. The rest of you, work on setting up and securing the location. We'll take the long way to get out there."

Alec opened one of the rear doors. Mercedes climbed in and sighed, laying her head against the seat. After the last few instructions, the team was off, and he joined her in the back seat. She'd already belted herself in and was leaning back with her eyes closed.

When he touched her hand, she opened them and smiled at him. "Alec," she murmured. Warmth spread through him. How was it just hearing her say his name made him crazy for her?

"You sure you're alright?" She looked so damn fragile.

Mercedes yawned. "I will be. I just need some sleep."

"Would you like this?" he asked, reaching behind the seat to take out a heavy faux-fur blanket. "We have a bit of a drive, so I grabbed it for you."

"Oh, that looks amazing."

Alec grinned at her and unfurled it over her. He could feel her eyes on him.

Declan got in behind the wheel and maneuvered the car out of its space. Alec moved to the other side and made to buckle in, but her voice stopped him.

"Do you think . . . maybe I can lean on you? Leaning against the window won't be as comfortable."

Another thrill of energy shot through him, making his heart jump. Did she realize what she was doing to him?

Alec shifted back to the middle seat and put his arm around her, drawing her in. Mercedes nestled her head against his chest, still vibrating with tremors.

She sighed. "Better be keeping a tally."

"A tally?"

"Mm-hmm." She yawned. "A tally of all the favors I owe you. I can't keep up."

He chuckled. Even in her exhaustion, she kept her sense of humor. Mercedes burrowed under the blanket, closed her eyes, and was asleep before they reached the motorway.

Alec kept turning his head to check the cars behind them, doing his best not to jostle Mercedes as she slept.

"I could keep a better lookout for tails if your fat head weren't in the way," Declan said, amused.

"That's probably true. Can't blame me though, aye?"

"Oh, aye. I noticed you didn't tell her there's a pillow in the back."

Alec caught his cousin's eye in the mirror and smiled sheepishly at him, saying nothing more.

"You doing all right? With, you know, everything?"

Alec shrugged. "I want to kill the son of a bitch. But my priority is getting her whatever she needs."

"What about when this is over? It's clear you still have a thing for her."

Alec looked at Mercedes, breathing softly against him, her face upturned in a way that allowed him to study her features in the fading evening light. She was as close to perfection as he'd ever met. Smart and kind, funny and talented. And so damn beautiful. She could leave him breathless with a look.

Yeah, he still had a thing for her. It didn't seem to be something he could control. No one but Declan knew how much it had hurt to let her go all those years ago. Long-distance relationships were always challenging, and theirs had been no exception. Add that he hadn't asked her to make it exclusive, and it all fell apart.

Months later, when Luke let it slip, Mercedes had introduced them to a new man. It had stung. He'd hoped she had found happiness in the person she had chosen. It was hard to swallow that Jason Marsh had been her choice.

Seeing her so shattered now ripped his heart into shreds.

How could anyone do so much damage to someone they claimed to love? It wasn't just the physical abuse, but the way he'd torn her down, stripping away everything she loved, everything she was . . .

Mercedes shifted. Her hand slid up his chest, coming to rest over his heart. She sighed and settled back to sleep.

Alec was getting hard again, and guilt washed over him. She was in crisis, for Christ's sake. He had to stop thinking of her that way. His cock disagreed.

He needed to get his shit together.

If they were to cross that line, it would mean cutting open his soul and leaving it bare for her to ravage. Alec didn't think he could go through losing her again.

He swallowed hard. "I don't know, Dec. I think the chance for anything between us is over."

PART II

CHAPTER FIFTEEN

This can't be happening. This can not be fucking happening. Jason's breath was haggard as he stood at the nurse's station, his heart racing in his ears.

"I want to know where the *fuck* my fiancée is. *Now.*" His voice was working up to a roar.

Adam put a hand on his shoulder. Jason wrenched it away.

"Sir, don't shout at me. You aren't her next of kin, so the only thing I can share with you is that Ms. Elliott is no longer in our care."

"But when did she leave? Who did you release her to?"

"Again. I'm not allowed to share that informa—"

Jason slammed his hands on the table with a growl. The nurse jumped.

"For fuck's sake, you'll get us arrested. There are other ways," Adam hissed.

Jason stared at the nurse, wanting to choke the life out of that smug face.

Instead, he strode away from the desk, his entire body geared up for a fight. He couldn't unload it on Adam, so he glared around, looking for a target.

His phone vibrated. He snatched it out of his pocket and put it to his ear. "You better have something for me."

"Cameras caught nothing," Patrick said.

Jason closed his eyes, cursing the utter incompetence. "Are you kidding me? Somehow she walked past two men and a dozen cameras without a trace?"

"Someone altered the footage. We know she was on the elevator with Adam, and they took her to the radiology department. But after that, she never reappears. And several cameras glitched out."

"So, what does this mean? She had help?"

"Professional help. They knew how to manipulate the system and recorded over various frames."

Jason's heart stopped. "Where is he?"

"Who? McKinley?"

"Fuck. Yes, McKinley!" Jason shouted.

"He's in Manchester."

"Are you sure?"

"Fairly sure, we expected him to stay several days. He hasn't been in his office. It's doubtful he's back already."

"Get eyes on him. I've read his file too many times to underestimate him. And Patrick," he growled, "you and Adam are on the hook for this. If we lose her, I'm gonna feed you to the wolves."

"Seriously? You first, asshole. We're here trying to clean up the mess *you* made."

Fucker.

He and Adam walked to the car park in silence. God damn her for this. It wasn't the first time she had run from him. She'd come back. He always won her back. Things would get better.

Jason hated himself for losing his temper on her, but the meeting with McKinley was crossing the line.

His fist curled as he thought of her making that call. Lying to him. Betraying all they had.

Mercedes was everything to him. Everything. Jason had to find her and bring her home. Without her, he was sure he would die.

CHAPTER SIXTEEN

Mercedes awoke to the sound of rain pattering against the windshield, the headlights of the oncoming cars illuminating the SUV's interior. Disoriented, she jerked in alarm, hissing in pain.

"Hey, hey. It's alright, you're safe," Alec soothed, his arm tightening around her. Her cheek was laying against him, her hand on his chest.

Mercedes hesitated before pulling away. God, she hoped she hadn't drooled on him. Thankfully, she saw no sign of any embarrassing pools as she sat up and stretched. Alec sat a little straighter, bringing his arm to his side to massage it.

"It's night already? How long have I been asleep?"

"Oh, about two hours," Declan answered from the driver's seat. "Snoring so loud we couldn't even hear ourselves think."

Mercedes's eyes darted to Alec. She was thankful he couldn't see her flush in the dark. "Really?"

"No, Declan's being an arse." Alec shot his cousin a look. "We hardly heard a peep from you the whole time."

"Aye, we started thinking you were dead. Alec had to poke you a few times to make sure you were still with us."

Alec's teasing grin shone in the dim light. "That's true."

She couldn't help but smile. "Where are we?"

"We've been driving around for two hours, but we're only about forty-five minutes from the hospital," Declan said.

She looked to Alec, who only shrugged. "You were sleeping well. We're almost to the house."

The scene outside the car had transformed. When she'd fallen asleep, they were in a bustling part of the metro area. Now, they were driving through the suburbs, where small eateries and shopping centers sprawled along the avenue.

She laid her head on Alec's shoulder. The nap gave her a little recharge of energy, but not nearly enough. She strummed her fingers against the soft fur of the blanket, the feel of it calming her wrecked nerves.

Relief washed over her as they turned into a quaint residential area. Declan pulled into the single garage of one of the brick homes and closed the door behind them. Alec jumped out of the car and came around to her side. He held his arms out to help her, which made her smile. But once she put weight on her feet, she was grateful he was there. Her legs were spongy, like she'd run a marathon.

She braced herself against him and they climbed the narrow steps into the house.

The moment the door opened, a savory aroma assailed her. Her nerves had kept her appetite away at the hospital, but now her stomach gave a turn to remind her she hadn't eaten all day. She was ravenous.

Alec took in a deep breath. "Ah, Mason has been at it, I see."

Mason waved from the small kitchen, a spoon in his hand. Shake was at work setting up a computer.

Cressida skipped down the narrow staircase. "Ah, there's my girl. Been hoping you'd be here soon." Cressida disentangled Mercedes's arm from Alec and held her own arm out for support. "I got this, Alec. I'll help her get cleaned up and human again."

She let Cressida lead her down the hall to a bedroom. Like much of the place, it was covered in busy floral wallpaper, reminding her of every movie she had ever seen involving a British grandmother's house.

A double bed sat in the center of the room, covered in neatly folded laundry. Everything she needed was there: day clothes, pajamas, socks, and even underwear and bras. Cressida set to work putting the clothes in the empty chest of drawers. "I hope I got your size right. I'm usually good at guessing, but you never know."

A heaviness formed in Mercedes's chest. This was everything she owned now. Her once tailored life had been reduced to a handful of outfits given to her by a stranger.

When Cressida finished with the clothes, she crossed to the bathroom and turned on the light. "You should have everything you need, and probably a few things you don't. There's a great makeup remover to scrub that cement off. And I should have a secure line for you after you eat, if you don't think it's too late. You can always do it tomorrow."

Nervous energy ran down her spine. "No, it has to be tonight. I want to get it over with."

Cressida smiled in understanding and left Mercedes to it.

The shower was sublime. Something about rinsing the grime of the hospital from her skin and the smell from her hair renewed her. While she dried herself, she caught a glimpse in the fogged mirror. Wiping away the water with her towel, she took stock of the damage uncovered by scrubbing away the concealing makeup. Thankfully, all the swelling had diminished, but fingers of purple and blue spread in blotches across her cheek and jaw and ran down to encircle her throat.

It would take work, but she'd get herself back. She'd allowed Jason to take over who she was for long enough. The call she dreaded making tonight was only the first step. She'd take them all.

She dressed in the tank top and pajama bottoms laid out

on the bed. When she emerged from the bedroom, a blast of cool air hit her. Crossing her arms to fight off the chill, she followed the intoxicating smell of food.

Mason was the first to notice her. "Ah, just the person I was looking for. I figured you could use some good American comfort food right about now. I got just the thing." He scooped ladles full of soup into a large bowl and handed it to her.

"Is this homemade chicken noodle soup?" The closest she got to homemade was the clam chowder at Boudin's Bakery in San Francisco.

"My gran's recipe. She always made it for us when we were sick. The trick is to make your own stock. I add a little cream to step it up a notch."

"Mason is the best cook in the lot. He insisted on cooking first," Alec said, coming up behind her and taking a bowl. "He never spoils us like this."

"Gotta make my countrywoman feel at home."

The meal was pure heaven. The company was just as lovely, with the group of friends laughing and teasing one another. The return to normal was exactly what she needed.

After they finished, Alec got up from the table and returned with a zippered hoodie with "Scotland Rugby" emblazoned on the chest. "Would you like this? Bit of a chill in the air."

Mercedes must not have been covering her shivers as well as she thought. His hands lingered on her shoulders before he returned to his seat. She inhaled the scent of him on the fabric.

"All right, lady," Cressida said. "You ready to do this?"

"Do what?" Alec looked between them.

"Kicking that piece of shit to the curb," Cressida said.

He frowned. "What's this now?"

"Sadie asked for a secured line to call Jason so she can tell him to bugger off." Cressida shrugged. "I have one for her."

Alec's eyes were dark as he looked at Mercedes. "Are you sure? You don't owe him anything."

Mercedes nodded. "I need to. I have to make it clear to him I'm done."

The corner of Alec's mouth lifted. "Of course. Is there anything I can help with?"

"I don't want to say the wrong thing. Where should I tell him I am?"

They moved into the living room and plotted out things to say and things to avoid. Her hand shook as she took the phone from Cressida.

"It'll look as if it's coming from your phone. If he manages to trace it, it'll say you're standing in the middle of Hyde Park."

Mercedes laughed.

Cressida had already primed the number. All she had to do was press call.

When Alec turned to leave, she stopped him. "Will you stay with me?"

Alec smiled and leaned against the wall.

Mercedes sat on the couch, trying to catch her breath. With a deliberate exhale, she made the call on speaker. She drummed her fingers on her knee anxiously while it rang.

"Sadie?" Jason answered.

She winced at the misery in his tone. "Hey, Jace."

"Christ, Sadie. I've been going crazy. You just disappeared. Where are you? I'll come get you and bring you home." His tone was wild with desperation.

"I'm . . . I'm in a safe place. I thought it would give me some closure to talk to you, to make things clear."

"What things? I'll give you anything. Just . . . just . . . fuck, please come home. We'll work it out," he begged. "I love you."

A tear rolled down her cheek. Earlier, she had been angry, but hearing his voice was harder than she thought it would be.

"Sadie, please? Babe, I need you."

How was she already losing ground? She caught Alec's stormy eyes. His jaw was tight with unspoken emotions, but he didn't move. He couldn't help her with this part.

It was Cressida who plopped onto the coffee table in front of her, knocking their knees together. She grasped Mercedes's tightened fists in her own. Cress's steady brown eyes bore into hers, hardening her resolve.

"No." Mercedes steeled herself. "I've got a lot of things to figure out, but I know you and I are done."

The silence on the line screamed at her.

Then he spoke. His voice trembled. "What? What do you mean?"

Was he going to pretend it hadn't happened? "You nearly killed me, Jace," she choked out.

"And I'm so sorry. But . . . you lied to me. I . . . I got so fucking mad."

"You think you can blame me for what you did? Is that the best you can do?"

"No, no. Shit." He paused. "I need you to come home, Sadie. I'll do the work. We can go to therapy, and you can . . ."

Mercedes cut him off. "No, I'm done. It's over, Jace." She gave him a second to take it in. "You can keep everything in the apartment. I'll call Cap and Vin and arrange for my last paycheck to be sent—"

"Where are you?" Jason demanded, his plaintiveness changing to anger.

"I told you . . ."

"I know you're not in fucking Hyde Park. So, where the fuck are you?"

Alec and Cressida exchanged a look. Did they not think the extra layer of security had been necessary?

"You don't need to know."

"Is this about McKinley?"

Even though she had been expecting it, it stunned her to hear him speak Alec's name. Out of the corner of her eye, she could see Alec tense. "Oh my god, you need to stop. He has nothing to do with this."

"Are you with him right now?" Jason challenged.

This time she was ready. "No. For fuck's sake, Jason, I'm not with him!" she cried. "But honestly, it's not your business who I'm with. Not anymore."

"It is my business, you fucking whore," he growled. "You think you can fuck whoever you want? That's not how this works, bitch. You're mine. You let him touch you again, and I swear, when I find you, I'll finish gutting you. And when I drag my knife through you, you'll wish you'd never heard his fucking name."

There wasn't enough air to fill her lungs. His words. The tone. The memories of the knife slicing through her skin, her warm blood pooling around her. Panic and revulsion welled in her, and the room swam.

Alec was by her side, her clammy hand in his. "Darling, breathe. You're safe," he whispered softly in her ear. "He can't touch you here. And he knows it."

The words grounded her. If Jason knew where she was, he'd already be here. She took in shaky breaths, hoping she could keep it together.

Mercedes waited for a pause in his tirade. "Are you done?" She allowed a tone of defiance to push to the surface.

"Don't fuck with me, Sadie."

"Mm, noted," she said dismissively. "The only reason I called was to let you know I'm moving on. I want nothing to do with you. Don't contact me again."

"That's not going to happen," Jason hissed. "You're mine. I decide what you do . . ."

Mercedes pressed the end button, cutting off the rest of his rant. Relief washed over her.

Free. Safe and free. It was real.

Overwhelmed, she buried her head in her hands and breathed in.

"Holy hell, that was brilliant!" Cressida exclaimed, rubbing her shoulders. "Don't be sad, love. You know you deserve better than that tosser, right?"

"I know. I thought I was going to lose it there."

Alec gently guided her chin to look him in the eye. "He was hoping you would cower to him, and you didn't. You were brave."

Mercedes could only hope it would be that easy. Alec didn't know the things Jason was capable of doing. Her stomach roiled at the threats he had made against her. The violence in him was tangible to her.

"Can I get you anything?" Alec asked softly.

"No thanks. I think I might go to bed, though. Feels like the longest day of my life." Had it only been a few hours ago she was being broken out of the hospital?

He nodded sympathetically. Then he put his arm around her shoulder and pulled her into him. "Before you do that, would you mind giving us a little more information about Jason? Something seems . . . off. I want to know what we're up against."

Mercedes told them about Jason's work, who he was associated with, and his access to surveillance technology. Cressida took notes as she and Alec worked through Mercedes's limited knowledge.

Alec stood and grabbed his jacket. "I was going to stay the night here and head back to the city in the morning, but I think it's best if I leave now and stay away for a few days. It's clear Jason thinks I'm involved."

Mercedes didn't want Alec to leave but couldn't find fault in his logic. They were likely staking out his apartment building and his office, waiting for her to show up.

Alec walked her to her bedroom and stopped at her door.

"I'll call and check in on you. Shouldn't be more than a few days."

"Can I keep your sweater?"

His eyes softened, stealing her breath. "Aye, for as long as you like."

Mercedes embraced him. Alec wrapped his arms around her in a tight, lasting hug.

"I don't know if I'll ever be able to thank you enough for all you've done. I'm pretty sure you've saved my life."

"Nah, you did that. I just offered a hand. You're the one who took it."

She smiled and stepped away. He leaned down and brushed a kiss on her forehead. "Get some rest. I'll see you in a few days."

And then he was gone. She snuggled into the bed with a smile on her lips and the warmth of his scent enveloping her.

CHAPTER SEVENTEEN

Jason paced between the living room and kitchen, aware of the exhaustion biting at his consciousness. Normally, he slept easy, even after an incident with Mercedes. His iron stomach never let him down.

But now, his gut churned with an unfamiliar wrenching. It had been three fucking days since she called him. It brought out a side of himself he didn't know existed. It was beyond jealousy. Now it was a torturous visualization, like a movie was on repeat in his mind.

What was McKinley doing to her right now? How many ways had he taken what was his? His brain spit the images out. Her chestnut hair cascading down her back. Legs spread while he went down on her. Fists grabbing his hair while she cried out under him.

God damn it.

"Will you sit the fuck down?" Patrick's voice broke in. "You're making me nervous."

Patrick had been eyeing Jason since he and Adam arrived. Jason pulled a chair from the table and dropped into it.

He had finally gotten his hands on a lead. It was weak, but

it was the only thing they had. The others were only half-ass looking for her. He'd used up all their goodwill.

He jumped up from the seat again, his muscles aching to move. "We need to tap into our assets now, before he moves her."

Patrick stared at him. "We've been monitoring McKinley, and we know she isn't with him. We're not gonna blow through our resources because you're worried she might be taking someone else's dick."

Jason launched at Patrick, but Adam stepped in his path. Patrick lounged on the couch, sneering at him.

These pricks didn't know their place. "This is my call," Jason growled. "And I say we go all in."

"Except this isn't your call anymore," Adam said.

Jason glowered at him. "The fuck you mean?"

"It's simple. You fucked this up for the last time. Now I get to be in charge of this shitshow. And I say, there's no justification for taking the risk."

"Like hell, there isn't!" Jason shouted, the blood rising to his head.

"Yeah, that's what you keep saying. But you being a jealous fuck isn't justification." Adam got up from the chair and grabbed his sweater.

Patrick stood as well and stretched. "By the way, you're welcome for the sanitation work we did for you." He nodded to the floor where Mercedes had lain in a pool of blood.

Jason couldn't look at the spot without his stomach turning. Instead, he glared at Patrick.

"Look," Adam said. "We can't take on McKinley without taking heat. You've been dangling the carrot for months. You got the goods? Now's the time to share. If *I* feel it's worth pursuing, *I'll* make the call. Otherwise," he said, shrugging. "we have to let her go." He reached for the door. "It doesn't matter who's pounding her, you or McKinley. Makes no difference to us. We won't move until we have more than your cuckold fantasies to go off of." Adam and Patrick shared a laugh.

Jason fantasized what it would look like if he pulled this asshole's tongue through a slit in his throat. He sat unmoving as they slammed the door behind them.

He sat on the couch, his fingers massaging his temples. The movie played again. This time McKinley was plowing her from behind, and his gut wrenched.

Fuck it. He picked up his phone and made the call.

CHAPTER EIGHTEEN

Alec's eyes burned from staring at the computer. He and Cressida sat together in his office, combing through the scant information they had gathered on Jason Marsh. The guy was a ghost. With each dead end, Alec became increasingly concerned with what they were dealing with. The social security number Mercedes had provided belonged to a Jason Marsh, but the birth year would make the man 102 years old. The company he worked for was a well-disguised shell corporation.

"Well, I think I see why she stopped reporting him to the police." Cressida slid her tablet over to Alec. "He almost convinced a police officer she was mentally ill and self-harming. Look, he nearly got her committed."

Alec reviewed the report written by the responding officer. They contemplated taking her in for a 5150, an involuntary commitment into a mental health facility. Jason reported the behavior, then talked the cop out of it.

"Can you imagine what that would have done to her career?" Cressida pondered.

Alec knew precisely what it would have done. Mercedes had worked at one of the most competitive legal firms on the

West Coast of the United States. A whisper of something like this, and the sharks would come out to feast.

Jason had her trapped long before he convinced her to move to London.

The stone in his gut continued to grow as he read the final medical report from San Francisco. Jason's name never appeared in it, but his stench was all over it. The hospital documented inconsistencies in her story, noting she was likely an abuse victim sheltering her abuser.

Alec sat back in his chair, sick to his stomach. *How could this have happened?*

"It's not her fault, you know." Cressida's voice broke him from his festering.

"I know. I'm just trying to understand what she saw in him."

"Dec told me the two of you have a history." It wasn't a question.

"We do." Alec took a breath and ran his fingers through his hair. "If I'm honest, it stings. When she was given a choice, this was who she chose. A manipulative abuser who held her hostage."

"She didn't choose an abuser, not over you or her sister or her career. She chose someone who doesn't exist." Cressida shook her head. "You heard him the other night. Crying about how much he loves her one minute, screaming he was going to gut her the next."

Mercedes's stricken face came to his mind, and his blood boiled all over again.

Cressida sighed. "He's a master at this. Every lie is designed to keep her off-balance. To manipulate her into believing he's everything she deserves."

Alec brought his hands to his face, massaging his brow. "You're right. I feel like such a prick for even thinking it."

"You're not a prick. It's not something everyone has experience with."

They sat quietly reading their various reports, the occasional soft click on a mouse and the whoosh of passing traffic the only sound between them.

Alec broke the silence. "Cress?"

"Hmm?"

"We're friends, right?"

"Mm-hmm," she confirmed, taking a sip of tea.

"So, if I asked you to pack your things and move to the other side of the planet just so you could follow my girlfriend around, would you do that?"

"Fuck no." She didn't look up from her reading. When he didn't say anything else, she glanced at him. "I mean, I love you and all, but you're going to have to pay me a shit-ton of money to move my arse anywhere."

Alec frowned at his computer. "The two men tailing her are American, right?" At her nod, he asked, "So how did Jason get them to drop everything and come to London only to follow Sadie around? Who has friends like that?"

"You think he's paying them? Why?"

Alec shook his head. "I know abusive arseholes like him don't follow a rule book or anything, but doesn't this seem extra crazy?"

"Oh, for sure. What do you want to do?"

"Let's pull the thread, see where it leads."

"You got it."

They were still working that afternoon when Declan came strolling into the office, a cup of coffee in hand. "Oi, we need to do something about that bed in the safehouse. It's the worst."

Alec grunted a response. That bed was everyone's least favorite part of staying there.

Declan turned his smile to Cressida. "Morning, lass."

"Good *afternoon*, Dec." She had a twinkle in her eye.

Declan looked at his watch. "Damn. Is it afternoon already?"

She shot him an exasperated look. "It's nearly three o'clock."

"Oh, well then. It's a good thing I got my work done before I drove all the way to the office." He cocked his head. "I have a present for you."

"Do you now?"

"Aye." Declan plopped a stack of files in front of her. "Got a couple of hacking jobs for ya."

"Ooh, gimme." Cressida grabbed them up and looked at Alec. "Do you mind? Won't take long."

"Go ahead. We have time on this."

Cressida jumped up and gave Declan a smacking kiss on the cheek, and hurried off to the office she shared with Shake. One of Cressida's favorite things was defeating the cyber systems of new or potential clients to demonstrate how easy it was to do. Declan's eyes followed her down the hall.

"Stop flirting with the employees," Alec warned.

"Stop flirting with the clients," Declan shot back, a mischievous glint in his eyes.

The color rose in Alec's cheeks. "You're an arse. And she's not a client."

Declan chuckled.

"How is she today?" Alec itched to see for himself, but it was better for him to stay away.

Declan shrugged. "Sleeping."

"Still?" Worry clenched in his chest.

"Aye, hardly heard a peep the whole time. Mason made her eat around ten this morning. Otherwise, she's been out."

"She's okay, though?" It had been four days. How much sleep was too much?

"Aye, she's braw. Mason's not worried at all. She's just having one hell of a lie-in."

Squeaking shoes outside the door announced Mrs. Downey was heading his way. She popped her head in his doorway.

"You have a visitor, Alec."

He frowned. "I do? The calendar is clear today."

"Och, I know, lad, but he said it was an emergency and hoped you would make an exception. Says his fiancée has gone missing, poor lad. She's a friend of yours."

Ice shot through his veins. He traded looks with Declan.

"Did he give a name?" he asked Mrs. Downey.

"Oh, aye. Jason Marsh. Should I show him in?"

The widening of Declan's eyes must have mirrored his own. *Holy shit, he really came here? Ballsy.* "Aye, show him in."

As she retreated down the hall, he pulled his gun from its place in his drawer, checked to see it was primed and ready, and put it in his holster. Closing his eyes, he inhaled deeply, allowing his mind to clear aside his feelings, moving the memory of Mercedes's battered body away from him. Even in his mind, he needed to keep her safe from this man. The rage he had built toward Jason shifted to indifference. Alec was a trained liar, someone who had perfected shutting his emotions into their individual compartments so the mission could come first.

Jason approached Alec's door, an apologetic smile on his lips. Alec had only seen him in pictures and surveillance videos. He was an impressive-looking bloke. Classically handsome face with a strong jawline, and light blue eyes, and blonde hair. Definitely someone who liked to hit the gym.

"Mr. Marsh, is it?" Alec walked around his desk and held out his hand. "Alec McKinley. Pleasure. This is my cousin and business partner Declan McKinley." Declan offered his hand.

"Please, call me Jason."

A less trained person wouldn't have seen it, but Alec caught the falter in his smile. Jason wasn't expecting a warm greeting.

"Please." Alec gestured to the chairs at his desk and walked to his own seat. "Can my assistant bring you anything? Cup of tea? Coffee?"

"No, I'm okay, thank you," Jason said, moving to the seat. Declan stayed against the window, leaning against the low bookshelf, watching Jason's movements from the side.

"I appreciate you taking the time to meet with me."

Alec waved it off. "Not a problem. My assistant said you were looking for someone, but I'm afraid I didn't catch the lass's name."

"Yes, my fiancée, Sadie. Mercedes Elliott? I understand you know her." Jason paused. "She told me you were helping her find a job."

Fiancée is a new development. Alec threw it into one of the compartments in his mind.

"Oh, Sadie. Aye." He pulled out his favorite memory of her. They were sitting on a rock next to a waterfall in Scotland. Mercedes's mouth was on his, his fingers tangled in her hair. The thought came and went in a matter of milliseconds, but the memory would be written all over his face. It had the desired effect. Jason's smile grew tight.

Alec cleared his throat. "I had coffee with her about a week ago. She didn't say she was engaged." Jason's jaw tightened. Alec had struck another direct hit. "You said she's missing?"

"Yes, I last saw her on Tuesday in our apartment. We had an . . . argument." He said this as if confessing something private and embarrassing. "I stayed the night away. When I came back home, she was gone."

Alec frowned. "Have you called the police?"

Jason sighed. "No. I— I didn't want to get them involved. She's been struggling a lot lately and . . . I'm worried police involvement would make it even harder for her to find work."

"Why would that be?" Declan asked.

Jason looked at Declan as if he had forgotten he was there. "She's had some mental health issues in the past. She's been known to harm herself whenever she's stressed. Especially when we've fought." He looked at his lap.

"Well, I haven't seen Sadie in a while, but she always seemed to be a fairly level-headed lass," Declan mused.

"She's good at putting on a show when she needs to. But over the last few years, the facade started to crumble. It affected everything. Her work, her social life . . . our relationship. On one occasion, the police wanted to take her to a psychiatric hospital. I talked them out of it."

"Have you called her sister?" Alec watched for any changes in Jason's demeanor. The fucker was literally wringing his hands.

"Charlotte and I aren't on the best terms. When we were in San Francisco, Sadie began behaving . . . erratically. I tried to reach out to Charlotte to tell her how concerned I was for Sadie's well-being. She didn't take it well."

"Oh, Charlie and I get on quite well." Alec reached for his phone. "I'd be happy to give her a ring. What time is it in California?"

The offer was a risk. He couldn't very well ring Charlotte with this bastard staring at him.

"No, that's okay. I wouldn't want to worry her unless I have to."

"Of course. The offer stands if you need it." Alec put his phone down and frowned. "Speaking of calls, I reached out to some acquaintances on Sadie's behalf. One told me they had already heard of her. They'd been warned against hiring her."

Jason nodded solemnly. "I don't know what she told you about leaving the practice in San Francisco, but I'd be careful about tying your name to hers."

"Really? She only said she made some mistakes, so they let her go."

"I guess you could say that." Jason smiled ruefully. "She got a man killed."

Alec stared at him. "What do you mean?"

"She had information on a whistle-blower who was helping them work on the lawsuit. One night, when she was drunk, she revealed the man's identity. They found him dead a few days later. They lost all the evidence the same night, so the case was tossed." Jason paused, letting it sink in. "That's why she was fired."

Alec frowned, wondering how much of this was true. He hadn't asked Mercedes for details about losing her job.

"I see. Well, she was a lovely person when I first met her and just as lovely the other day." He let a soft smile play on his lips at the mention of her. He didn't miss Jason's hand curling into a fist on his lap. "Unfortunately, I haven't seen her since we had coffee. I gave her the names of my acquaintances, and we went our separate ways." He lifted his shoulder.

Jason stood. "If you see her, will you please tell her . . . Tell her I miss her, and I— I love her." His voice broke, and he swallowed hard.

Jason spitting out fake emotions over Mercedes was testing Alec's control. "Of course. But I don't know I'll see her before you do."

Jason smiled and held out his hand to Alec again. In shaking it, Alec noted a scab and purple streaks across the top of Jason's knuckles. Mercedes's tearstained face, mottled with bruises, flashed in his mind. These were the hands that had pummeled her, frightened her, and tried to shatter her.

He squeezed a little harder than he meant to, fighting back the urge to end this man.

Jason didn't appear to notice Alec's struggle. He pulled out a business card. "Will you call me if she reaches out to you?"

"I will." Alec took the card and laid it on his desk.

Jason shook Declan's hand and turned to leave.

"One last thing." Jason turned back to them at the door. "She's good at making people believe things that aren't real. That she's been mistreated, or people are after her. I think she believes what she says. Again, you may want to think twice about supporting her. My understanding is your company has an excellent reputation."

"I appreciate the heads up, but I've a pretty solid bullshit meter." Alec smiled amicably.

Jason returned the smile with a nod and walked out of the office.

Alec turned to Declan, who shrugged. Alec nodded toward the cabinet in the corner where they kept some of their smaller equipment. Declan pulled out the sensor and swept the room. Nothing.

"That was some crazy shit," Declan said quietly. "There had to be a reason for that visit."

"Aye, there was. He was studying me. He wanted to throw me off balance and see for himself if I'd lie about where she is. Bastard's getting desperate."

"You almost lost it there at the end."

Alec grimaced. "Fucker had bruises on his fists." A wave of disappointment ran through him. "I'd better stay put another night or two. I don't think it's safe to go to her." *Damn it, so close.*

"I'll let Shake and Mason know."

Alec tried to get some research done, but he struggled to focus on the documents he was reviewing. The visit from Jason was unsettling. The man was effective in getting into people's heads.

His cell phone vibrated, breaking into his thoughts. It was a text from Mariah.

Hey. I'm free tonight. Dinner?

Alec contemplated the text for a moment. Mariah Costa had been an operative at another risk management firm in London. They had met at an art auction six months ago.

Tall and slender with long blond hair and rich brown eyes, Mariah knew she was beautiful. She'd smiled at him while they waited for their clients. Once the job was done, he offered to buy her a drink.

One drink turned to three. Before he knew it, he was rummaging for a condom in his wallet at her flat. Alec wasn't much into one-night stands, but she was enthusiastic, and it had been a while.

For several months, they kept up a casual relationship. One of them would text the other with an invitation for a drink or dinner. Usually, he'd end the evening in her bed. He never stayed the night, and Mariah never expected him to.

One afternoon, Mariah confessed to being unhappy at work and asked if he had room for her at his company. Alec knew she'd make a great member of the team, but they'd have to end their relationship. He didn't sleep with subordinates. Although she was prone to flirting a little too openly with him at the office, she respected the boundaries he put in place.

They'd had dinner a couple of times since ending their physical relationship. Mariah appeared as comfortable as he was with their professional friendship.

As disappointed as he was that he couldn't see Mercedes tonight, he had to admit going out with another woman might show his shadows he was living his life and not squirreling away the woman they were looking for. He shot her back a text and made plans to meet up.

When Alec arrived at the restaurant, Mariah had already gotten them a table. He gave her a friendly kiss on the cheek when she rose to greet him.

"How are you?" Her dark eyes sparkled in the dim lighting. "It feels like forever since we've had a chance to catch up."

"It has been a while. How was the Goodwin job? I hear they were happy with their delivery."

She rolled her eyes. "The son was a prick, but I managed not to kill him."

Alec laughed. "That's good. I'd hate to get a bad reputation for murdering spoiled rich kids."

They fell into an easy conversation. Alec ordered a bottle of wine he knew she liked but nursed his glass.

"I noticed you had a safehouse blocked off for this weekend. You're not hiding someone famous, are you?" Mariah's eyes sparkled with curiosity. One of her favorite things about their job was the occasional protection of famous people.

He wasn't going to share the real reason he'd scheduled the house. "Not unless you consider Declan a celebrity," he laughed. "Our aunt is having a birthday celebration nearby, so Dec and I thought we'd rent the house. Give the cousins a place to stay."

"Oh, sounds fun. Are you going up soon?"

Alec shrugged. "I hope to in the next day or so. I have some projects I want to finish first."

The waiter cleared and prepped their table for their upcoming meal. When he walked away, Mariah gently took his hand. Alec froze, staring at her polished fingertips stroking the back of his hand.

Well shit. "Mariah . . ." Alec shook his head at her.

"Alec, I know I agreed our relationship would end if I took a job, but . . ." She squeezed his hand. "I think maybe it was a mistake. I can't stop thinking about you. About us. We had a lot of fun together, right?"

"We did," Alec agreed. "And I'm flattered. Truly. But I meant it when I said I wouldn't date someone from the office. It wouldn't be right."

"I know, but if I had known how much I'd miss you, I might have reconsidered taking the job." Her wide, brown eyes were pleading. She was beautiful and used to getting what she wanted.

Maybe there was a time when he'd have accepted such an offer, subordinate or not.

But Mercedes was in his life again. She might never be his, but he wouldn't kill the already slim odds for a quick shag with Mariah.

"I'm sorry, but no. It's not a good idea."

Mariah's eyebrows pulled down, and she looked away. Blinking rapidly, she picked up her glass for another sip. Alec tried to think of something to say, but the words stuck in his throat. The waiter arrived with their dishes, breaking the tension between them.

"I'm sorry." And he meant it. It sucked that he was hurting her.

"Forget it. I'm sorry too. I knew it was a risk. We can still be friends, right? Have dinner every now and again?"

"Of course."

She poured herself more wine and changed the subject. It took a few minutes for the awkwardness to subside, but by the end of the meal, she was laughing easily again. When they finished, he walked her to the street, and she hailed a cab.

"One last chance?" She said it jokingly, but her eyes told him she wasn't playing. If he wanted, he could take her home and have her all night.

Shaking his head with a smile, he reached to open the door for her. Without warning, Mariah's mouth found his, pulling him into a kiss. It stunned him enough that he didn't immediately respond. When she used her tongue to coax him into kissing her back, he pulled away.

"I meant it." Alec peeled her hands from around his neck. "Goodnight, Mariah."

She pouted but turned to the cab. Alec helped her into the car and shut the door.

Alec touched the back of his hand to his mouth, annoyed. This wasn't how he thought the night would go.

Maybe she had done him a favor. Kissing another woman on the street would send his shadows the message that Mercedes wasn't in his thoughts at all.

It had the opposite effect on him. The kiss only made him ache for Mercedes more. He needed to get it together before he saw her again. The last thing she needed was for him to be horny for her when she needed him to be her friend.

CHAPTER NINETEEN

Mercedes had been sleeping for days, only waking when one of her new friends wanted to make sure she hadn't died on them. When they were satisfied she wasn't at her end, they'd feed her and let her return to her comfy nest where she'd fall right back to sleep again.

On the fifth day, she awoke on her own, her energy level nearly restored. She probably couldn't run a marathon, but she could have lunch at the kitchen table like a normal person.

The days had lessened some of the bruising, but they had a ways to go. Cressida had left the small makeup bag, so she experimented with covering up the worst of her battered face. A little eyeliner and mascara had her feeling a little more human.

Shake sat at the kitchen table, his fingers dancing over the keyboard of his laptop. He gave her a huge grin. "Hey, look at you. Out of bed and everything," he teased. He stood and walked to her, lifting her chin to scan her concealing work. "Not bad."

"Maybe I can get a job in the West End?"

He laughed. "You could. It's all about slathering the stuff on like mortar on a brick wall."

Shake helped her hunt down something to eat, and they sat at the table munching on sandwiches.

"So, I meant to ask you," Mercedes said between bites. "How did you get the name 'Shake'?"

Shake gave her an amused smile. "Well, you remember Cress and I are twins, right?" At her nod, he continued, "Well, our mum's a bit of a nutter. She was going through a big Shakespearean period when she was expecting us, so she pulled our names from his work. Cress's name comes from *Troilus and Cressida*."

"Sooo, what's your name then? It's not Romeo, is it?" she teased. "Oh my god, it's Hamlet."

He gave a dramatic sigh. "It's Lysander."

"Lysander?" She couldn't remember that one.

"*A Midsummer Night's Dream*."

"Aww, I like it!" she exclaimed. "Is that why you had Sandy on your name tag?"

"Oh, for sure. My nan calls me Sandy. My mum calls me Lysander, though."

"So, the nickname Shake . . ."

"My mates at school. *Nobody* wanted to call me by my name. I started out as Shakespeare, but that's a mouthful, so they cut it down to Shake."

"I'd like to meet your mom someday. She sounds fascinating."

"Yeah, she's a crackpot, but she's really sweet. Oh hey, got some good news. Alec and Dec will join us today. Finally." Shake rolled his eyes. "Alec's been getting antsy."

A gentle flush crept up her cheeks. "I thought he'd be here days ago."

"He was planning on it, but he was waiting for them to give up following."

Mercedes frowned. "Were they actually watching him? I thought it was a precaution?" She took a bite of her sandwich.

"Oh, they were watching him all right. Jason even paid him a visit a couple of days ago."

She coughed, the bite turning to lead in her throat. "What? Is Alec okay?"

"Ah, I didn't mean to alarm you. All is well. Alec handled it," he reassured her, pushing her glass of water toward her. "Declan was there. Jason told Alec you were a missing mental patient."

"He *what?*" she cried. *That asshole.*

"Yeah, he tried to say you hurt yourself, and he was concerned for your safety, yadda yadda." He made a jerking-off gesture with his hands.

Mercedes's fingers tapped on the table. "So . . . they didn't believe him?" Jason was so good at manipulating people.

Shake grinned. "What do you take us for? Of course not." She must not have looked confident. "Alec knows what happened. We all do. You don't need to worry about being believed here. We know total shite when we see it."

Mercedes was playing poker with Mason and Shake when Alec and Declan's car pulled into the drive. A minute later, Alec emerged from the hall, and his eyes searched the room until they landed on hers. He smiled, warming her to her core.

She tried to focus on her cards while stealing glances at him. *Jesus, he's delicious.*

Alec had on a black wool jacket and a dark blue scarf that brought out his eyes. He hadn't lost the habit of running his hand through his hair. The soft dark waves were tousled. There was a scruffiness to his unshaven jaw she couldn't get enough of.

Mason folded his hand and joined Alec. Mercedes didn't know what they were saying, but it didn't matter.

Alec was listening to Mason while he shrugged off his jacket and hung it in the hall closet. The way his body moved fascinated her. For such a big man, he had a gracefulness about him. The polo hugged his powerful upper body beautifully. And his shoulders. She imagined draping her leg over his shoulder while he drove her wild with . . .

"A-HEM," Shake said. Mercedes jumped, and an instant heat washed over her face. Shake's mouth quirked into a knowing smile. He laid out his cards. "Two pair."

Flustered at being caught having an X-rated daydream, she stared at her hand. She'd completely forgotten she had a straight.

Shake's mouth dropped open when she laid them out. "You *have* to be cheating. Hey Alec," he called. "You failed to mention Sadie was such a dirty cheat at cards."

"Nah. You're just rubbish, mate," Alec called back.

"Complete rubbish," she agreed. Mercedes snorted when Shake shot her a warning look.

"Ah, a gang-up, is it? Should've known." Shake sniffed as he stacked his cards and stood. "It's a good thing I already have plans with a gorgeous bloke, or I'd stay here and have another go. Next time, I guess."

"I'll beat you next time too." Mercedes fluttered her eyes.

"Oi, you're a cheeky one," Shake grumped. He leaned down to her ear. "Don't worry, love. He looks at you the same way." He gave her a kiss on the forehead. "Take care. I'll see you in a few days."

Mercedes flushed again and wished Shake luck on his date.

Alec and Declan had brought pizza with them for dinner. While they ate, she caught Alec sneaking a look at her from time to time, sending a shiver of pleasure down her spine. Good lord, he was killing her.

After dinner, Declan excused himself to go upstairs, leaving her and Alec alone for the first time since he visited her hospital room. Mercedes took in a deep breath, the clench of unexpected nerves in her stomach. At least she wasn't shuddering like a butterfly or wanting to pass out with exhaustion this time.

Her fingertips found the rhythm she searched for.

"You look *a lot* better. How are you feeling?"

"Sore, but good. The cuts are starting to itch. Mason gave me some cream to put on, which helps." Mercedes braved the subject. "Shake said Jason came to see you."

Alec's shoulders tightened. "Yeah, he did."

"He told you I was unstable?" Her heart was racing. Would Alec regret offering his help? No one needed this kind of drama in their lives.

"Something along those lines."

"Yeah, he likes that one." She looked at her hands.

"I can see why. He can be quite persuasive."

Her heart sank. "Can he?"

"Oh, aye. It was strategic. I might have bought it if I didn't know better."

Mercedes shot a look at him. "You didn't believe him?"

Alec frowned at her. "Of course not."

She smiled at the affront in his voice. "Sorry, I've just had some experience with his lies."

Alec nodded, fidgeting with his napkin. "He also told me you were engaged to him."

Mercedes rolled her eyes. "He likes to say that too. He thinks it legitimizes him or something."

"So, you weren't engaged?"

Her breath hitched at his tone. Did it matter to him? "No. Not for lack of asking on his part. He had a lot of plans I wouldn't go along with."

Alec's eyes narrowed. "Like what?"

"He kept asking me to have a baby," she said. Alec winced and looked away. "When I'd refuse, we'd get into a huge fight. One day, I found my pills had been tampered with."

"Jesus." Disgust was thick in his voice.

"Yeah," she agreed. "The thing is, he doesn't even like children. It was another trap he could lay out for me. So, I went to my doctor and got on something he couldn't mess with. He never knew."

"Oh, smart."

Mercedes gave him a wry smile. "If I was smart, I would have left."

Alec's eyes met hers. "You did."

Mercedes breathed out sharply. "I did."

Sometimes it didn't feel real.

After they cleaned up the kitchen, they settled in the living room.

"There was something he said I wanted to ask you about." Alec sat across from her on the couch. "He said you'd made mistakes at your work and someone died. Can you tell me about that?"

Mercedes's stomach turned, and she closed her eyes against the nausea. Of course, Jason had told Alec about the worst thing possible.

"You don't have to tell me if it's too hard. I just thought . . ." Alec started.

"No, it's okay. You should know." She exhaled slowly, bringing her knees up to her chest. "I was working on a huge lawsuit between two pharmaceutical companies. Our client was suing Cooper Pharmaceuticals for breach of contract and a whole slew of ethical violations."

"I remember this. It was the case you landed before you came to Scotland?"

"It was." She was surprised her remembered. "A whistle-blower came forward with some pretty damning evidence. We had a solid case.

"One night, a partner at my firm had a retirement party. I had too much to drink, and Jason took me home to sleep it off.

The next morning, I woke up to dozens of messages. Somehow, I'd managed to unmask the whistle-blower."

She couldn't look at Alec, so she focused on her fingers, moving melodically on the fuzzy fabric of her pajama bottoms.

"They found his body three days later. He'd been executed and thrown into the bay." She had a hard time meeting his eyes. When she braved a look, they were filled with sympathy she didn't deserve. "We had to drop the case, and I got fired."

"I'm sorry you went through that."

"Thanks." She wiped her eyes with the back of her fingers. "I'm not surprised Jason wanted you to know. He knows I'm utterly devastated by it."

There was a time Jason had been her confidant, but he didn't like to be reminded of the incident once they moved to London. When visions of Seth's mangled body haunted her dreams, Jason would tell her to go to the couch so he wouldn't have to listen to her crying.

"Can we talk about something else?"

Alec moved the conversation away from her career. They fell into that easy companionship they had always enjoyed. He showed off a picture of his sister's baby, who had recently turned four months old. Isla Grace was draped over his shoulder. Alec was grinning, completely ignoring the stream of drool touching the top of his shirt. This little girl had him wrapped around her tiny little fingers.

"I didn't even know Katie was expecting."

She should have known. Luke and Katie were close. But she hardly ever talked to Luke anymore. Every day, she was coming to terms with how much control she had given to Jason.

Alec was watching her face. Sometimes the way he looked at her left her breathless. "I have something for you."

He went to the other room and returned with a large cardboard box filled to the brim with packing paper. Confused, she stared at him. He waved his hand for her to open it, an encouraging smile playing on his lips.

Mercedes rummaged around the packing paper. When her hand landed on the hard, bumpy surface, she stopped. She shot a look at Alec. He was watching her apprehensively.

"Oh my god, you didn't have to buy me this. They're expensive, and I can't pay you back. You should return it." She pushed the box back to him.

His mouth quirked up into a crooked smile. "First, I'd never expect you to pay me back. It's a gift. And second, it's not *really* from me. My part in it is pretty small. But when I found out she had it, I asked her to send it, and I'd see it safely delivered."

"Wha—?" Then it hit her. Frantically tearing through the paper, she pulled the violin case free.

It wasn't just any violin. It was *her* violin. The one her foster mother had given her.

With shaking hands, she turned the case over. The hot pink nail polish was as bright as the day she had scrawled *Mercedes Rose Elliott* along the side. Fumbling with the latches, she opened the case. The smell of the velvet lining hit her.

Hers. It was one of the first things that had truly belonged to her and her alone. She touched the smooth wood of its body. "Where did you get this?" she whispered.

Alec sat down next to her. "Charlotte. She was heartbroken when you told her you pawned it. So, she and Luke combed all the shops in your neighborhood until they found it and bought it back."

Tears blurred her vision. "She's had it all this time?"

"I believe so."

Mercedes met his eyes. "Thank you. I can't believe you all went through the trouble for me."

"Why wouldn't we?"

She looked back at the instrument. "I know why Charlie

would and even Luke. But this must have been a hassle for you."

"Not at all." Alec ran his fingers across the wood surface. "I found out they had it the day we had coffee. Charlie must have sent it straightaway." He looked into her eyes again. "Anyway, I thought you might enjoy having it while you recovered."

Warmth washed through her body. Mercedes thought she had made her peace with never seeing this part of her life ever again, but tears threatened to spill over. She set the case aside and wrapped her arms around Alec in a tight hug. The feel of his body against hers was everything she needed. She breathed him in and let the tears fall. His hands roamed her back slowly, letting her take her comfort against him.

"This is amazing." She pulled away to look up at him. "I don't know what to say."

"I'm glad it makes you happy." Wiping a tear off her cheek, Alec leaned toward her. Mercedes thought he might kiss her, and her breath caught in anticipation. He stopped and pulled her to him in another embrace, his heart racing in her ear. She rested her head on his broad shoulder and sighed.

If she could stay right here forever, she'd have done it.

A rustling behind them made her pull back again. The shyness returned as Declan sauntered into the room and flopped onto the lounger, a slice of pizza in his hands.

Alec cleared his throat. "Dec helped too."

Declan grinned at her. "Aye, I did. It was tough to carry it in from the car."

"Aw. Thank you, Dec." She walked over and gave him a hug, too, then gestured at the violin. "Do you mind?" Her fingers itched to play. Alec nodded for her to go for it.

Mercedes picked up the bow and examined it. She dug through the case, found the amber rosin, and slid a few passes across the fine hairs of the bow. She played a few tuning notes, making string adjustments.

When it was tuned, she placed it under her chin and let the instrument decide what it would say.

There was always a calm that washed over her when she played, quieting her anxious energy. Losing all sense of time, she healed herself. The music was a balm against her open wounds.

No one could understand why she didn't stick with a music career. Her abilities were well beyond that of her peers. She'd had both teachers and producers tell her she was wasting a gift others would kill for.

For years, her talent paid her way through school. It was a way to get herself, and later Charlotte, out of the squalor their drug-addled mother left them in. But it came at a cost.

Once her legal career took off, playing for money was no longer needed. She took her music back. Now she chose who she shared it with.

Mercedes finished the last notes to Vivaldi's "Winter" from *The Four Seasons* when she remembered she wasn't alone. She cleared her throat. "I'm sorry. You probably want to go to bed."

Alec had settled onto the couch, his eyes soft as he watched her, but Declan was sitting forward in the chair. "That was brilliant. I forgot how good you were. Can you play anything?"

"Pretty much. If I don't already know it, I just have to hear it a few times to pick it up."

It was a favorite game to play with friends. They would call out random songs, hoping to stump her with one she didn't know. Declan tried his hardest but was no match for her vast knowledge of music. It wasn't long before she was giggling at his suggestions, which ranged anywhere from rap to heavy metal.

Eventually, fatigue began to creep up on her, and she was forced to admit she needed a break for the night. Mercedes promised Declan he could try to trip her up again in the morning. He left, and Mercedes packed the instrument into its case and closed the lid. "I can't tell you how much better I feel. Thank you."

"I was happy to do it."

Alec was so close she could feel his breath brush her cheek. She could kiss him. Maybe he'd let her. The temptation burned through her, but she resisted. Life was complicated enough. Her fragile ego would crumble if he rejected her again. And to be honest, she didn't need the hassle of another messy relationship.

She picked up the case.

Alec stood, and like the first night in the house, he walked her to her room, stopping outside the door. "If you need anything, you know where I'll be."

Mercedes stepped in to give him a hug at the same time he leaned forward. They both stopped and awkwardly moved toward each other again, laughing. Alec leaned down and kissed her cheek, letting his lips linger.

"Well, goodnight," she sighed.

"Night," he called as he turned the corner to his room.

So much for not needing the hassle.

CHAPTER TWENTY

The smell of sausage and bacon greeted Alec as he opened his bedroom door the next morning. The sound of a playful fight happening between Declan and Mercedes reached him as he came down the landing.

Alec leaned against the doorway and took in the sight of her. She was so beautiful it made him ache. Her chestnut hair was loose and flowing down her back. Her fair skin, smooth and delicate, was restored to its natural radiance. The morning light caught her hazel eyes and gave them a warm, whisky glow.

Mercedes held a pair of tongs out like a weapon. She snapped the tongs at Declan in warning, giggling when Dec shot back a joke about her abysmal cooking skills. That laugh was mesmerizing.

Alec was growing hard. He cursed his lack of control.

"Holy hell, what's wrong with you?" Declan said.

Alec gave a start and glared at him. Mercedes turned to him and looked him up and down with an amused expression. Shit, he hoped she couldn't tell she'd made him hard by simply laughing.

"Nothing," he grumped.

"Aww. I forgot you're not a morning person," Mercedes teased. She reached for a mug and poured him a cup of coffee. "Here." She gave it a little push across the counter.

Alec grunted at her and picked it up. There was that giggle again. Jesus, she was adorable.

"You sure she should have those, Dec?" Alec tilted his head to the tongs in her hand. "We don't want meteorites for breakfast."

Mercedes sent two snaps his way. "Watch it, McKinley. I might burn yours to spite you."

"Sure, *that's* why you'd burn it."

Mercedes gave him a glare and turned back to the stove. "You didn't sleep well?"

"Not really."

"I'm sorry. I've slept like the dead since I've been here."

Alec scoffed. "I heard."

She shot him a wry smile.

"Well, you had a four-day lie-in," he teased.

Ignoring him, she went on. "Do you want to switch rooms? My bed is amazing. Maybe that's why you didn't sleep well?"

An image of Mercedes writhing underneath him in the guest bed flooded his mind. He took a long gulp of hot coffee and prayed his body would knock it off. "No thanks. I'll be alright."

"'Brain Damage,' by Pink Floyd," Declan declared.

Mercedes looked at Declan in sympathy, but it was Alec who answered. "She can play that one, mate."

She caught his eyes and held them. The corner of her lips turned up, and she looked away. A soft pink came to her cheeks. When they'd been together, on one of their video calls, he had requested every Pink Floyd song he could think of. He could no longer hear "Wish You Were Here" without thinking of her.

After breakfast, Declan excused himself to the formal living room to read. Alec rose to clear the table and was surprised to see Mercedes bringing dishes to the sink. "You don't have to do that. Cooks don't do the dishes here."

She rolled her eyes. "So I've been told. But I have to earn my keep somehow."

Alec washed, and Mercedes hummed while she dried dishes. It was clear she was oblivious to the effect she had on him. He wanted to pull her against him and taste her mouth again. It had been so long since he'd kissed her, but there was no forgetting the feel of her lips or how her body felt pressed against his.

Alec sighed, feeling like an absolute shit-heel. She wasn't here to satisfy his fantasies. Even if she was receptive to it, nothing but hurt could come from it.

Mercedes shot him a glance. "How long do we have in this house? I know you have a business to run, and I don't want to overstay."

"It's up to you. You can stay as long as you like."

Mercedes snorted. "A team of highly trained operatives hanging out with a broke American just in case her psycho ex takes another run at her? I thought you were a clever business-man, Alec," she teased.

He gave her a sideways look, taking it in stride. "I do alright. But that's why I took some holiday time. It'll be mostly me and Declan from here on out."

She stared at him. "You didn't have to do that."

"I know. I wanted to."

Mercedes was quiet for a moment as she wiped the counter. Then she said, "We haven't talked about what I'm going to do next."

"There are a couple options. Option one is to take you to the embassy. We'd get you a new passport and a ticket to the States. You can go back to San Francisco if you like. I'm sure Charlie will have a place for you."

"What's the other option?"

Alec leaned against the counter, drying his hands. "You could stay in London. We'd file charges and a restraining order against Jason. I'll provide security for you until you're safe. When you're feeling tip-top, I'll make introductions to anyone and everyone I know to secure you a job." He wanted so badly to talk her into staying, but he wouldn't.

"I don't have grounds for an order."

"That's not true," he said. When she looked up in surprise, he added. "You don't think Cress set you up a secure line without recording it?"

Mercedes's eyes widened. "I was so exhausted, I didn't think of it." She bit her lip and turned back to wiping the counter.

"I'm sorry. Neither choice is ideal." Alec wished he had more to give her.

"It's not that. It's nice to make some choices for myself again. It's . . . I don't think I can ever be free of him. If I go home, he'll know I'm with Charlie and Luke. They aren't equipped to deal with him. If I stay here, he'll figure out you're helping me and come for you. No matter where I go, I put people I care about at risk."

It didn't go unnoticed that she'd included him with the people she cared about. "Sadie, I'm equipped to deal with him. Please don't worry about me."

Mercedes's brows pinched together. When she looked up to him again, the fear in her eyes gave him a pang. "Alec, please listen. No matter what I decide, he'll think you had something to do with it. He . . . he hates you."

Alec frowned. He was under no illusion that he and Jason would ever be mates. He had a solid loathing for the man as well. But that was rooted in what he'd done to Mercedes. "Did he have a reason for hating me before last week?"

Mercedes looked at the towel she was twisting in her hand.

"When he and I first got together, he knew you'd been important to me. He didn't like sharing any part of me with anyone, even someone I didn't talk to."

Alec's heart lurched. Jesus, she was twisting the knife and clawing away at old scabs, pouring salt into the festering wounds.

"He hid his jealousy for a time. But when we'd fight, he'd bring you up to hurt me. When we moved here, he'd warn me not to see you. Even if I saw you on the street, I was to pretend I didn't know you."

Mercedes swallowed hard and met his eyes again. "He hates you, and he's dangerous." She took a step toward him, the smell of her shampoo filling his senses. "No matter where I go, he'll think you had something to do with it. My biggest fear is he'll come for you or Charlie."

Alec would love nothing more than to take a piece out of Jason Marsh. He figured it would be cathartic to beat the shit out of that short little fuck. But the fear in those hazel depths was more than he could handle, so he tucked away his own ego to reassure her. "I'm sure it won't come to that, but if it does, I'll be ready. Just make the best choice for you, aye?"

"Okay," she said, but her expression was strained.

OVER THE NEXT SEVERAL HOURS, THEY WATCHED A MOVIE AND binge-watched a British bake-off show. Now that she was feeling better, Alec could sense Mercedes was getting stir-crazy.

"Can we go for a walk?" Mercedes asked.

"Sorry, no. I don't want to take a chance."

"Ugh."

Alec understood. Staying in a safehouse could be such a drag. "How about a lesson?" He gestured to her violin.

"Really?" Mercedes's eyes lit up. "You want to learn how to play?"

"Well, I don't think we'll be here long enough to learn how to play, but I can get some basics, right?"

Mercedes's face was alight with excitement. Guiding him to the ottoman, she perched on the couch in front of him. She showed him how to tighten the bow and explained how the horsehair worked. Alec barely heard any of it. She was stunning.

Alec took the violin and did his best to hold it the way she had explained. The neck of it seemed tiny to his large hands.

"Here, can I just . . ." Mercedes gestured that she'd need to touch him.

Alec's breath caught. "Oh, yeah. Course." She came around the back of the ottoman and put her hands on his shoulders, pulling them back.

This was turning out to be one of his best ideas.

"Sit up straight," she teased.

Laying her hand on his, she placed his fingers onto the bow. Her searing touch lingered, scorching his skin as she moved to his other hand to guide it up the neck of the violin. She placed his fingers to cover one of the strings.

"There you go." Mercedes walked back around in front of him.

"Alright, now what?"

"Now, run the bow across this string." She pointed to the one she meant.

"Right." A god-awful squawk erupted from the instrument. "Christ. That's not right." He tried once more, and again it sounded like a cat was being beaten in a bag.

Mercedes bit her lip to keep from laughing.

"Aye, you laugh. But the student is the reflection of the teacher." He squawked some more notes out and glowered at the instrument. Mercedes erupted into a fit of giggles. Her laughter was intoxicating.

"It's a pretty normal thing when you're starting out. It's . . . the look on your face. It's . . . adorable."

Alec grumbled and tried a few more runs of the bow across the string. A series of screeches and squeals filled the room. He frowned at the bow in his hand. *Why is this so hard?*

"Sounds good, mate," Declan called helpfully from the other room.

"Ach, feck off, aye!" he called back. "Prick."

Mercedes wiped a tear from her eye, getting herself under control. "Let me help you."

Coming up behind him again, Mercedes pried his fingers from the neck and moved them a fraction of a centimeter. "You want to hold it right here." Her voice had grown softer, the laughter gone.

This time, she kept her hand on his when she moved to his other side. Her energy thrummed through him, and he took an even breath to calm his heart.

She put her knee on the ottoman next to him and leaned in. The feel of her body pressed against his back sent a shock through him, adding to the pressure building in his groin. *Christ, he wanted her.* He closed his eyes, resisting the urge to lean back into her.

Mercedes touched under his bow arm and lifted his elbow up, hesitating before she moved again. Her fingertips grazed the bottom of his forearm, and she rested her hand on his. She left a wake of fire as she went. Did she know what she was doing to him?

Her breath was soft against his cheek, and he felt her body shiver.

"Ready?" she whispered.

Alec's voice refused to work, so he gave a single nod. Mercedes guided the bow along the string, her fingers pushing then pulling on his hand. He had no idea what it sounded like, every thought consumed with her touch. He shifted in his seat to ease the discomfort her closeness had brought on.

He couldn't keep kidding himself that he didn't want her. Every part of him ached for her. The desire to take her mouth with his had reached a painful peak, and he needed to act or leave.

Alec stopped the bow and lowered it. Mercedes's hand stayed in the air, and he thought she'd back away. She didn't. Instead, her hand came to rest on his chest. He turned his head and caught her eyes.

Disappointment coursed through him when she pulled away. She didn't speak, making him feel like an absolute arse. Alec stood, setting the violin and bow on the ottoman.

Her eyes were downcast, conflict written on her face. Had he hurt her? Was she angry he was taking advantage of her?

"I'm sorry," he murmured. "I don't want to make you uncomfortable."

Her eyes jumped to his. "You didn't," she breathed.

Mercedes rose and brushed a tentative hand across his brow, sweeping an unruly lock of hair away. Her hand lingered on his temple and slid to cup his cheek. Alec closed his eyes, reveling in the feel of her. Turning his cheek into her touch, he let his parted lips slide against her fingertips. She shuddered.

When he opened his eyes again, she was watching him, the flecks of amber hidden below the moss green. Her breath caught, and he was lost.

Alec's heart raced as he pulled her to him, molding her body against his. He moved his hands along her shoulders and down to the small of her back. If she hadn't known what she was doing to him, she did now. Instead of giving him relief, it made him throb for more. Mercedes slid her hand up his body, letting her fingers tangle in his hair.

Alec grazed his lips along her jaw, teasing his way to her mouth. Her breathing became labored the closer he got. When his lips brushed hers, she closed her eyes and sighed.

"Jesus, Sadie," he moaned and dipped his head to satisfy his need to taste her.

The sudden, piercing chime of the doorbell cut through the air. The fog of desire dropped like a lead veil. Mercedes's eyes searched his, wide with terror. No one was expected. No one on the team would ring the doorbell. She broke from his arms and bent to pick up the violin. She looked to him, waiting for him to move.

Alec was still. There were innocent possibilities. It could be the post or a neighbor. He waited to hear a delivery truck pulling away or for the neighbor to leave. Instead, an insistent knock thumped on the door.

Alec grabbed his gun from the end table, wrapped his arm around Mercedes's waist, and swept her into the darkened hallway. An alcove in the hall provided a space for her to remain hidden from the living room. He pressed her back against the wall, shielding her with his body.

Mercedes clung to him, her head buried against his chest. "He's found me?"

"No, no. It's okay, it's going to be okay."

She nodded, but he doubted she believed him.

Declan appeared in the hallway, his own gun drawn, slowly approaching the door. The bell rang again. Declan placed the drawn weapon behind his back and peered out the window.

He drew a breath. "What the hell?"

The door swung open, and a feminine voice carried down the hall. "Hey, Dec."

"Mariah. What brings you out here?"

Oh, shit.

"Alec said he'd be here this weekend. I thought he and I could . . . spend some alone time together." The implication in her voice was clear. Mercedes's body went rigid.

Fuck. Fuck. Fuck. What the bloody hell was she doing here?

Alec met Mercedes's gaze. The fear was gone. Anger and distrust had taken its place. There was no time to explain. She wouldn't believe him if he told her anyway.

She looked away from him and gave him a shove.

God. Fucking. Damn. It.

CHAPTER TWENTY-ONE

Shattered. That was probably an accurate word. Mercedes had felt safe, like maybe she'd escaped and could rebuild the life she'd lost. These people had given her hope. Alec had given her hope. Now it was scattered into pieces, like the illusion he'd been.

He looked as if he wanted to say something but stopped himself. Laughter from the strange woman carried down the hall.

"Go to your room. I'll get rid of her." Alec holstered his gun behind his back. Without another word, he strode away, leaving her alone in the hall.

He greeted the woman warmly, stabbing her in the heart. She restrained herself from slamming the bedroom door, instead clicking it quietly shut. Her pulse raced. What should she do? Her head spun from the sudden change in the evening's events.

Emotions screamed through her. Which was winning, the hurt or the anger?

Anger. Anger was pulling ahead.

Mercedes strode to her bathroom and pulled open the makeup bag. Pumping out the concealer onto the brush with unnecessary aggression, she swept it over her cheeks. Once the bruising on her face and neck were covered, she added a touch of eyeliner and mascara. She'd be damned if her already tiny world would be reduced to hiding in a single bedroom while Alec entertained another woman.

Did this she already know all about Mercedes and her situation? Rage coursed through her veins, making her heart thunder. Alec could have been talking to this woman about her. Maybe they had been talking about how stupid and weak she had been.

Why had he almost kissed her if he was seeing someone?

Mercedes jerked a brush through her long hair, happy it still had a curl to it. Not a great one, but it would work. She took a cleansing breath before turning the door handle. Raging like a crazed woman would do her no good.

When she approached the kitchen, she could hear the woman saying, "I know you said you were busy, but I thought we could talk about things."

Declan was the first to see Mercedes. He strode across the kitchen toward her, blue eyes wide with a warning.

"Sweetheart. You're awake." His long arms enveloped her. She froze for a beat before she realized his ruse and wrapped her arms around him. When he pulled away, he murmured into her neck, but loud enough for the room to hear. "You look beautiful."

Mercedes played along by squealing at his playful nuzzling. When he pulled away, he had a twinkle in his eye.

"Dec. You have a girlfriend?" the stranger gushed.

"Oh, aye. It's a fairly new thing."

Mercedes turned to acknowledge the woman. She was beautiful. Long blonde hair and brown doe-like eyes.

Mercedes offered her hand. "I'm so sorry, my manners. I'm Emma."

And she saw it. Right there in this stranger's eyes. A faint tic. It was so quick and subtle, she almost missed it.

"Emma?"

"Yep, Emma Woodhouse." Mercedes smiled brightly, wondering if the woman was a reader of the classics. She didn't think so.

"I'm Mariah Costa. Nice to meet you."

Mercedes wrapped her arm around Declan's waist, letting her head fall onto his shoulder. "What brings you by?"

"Oh, well. I wanted to spend a little time with Alec. He told me he'd be at a family party this weekend, so I thought I'd catch him up."

"Alec, you didn't say you were seeing anyone." Mercedes looked up at Declan, fluttering her lashes. "Did you know?"

"Nope." Declan shook his head.

"Alec has so many secrets." Mercedes rolled her eyes. Alec shifted in his seat, not saying anything. Mercedes avoided looking right at him, but she could feel his gaze on her.

"Well . . . We were seeing each other casually for a few months. We ended it when I started working for him." Mariah reached over and took Alec's hand. He pulled away as if it had burned him, but Mariah was unperturbed. "When we had dinner the night before last, I told him how much I missed him and wanted to be with him. For more than for just . . . well, you know what I mean," Mariah said as an aside to Mercedes. Alec winced.

"Mm-hmm." Mercedes nodded back knowingly, wanting to scratch the woman's eyes out.

"And with what happened after dinner the other night . . ." Mariah gave Alec a shy smile.

Realization hit Mercedes like a truck, and her stomach lurched. That's where he'd been? Screwing another woman instead of at the safehouse with her? It hurt more than she had a right to feel.

She thought of the moment they had shared before the doorbell rang. He'd been playing her, just like he had before.

Only this time was worse. This time, he put her safety in jeopardy by bringing this person into her little haven.

God, she was an idiot when it came to men.

Declan grunted softly. Mercedes had dug her fingers into his ribs. She loosened her grip and gave him a little pat as a silent apology.

"Aww, that's sweet. You know what?" Mercedes gazed up at Declan. "Dec and I'll get out of your hair. It sounds like you have some catching up to do. What time are we leaving?"

"Leaving?" Declan and Alec said together.

"To the party?" Mercedes rolled her eyes.

"Oh, an hour, I guess?" Declan said.

"An hour's perfect." Mercedes shifted her gaze to Alec. "I'd like to be out of here in an hour." She hoped he picked up her meaning.

"Come on, love." She took Declan's hand, heading for her room. He had other ideas, tugging her to the formal living room.

Declan, an avid reader, had created a cozy reading nest out of blankets and pillows tossed on a loveseat. They had a direct view of the kitchen table where Alec and Mariah sat. Alec was leaning toward her, talking in hushed tones. Mercedes couldn't make out his words.

Declan sat on the loveseat and pulled her into his lap. Mercedes let out a playful yelp and a giggle. Snuggling against him, she was grateful for the quiet moment to talk.

"What the hell, Dec?" she hissed.

"I don't know. Something's not right. Alec gave instructions to keep this locked down. Even his assistant doesn't know what he's doing here."

"Maybe his girlfriend doesn't count in that."

"Mariah isn't his girlfriend or anything close to it. They've never been serious."

"Serious enough for him to put off coming here one more

day to screw her." She couldn't keep the bitterness out of her throat.

"That's not why he put it off, and I doubt he screwed her."

"She seemed pretty proud of the fact."

Declan rolled his eyes at her. "She didn't *say* they slept together recently, only that something happened after dinner. You're the one spinning it, lass."

Mercedes glared at him. "Humph."

She wasn't in the mood to listen to his reasoning. Not while Alec and Mariah were bent together, whispering. Alec's jaw was set. Mariah was smiling up at him. No, not smiling.

Simpering.

Mercedes had to look away.

"No way he slept with her," Declan said. "Not with you back in his life."

"You don't know that."

He gave her a pitying look. "Come now. He's thought of little else but you since you asked him to come by for coffee. You have him by the bollocks, and you don't even know it."

Her heart lurched. *If only that were true.* "Whatever."

Declan turned to her, his blue eyes sparkling with mischief. "Want me to prove it to you? Give me a little snog. You'll see."

"You want me to kiss you?" She scrunched her nose at him.

"Oh aye, a decent little make-out session would make his blood boil." He grinned at her. "Oh my god, it'd be hilarious."

"Um . . ."

"It wouldn't be like that, you dolt. No offense, but I don't think of you that way. You've been off-limits since the day I met you."

Mercedes wasn't convinced. He tilted his head toward Alec. "The man's got it bad for you. But hey, if I'm wrong, it won't matter, will it? Just a friendly kiss between friends." He shrugged. "Besides, if he reacts the way I think he will, he'll get her out of here quick."

That caught her attention. A streak of recklessness stiffened her spine and she thought quickly. It certainly wouldn't matter to Mariah. If anything, it would make their ruse more believable. She didn't like how Mariah kept shooting glances at the two of them on the couch.

Mercedes wanted her gone.

"Alright, I'm game." With more confidence than she felt, she tilted her head up and pressed her lips to Declan's. He responded in a way she could only describe as polite. She fought the urge to laugh, despite her anger. She opened her mouth, coaxing Declan to kiss her back so it wouldn't look like two schoolkids playing spin the bottle. He took the hint and put more effort into it, lacing his hand through her hair.

The sound of the chair thrusting back and hitting the wall made her jump. Mercedes broke away in time to catch Alec's glare as he stormed out of the kitchen, Mariah following behind.

"Too easy," Declan snorted.

With Mariah outside the house, it was time to pack it up and go. Mercedes got off Declan's lap and stalked to her room. Declan followed her, chuckling.

Opening the drawers with a jerk, she pulled the folded clothes from inside and threw them on her bed.

"Why ya doing that?" Declan asked.

Ignoring him, she stuffed her clothes anywhere they would fit.

Mariah's voice carried to her window. Mercedes stopped to peer out at them. Mariah was yelling at Alec, and he was giving it right back to her. Mercedes couldn't make out the words, but it didn't matter. She turned back to her packing. "Can you take me to the embassy tonight?"

Declan's brows were creased together. "You don't need to go anywhere. You and Alec can work this out."

"Nope, not happening." She stopped and looked at the clock next to the bed. "How long has it been since she arrived at this house?"

"I don't know, fifteen, twenty-minutes? Why?"

Mercedes rushed to the bathroom and gathered the various items on the counter, shoving them haphazardly into the makeup bag. Those, too, were crammed into the backpack. "We might have fifteen minutes. Unless he's staged nearby. Then it could be any minute."

"Who?" Declan asked.

"Jason."

"You think Jason's on his way? Here?" Declan said dubiously.

"Yes."

"Why?"

She spun on him. "Because that woman *knew* my name wasn't Emma."

Declan looked unconvinced. "She's worked for us for months. How would she even know Jason?"

"I don't know, but he always finds a way to get to me."

Declan pursed his lips.

Mercedes didn't stop. "Look, I know how bonkers this seems, but I'd rather be safe. Forgive me if I don't want to put my life in the hands of someone like Alec at the moment."

"Hey, now. What do you mean by that?" Declan frowned. "Alec's always been there for you."

"Oh sure, right." Her tone was laden with sarcasm. "He was really there for me years ago, when he decided I wasn't even worth a god damn *text message* saying he was no longer interested in me anymore. Super trustworthy. Never mind, he invited his fucking booty call to my safehouse. Yeah, that's the guy I'm throwing all my trust behind."

Declan's face turned stoic.

"I'm— I'm sorry." She willed herself to calm down. "He's your cousin, and you love him. I get that. But this is my life. I knew running from Jason was a risk, and looks like I chose wrong. Again." She crammed a few more things into the bag.

Declan didn't say anything. Mercedes pulled the violin case from the chair she'd propped it on. She opened it to make sure it was secured and closed it quickly.

"What did you mean by that?"

She turned to see Declan tilting his head at her. "By what?"

"You said he didn't even message you saying he wasn't interested. What did you mean by that?"

"I meant exactly what I said. He didn't even bother with a 'Hey, it's not you, it's me' line."

An engine revved. Mercedes peered out the window in time to see Mariah's car accelerate down the street.

When she looked back, Declan had left the room. The screen door slammed, and raised voices carried to her through the hall. Declan and Alec were having it out.

Mercedes ignored them. She only needed another minute, and she'd be ready to leave. She'd walk to a bus before she'd stay another night in this house.

CHAPTER TWENTY-TWO

Alec's heartbeat thundered in his ears as he flung Mariah's door closed and turned away. She revved the engine as she pulled off, but he was already striding back to the house.

He was going to fucking kill Declan. That arsehole knew damn well what he was doing. Between Mariah's unexpected appearance, the look on Mercedes's face, and seeing Declan's mouth on hers, his temper was at an end. He hurled the door shut behind him and locked the deadbolt.

Declan came through the hall, and he let it out. He grabbed Declan by the collar. "What the fuck were you doing?" Alec's voice shook with rage.

Declan was quick, bringing his hands through Alec's hold and giving him a shove. "Me? What the fuck were *you* doing, ya wanker? *Mariah?* You didn't think it'd be a bad idea to have her pop by? Smart."

"I didn't invite her here," Alec said through his teeth. "She knew we had the safehouse, so I told her we had a family party. None of that excuses what you were doing."

"Oh, please. Like kissing my sister, and you know it. But

you've got bigger problems than me kissing her. She's in there packing."

This landed like a punch to his gut. "What? Why?"

Declan looked at him like he'd lost his mind. "You're kidding, right? I believe her exact words were, 'He invited his fucking booty call to my safehouse.'"

"Shit." Alec pushed past him and stopped outside her bedroom, his anger waning. She had every right to be pissed, but she needed to know it hadn't been intentional.

Alec pushed open her door. She was shoving clothes into the backpack so hard he thought she might tear the seams.

"Sadie . . ."

She stopped and glared at him. Alec was taken aback by the fury blazing in her eyes.

"Thank you for getting me out of the hospital and letting me rest." She went back to packing, her words laced with fire. "I *very* much appreciate it."

"Wait! I didn't ask her to come here. Nor did I want anything to do with why she was here."

"No? Well, you know what? That's none of my business. I mean, really, it's not. You're free to fuck whoever you want."

Alec flinched, his heart pounding in his ears. "I didn't sleep with her. Well, I mean I did . . . I dated her a while ago, but . . ." Her eyes flashed at him, so he stopped and tried again. "I only went to dinner with her. As *colleagues*, nothing else. Afterwards, she kissed me and—"

"I don't need to hear this," Mercedes interrupted.

"But I told her no, that was it. I went home. *Alone.*"

"Cool. My problem is you brought your little bed buddy to the one place I felt safe—the one place where I was supposed to recover and get myself back together. And just like that, it's compromised. No doubt he's already on his way." She struggled with the bag's zipper, mashing the pile of clothes down.

Alec cocked his head at her. "Who? Jason?"

Mercedes scoffed and rolled her eyes but didn't answer.

She kept trying to close the zipper, but her trembling fingers were slipping off the pull.

Alec longed to comfort her, to ease her mind. "We'll go somewhere else if you don't feel safe, but I *will* protect you, Sadie."

She finally wrenched the bag closed and slung it over her shoulder.

"No, you won't. It's over."

Alec's heart wrenched at the words. *This can't be how it ends.*

Mercedes tried to walk past him, but he put an arm out to stop her. Her nostrils flared, the heat of her anger radiating to him.

"Sadie, it's not over. I promised you I'd help you. I intend to see that promise through."

"Are you going to hold me against my will then?" she challenged him.

"No." Alec flinched at the implication.

"Then you have no say." Mercedes tried to push past him again, but he stood before her for one more try.

"Where will you go? You have no money, no way to get out of here. I know you're upset at me, and I can see why you are, but you have to be reasonable here. It's nearly dark outside and starting to rain. You'll not get far."

"That's a very 'Jason' thing to say," she spat.

The words knocked him back, stealing his breath. "That was low."

Mercedes winced but quickly covered it. "I've asked Declan to take me to the American embassy tonight." She lifted her chin. "I'm leaving. Now."

He opened his mouth to respond, but Declan cut him off from the other room. "Alec! You need to see this."

Christ, what now? "Wait. Just wait, okay?"

Mercedes glowered at him as he left.

Declan was in the kitchen, compact device in his hand.

"What?" Alec barked, impatient to get back.

Declan looked up at Alec and turned the device so he could see the red beacon flashing. Alec's heart dropped out from under him. He walked to the table. Bending low, he peeled the tiny listening device from the lip.

How the mother fucking hell did this happen?

Mercedes had followed him into the kitchen. She leaned against the wall, her head back, fear and resignation in her eyes. "I told you he'd find me."

Alec's blood ran cold. He had failed her.

He locked eyes with Declan. "Two minutes. Go."

Declan grabbed Mercedes's bag and violin case from her hands and disappeared down the hall. Alec pulled a kitchen knife from the drawer. Using the sharp edge, he broke the listening device in half.

He and Declan worked silently to break down the site. Computers and weapons were the priority. The rest could be managed later. Pulling his weapons bag out of the closet, he strapped his drop leg holster to his thigh, adding his back-up .9mm and extra magazines to the dock.

He could feel Mercedes's eyes following him as he moved. She'd wrapped her arms around herself. The spark in her eyes had gone out.

Fuck.

Alec took a step toward her, but a sound stopped him. He drew his sidearm, listening.

Someone was in the front yard.

They had to go. Now.

Alec held his hand out to Mercedes. She hesitated. For a beat, he thought she was going to gut him with a refusal. Relief washed over him when she stepped to him and took it.

The crack of a breaking window cut through the silence. Then all hell broke loose.

CHAPTER TWENTY-THREE

A volley of gunfire erupted. All the windows in the living room shattered. Alec spun Mercedes into the kitchen, taking cover behind the arched wooden frame.

Bullets tore through the walls, reaching the ceiling. Broken glass and plaster skittered across the floor.

"Hold on to me. Move when I do!" Alec shouted to Mercedes. She clutched the back of his shirt.

Declan had sought cover behind the kitchen wall opposite of the arch from Alec. They needed to retreat, but Declan was stuck. He couldn't move across the archway.

A pause in the gunfire left nothing but the sound of his heart pulsing in his ears. Alec peered around the corner. The acrid smell of gunpowder permeated the air. The blown-in windows remained dark.

Where were they?

Gunfire erupted again, and he pulled back. The shots remained high up. Plaster rained on their heads. They were not aiming to kill. They were doing something else.

A god damn distraction. "Fuck!" he growled.

It was too late. The footsteps were already approaching from behind.

Alec shoved Mercedes away, bracing for impact. Jason Marsh's weight crashed into him, throwing him against the wall. His gun flew from his hand, skidding under the table. Jason's blow to the ribs stole his breath. Alec blocked the next hits and returned them with matching speed.

Jason didn't move like a computer programmer. He moved like a soldier.

Kicking off the wall, he pushed Jason away and landed two hits into the man's gut. His fist bounced off.

The bastard was wearing a bulletproof vest.

Jason locked his hands around Alec's neck, spinning him into the kitchen counter. Hip bone met tile, and Alec grunted. Kicking out, he dug his heel into Jason's knee. It gave way. Jason let out a cry and stumbled back. He caught his balance and glared at Alec.

Then Jason pulled a long knife from his belt.

When he charged, Alec caught him by the wrist, the blade centimeters from his chest. Eye to eye, they pressed together, Alec's muscles straining. Jason had better footing, bringing all his weight onto the knife.

The tip of the blade tore into Alec's flesh, a burning agony.

The bastard smiled and twisted the knife. "I knew you'd be a pussy."

"Fuck you," Alec growled and drove his knee up into Jason's thigh. He faltered enough for Alec to shove him off.

Alec scanned for a weapon and grabbed a metal tea kettle off the counter, and swung, striking Jason across the face with a *crack*. He stumbled backward, blinking, blade in hand.

Jason swung the knife blindly. Alec moved, capturing Jason's wrist and elbow. He twisted Jason around and pinned his arm behind his back. Then Alec gave a sharp thrust, and the joint came free with a *thunk*.

Jason yelled and let go of the knife. It clattered to the ground. Alec kicked it away.

Grabbing a fistful of hair, Alec slammed the fucker's face into the corner of the counter with a satisfying crunch.

"Fuck!" Jason yelled, dropping to the floor. Blood poured from his nose.

Alec pulled his .9mm, ready to end it, when a scraping sound caught his attention.

Declan.

He turned his gaze to the living room.

A figure in black straddled his cousin. As he watched, the man grabbed Declan's weapon from the ground next to them, turning its aim on Declan.

Alec pulled the trigger on the swing up. *Double tap to the chest. Head shot.*

All three bullets hit their targets. The man's body convulsed and slumped to the side. Declan scrambled to his feet, snatching up his gun as he dove to cover again. Rapid fire of his gun rang out. Someone was still shooting from the outside.

A shattering of glass and a scream brought his attention back to Jason.

He was holding Mercedes in front of him, using her as a shield, his large hand wrapped around her throat.

Jason sneered at Alec as his fingers squeezed, knuckles white with tension. Mercedes gagged and fell silent. She dug her fingernails into his hand, trying desperately to peel his fingers away, her mouth opening and closing in mute screams.

"If you care about her at all, you'll put your gun down and let me take her," Jason said, "because if you don't, you're gonna watch her die. Right now."

"I thought you said you loved her?"

Jason's lips pulled up even further. "I'd rather see her dead than fucking you."

Bolts of energy pulsed through Alec's veins. He slowed his breathing and moved his aim down her body. He could graze her thigh. Once she fell, he'd have a clear shot at this fucker's head.

A shimmer of metal caught his eye. He stopped.

Mercedes had Jason's knife. It was clenched against her side. Her fingers trembled. She didn't have much time left. If she didn't act, he'd have to shoot her.

Alec met her eyes. "Do it," he said through gritted teeth.

She brought the blade up and back into Jason's thigh, sinking it into his muscle a good two or three inches. He cried out and dropped her, doubling over in pain.

Mercedes lunged at Alec. He caught her but lost his shot at Jason as he spun them both toward the hall. Mercedes clung to him, gasping for air. She staggered.

Oxygen deprivation. If Jason had damaged her trachea, she'd need immediate care. "Talk to me," he demanded, listening to her breath through the commotion.

"I'm okay," she rasped through the coughing.

"Dec! Fall back."

Declan was poised at the window, holding off the men outside. At Alec's call, he hustled toward them, covering their escape toward the garage. Declan met them at the garage door.

"Clear it," Alec said. "We'll be right behind you."

As Declan moved past them, Jason popped his head around the corner, and Alec took a shot. The bastard ducked, and the plaster on the wall behind him exploded.

"Clear!" Declan called.

Alec pulled Mercedes into the garage, securing the door behind him.

He guided her to the front passenger seat of the SUV and ran around to the driver's side. Declan climbed into the back seat, his gun trained on the door to the house.

Alec started the engine, slammed the car into reverse, and floored the gas pedal. The SUV crashed through the garage door, the metal screeching over the roof.

Jason and the other man were running across the lawn outside. Alec grabbed Mercedes and pulled her head into his lap. Not a second later, a bullet hole cracked the windshield open as the SUV screeched onto the street. Alec threw it into drive, the tires squealing.

Alec watched the rearview mirror. The lights of Jason's car swung into view.

"There they are." Alec's foot pressed down on the gas pedal. "You got the rifle?"

"Aye." Declan switched his weapons, now aiming a long-barreled gun on the advancing car.

Mercedes's head was still in Alec's lap. He pressed his hand on her exposed ear, muffling the sound. When the shot came, she jumped. Shattered glass cascaded down the back window. Declan loaded the next shot into the chamber with a click. Alec put pressure on Mercedes's ear again as the next shot reverberated through the car. In the rearview mirror, the car behind them pitched one way and then the other, crashing into a parked car.

Alec pulled the wheel to the right, drifting around the corner, and took another sharp turn onto the main avenue.

A minute passed with no sign they were followed. He rubbed Mercedes's shoulders, and she sat up.

"Either of you hurt?" Alec's heart was hammering. It would be another minute before his own injuries made them-selves known.

"Oh aye, gonna feel like I got kicked by a horse tomorrow. But I think I'll manage," Declan said.

Mercedes didn't respond. She stared at her hands, her mouth open.

"Sadie, say something," he demanded.

She blinked. "I— I think I have a couple of cuts from glass but not too bad."

Relief washed over him when she took in a full breath. No damage.

She ran a hand through her hair. "Oh. My head is bleeding."

Alec turned on the overhead light. Her shaking hand was wet with blood. The back of her head was a sticky tangle, drops of red falling onto her shirt.

"Christ! Dec!" Alec cried. "Can you see how bad?" *Had a bullet struck her?*

Declan shot forward, scanning the top of her head by the light of his cell phone.

"Do I need to pull over?" When Alec didn't get an answer, he yelled, "Declan!"

"Aye, I hear you!" Declan shouted back. "Give me a second."

Mercedes whimpered, and Declan pulled back, a bloodied shard of glass held between his fingers.

"How the hell did you get this?" Declan asked.

"Jason threw me into the china cabinet," she whispered. "I don't feel good." She leaned forward, breathing in shallow pants.

"Breathe, Sadie," Alec ordered, rubbing her back.

"She's bleeding a lot, but head wounds do that," Declan said. "She might need stitches. I need a rag or something."

"Here." Alec ripped at his shirt, ignoring the buttons popping off. "Use this."

Declan got Mercedes to sit back, the shirt pressed to her head to stem the bleeding. "Did you stab that fucker with a knife?"

Alec let out a breath. "Aye, she did."

"I didn't think I could do that." Her voice was hollow, but her lips turned up in a smile.

Alec's chest throbbed. His fingers felt where the knife had entered his chest. It was seeping blood. Adrenaline was fading along with the mental chaos it brought.

What was their next move? Nothing was secure. The other

safehouses were useless. Mariah had access to most of their internal protocols. Most, but not all.

Shit. "We have no choice, do we?"

"Nope."

"Fuck!"

Alec pulled his phone out and dialed.

It rang twice and clicked. Cressida's voice came on the line. "Artemis here."

"Artemis, this is Renegade. We've been compromised."

A brief pause. "Go."

"Safehouse was breached. All members accounted for. All sustained minor injuries. At least one deceased assailant. All priority gear stripped, secondary items left. All communication forms are unusable. We will be moving to November. Confirm." Mercedes's eyes were on him, but he didn't have time to explain.

"Moving to November. Affirmative. Other instructions?"

"Strip everything from Mariah Costa immediately. She's a mole and should be treated as hostile. Under no circumstances is she to gain access to any part of our system. Any avenue she has been a part of has been compromised."

"I want one of the twins," Declan said. "Something I need to look into."

"Take them both. And tell Matrix as well," Alec said, using the code name for Mason. "Everyone goes dark until further notice." He didn't want any loose ends until they regrouped.

After everything was repeated and affirmed with Cressida. She promised to update him when she knew more.

Mercedes was looking out the cracked window. He wanted to talk to her, to reassure himself she was all right. He wanted her to let him apologize for not keeping her safe.

He knew better. Mercedes wanted nothing to do with him at the moment, and he didn't blame her. Still, she was breathing. She was alive. If there was anything to be grateful for, it was that.

CHAPTER TWENTY-FOUR

The dim light dulled the crimson threads of blood smeared on Mercedes's palms. Wind from the blown-out windows thundered through the cab.

It wasn't real. It couldn't be real.

The god damn shaking had returned. The back of her head burned, and a dull ache was seeping through her body, amplifying every new bruise and mark.

She tried to think of a song. Something that would help settle her stomach and relax her stiff muscles. Her fingers did nothing. Her mind was too splintered.

Just this morning, she and Alec had discussed her options. Staying here or going back to San Francisco. It was clear she couldn't do either.

Jason had lost his damn mind. If he was willing to do what he had done tonight, there was no way he'd let her go. Alec couldn't beat Jason back forever.

Alec.

Holy hell.

Mercedes had always known about his abilities. It wasn't like it was a secret. He had shared stories with her, some that made her stomach turn. She knew he was a well-trained soldier.

But watching it in action was something entirely different. There was a violence in him she'd never seen before. Every movement he made had a purpose. The gruesome sound of Jason's shoulder being ripped out of joint reverberated in her head. Alec hadn't even flinched.

Where Jason was chaos, Alec was composed.

A gunshot and a thick crunch of bone echoed in her mind. She hadn't seen it, but Alec had pulled the trigger. Her gut wrenched.

"Oh my god, you killed someone." She stared at him.

"Aye." Alec shot a look at her. His eyes were hard. "And I'd do it again."

Her pulse leapt at his intensity. "I'm sorry you had to do that because of me."

Alec stared out at the road, his hands gripping the wheel. When he finally spoke, his voice was quiet. "I told you, I'd do anything for you."

Her breath caught as a spark of warmth ran through her.

Mercedes closed her eyes, breathing in the rain-drenched air whipping around her. Time wasn't making sense. Was it only minutes ago he'd brushed his lips against hers, a gentle teasing before a kiss that never came?

Because of the doorbell.

And fucking Mariah.

The ache of betrayal rushed through her. Alec had made her believe she meant something to him. And like an idiot, she had fallen for it. Again.

I told you, I'd do anything for you.

Nothing more than honeyed words.

"How did you know, Sadie?" Declan's voice made her jump.

"Know what?"

"That Mariah was working with Jason."

Mariah Costa's smug smile gnawed at her. If she was being honest, she'd say it was straight-up jealousy that made her instantly distrust the woman. But she'd never admit to that.

"It was in her eyes." Which was also true. "She didn't think we'd lie about who I was. And every time she talked about being with Alec, she was watching me. She wanted a reaction out of me."

Mercedes didn't miss the jerk of Alec's head from the corner of her eye. His grip on the wheel tightened.

An hour later, Alec pulled into an industrial park. While a few cars were passing by on the main street, the buildings were quiet. The SUV stopped in front of a warehouse with a large roll door. The headlights against the side of the building reflected into the darkened cab, illuminating the cracks along the windshield.

Mercedes peered. "Where are we?"

"The last safe location we have," Alec answered. "We own this building, but it's not on the company books. Mariah doesn't know about it."

The hurt in her heart bubbled to the surface, lashing out. "You sure? She seemed to know a lot about you." She was being a petty asshole, and she knew it.

Alec stopped and looked at her. She held his gaze. Her pulse jumped at the mix of anger and regret she read in his eyes. He pursed his lips, shoved his door open, and stalked to the warehouse.

"Damn, that was salty," Declan scoffed.

"Shut up, Dec," she said without heat. He chuckled.

Alec opened the large warehouse door and walked back to the car, the headlights illuminating his powerful frame. His plain white T-shirt was stained with streaks of blood, and the thin cotton fabric clung tightly to his sculpted chest. Warmth tingled down her spine, pooling in her core.

God, he was incredible.

She had to look away. It did her no good to be distracted by this attraction she had for him. She needed to keep her eye on reality.

Alec climbed back into the driver's seat and pulled the battered SUV into the warehouse. The large overhead lights gave the room a blue glow as they warmed up. He shut off the car and climbed out without saying another word.

She pushed open her door and held onto it as she gave her legs a test run. Grateful they weren't as jittery as they'd been during her hospital escape, she wrapped her arms around her waist and took in the building.

There was a collection of vehicles parked around the space. Some were basic black sedans, while others were classics. Alec loved working on cars. These were clearly a mixture of business and pleasure.

Alec pulled a first aid kit from a nearby cabinet and set it on a low card table.

"I need to have a look." Alec gestured to her head. "Come sit here." He pulled a folding chair out from the table and turned it around in front of him.

Mentioning the injury made it throb. Mercedes sat in front of him, biting her lip to keep in a grunt of pain when he started searching through her hair. His fingers were gentle, but she winced when he separated her hair from the wound at the crown of her head.

"Sorry," he murmured. "The bleeding has stopped. I don't think I'll have to stitch it. Let me know if you feel it start up again."

Alec came around and knelt in front of her. His hand reached for her throat, and she pushed back in her chair, terror ripping through her. Her fist struck out, but he caught it before she could land a punch.

"Hey, hey, hey, it's alright. It's alright." Alec's voice was gentle. "I want to make sure you don't have any swelling."

She sucked in gulps of air, desperate to calm her thundering heart.

He kept her hand, his eyebrows furrowed. "You're okay. You're safe here. Breathe in. Focus on my voice," he coached in soothing tones.

Mercedes shuddered uncontrollably, a cold sweat beading on her forehead. Declan brought over an ice pack and pressed it against the back of her neck.

"Better?" Alec's blue eyes were anxious.

"I think so. What the hell just happened?"

"You had a panic attack. It's no wonder after everything that's happened." His hand brushed her hair from her face. "I'm so sorry. I shouldn't have come at you like that."

"It's okay. I've never had one of those before."

"They can be pretty intense." His face was only inches from hers. "I want to check your throat, if you think you can manage?"

Logic told her Alec would never hurt her. But she was terrified of having another reaction like that.

Mercedes took a breath. "Go ahead." She tried to relax as he gently examined her throat, wincing when he hit a tender spot.

"Sorry," he mumbled, probing gently. "Everything seems okay. You can breathe normally, right?"

Not at the moment. She gave him a curt nod.

"Good, we'll be out of here soon."

"What about you?" She put her hand on his chest, next to the bloody tear in his shirt. She could feel him tighten under her fingers. "You might need stitches."

"Aye, I might. Declan will look at it. It's not the same as having Mason around, but he can thread a needle if needed."

Alec stood and walked to the first aid kit, taking out various gauzes and medical paraphernalia. He stripped off his bloody shirt and sat on the table in front of Declan, who handed him a wet towel to clean the blood off his chest. The nearness of Alec without a shirt would usually give her a thrill, but all she could see was the crescent-shaped gash on his chest. It was about three inches long and deep. Jason had narrowly missed adding to his puckered scar, a reminder of the bullet Alec had taken in the war. Other silver scars, long since healed, decorated Alec's muscular torso and arms.

The thought of Declan pulling a needle through Alec's flesh made the room spin. Mercedes held her breath while they examined the wound.

"I think a closure bandage will do the trick," Declan muttered. "Sadie, come hold this towel, please."

Mercedes took the towel. Her hand shook as she held it against Alec's chest. Declan used a squirt bottle of saline to clean the wound while Mercedes caught the runoff. She put her other hand on his shoulder to steady herself, feeling the warmth radiating from him. His body tensed with each stream of solution that hit it. Mercedes winced at his quiet hisses of pain, each sending a dagger into her heart.

"I'm okay, lass," Alec said. "Just stings a bit."

Mercedes was clutching his shoulder. "I know. But I don't like it," she whispered.

"Aye, I know how that is."

Once it was clean and dry, Declan made quick work of bandaging it and added a clear adhesive wrap to cover it.

"Good thing you were here, lass. Normally he swears at me like a sailor." Declan smacked Alec's good shoulder with a grin.

Alec sent Declan a smirk as he hopped off the table.

Normally? Was this just another day for them?

Mercedes watched them silently as they pulled bags and items from cabinets. They spoke in low tones about next steps, how to clean up the mess at the house, removing the damaged vehicle from the warehouse.

"There's a bathroom in the back." Alec gestured behind him. "You should wash up and change."

Mercedes gathered clothes and her makeup bag and found the small restroom. She was a wreck. Smears of blood were on her cheeks and chin and crusting on the fabric of her shirt.

Who the hell is this woman?

What she wouldn't give to go back to when her biggest concern was submitting a brief on time or how short to make her hemline for a company cocktail party. Now she was wondering how to dispose of a blood-soaked shirt.

Mercedes scrubbed her hands and face. She tried to rinse the blood from her long hair, but it wasn't easy with only a pedestal sink.

Alec knocked at the door as she added the final touch. "It's time for us to go."

The table of supplies was neatly packed up. Declan was loading an older model jeep with bags, and she walked to the passenger side.

"We're over here, lass." Alec's voice was quiet. He was standing in front of a sleek black muscle car.

"What's that?"

Alec glanced down at the car. "It's a Camaro."

"I can see that. Won't it draw attention?"

He smiled. "Aye, it's a *very nice* Camaro. But they didn't use satellite systems in 1969." He frowned, regret clear in his eyes. "I'm not taking any chances."

Mercedes looked to where Declan was throwing one last thing into the passenger side of the jeep.

"Dec's not coming with us?" Why was she only now catching on to this?

"No, you and I are going out on our own."

Her stomach sank. "Just the two of us?"

"Aye." He was studying her.

She swallowed, her throat scratchy. "I thought I was going to the embassy with Declan."

Alec's face darkened. He took a step forward. "Why would you think that?"

"Because I *told* you I was going to the embassy with Declan."

Alec winced, his eyebrows drawn together. "I know you're angry with me. You have every right to be. But it's not safe to do that tonight."

Mercedes hesitated, but not for the reason he thought. Her anger had slipped away when she saw him bleeding. Blood he had shed for her. But she couldn't go with him. Alec had a way of scraping her heart raw. It was too hard to be alone with him.

"I can't let you go on without me. I have to see you safe." He cleared his throat. "Please."

Mercedes looked away, torn. Declan had said he wanted to go on his own with the twins. A trip to the embassy might be pointless anyway. She had no idea if they could accommodate her at the last second.

At least Alec seemed to have a plan.

She looked up at him again and sighed. "Okay."

Alec let out his breath all at once. "Let me take your bag." Mercedes slipped the strap off her shoulder and handed it to him.

She walked to Declan and gave him a hug.

"Can't you come with us?" she asked in a last-ditch effort to put a buffer between her and Alec.

"I'm sorry, I can't. I have something I need to do. It's important." Declan smiled apologetically. "You'll do fine. No one wants you safe more than that man over there."

Mercedes followed his gaze to Alec as he got into the car. The engine roared, reverberating off the metal walls. If only she knew what to believe.

Declan gave her a kiss on the cheek, and she joined Alec in the car.

She had no idea where they were going. It didn't matter. One thing today had taught her was that she'd be stupid to let her guard down again.

CHAPTER TWENTY-FIVE

Vodka doesn't do shit for pain.

Jason took another pull from the bottle as Patrick snipped the last suture. He'd dug the needle into Jason's thigh a little more aggressively than necessary, but at least the job was done. It was going to be a bitch to walk for a few days.

The other injuries were a problem too. His broken nose had been set, but the purple and black discoloration had already seeped under his eyes. By morning, he'd look like hammered shit.

Then there was his shoulder. It had popped back into place on its own, but muscle spasms threatened to throw it out of joint again.

It hurt like hell.

"Finished," Patrick said.

Jason slid off the conference room table and pulled his pants up. The world spun as a wave of nausea hit him. *God damn it. I don't have time for this.*

The darkened offices had given him a reprieve after everything had gone sideways, but they couldn't stay here long.

Mariah was leaning against the glass doorway, looking amused.

"Where's my icepack?" Jason growled at her.

She sneered and tossed it at him. His hand moved automatically to snatch it from the air, searing his injured shoulder. The world lurched again.

Bitch.

Mariah smirked as she pulled out a chair from the table and flopped into it. "I don't know why you're so pissy with me. You're the dumbass who tried to take him on."

"Shut the fuck up."

She rolled her eyes at him.

Jason slumped against the table and pressed the pack to his face. He had to get it together and make a plan. But between the throbbing of his injuries and the rage coursing through him, he was drawing a blank.

Fucking McKinley.

That piece of shit told Sadie to stab him. And she did it. What had that bastard done to her? There was no way Sadie, *his Sadie*, would have ever hurt him on her own.

She loves me. She's just confused.

The bang of a distant door brought him back to the present.

"Shit, here we go," Patrick muttered.

He turned to see Adam's broad form striding toward them. Jason stood, straightening his back and pushing the ice pack away. Adam wasn't a man you showed weakness to. He thrived on it.

"What the fuck did you do?" Adam ground out as he strode into the conference room.

Jason put his chin up. "I told you I'd find her."

Adam stepped up to him, glaring down into his eyes. "You were told not to engage McKinley," he snarled. "Do you know, or even care, how much you cost us tonight?"

"We needed to know where she was," Jason said.

"No. What we needed was for you to not beat the shit out

of her and send her back into the arms of a fucking MI6 officer, you stupid bastard." Adam's face was reddening with
every word. "Years of our work, gone."

He stepped away from Jason with a huff and turned his
attention on Mariah. "And you."

Her wide dark eyes watched Adam warily.

"You were directed to have dinner with McKinley and test
the waters. How the fuck did you end up at that house?"

Mariah lifted her chin. "Romeo over there said I needed
to get eyes inside to confirm the asset was there. I did that."
She shot a glare at Jason. "I *thought* I was following orders."

Adam gritted his teeth. "He didn't have the authority to
give that order."

She shifted her gaze back to Adam. "And how the fuck
was I supposed to know that?" She stood and came around
the table. "It would've been nice to know there was a change
in management before I got sent in to blow my cover."

A smirk played on Jason's lips. It was Adam's fault. *This is
what the asshole gets for running a sloppy ship.*

Mariah turned back to Jason, narrowing her eyes. "What I
want to know is *why* did I have to blow my cover?" She walked
closer and tilted her head at him.

Jason stared at the floor, his jaw clamped tight. There was
no way he was going to give them anything.

"What did you think was going to happen?" Mariah
studied him. "You were going to go in there, machine guns
blazing, kill Alec and Declan McKinley right in front of her,
and she'd somehow swoon into your arms?"

They were watching him, three sets of eyes evaluating his
every movement. He'd have to be careful.

"We still need her, don't we? I made the call to get her
back. Once we had her, we could do what was needed."
Jason's stomach turned to think of what they might have to do
to her.

"It would have been easier to know what they were doing if I were embedded. Cressida's already stripped my access. We're blind now."

Damn it. There had to be another way.

"McKinley has a sister, doesn't he?" Jason said. Mariah's eyes widened. "And a little niece? Where are they? In Scotland?"

Her mouth dropped.

"Jesus," Patrick murmured.

"Tell me McKinley wouldn't trade Mercedes for the two of them."

"You're a sick fuck, you know that?" Adam's eyes were filled with disgust.

Mariah glared at him. "It won't work, anyway."

"Why not?"

"After all this time, I still don't think you have a fucking clue who you're dealing with," Mariah scoffed and shook her head. "How would he even know we have his sister and her baby? Alec isn't going to call his mum and check-in to see how the family is doing.

"He's going dark, and he's taking Mercedes with him. If anyone knows how to fall off the grid, it's Alec. He could, at this very moment, have her on a charter jet to America, or France, or fucking Morocco. They could be going anywhere. It could be weeks before he makes any sort of contact with his team. And because we've lost access, we won't find them until he's ready to resurface." She scowled. "That's how bad you've fucked us tonight."

"You're just sad to lose your little fuck buddy." Jason sneered.

"Ha. Not at all. I don't get attached the way some people do." She cocked her head at him. "You know, he's quite good in bed. I'm sure Sadie is *really* going to enjoy herself."

Fire lashed through his gut. He lunged.

Click-click. The sound of a bullet entering a chamber

stopped him. Adam had his .9mm aimed at the side of his head.

Jason met Adam's dark blue eyes and froze.

"One of my men is dead. The cops are all over that house, leaving us with a mess to clean up, and now we're blind." Adam pressed the barrel against his temple. "We've barely been able to stay a step ahead of McKinley, and he doesn't even know he's playing the game. There's no doubt he's about to catch on, and then we're fucked. Explain to me why I shouldn't put a bullet in your brain and be done with you."

"I can get what we need."

"How?" The cool metal pressed harder. "Kidnapping babies?"

"No. Mariah's right; it wouldn't work, anyway." Jason leaned back to lessen the pressure on his bruises. "But *you know* there are loose ends we haven't tugged on. Let me work them."

Adam stared at him, clearly contemplating his choices. "You've made a lot of promises."

"I've *kept* a lot of promises," Jason shot back.

The gun lowered. "This is your last chance. No more fuck-ups, or I end you." Adam turned to go but stopped and looked Jason in the eye. "And if I hear anything has happened to the sister or the kid, I'll tear your tongue out through your throat. You get me?"

Jason swallowed hard. "Understood."

Adam looked to Patrick. "You stay with him. Make sure he doesn't do anything else stupid."

Patrick nodded. Adam stalked out of the room, Mariah following behind.

Jason let out his breath in relief. *Shit, that was too close.* He brought the ice pack back to his face, his mind racing.

He needed to find Mercedes or find what they were looking for. There were no leads on either.

One way or another, he had to get to Mercedes before Adam did.

CHAPTER TWENTY-SIX

The city had fallen away to the darkness of the country motorway. The only sounds were the heavy rumble of the engine and a nineties radio station playing quietly.

The ache in Alec's gut hadn't eased since they'd left the warehouse. Every mistake he'd made replayed over and over in his mind. He should have known, should have seen the attack coming. Mercedes had trusted him to get her away from that fucking madman. And he'd failed her.

It was unforgivable.

Alec stole a look at her. The dim lights coming off the dashboard washed her in a soft glow. Her head rested against the window while her fingers danced against her thigh. A lock of chestnut hair fell forward, and she brushed it back behind her ear.

The simple movement made his breath catch. *She's every-thing. She doesn't even have to try.*

An image of that fucker's fingers squeezing her throat assailed him, and his stomach roiled. Her nails digging into an unrelenting grasp. Panic in her eyes. The weight of her terror was hanging onto him, sucking away his ability to breathe.

Fuck.

How had they gotten so god damn close? Why hadn't he known?

Mercedes hadn't spoken much since she'd chosen to come with him. There was no doubt in his mind she was regretting the choice.

Alec could feel her slipping away from him again.

He cleared his throat. "Sadie," he choked out. "I owe you an apology,"

She didn't answer right away. "Yeah? For which part?"

He swallowed, his throat dry. "For all of it. I made a promise to you, and I didn't keep it. I got outplayed." Alec took his eyes off the road to meet her gaze. "You know the things I've seen. The things I've done." He shook his head, his voice thick. "It shouldn't have been possible to play me like that. And they did. I underestimated him. He hurt you again because I fucked up."

Another agonizing silence lingered between them. When she spoke again, she had lost the heat that had peppered her tone since the warehouse. "I know you're doing everything you can."

"It wasn't enough." The words were suffocating.

Mercedes exhaled sharply and put her head back against the seat, staring at the ceiling. He didn't miss her dabbing the corner of her eye with her finger. When she turned to him, tears were threatening to spill.

"Alec." Her voice shook with emotion. "If it weren't for you, I'd be sleeping next to him right now. I'm grateful that I'm not."

He jerked his head to look at her. "You would have gone back to him?" he asked, his voice strangled. The thought of her lying next to him made his stomach lurch.

"I wouldn't have had a choice, would I? You've seen how they work. I'd never have made it out of the hospital on my own." Her lips turned up. "I needed help, and you gave it to me. I'm not happy about having to run again, but I always knew the risks."

The knot tightened again. They were only on the run because of Mariah. He knew how it looked, what Mariah had made her believe. The fact he was about to kiss Mercedes when everything went to shit made it all seem worse.

Christ, that doorbell couldn't have come at a worse time.

"About Mariah . . ."

"No," Mercedes shook her head. "I'm not ready to go there yet."

"Sadie, I . . ."

She stopped him. "Alec, please. I can't right now."

God, this was going to kill him. But he'd do it if she wasn't ready to talk about it. He bit his lip and nodded.

They let the road and the radio lull them.

The shrill sound of a phone ringing broke the silence, and Mercedes jumped.

"You have your phone?"

"It's a burner phone. Only Cress and Dec know about it." He pulled it from his back pocket and answered.

Cress's voice came through. "Good evening, Renegade. Busy night?"

He scoffed. "Aye, Artemis. What do we know?"

"Well, I have a few updates. The safehouse has one deceased male. He isn't one of Jason's known associates. The police are all over the house. The press is also on the scene."

"Shit."

"Rebellion will cover police statements and press releases. It should hold them off of you for a while. Everyone is going quiet."

"Good. What lodgings did you secure?"

"I have some unfortunate news there. There's no availability in isolated properties, so you'll have to be wary. I've done a background check. It's a solid location. You have a map in your encrypted messages."

"Let me verify." He slowed the car and pulled onto the shoulder of the road to scroll through the phone and find the map.

"Confirmed. Establish new comms as soon as it's safe to do so."

"Will do. Stay safe."

"You as well."

Alec hung up and studied the map. Once he had it memorized, he opened his door, walked in front of the car, and tossed the phone in the dirt. He pulled his gun, and shot two rounds into the phone, and tossed the remaining pieces into the night.

"Why did you do that?" Mercedes's eyes were wide. "Now we don't have a way to contact them."

"Aye. Now we're dark."

She closed her eyes and took a deep breath. There was no turning back.

Pulling back onto the highway, he figured now would be a good time to go over what she should expect.

"Unfortunately, Cress couldn't get us a place on our own, so we will have to interact with people. My name will be William Cameron. I'm an investment banker in London. I don't have identification for you, so you can pick a name to go by. When you speak, people will know you're an American. There's no reason to pretend you're not. In fact, stay as close to reality as you can."

"Lies are hard to keep track of." The hollowness of her words hit him. How many lies had she told to keep what that asshole had done to her a secret?

Alec swallowed. "What shall I call you?"

"Elizabeth. Elizabeth . . . Carter." She scoffed. "It'll be an improvement on Mercedes."

Alec cast a glance at her. "Mercedes is a beautiful name."

A ghost of a smile played on her lips, but she wouldn't look at him.

"We have a few hours left. You should get some rest."

Mercedes leaned forward to take off the sweater she had borrowed from him. She balled it up and laid it on the window to use as a pillow.

It took a while before her strumming fingers quieted, settling against her thigh. Even though her face had softened and her breath had evened out, there was no way she'd get a restful sleep like that.

Guilt gnawed at him. Mercedes deserved to be sleeping in her own bed. Not leaning against a cold car window, injured and running for her life. She deserved the whole fucking world.

A GENTLE SHAKE OF HER SHOULDER WOKE MERCEDES. "SADIE, we're almost there."

She rubbed her eyes and sat up, her neck tight. The night was an inky black. Only a few sparkling lights twinkled at them in the distance.

Mercedes snuck a look at Alec. His brows were furrowed, and his jaw set tight. The heaviness between them was taking a toll on them both.

"There isn't anything out here," she said.

"We're pretty far from any sort of city, that's true. There's a town just over this hill. Hey, can you reach into the back seat and get that beanie?"

Mercedes grabbed it and held it to him. Alec shook his head. "It's for you. There's some blood in your hair."

A few turns later and a charming little village came into view. Tall stone shops and houses lined the deserted cobblestone roads, illuminated by decorative street lamps. The rumble of the car's engine cut through the slumbering streets.

They turned onto a long drive. The sight of the inn breaking through the trees made Mercedes draw in her breath. The sprawling house wasn't a castle but a large manor lit from below to showcase the red and cream brickwork. A stone sign announced they had arrived at Kennison Manor Inn and Spa. Alec pulled the car into the mostly empty parking lot.

Mercedes opened the door and was immediately struck by the freshness of the air. Gone were the sharp scents of cars and people. A soft and earthy essence filled the night.

She covered her hair with the cap and followed Alec into the inn. The scent of cookies warmed the entryway. It had the feel of a comfortable cottage rather than a large estate.

"Oh-ho lad, I'll be right with you," a voice called from the adjoining room. A tall white gentleman emerged, brushing crumbs from his shirt. He was older, perhaps in his early seventies, with closely cropped gray hair and a salt-and-pepper beard.

"You caught me whilst I was stealing one of my wife's biscuits. Supposed to be for tomorrow, but she'll never miss it. Can I get you one?"

"Oh, no, thank you." Alec smiled. "I believe my assistant called and made a reservation for Cameron."

"Aye, she did. You must be the young lovers looking for a romantic getaway. My name's Gavin Kennison."

Alec gave a short cough to cover his surprise. Mercedes winced and pursed her lips. She knew exactly who to thank for that.

"Aye sir, I'm William." Alec extended his hand, which the man took heartily. "And this is Elizabeth Carter," he added, putting his hand to the small of her back.

The man turned his twinkling eyes toward her, and she couldn't help smiling at him. He shook her hand as well, giving it a cheery pat.

"Thank you for fitting us in on such short notice and so late," Mercedes said.

"Oh no, no need to worry about that, lass. I'm a night owl,

and I don't mind a bit." He gave Alec a tap on the shoulder. "Come, we'll get you all signed in."

"Remind me I need to sack Cressida the next time we see her," Alec muttered into Mercedes's ear before following the man to the desk. Mercedes chuckled softly.

She examined the architecture and artwork of the room around her. A painting of the estate in the late 1700s caught her attention, and she moved in to study it.

"Hello, I heard we were having latecomers," a male voice said behind her.

Mercedes yelped and leapt away from the stranger, her heart racing.

He stepped back with his hands up. "Oh, so sorry, lass. Didn't mean to give you a turn." His rich brown eyes were surprised.

Alec was more than halfway across the room to her when she met his gaze and gave him a small shake of the head. He stopped, fists clenched at his sides.

She felt like an idiot. "It's okay. Sorry, I'm a little jumpy."

Alec narrowed his eyes at the man but backed away, returning to the front desk and their host.

"I'm David Kennison. My parents own the inn." He offered his hand to her. The corners of his eyes crinkled when he smiled. She took it, noticing the roughness of his palms.

"Elizabeth Carter." The name sounded so strange coming out of her mouth. She made a snap decision. "You can call me Eliza."

"Eliza, lovely. You're an American?"

"Guilty."

David's mouth was turned up in a pleasant smile. He was attractive. Maybe he didn't have the chiseled handsomeness of the McKinley cousins, but he had a certain charm.

"I've always wanted to go there but never have. Whereabouts are you from?"

Alec had told her to stick to the truth as much as possible. "San Francisco, originally. Now I live in London."

"Oh, brilliant. San Francisco's on my bucket list for sure."

A wave of homesickness washed over her as she thought of home. She was so out of step with the world she was in now.

Alec had finished with the check-in and joined them.

"William Cameron." He offered his hand to David with a smile that didn't meet his eyes. He was studying the man's face intently. David took it and seemed to take the measure of Alec as well.

"I was saying to Eliza, I have always wanted to travel to the US. San Francisco is on the top of that list. She was about to tell me some of the best places to go. I'd love to finish up that conversation while you're here. Maybe it will inspire me to buy a plane ticket."

"Of course. Be happy to," Mercedes said.

David flashed her another smile and tilted his head at her.

Alec cleared his throat. "Well, it's been quite a long day. Darling, we should head to our room."

Her pulse leapt. The "darling" threw her. It was the only pet name she'd ever loved, and only from his lips.

She flushed. "Of course." She turned to David again. "It was lovely to meet you. We'll chat soon."

She took Alec's hand, and he led her to the grand staircase and to their suite. It was stunning. Large fireplace with a sitting area around it, perfect for reading in front of the fire. Floor-to-ceiling curtains that perfectly matched the modern red and cream decor.

Except there was only one bed.

Since Cressida had told the owner this was a romantic getaway, there was a tray perched at the foot of the fluffy cream down comforter. On it was a variety of chocolate truffles, a bottle of red wine, and two glasses.

Alec frowned at it like it might jump and bite him.

Mercedes walked to the tray and picked up the card that was tented on it.

Enjoy you two

~ C & D

"Well, it looks like she had help." She handed the card to Alec.

"My next communication with them should be fun," Alec grumped.

The bed was large enough to fit them both. But given the state of their tattered relationship at the moment, Mercedes doubted they would both be sleeping on it.

She'd worry about that later. Right now, she needed a shower. Jason hadn't had his hands on her for long, but she could still smell him on her.

The water stung when it hit the crown of her head. She washed until the suds no longer came back pink in her hand.

When she left the bathroom, he had lit the fire and set up blankets and a pillow on the rug for a makeshift bed.

"You don't have to sleep down there. There's no way you'll get any rest."

"It's fine."

Mercedes frowned. "You're paying for this room. It's not right you're sleeping on the floor." *This is silly.*

"I don't mind." Without warning, he stripped off his shirt and tossed it in his bag. "I've slept in worse places."

The firelight flickered on his skin, shadows dancing around his taut muscles. Pure need washed through her, pooling heat between her legs. *Lord, help me.*

He gathered his clothes and went to the shower, seemingly unaware of what he'd just done to her. Mercedes rubbed her temples, willing her heart to slow down.

Yeah, he should probably sleep on the floor.

The bottle of wine caught her eye. *Perfect.* She poured a glass and snagged a chocolate truffle from the plate. It was a little piece of heaven. With the chaos of the night, they hadn't eaten anything since lunch. She wasn't about to disturb the hosts, so this was probably all they would get until breakfast.

Mercedes curled up on the loveseat, letting the wine and the heat from the fire lull her.

That is until Alec emerged from the bathroom.

He still wasn't wearing a damn shirt. His dark hair was tousled from towel drying, and his scent lingered throughout the room. Tea tree and mint. It was the first time she could identify what made him smell so amazing.

Mercedes tried to focus on the glass of wine in her hand and not on how beautiful he was. He created a lovely ache in her. One she'd forgotten existed.

She took another sip of wine. Her best course of action was to polish off the glass quickly and go to bed. It would be harder to ogle him if the lights were off.

Alec had other ideas.

"Sadie, can we talk?"

Mercedes's heart sank. "Do we have to? We talked in the car."

"I need to tell you what happened with Mariah."

Jealousy clawed at her gut. She had no right to feel it. Alec wasn't hers. He never had been. Her brain understood this. But her heart refused to feel nothing.

Mercedes shot a glance at him, the refusal on her tongue, but his expression caught her attention. His eyebrows were pinched tight, his jaw clenched. In fact, his entire body was radiating tension.

Maybe he was right. Better to get it over with now.

Mercedes stood and walked to the dresser. Setting the wineglass down on top of it, she turned and leaned against it. "Alright." She crossed her arms and waited.

Relief crossed his face, and he jumped right in. "She wasn't lying. We had a relationship. It wasn't serious, mainly just . . ." He stopped, clearly not knowing what to say next.

"Just banging?" she supplied helpfully.

Alec flushed. "It wasn't like that."

"Look, I appreciate what you are trying to do, but you don't have to tell me anything about your relationship with her. It isn't my business." It was breaking her apart to hear about it.

"You seemed pretty upset."

"I was, I *am*. It's just . . . I had thought we were . . ." What did she think they were? "When Mason and Shake told me you couldn't come for a few more days, I was disappointed. I'd been looking forward to seeing you. I thought you felt the same."

Alec's eyes softened.

"And right before she showed up, you were about to . . ." Mercedes's voice choked off. The moment replayed in her mind. There was no way she misread what happened.

"I was going to kiss you," he finished for her.

The confirmation hit her in the chest. At least she hadn't imagined it. "Then she comes in, and I realize you'd been with her. It stung," she admitted.

"I didn't sleep with her."

"Again, you don't have anything to . . ."

"I was disappointed too," he said. "I'd thought of little else but getting back to you. But Jason had come to my office, and it wasn't safe to come out yet. So when Mariah invited me out, I thought it would provide more of a cover. She and I hadn't been . . . you know, in months."

Her heart wrenched again. "So, you're saying you went out with her for me?"

Alec scoffed. "Aye, I know how it sounds. But I swear, it's why I did it. I've no interest in her."

"But she knew you'd be there."

"Aye." He nodded. "She saw we'd blocked off the safehouse for a time and asked about it. It's not an unusual question, but I lied to her anyway. If I had told her the truth, Jason would have found you that night. And I wouldn't have been there."

Mercedes took this in. She'd always known Jason had a long reach. When she'd try to leave, there was always someone there to help him.

A thought occurred to her, and she frowned. "How long do you think she was working for Jason?"

Alec winced and looked down.

Her heart dropped. "You don't know, do you?"

He shook his head, his lips tight. "I have a few theories."

"What would those be?"

"Best case scenario is he met her and paid her off in the last two weeks."

"And the worst case?"

Alec's brows furrowed. "You would have just been moving to London when I first met her."

Ice hit her veins. "Oh my god," she whispered. "You think he planted her months ago?"

"Given what I've seen, it's possible."

Why? Why would Jason even think to do something like that?

Mercedes pressed the tips of her fingers to her forehead, taking a moment to breathe. When she looked back up at Alec, most of her anger had slipped away. It was replaced with guilt. She'd dropped into Alec's life and brought a shitstorm with her.

"God, I'm sorry, Alec."

He tilted his head at her. "Why are you sorry? It's not your fault."

"But it is. I knew . . ." She stopped herself. "You didn't ask for any of this."

Alec was quiet for a moment. When he spoke, his voice was tight. "I don't know if you'll believe me, but I haven't been able to stop thinking about you since I first heard your voice again."

"You haven't?" The oxygen was swept from the room, leaving her dizzy.

Alec took a step toward her. "At the shop, I asked to see you again, even though you were with someone else because I enjoy spending time with you. I was willing to be friends with *him* if that meant I got to see you. That's how much I want you in my life."

He swallowed. "When I found out what he'd done to you, all I could think of was getting to you. I had to see with my own eyes you were alive." He shook his head, his brows drawn together. "I honestly don't know that I could have walked away if you had told me to go."

A silence fell between them. Mercedes's breath had grown shallow, and her heart pounded in her ears.

"I knew he was jealous of you," she said. "And that when we moved to London, you were off-limits. He told me more than once. I knew, and I called you anyway. But I thought the consequences would be mine."

Alec cast his eyes away, his brows knitted together.

"The truth is." The words were getting harder to say through the tightness in her throat. "He was right to be jealous of you."

Alec's head snapped up. "He was?" he whispered, his blue eyes wide, searching her face.

"If I'd had a notion you would ever want to be with me, I'd have . . ."

"You'd what?" His voice had grown rough.

Mercedes blinked back the tears that threatened to spill over. There was no turning back. "He never stood a chance against you."

Alec closed the distance between them. She only had time for a hitched breath before his mouth was taking hers. She responded immediately, opening to him. His tongue relentlessly stroked hers, working her. Each lash a promise of what he could do. She moaned into his mouth. Alec groaned, deepening the kiss.

It was everything she needed. No matter the lies she told herself, this was what she'd wanted. To feel his body against her, his kiss taking what belonged to him.

The slam of a distant door made his body tense, and he broke away. His eyes darted to the door, and his labored breathing stilled. Mercedes's heart thundered in the quiet. She waited for some sort of sign of what was happening.

Laughter carried down the hall, and Alec's straining muscles relaxed. It was other guests returning to their rooms.

He looked at her as if he just realized she was wrapped in his arms. Her hand was intertwined in his hair, and she ran fingers through it.

There was conflict written all over his face. Did he regret kissing her? She hoped not. It had been the best part of her year.

Alec moaned and kissed her again. Mercedes answered him, desperate to sate the hunger she had for him. The hard ridge of him pressed against her. Making her aching and ready. Kissing wasn't enough. She wanted more.

Her heart sank when he pulled back this time, gently easing her away from him, his breathing ragged. "Sadie, we have to stop."

"What?"

"Shit. I can't. I'm sorry, but I can't." Alec stepped away from her, his face turned away. When he finally looked at her, there was turmoil brewing in his eyes. "Damn it. I shouldn't have kissed you."

A crack formed in her heart. "Why not?"

"Because I fucked up today." Alec's mouth moved, but the words seemed trapped. "And you nearly died." He paced the room.

When he turned back, frustration was written across his face. "All the mistakes I made, every *single* one, was because my thoughts were of you." His voice was thick. "*I* should have heard Mariah coming up the steps. I didn't. Because I couldn't think of anything but kissing you. *I* should have seen her reaction to your name or the way she watched you. But I didn't. Because I was worried about how what she was saying might hurt you."

Alec pulled his hand through his hair. "And *I* should have realized Jason was on his way. But I didn't. Because I was so scared you were going to walk out of my life again, and I couldn't bear it."

His words lay between them, and she tried to make sense of them. He thought it a mistake to kiss her, but it scared him to lose her. They were in direct conflict with one another.

Alec stared into the fire. She ached to go to him, to wrap her arms around his neck and kiss him.

Instead, she put her hand on his. "Alec . . ."

"I almost shot you tonight, Sadie."

Her stomach dropped to the floor. "What?" she whispered.

"He had you. And you were going to die." Alec's eyes squeezed shut. "If you hadn't stabbed him, I'd have done it."

Mercedes stepped back, the twisting in her gut leaving her dizzy.

Alec turned to her. "When I'm with you, I can't think straight. Look what distraction almost cost us. I have to focus everything I have on protecting you. I can *never* be that desperate again."

He leaned down and kissed her on her cheek. "Goodnight, Sadie." And he stepped past her to the bed he'd made on the floor.

Heat rose to her cheeks. She'd been dismissed.

The room was hot and stifling. Mercedes grabbed her sweater and headed for the door. "I need some air."

"Wait. I'll go too."

"No," she said. "I need a moment away from you."

"I know you're upset, and I'm sorry . . ."

"Upset?" Humiliated was probably a better word. "Jesus, Alec. I've lost everything. I've been beaten and left for dead. My psycho ex keeps trying to kill me, and I'm terrified. All the time." A sob left her chest. She took in as much air as she could to calm it. "I don't have the emotional storage to deal with more heartache. If you can't decide what I am to you, then don't touch me again."

Mercedes turned and was out the door before he could say anything else.

CHAPTER TWENTY-SEVEN

The force of the door closing behind her echoed down the corridor, making Mercedes wince. She tried to fill her lungs with air that wasn't interwoven with Alec's scent. Throwing her hoodie over her shoulders, Mercedes strode down the stairs and across the lobby, spotting an exit with a sign to the garden.

Perfect.

The whoosh of night air soothed her heated cheeks, and she sucked in the floral scent. The path opened up to a patio with a large firepit at its center. Sitting on one of the chairs, she drew her knees to her chest, her arms holding them tight.

A bitter recounting of all the ways her life had collapsed in the last three years ran through her mind. She fought back the tears. Each trauma weighing down her heart.

It was too much. She was falling apart.

Mercedes touched her lips, imprinted with the scalding heat of Alec's mouth commanding hers. Why the hell would he kiss her like that if he didn't want her?

There was more to it than just keeping her safe. She'd felt him resisting, even in the moments before the doorbell.

It had never been that way before. Three years ago, she

hadn't questioned how much he wanted her. He'd gone out of his way to be near her, to see her wherever there was an opportunity. Then there were the come-fuck-me eyes they tossed at each other across a crowded room. Flirting was one thing, but the first time he'd kissed her was forever seared in her mind.

As the pre-wedding madness descended on Edinburgh, Mercedes had found herself overwhelmed with the size of the McKinley family. Luke and Charlotte were meeting with the clergyman that morning, and Mercedes had been looking forward to catching some much-needed sleep and maybe exploring the city after. That was until Alec called and invited her on a hike. She wasn't exactly outdoorsy, but spending the day with Alec was definitely appealing.

"There aren't any bears where we're going, are there?" she asked, only partially kidding. Bears freaked her out.

Alec pulled a pack out of the trunk of the car. "Oh, aye. We'll have to be careful. Big bastards and vicious too." His blue eyes were wide and serious. "They say their claws can cut right through metal." He tapped the hood of the car.

Holy shit.

His lips twisted up into an impish smile.

Mercedes gasped. "That's not funny." She gave his shoulder a gentle punch, laughing despite herself.

Alec chuckled. "Oh, I disagree. It's very funny."

"Go easy on me. My idea of a hike is a walking trail in Golden Gate Park. I'm a total novice here."

The rustle of a nearby bush made her heart jump. She grabbed his arm, ready to bolt to the car.

Alec wrapped his arm around her waist and laughed. "It's just a squirrel."

Mercedes held her breath until a red-coated squirrel burst from the bush and scurried up the neighboring tree. "Oh my god, he's so cute. He's different from the ones at home."

Alec hadn't let go of her waist. Mercedes met his gaze, not

stepping away. He was so close. She swallowed hard. "Are you sure there aren't any bears here?"

A smile played on his lips. "Quite sure."

"How do you know?"

Leaning down, he whispered in her ear. "Because there aren't any bears in all of Scotland."

His voice had a gentle hum to it that made her breathless. Until she registered what he said. She popped back in surprise, her eyebrows furrowed. "Really? None?"

Alec chuckled. "I promise, Sadie. You'll be safe." He slid his palm down her arm, interlacing his fingers with hers. He shot her a look, silently asking if his touch was okay. She parted her lips, squeezing his hand in response.

Walking through the wilderness with a tall, handsome Scotsman was an experience she hadn't known she needed in her life, but there she was. Maybe she should take up hiking after all.

They talked the whole way, laughing and teasing one another. Occasionally, he'd help her with a tricky step, his touches lingering on her longer than necessary. Not that she minded. The constant flickering in her soul made it clear how smitten she'd become.

As they rounded a bend in the pathway, they came up to a stair-stepped waterfall hidden amongst the dense green foliage. Mercedes stopped, her mouth agape.

"It's so beautiful," she whispered.

"Aye, it is," he said softly, his gaze on her. A flush rose on her cheeks.

Alec led her to a crop of rocks on the riverbank at the base of the falls. The breeze carried an occasional mist of spray to her face. He found a large boulder to sit on, turning Mercedes to settle in front of him. The feel of his powerful arms folded around her kindled a deep burn in her core. Taking slow, deep breaths, she was lulled by his clean, earthy scent mixed with the water and trees around them—a moment of perfection.

"What is this thing you do with your fingers?" Alec murmured in her ear. She froze. She hadn't realized she had been tapping her rhythm on his wrist.

Mercedes bit her cheek. "Sorry. It's a weird thing I do."

Pulling their hands up to examine them, his fingers ran slowly up and down the length of hers. "There's a pattern to it, isn't there? I've watched you do it several times. It isn't random."

A shot of warmth ran through her. Alec had to have watched her for a while to know she did that.

"Sometimes, a song comes to my mind, and my fingers itch to play it."

The stroke of his touch electrified her, distracting her from what she was saying. "Ah, I heard that about you. You can play all sorts of instruments, and you're quite good."

Mercedes smiled. "Something like that, I guess." Alec's fingertips brushed her wrists, making her voice husky. "I have synesthesia. It's hard to describe, but music comes to me easily. Sometimes I lose myself in it."

"So what song were you playing?"

She shivered as he nuzzled against her, his breath soft against her cheek. "It wasn't anything that's been written." She shot him a shy smile. Most people never noticed her weird quirk. "It was the waterfall. The sound of the water tumbling over the rocks makes a rhythm. I was adding to it."

Alec turned her chin to face him. "You're incredible." The rumble of his words made her exhale sharply.

She scoffed. "I don't know ab—"

Alec dipped his head and kissed her, his soft mouth teasing hers. He broke away, his eyes piercing, his hand on her cheek. "Incredible," he repeated, barely above a whisper.

Mercedes let out a shuddering breath as his mouth crashed onto hers. There was no hesitation in his kiss but a demand she was ready to match. The roar of the waterfall fell aside, mingling with the rushing heartbeat in her ears.

Mercedes let out a gentle moan, opening to him. Delicious heat rushed through her as he caressed her tongue with his.

Alec responded with a groan of his own, bringing his fist into her hair. The fire he ignited shifted into an inferno, making her eager for more. She burned for him to slide his fingers between her thighs, to massage the ache he was creating.

The sound of approaching hikers was the only thing that kept her from allowing scandalous acts to be done to her in public. He tore his searing kiss away, his soft pants arousing her even more.

Looking back on it now, little had changed in the last three years. Alec could hold her attention the way no other man ever had. It wasn't just his stunning good looks or the toe-curling accent.

Sometimes he made her feel like she was the most important person in his world, that he'd do anything for her. The next thing she knew, he was dropping her without a word, repeatedly reminding her how forgettable she was.

The chill of the night air had broken through the heat of her inflamed body. It would be too cold to stay out here soon. She inhaled again, wanting to take one more moment before his closeness stole her breath and common sense.

A door squeaking shut behind her brought her attention to reality. Someone, most likely Alec, was coming up the path to the firepit.

Shit. She wasn't ready to face him again.

Sniffing, she hastened to wipe her cheeks and brush back her hair. She'd be damned if her dignity would be on the ground.

"Hello, lass." The strange voice made her jump from the chair, her pulse screaming alive.

"Oh! Damn, so sorry!" David Kennison appeared in the light, a chagrined smile on his lips. "I heard you come out.

Thought maybe you could use a dram." He held a bottle of whisky and two crystal glasses in his hand.

Mercedes cursed herself for being so far away from Alec. She looked at the manor house, contemplating how quickly she could get back inside.

David cocked his head. "I mean, I'm not sure if you're a drinker or no. No trouble if you're not. I also brought out a blanket if you're cold." He set the bottle and glasses on the edge of the firepit.

Cress cleared this place. He's the owner's son. You are safe.

Exhaling sharply, she let out a nervous laugh. "Actually, they both sound great. Thank you."

Beaming at her, he unfurled the blanket and handed it to her. She tugged it around herself, grateful for its warmth. Pouring a finger of amber liquid into the crystal glasses, David passed one to her. "*Slàinte.*"

Mercedes held her glass up in response and took a sip. The smoky flavors mixed with the sharp heat of the whisky spread warmth through her.

"Rough night, lass?"

She wasn't used to anyone but Alec and Declan calling her that.

"Something like that." At least David hadn't come at the height of her ugly cry. "Have you ever had one of those moments when everything seems to go wrong?"

"Oh, aye." He took a sip of whisky. "My girlfriend gave birth to my daughter and announced three weeks later that she wasn't cut out to be a mum."

"Oh." Mercedes lifted her brow. "I'm sorry to hear that."

"It gets better every day." David shrugged. "What about you? You think you and your lad will work it out on this trip?" At her look, he added, "You'd not be out here crying alone in the cold if things were right with your man."

That's the truth. "We'll be okay. Things between us are . . . complicated."

"It'll get better. It always does."

She smiled at his optimism, but her outlook was pretty bleak.

When Mercedes had drained her glass, she stood. "I should turn in now. It's been a long day. Thank you for the drink and the company."

"Anytime. We'll chat about that trip another time." David took the glass from her hand, and they walked to the house together.

Once inside, Mercedes shrugged out of the blanket and handed it to him. She pulled the hood of the sweater off, running her hands through her damp hair. She looked up and saw David was staring at her with narrowed eyes.

Shit.

She'd washed her face in the shower. Her healing bruises were on full display.

Mercedes touched her temple, where most of the yellowing marks were visible. "Ah. I was in an accident about two weeks ago now. Totaled my car. The airbag hit me pretty hard." She closed the sweater around her neck, unsure if the recent assault had led to new bruising.

David's eyes went wide. "Oh, well. You're lucky to be alive by the sounds of it."

She smiled at his spot-on assessment. "I'm lucky to be alive, for sure."

"Well, goodnight, Eliza."

Her fake name gave her a start. "Um . . . goodnight David. Thanks again for the drink." Mercedes hurried up the stairs so he couldn't examine her any further.

She opened the door quietly and slipped into the room. Alec was lying on his makeshift bed in front of the fireplace, his back to her. Mercedes pulled off the sweater and climbed into bed. Huddling under the blankets, she let the whisky and wine settle her into sleep, the song of a long-ago waterfall playing in her head.

CHAPTER TWENTY-EIGHT

Clenching his fists and inhaling deeply, Alec struggled to ignore the deep throbbing of the wound on his chest. His entire body ached from the smaller bruises that were now making themselves known. Not to mention Mercedes's scent was lingering on his skin, making him hard as hell. Shifting in his seat at the window, he sought to relieve the discomfort. No luck.

Christ, what a clusterfuck.

He should have let her go to bed instead of trying to hash things out when they were both wrung out and raw.

Why the hell had he kissed her?

Alec had spent hours in the car coaching himself on how to let her go again. To distance himself from how she made him feel and focus on keeping her safe. It had only taken an hour to blow that plan to shit.

In his heart, he knew why he'd done it. Because she'd said something he'd needed her to say for three years.

He was right to be jealous of you. He never stood a chance.

Alec closed his eyes and swallowed hard, trying to clear the tightness in his throat.

If he thought it was true, he'd move heaven and earth to be with her. To let the wall down and be her everything.

But it wasn't true.

She'd already made that choice once. And she'd walked away without giving Alec a chance to fight for her. All the plans they made, the trips they wanted to take, it hadn't been enough. Without warning, the phone calls stopped. Texts went unanswered. It was so unlike her. He had reached out to Luke to make sure she was alright. Luke said she was fine, but she was working a lot.

Alec let it go on for nearly two weeks before he threatened to get on a plane. He was at least owed the courtesy of knowing what was going on. If she wouldn't tell him by phone, she could do it face to face.

That finally provoked a response. A series of short text messages was all she offered him. All he was worth.

The distance was too much. She'd found someone else. Someone who loved her and wasn't a half a world away. She was sorry. She'd never meant to hurt him. Please don't get Charlie and Luke involved. Maybe someday they could be friends?

Alec had never been so blindsided. But Mercedes had asked him to respect her decision, and he had. It had ripped his fucking heart out.

Throwing himself into his work, he trained harder and worked more hours than anyone—anything to keep her out of his head. After time had lessened the pain, he recognized his own mistakes. He'd thought her feelings had matched his. It never crossed his mind that she was having doubts. He should have said the words out loud, told her how much he needed her in his life. Maybe if she'd known, she wouldn't have looked for it in someone else.

He'd been afraid to scare her off. How do you tell a woman you hadn't seen in months you were falling hard for her?

The whole affair was nothing more than a painfully lost opportunity.

Now she'd crashed back into his life. Traumatized and shaken, but just as incredible as ever. It had been too easy to step right back into that soul-shaking connection. The pull toward her was as strong as it had always been. It didn't help that she looked at him the way she used to. Like nothing had changed between them.

That little moan she'd made when he kissed her came to his mind, and he grew even harder. Holy hell, he wanted her. Just one taste was an intoxication, an addiction leaving him seeking more.

If you can't decide what I am to you, then don't touch me again.

Alec knew damn well what she was to him. A beautiful ray of light that would draw him in then tear his world to shreds.

Mercedes was fucking dangerous.

He couldn't do it again.

He had to keep his bloody hands off of her until she was safe and back to living her life.

The door to the house squeaked open, and Alec's body tensed. A tall figure walked across the patio to the firepit. He held himself ready to sprint to her, but the light caught the man's face as he turned. He recognized the innkeeper's son, and his muscles relaxed. Cressida would never have sent them here if she hadn't cleared the family and staff.

That didn't stop Alec from pulling his gun and resting it on his thigh.

He couldn't hear their words, but David sat away from her, putting his feet on the wall of the firepit.

Now there was a man who didn't know how to keep his thoughts from being broadcast across his face. It was clear from their first meeting that David liked what he saw when he looked at Mercedes.

Join the club, you poor bastard.

Alec was about to go downstairs when they started back

for the house. The lights shone on her face, and he could see a flash of the smile she gave David. A thrum of unreasonable jealousy plunged through him. God damn, she made him crazy.

Alec turned away and pulled the curtains closed. Taking off his shirt and tossing it on his bag, he lay on the bed he'd made on the floor. When the door opened, he let out the breath he'd been holding. She was safe. Now he could finally get some sleep.

———

THE NEXT MORNING, ALEC WOKE UP SHIVERING. THE FIRE HAD gone out, and his thin blankets weren't doing the trick. Stretching, he tried to relieve some of the pain the floor had caused to his battered muscles. Sleep hadn't been easy. Even with the fluffy rug, it was uncomfortable as hell, and his overly alert mind wouldn't settle for the night.

Mercedes was curled under the down comforter, breathing in slow, even breaths. Her chestnut hair splayed out across the white pillow. Sleep had softened the lines of worry and anger on her face. She needed all the rest she could get.

Alec pulled on his shirt and shoes and slipped from the room. The lobby of the manor house had a quiet buzz to it. Guests had started to stir, and the clanking of teacups and the scent of breakfast filled the air. He wandered the rooms. There was a wing dedicated to a spa and a spacious parlor that had been turned into a library.

Alec took in the tall shelves filled with leather-bound books. A baby grand piano was situated in the corner.

A young woman was helping guests as they browsed the room.

Alec caught her eye, and she came to greet him. "Morning, I'm Cecily. Welcome to the Kennison Library. Let me know if I can help you find a book."

"Thank you." Alec looked to the corner of the room. "Can you tell me if that piano is tuned?"

"Oh aye, we play it every evening during our wine and cheese hour. You should come by," she said.

Cecily's eyes roved over his figure. Alec cleared his throat. "Is it possible for a guest to use it?"

"Aye, as long as they're good. Don't want to drive away the guests. Do you play?"

"Ah . . . my girlfriend does actually." Cecily acknowledged this with a little nod, not looking too disappointed. "Do you think she might be able to play during our stay? She's classically trained."

"Oh, brilliant." Cecily's eyes lit up. "I'm sure we can arrange that."

Alec hoped Mercedes would enjoy a chance to play. He'd brought her violin as well. With any luck, she'd find the stay here a peaceful distraction from the reality of their situation.

Leaving the library with a book in hand, Alec turned a corner and nearly ran into David Kennison.

"Pardon me, mate," David said, his smile polite. "Oh, good morning, Mr. Cameron, is it? I see you've visited the library."

"Aye. I haven't read Burns since I was a lad. I thought Eliza might like it." In truth, he needed something to do besides look at Mercedes.

"And how is Eliza this morning?" David asked.

"Quite well. She's knackered from the drive up. I was going to pick up some coffee for her." Alec waved his hand toward the dining room.

David followed his steps as he sauntered to the buffet table. "I was sorry to hear about the car accident she was in. Lucky to be alive from what she said."

Alec's heart dropped. *Shit. What had she said to this man?*

He took two paper cups from the stack and poured the

coffee. "Aye, scariest phone call I ever took," he said with perfect honesty.

"How long ago was it?" David's dark eyes watched Alec's face. Alarm bells were ringing in Alec's head as he stared at the cream. What was this man getting at?

Stick close to the truth; that's what he'd told her.

"Around two weeks now." Alec tossed the wooden stirring stick into the trash and picked up the drinks, eager to get away from David's dark eyes. The last thing he wanted was to keep talking about Mercedes's supposed car accident.

David's eyes had moved to the cups in Alec's hand, his expression sharp. It passed quickly and was covered up by a nod.

What else had Mercedes and David Kennison talked about on their excursion to the firepit last night?

ALEC RETURNED TO THEIR ROOM AS MERCEDES WAS STIRRING. She smiled dreamily at him. Then the smile fell away, and she sat up.

Alec held a cup to her like an olive branch. "Coffee?"

Mercedes took the drink and sipped from it, wrapping her palms around the cup. Alec sat on the edge of her bed, but she wouldn't look at him directly.

"I'm sorry about last night. It'll remain professional from here on out."

"Professional," she said dully. "Just a bodyguard and his . . . what's the word? Protectee?"

Her words had enough of a bite to hit his heart. She was so much more than that, but telling her wouldn't help. Instead, he shrugged. "We prefer the term close protection officer."

Mercedes's mouth curved up into a smirk. "If that's the way you want it." She set the cup down. "I think I want breakfast downstairs."

She untangled herself from the bed, gathered her clothing, and walked to the small water closet to change.

Alec moved to the large windows and pulled the curtains. The daylight exposed the beauty of the landscape beyond the patio where Mercedes had spent the night before. The well-kept grounds held an English-style garden complete with a maze of short shrubs and a wide variety of flowers. Past the cultivated land, a sun-sparked river broke through a dense copse of trees.

Alec heard Mercedes's intake of breath and turned. She was staring out the window in wonder. "Where are we?"

"The Borders." At her frown, he added, "Scotland."

She joined him at the window, her face soft, "It's beautiful."

"Aye, it is. Cress chose well." Alec's lips pulled up into a crooked smile. "We can go out. You don't have to stay cooped up in the room like you did at the safehouse."

Mercedes's eyes, greener in the morning light, were wide and hopeful. "Really? Oh, thank God." She grabbed her makeup bag and dashed to the mirror. Her excitement made him wish he'd thought to bring her to Scotland before.

On the way downstairs, Alec took Mercedes's hand. She stopped and pulled it away, glaring at him as if he'd burned her.

Alec looked around, grateful no one was around. He leaned close to her ear, the scent of her hair enveloping him. "We have a show to put on, darling," he murmured. She inhaled sharply, her shoulders tense. He waited until she finally met his eyes. "Unless you want to go back to the room?"

Mercedes's expression darkened. Her gaze moved down to his mouth and back up to meet his eyes. Alec's breath caught at her look of pure lust. She stepped toward him, pressing her body against his. Heart pounding, Alec's mouth parted as she brushed her lips against his cheek, ready for her kiss.

"How am I doing? Good enough for the show?" she whispered. She pulled back, her eyes wide with a coy innocence.

Christ, was she really going to fuck with him?

"You little shit," he breathed. Mercedes's lips turned up into a smirk as she backed away.

He could play that game too. Slipping his hand around her waist, he pulled her to him, pressing her against his growing hardness. Alec's lips swept along her jawline, and her body shuddered. He pulled back to look into her eyes. The teasing smile had faded, and the lust had returned, leveling him.

"Careful, Alec." Her voice was thick. "Wouldn't want to be an unprofessional bodyguard, would you?"

Alec wasn't taking the bait this time. "I didn't start this, Mercedes. But you're right, we should probably stick to holding hands. What do you think, *darling*?" He released her, willing his heart to stop racing. He walked a few steps toward the reception room and turned, holding his hand out.

Mercedes took a steadying breath before she put her hand in his. It gratified his ego to see he was affecting her. As much as he secretly enjoyed the exchange, he hoped that was the last of its kind. If she kept that up, he'd have her underneath him by sunset.

They were seated next to the window overlooking the gardens. Mercedes stared out at the lush scenery, her fingers tapping against the table. Alec wanted to ask what she was thinking, but that would cross the line into the personal again.

David Kennison appeared in the dining room carrying a baby on his hip.

"Eliza," David called. "Good morning."

Mercedes smiled at the baby. "Hi, who's this?"

"This is my Hannah."

"Hello, lovey," Mercedes cooed. The baby's wide, dark eyes mirrored her father's. Hannah cycled her legs in excitement. Mercedes obliged by opening her arms to take the squirmy baby onto her lap.

A chubby fist locked onto one of Mercedes's curls, twisted, and tried to bring it to a drooling mouth. Alec couldn't help smiling at the little one. He had a soft spot for babies.

"No, no, my love. You don't want to eat that," Mercedes giggled, unwinding the baby's tiny fingers from her hair.

God, her laugh is beautiful. Where was the lassie's mother? Alec looked around, hoping he'd see a wife or girlfriend somewhere nearby.

David's voice cut into his thoughts. "Maybe this evening we can meet up and talk about it?"

"What's this, now?" Alec frowned, cocking his head at Mercedes. Clearly, he'd missed something.

Mercedes smiled. "Oh, David invited us to the fire tonight. We thought maybe we could chat about California while we were there."

For Christ's sake, I'm sitting right here, mate.

Alec forced a smile, leaning across the table to scoop up Mercedes's free hand. "But darling, I . . ." Sparing a glance at David, Alec gave her a meaningful glance. "I had . . . plans for us this evening." He let the words fall in a way that left no room to doubt their intimacy. His hand moved across hers in long, delicate strokes. Mercedes flushed, letting out a soft exhale.

"Um, we'll have to see. I guess it'll depend on the plans Will has tonight," she said to David. Alec continued his assault on her hand, turning it over to sweep his thumb across the soft skin on the inside of her wrist.

David's gaze was on their intertwined hands. He gave a tight smile. "Aye, I understand. I'll try to catch up with you then." Reaching for his daughter, he said, "Come on, lassie, let's go find a snack. You two enjoy your breakfast."

Mercedes's smile stayed on her face until David turned the corner. She dropped into a scowl. "Was that necessary?"

"Aye, it was." At her exasperated look, he said, "You and I are here on a 'romantic holiday,' and this bloke is hitting on you."

"No, he's not," she scoffed.

Alec's brow went up, but the waitress arrived with their food, so he let it go. They ate in silence, Mercedes avoiding his eyes. When they got up from the table, she was the one that reached for his hand. There was a coolness to it, like she was performing a duty. In a way, she was.

A pang of regret shot through him. Alec didn't want it to be this way with her, but he'd lost the ability to talk to her.

With any luck, they could work out a peace between them. One that kept them both safe.

CHAPTER TWENTY-NINE

Sunlight danced through the dense leaves, swaying along the path. A breeze running through the chilly shadows cooled Mercedes's heated skin, a sensation she welcomed. The brisk walk along the river was her first attempt at exercise since leaving the hospital, and she was feeling it. It was a perfect jogging trail, but she was afraid she'd keel over if she pushed too hard. It would take time to get her endurance back.

Shooting a glance at Alec, Mercedes noted he was unaffected by their pace. The chill had added a trace of pink to his nose and cheeks. His breath was coming in even puffs. The way he held himself had shifted since yesterday. He had his hands stuffed in his pockets and, he was unusually quiet.

He was probably pissed at the way she had baited him on the stairs. It had been a jerk move, especially when she'd been the one to tell him not to touch. As wrong as it was, the feel of his arms around her, of their bodies pressing together, had made it worth it.

Back at the manor house, the river flowed steadily through the level farmland. But the further they walked upstream, the more the rapids crashed against the rocks, twisting in and out of the trees.

A small cottage came into view. The trail was interrupted near the top of the house's driveway and picked up again close to the main road. An ornate iron gate closed the gravel drive to stray cars and hikers enjoying the river trails. The house was adorable. Every detail could have been pulled from a fairytale. The white plaster exterior was accented with black trim and a red door. Flowers danced along the brick sidewalk and skirted the base of the house. The river curved away from their trail, nestling the house against its banks.

Alec had stopped with her, taking in the house. His gaze turned toward the road. A sign for a real estate company was displayed at the entrance. A plastic box held fliers, and he took one out. Mercedes waited for him, where the path continued.

"Are you thinking of moving back to Scotland?"

He scoffed. "Nah. But I'm pretty sure I need a new safe-house. This might be a little too far from the city, though."

A pang of guilt ran through her. "I'm sorry."

"Don't be. It's not your fault."

It was her turn to let out a sharp exhale. "Well, you weren't the one who brought a lunatic into your life."

Alec's eyes were thoughtful. He pointed to a large boulder next to the flowing water. "Do you mind sitting for a moment?"

"Are you tired already?" she teased, although her body ached with the morning's exertions.

"No, but we need to talk."

Something in Alec's tone made her heart bottom out. *What now?*

Mercedes sat on the rock. Alec perched next to her but seemed to take care not to touch her. Blood pounded in her ears as she waited for him to say what he needed to say.

"David Kennison appears to be infatuated with you."

Mercedes rolled her eyes. "I doubt that."

Alec angled his head toward her, eyebrows raised. "He is. Which means he might ask questions about our relationship. We need more background."

Mercedes lifted her gaze to the rushing rapids. "I think we have plenty of history that's easy to sell. Your cousin married my sister. We met at the wedding. We carried on a long-distance relationship for three years." The words were getting harder to say. "I moved here six months ago to be with you. No one needs to know more than that."

So that was it. She was going to have to pretend. Not only that she was with Alec, which was hard enough, but that they'd shared the life she'd dreamed of for three years. That he'd loved her enough to make it work. The irony of it all scraped her heart raw.

Alec was leaning forward, his elbows on his knees. The muscles of his jaw were clenched tight. Clearly, he didn't like the reminder of what had happened between them.

Why did you walk away?

The question burned in her chest. She deserved to know, but could her soul take the answer?

Swallowing hard, she opened her mouth to ask when Alec's quiet voice stopped her. "There's something else I need to tell you. I'm not quite sure how to do it."

Once again, her stomach sank.

"You know Cress and I did a background check on Jason." At her nod, he continued, "We found some inconsistencies in the information you gave us. The company he said he worked for as a consultant doesn't exist. It's a shell corporation."

Mercedes's mouth fell open. "That can't be. He's worked there for years. His job is the reason we moved to London."

"Aye, but it appears to be a front."

She stared at him. "For what?"

"We don't know," Alec admitted. "He may be a part of a

drug ring, or perhaps human trafficking. There are a lot of possibilities."

Mercedes's gut lurched, and she put her hand over her mouth. *Human trafficking?* "That can't be right," she whispered.

"We're missing a lot of information, but the markers are all there for a larger organization to be behind him. We just can't say what they're doing."

Dread curled in her stomach. Jason wasn't a Boy Scout, but she didn't think his work was illegal. Mercedes had met him for lunch at his office more than once and attended several holiday parties. It appeared so normal, boring even.

"There's more," Alec said. "We're almost certain he's using an alias."

"What?" The blood drained from her face. "What do you mean?"

"The American social security number you gave us is for a dead man. Before we left the safehouse, Cress was digging around to find out more. Not only on him but the two guys that follow him around." He paused, watching her. "I wasn't going to say anything until Cress had time to search, but I don't know how long it'll be before she can re-establish our communications. I didn't want to surprise you with it."

Mercedes sat forward. "Is it possible she got it wrong somehow? Or maybe I messed up when I wrote the number?" Her mind was frantic, struggling to make sense of it.

Alec shook his head, eyebrows creased. "It's possible we have some things wrong. But the dead man's name *was* Jason Marsh. He died five or six years ago."

"So, who . . ." Mercedes choked. "Who have I been with all these years?"

There was a pause. "I don't know."

Mercedes stared at Alec.

Jason isn't Jason.

He was a complete stranger.

A stranger who'd shared her life. Her secrets. Taken her body.

That thought sent a flood of revulsion through her gut.

A man whose name she didn't even know had been inside her. For three fucking years.

Mercedes didn't know how to deal with this information. It was one more violation of her body she'd have to process and learn to live with. Mercedes inhaled the fragrant air deep into her lungs. Anger, terror, defilement . . . the roil of emotions threatened to overwhelm her. Blinking, she cleared the tears that welled in her eyes.

Fuck that.

She would not be broken by this.

Alec's hand slid over hers. It was tentative, like he was ready to pull back at the first sign he was crossing the line. Mercedes stiffened, unsure of letting him see her turmoil. There was a vulnerability that had been ripped open, one she was desperate to not let anyone else into.

But his quiet strength drew her in.

Alec knew.

She didn't have to pretend to be okay.

Who else could understand but someone who'd lived it? If his theory was correct, Mariah had used him the same way.

Instead of the shock of jealousy she expected to feel when thinking about that woman, she felt a surge of protectiveness. Alec didn't deserve that. Neither of them deserved to be manipulated that way.

"Sadie, we *will* find out who he is. Then we'll know how to deal with him." He sounded confident, but his eyes told her he was worried too. His thumb stroked the back of her hand.

Suddenly, the fight they'd had seemed so insignificant. Mariah's appearance at the safehouse, the way he kissed her, then let her down again. None of it mattered. Hurt feelings were a luxury she couldn't afford, and the resentment she carried was putting them both at risk. She had to set it right.

"I . . . I'm sorry about this morning." Mercedes bit her lip. "I shouldn't have been such an ass."

Alec let out a short, unexpected laugh. "Aye, well. I rather enjoyed this morning."

Mercedes's mouth curled up in a smile. The simple jest cracked through the ice between them.

The two of them fell quiet. Her hand rested in his. Mercedes didn't want to pull back, afraid to lose the thin connection they had.

When he spoke again, the teasing was gone from his voice. "I know there's a lot you and I need to say to each other. We have a history we can't ignore forever." He looked at their hands. "But for now, I think it's better if we wait. There are other things we have to put first."

As much as Mercedes wanted to get it all out in the open, she recognized the wisdom in his words. Their tattered relationship was already hanging by a thread, making their pretense difficult enough. Bringing up past hurts could make it impossible.

She bobbed her head. "We've gone this long, I guess. Besides, I know how important it is for people to believe us. Especially now. You won't have to remind me again."

Alec dipped his head in acknowledgment. He got up from the rock and helped Mercedes to her feet. Even though no one was around, he kept her hand in his. Mercedes didn't pull away this time, though his touch sent shivers of fire through her body. She had to get used to the feel of him again.

They were quiet on the walk back to the main house. The news of Jason's possible double life spun through her brain.

Was anything real?

Was she just a part of his cover, a pawn whose connections concealed his crimes? What if Cressida couldn't find who he was? Would she have to live with never knowing?

Alec tightened his hold on her hand. "Are you alright?" He was watching her with knitted brows.

"No," she said honestly. "But I will be."

The wooded path opened up, and the inn came into view. This was the perfect location for lovers to run away to. Mercedes tried to imagine having a life like the one they were trying to pass off. How could she pretend to have everything when, in fact, she had nothing at all?

CHAPTER THIRTY

The evening fire was quite an attraction for the visitors at the manor. The sun had set behind the trees, cooling the air once again. Alec picked up a blanket from one of the baskets at the edge of the patio and joined Mercedes at their seat. He unfurled the blanket over them both and settled in next to her.

Her lips turned up into a pleasant smile. It was for show. She was reeling from their talk this morning and had grown quiet since they had returned to the inn. Staying true to her word, she no longer pulled away when he touched her. In fact, she seemed to lean into their contact, reaching for him even when they were alone.

Not that he minded. Having Mercedes touch him would always feel amazing.

The Kennison family had gathered, chatting with guests and tuning instruments. The hum of the conversation was mixed with the occasional strums of guitars. Alec wasn't sure how many children the Kennisons had, but it was quite a brood. David Kennison sat next to a teen boy who shared his dark eyes and black hair. Each held a guitar, and David looked to be coaching the young man.

Alec caught sight of Mercedes's hands, the weather vane to her feelings. She'd been calm a moment ago, but now her fingers were tapping against the stem of her wineglass on her knee.

He leaned toward her ear. "Are you alright?"

"Mm-hmm," she returned. She looked at her own hands, and seemed to recognize what she was doing, and clenched them tight together.

"What's going on?"

"It's silly." At his pointed look, she sighed. "That boy's guitar is seriously out of tune, and he's about to throw a string trying to fix it."

Alec followed her gaze to the lad sitting with David. Mercedes's knee bounced as she watched the kid turn the pegs at the top of the guitar.

"Maybe you should go help him."

"Would that be okay?"

At his nod, Mercedes jumped up and set the wine on the table, relief clear on her face.

David's eyes lit up like a Christmas tree when Mercedes approached, but it was the boy who seemed the most grateful, handing her the guitar without hesitation. She made quick work of the tuning and held it to the boy. He gestured for her to play for him.

Mercedes hesitated, looking at the guitar. She turned her eyes to Alec in question. He knew why.

The moment she played, people would know how talented she was. It could give her away. He nodded, motioning she should go for it. Her smile broadened. The first genuine smile she'd had since they'd arrived.

David Kennison studied Alec, then turned back to Mercedes. She was playing a few chords for the boy, who was bobbing his head along with her. David stepped to them, his face softening as she played.

If this man was some sort of operative, he was doing a shit

job. Blatantly gaping at his targets was a sign of a complete amateur. Was there any recognition in David's eyes? Or was he just an enamored prat who was trying to figure out how committed Mercedes was to her relationship? Either way, Alec couldn't let it go unchecked.

Mercedes laughed at something the kid said. David's eyes never left her.

Yep. An enamored prat was looking to be more likely. It was a sign of how unconvincing he and Mercedes had been when they'd arrived last night. It didn't help that David had come upon Mercedes when she was upset. That fight was costing too much. They were going to need to do a little damage control.

Mercedes handed the young man his guitar and returned to Alec. He held his arm out to her. She settled in at his side, adjusting the blanket across their laps. A bagpipe rang out, signaling a beginning to the evening's entertainment.

With Gavin Kennison at the helm, they shared stories and sang ballads of Scottish lore. The darker tales of selkies and kelpies were broken up with the charm and humor of the Kennison clan. Alec smiled, knowing many of the stories from his youth. Gavin sang the songs in a rich voice, sometimes in Gaelic. David and the young man accompanied on the guitar. It didn't feel like a show being performed but an intimate family gathering they had been welcomed into.

Mercedes was enchanted. Snuggled up against Alec, she laughed and gasped along with the others. When the piper played the bagpipes, she leaned forward a little, trying to see how it worked. It was one of the few things she couldn't play. Yet.

David's eyes darted to them occasionally. Alec made a point of gently stroking her hand. When a lull came between songs, he stroked her cheek, turning her face to look at him. She stiffened enough for him to feel, but she didn't pull away.

Alec leaned toward her. "We have a problem, darling."

Her eyes widened. "What problem?"

"Your new friend is watching us like a hawk."

"Who, David? He's harmless, right?"

Alec's lips turn up into a wry smile. "Aye, most likely. But I'd rather put a stop to his nosing about."

Mercedes looked at him expectantly. "Okay, so how do we do that?"

Taking in a deep breath, he brushed the hair from her face. "We need to be better at selling this. I know you're not big on public affection, and I get that, but we have to step it up. If we don't, he'll get brave and I'm not sure what he might do, or say to you to get . . ."

Her hand moved to his cheek. "Alec, stop," she said, interrupting his ramble. "I get it." Her thumb played with his temple.

Christ. The way she was looking at him, Alec had to remind himself that they were both playing a part, nothing more.

"Is he turned this way?"

Alec nodded.

Mercedes tilted her head and pressed her lips to his. The kiss was soft and slow. Alec's body flooded with heat, and he leaned into her, knowing this wouldn't last. Wanting to seize more. She took her time, running her hand up his neck and into his hair. Then her tongue swept his, an unexpected invitation for him to do the same. He couldn't help but respond. A whisper of a moan came out of her.

Fucking hell.

His heart was thundering when Mercedes ended the kiss. Alec rested his forehead on hers, inhaling slowly. Her fingers remained intertwined in his hair, but she made no move to withdraw.

"Think that will work?" she whispered, her chest lifting with each panting breath.

"I think so." Clearing his throat, he leaned back to look

her in the eye. "I'm sorry we had to . . . you know. Especially after last night."

Mercedes shook her head, giving him a smile. "Don't be. Kissing you is the easy part."

Alec's heartbeat jumped to his throat. "Is it?"

"Yeah." Mercedes looked at his mouth and looked away. Leaning over, she picked up her wine and settled against him again, the smell of her hair filling his senses. "The hard part is knowing it isn't real. That's what I'm adjusting to."

Alec tried to think of something to say, but the words wouldn't come. She was right. Kissing her was a glimpse of a life he'd been missing out on. Letting her believe it meant nothing was killing him.

CHAPTER THIRTY-ONE

A soft breeze brushed Mercedes's cheeks. She turned her face up to take in the rays of the sun. Her bare feet dangled off the edge of the bridge, the current of the river surging under her.

"How's the fishing today, lass?" Mercedes jumped at Alec's voice, but she didn't turn around. She didn't know how the fishing was. Had she ever fished here before? She didn't even know how to fish.

His steps were quiet as he came up behind her, touching her. The warmth of his hands on her shoulder made her sigh. Mercedes couldn't help leaning back as he massaged her tense muscles.

Alec's hand slid past her collarbone and gently caressed her neck. Fingers guided her head toward him. She let him, wanting the feel of his lips on hers.

"You're a fucking whore."

Her eyes snapped open, and she gasped. The river was gone. She was in her room. Jason's icy glare loomed over her.

Mercedes screamed, trying to kick. Her body was made of lead.

"Alec!" she cried. "Alec, where are you?"

Fingers clenched around her jaw, digging nails into her flesh. "What was I supposed to do, huh? I had to do it. You left me no choice. I had to."

Jason pushed his hand down, forcing her head toward the fireplace.

Alec's lifeless blue eyes were staring at her, his body bruised and twisted. A hand clutched at his torn throat. Blood covered his hands and arms, soaking the rug on the floor.

No, no, no, no!

"Look what you made me do," Jason's voice growled in her ear. "Why did you do that?"

"Alec!" she screamed.

The hand tightened around her throat. The next breath wasn't coming. She had to fight. Her fist struck out, but he caught it.

"Christ, Sadie. Breathe."

She couldn't.

"Breathe," he said again. "Darling, you have to breathe."

The grip on her throat released. She gasped. It was impossible to fill her lungs. The weight on her body pinned her down.

"Sadie, open your eyes. Look at me, lass."

Forcing her eyelids to open, she couldn't see anything in the darkness. But he was here. She could feel him.

Alec.

Sitting up, her fingers grappled at Alec's neck. He gave a little cry of surprise, but he let her feel around.

"Are you okay?" Her voice came out shrill.

"Yes, darling, he's not here. It was a dream." Alec was speaking to her in a low, soft tone. She inhaled deeply, taking in as much air as she could. "Watch your eyes." He leaned away from her, and the room was flooded with the soft light of the bedside lamp.

It took a moment to adjust. The makeshift bed came into focus. It was empty, the pooling blood gone.

"It felt so real." The sweat chilled her skin, and she shivered.

"Aye, I could tell. You're safe now." Alec pulled her against his chest, and she gratefully complied. He held her until her muscles eased.

"Do you get them a lot? The dreams?"

"Yeah, a few times a month, maybe? Although it is always worse right after an . . . incident." She pulled away from him to sit up straight, stretching her back and wiping her tearstained cheeks. "Did I say anything?"

"You just kept screaming my name." Mercedes's eyes went wide. Alec winced, a flush overtaking his cheeks. "That came out wrong."

She gave a little chuckle despite herself. "I'm so sorry I . . ."

Mercedes didn't get to finish her apology. A pounding at the door stopped her.

Alec was off the bed like a shot.

"Who is it?" he called.

"It's Gavin and David, Mr. Cameron. One of the other guests said there was a disturbance up here. Is everything alright? May we come in?"

Shit.

"Aye, of course. Just a tick," Alec called. Turning to Mercedes, he said, "Fix the bed."

Mercedes leapt off the bed and hastily gathered his bedding from the floor. Tossing his pillow next to hers, she threw the thin blankets into the closet as Alec opened the door.

"Is everything alright in here, sir?" Mr. Kennison asked.

Alec's voice was friendly and apologetic. "Aye, Eliza had a nightmare. We're so sorry to have disturbed your guests."

"Where is she?" The edge in David's voice made it clear he didn't believe it. "Can we see her?"

Alec's shoulders tensed.

"I'm right here. Come on in," Mercedes said, touching Alec's back to move him out of her way.

Gavin Kennison's brows were furrowed in concern, but David was glowering at Alec.

They stepped into the room and looked all around them.

"I'm so sorry. I've suffered from horrible nightmares since I was a kid." Mercedes wrapped her arms around Alec's waist. Suddenly, she was acutely aware he wasn't wearing a shirt. "I didn't mean to wake the whole house. This is so embarrassing."

Both of the Kennison men sized them up.

Gavin frowned. "Where did you get all those marks, lad?"

Mercedes's gaze was pulled to Alec's abdomen, peppered with dark bruises. He wore the bandage on his chest from the knife wound.

"I'm training to be an MMA fighter," Alec said without hesitation.

David's frown deepened, but he said nothing.

"Well, I'm glad you're okay. We'll let you get back to your evening. Come on, David."

David met Mercedes's eyes as if trying to determine if she was hiding some horrible injury. His gaze shot to Alec, expression hardening. Alec didn't look away, the tension between the two, ready to snap.

David turned back to Mercedes. "If you need anything, you only have to ask."

"Thank you. I promise everything is fine."

Alec's lips were pressed together tightly as he waited for them to pass through the doorway. When the door was firmly locked, Alec turned and leaned against it.

He looked exhausted.

And no wonder. He'd been sleeping on the freezing floor and woken by a crazy woman screaming her head off at one in the morning.

Guilt for all he was going through for her swelled in her chest. "I'm sorry."

He walked to the bed and grabbed his pillow. "You had a bad dream, Sadie. It's not your fault."

The contrast between Alec and Jason struck her once again. They handled every aspect of their lives differently.

Mercedes walked to him, took the pillow from his hands, and tossed it back on the bed. "No more sleeping on the floor."

He grimaced. "I'm fine on the floor."

"No, you're not."

"Sadie, I'm . . ."

"It's uncomfortable and cold and *really* unnecessary. You can't do your job if you're dragging ass all day. We're perfectly capable of keeping our hands to ourselves." She pulled back the comforter on the bed. "Get in."

Alec looked at the bed and back to her. He opened his mouth to speak again, but she raised her eyebrows. This wasn't up for discussion. She couldn't stop her nightmares, but she could help him get the rest he needed.

He sighed. Shaking his head, he crawled into the bed, and she laid the covers on him. Mercedes stoked the fire and added another log before she got in.

She'd thought the bed was huge, but with Alec in it, it seemed so much smaller.

"Sadie?"

She turned to him, the firelight dancing on his face. "Hmm?"

"When this is all over, I want you to promise me you'll seek some help. You've experienced a lot of trauma. There's no doubt it has left its mark on you. A great therapist can help."

"The dreams usually get better on their own."

"They might ease, but it'll be so much easier if you talk to someone." He eyed her sympathetically. "I had to do a lot of work when I came home from the war. And later, we did some training to spot the signs of PTSD."

Mercedes scoffed. "It's not nearly as bad as that." The comparison was ridiculous.

Alec turned his body, so he was facing her. "So, what you've gone through wasn't traumatic?"

"It was. But it's not as bad as war."

"You're minimizing what happened to you."

"No, it just isn't the same."

"I mean, I only saw *a couple* of my mates die; that was hard. And they shot me in the chest, which hurt a lot. But I got to stay at my mum's house, and my little sister stole Dec's shortbread biscuits for me. I made a full recovery and went on with my life. Other people had it much worse, so getting shot wasn't so bad." He smiled wryly. "See, I can do it too."

"Point taken," she conceded.

"I don't think you've realized it, but you're experiencing it right now as we speak. This place is beautiful, but we aren't on holiday."

She hadn't thought of it that way. Her survival mode had kicked in long ago. She was dancing between terrifying moments.

"Just promise you'll look into it. Okay?"

"Okay."

Alec stifled a yawn. "Good. Now don't hog all the blankets, aye?"

Mercedes snorted. "Just stay on your side of the bed, McKinley."

"No promises."

———

He didn't stay on his side of the bed.

Mercedes awoke pressed against a solid, heated mass. It took a moment before she realized it was Alec's back.

Although her arms were tucked between them, she was pretty much spooning him.

Ugh. She rolled her eyes. *How did I end up the big spoon?*

Not only that, she was inches from falling off the bed.

Good lord, man. Were they going to need a pillow barrier between them?

Clearly, he wasn't used to sleeping with someone else. The thought gave Mercedes a little tinge of happiness. If that were the case, she'd take teetering off the edge every once in a while.

She snuggled against him. He felt so good. So warm and strong. Mercedes might not be able to move much, but she was certainly cozy. And really, she didn't take the time to appreciate his toned back nearly enough.

She'd stayed too long. Her mind was consumed with ways she could wake him up and end their "professional" relationship.

Time to put some distance between them and let the man sleep.

Proud of herself for getting out of the bed without tumbling to the ground, Mercedes quietly dressed and added a touch of makeup. She stole one more glance at Alec before she slipped from the room to let him rest.

CHAPTER THIRTY-TWO

A lec woke to the sound of a vacuum whirring back and forth in the hallway. He blinked, not making much sense of it. Their room was much too dark to have the cleaning service working already. He looked to Mercedes and found only the edge of the bed.

How the hell did I get over here?

Lurching up, he realized he was alone.

"Sadie?"

Nothing.

It was already nine-thirty. His heart shot to his throat. How long had she been gone? Jesus, anything could have happened to her.

He dressed as quickly as he could. Wrenching open the door, he saw the little sign refusing cleaning service hanging on the handle. Mercedes had wanted him to sleep in? He didn't know if he should find it sweet or be irritated she'd left without telling him where she'd be.

Alec bounded down the stairs and scanned the lobby. A handful of guests were milling around, but she wasn't amongst them. He turned to head to the dining room when the music stopped him. It was much too loud and clear to be played by a sound system. He sighed with relief.

She'd found the library.

Alec rushed to the double doors, needing to see for himself that she was okay. Seeing her seated and playing stopped him in his tracks. Something about her changed when she played. Her face was softer, more relaxed. Every once in a while, she'd bite her lip. He could watch her all day long.

A handful of guests had stopped to listen, as had Cecily Kennison, who stood next to the piano.

Mercedes finished her song and saw him in the doorway. Her eyes lit up. "Hey, there you are. Cecily found me this morning and let me know they were happy to let me play whenever the library was free. Thank you for arranging that." She beamed up at him.

He couldn't help but smile too. "Of course." He'd talk to her about not giving him a heart attack later.

Mercedes tilted her head at him. "You okay?"

"Aye, why?"

"Well, you've got this sort of wild look going on." She gestured to his head.

Alec ran his hands through his hair, realizing it was mussed from bed. He flushed. "I ah . . ."

"Oh, don't get me wrong. It's a good look for you." Mercedes looked to Cecily, who nodded her agreement.

When Mercedes's eyes met his, he held them. The familiar spark of energy sizzled between them.

Cecily gave a delicate cough, breaking Alec's attention. "Eliza said you were interested in the river cottage. We were using it as a vacation rental until recently. It's a sweet little place. I could have my Da give you a tour later."

"That would be great, thank you."

Cecily stepped away from the piano but stopped and turned back. "Oh, I almost forgot. A package arrived for you at the front desk. You can stop by and pick it up anytime."

Mercedes's smile faded, and her eyes went wide.

Alec squeezed her shoulder. "I was expecting a package from work. Darling, why don't you stay here and play. I'll take care of some business and meet you back here when I'm finished?"

Mercedes bit her lip. Alec leaned down and kissed her. It was brief, nothing but a quick goodbye. But the feel of it lasted on Alec's lips long after he had left the library.

After retrieving the package from reception, he took it to their room. Inspecting it, he was confident it was what he'd been waiting for.

He was right. Cressida had sent him a phone in a leather case. Turning it on, he found the only video conference line pre-programmed and called in. It took a few rings to answer. When she did, their screens remained black.

"This is Artemis. Please verify access code."

Alec responded with the code that meant he was safe. "Isle of Skye. Confirm?"

"The River Seine."

The screen lit up, and he turned on his camera. Cressida and Declan appeared on the screen. Seated at a desk, they looked to be in a rented house. "There's no way anyone can trace this call so we can speak freely."

"What's your status? Is the team secure?"

Declan answered. "Aye, we're all together. We can't be completely dark, but we're low profile. Mrs. Downey is managing daily operations at the office."

Alec sighed with relief. He was going to need to give his assistant a huge bonus when this was over.

"The safehouse?"

"We're working with the local police. But they haven't been as . . . aggressive at investigating the incident as one might imagine." Declan's brows went up, letting the implication land.

Alec looked up at the ceiling. *Fuck.* Was there nothing that wasn't compromised by these people? "Alright then. Tell me about Jason. What have you found?"

"We've had some breakthroughs on that front," Cressida said. "But there's a lot of work to do. We were right Alec, none of them are who they appear to be. Their organization is moderately sized, maybe twenty members total. But they're active."

"What's their focus? Drugs? Trafficking?"

Declan shook his head and grimaced. "Nah, mate. Corporate espionage."

Alec sat back in his chair, letting this wash over him. "Oh shit. How long?"

They didn't have to ask what he meant. Cressida looked up at Declan. Alec didn't miss the little shake of Declan's head. They weren't ready to share that yet.

"A while," Cressida said. "But the timeline is unclear. As are their true identities. We're almost there, but we need more time. I've arranged for us all to join you at your location in the next few days. Our goal will be to provide a full briefing then."

Alec didn't want to wait, but he nodded. "I already told Sadie that Jason was using an alias. It's been tough on her. I want to know who the hell he is. She deserves to know."

"Understood. I'm doing everything I can to find the answers she needs," Cressida said.

"I know you are. Thank you," Alec said. "Now, let's talk about our accommodations." He tilted his head at the camera.

Cressida suppressed a smile. "Is it not to your liking? I've stayed there a few times myself. It's a beautiful place."

"Aye, they have a very uncomfortable floor."

Declan chuckled. "I told you," he said to Cressida.

"I know," she sighed. "Look, I actually *was* limited on locations. The inn was the best of my options, but they don't have rooms with twin beds there. I knew you wouldn't want to stay in a separate room."

"Mm-hmm," Alec grumbled. "Tell me about the Kennison family. How deep is your background on them?"

"Very," Cressida said. "Gavin Kennison is a former investigator who retired to take over the inn when his older brother died. They have five children. One is a police officer in the village, one is an accountant who recently moved home, and the others live and work on the estate."

"David is an accountant?"

"Yes, he moved home with his infant daughter. You've met him?"

"Aye, he's taken a liking to Sadie."

Declan scoffed. "If this bloke thinks he has a chance with Sadie, you aren't doing your job, mate."

"Aye, I know. We're working on that." Alec wasn't worried about the ruse. They were becoming more natural together. Sometimes a little too natural. But there were other ways they could blow their cover. "Sadie had a nightmare last night, which woke the neighbors and brought the Kennisons to our door. It's not sustainable to stay around other people."

"Poor lass," Declan murmured.

"Aye. She's tough, but this is wearing on her. Kennison has a cottage within walking distance. They were using it as a vacation rental but, it's currently for sale. It's a perfect location to move her if they'll let it to us."

"I chose that inn because I knew we could trust this family," Cressida said. "If your identity were exposed to Gavin Kennison, I'm ninety-nine percent sure you'd be safe. It's been over ten years since he retired, but he did a lot of work at the Specialist Crime Division, including work with victims of domestic abuse. And the inn's location is obscure enough to be outside of Jason's circle of corruption."

Alec contemplated this information. The way both father and son had evaluated them last night meant they were likely already suspicious. It was a risk to bring more people in on this, but Gavin Kennison might have resources that could keep Mercedes hidden.

"I'll think about it," Alec said. "I'll see you all in a few days?"

"Aye, keep the phone nearby and message if you need us."

Alec closed out the meeting and tucked the phone into his pocket. The call brought more questions than answers, but at least he knew more background on his host.

ON HIS WAY TO JOIN MERCEDES, ALEC STOPPED AT THE reception desk and asked if he could make an appointment with Gavin Kennison to see the cottage. He'd start with trying to rent it. Ideally, he could do that without telling him who they were.

When Alec returned to the library, David Kennison was sitting next to Mercedes, talking to her in hushed tones. She was shaking her head, whispering to him. Heat rose in his chest. *What the hell is up with this dobber?*

As Alec got closer, she whispered, "You have this all wrong. Really."

"No, I don't think I do," David said, equally as hushed.

Alec approached them, watching as David earnestly tried to talk Mercedes into something.

She turned her wide eyes to him, brows furrowed in alarm. Alec's heart rate kicked up as David looked around. Seeing Alec, he stood, blatant dislike in his eyes.

Alec gave him a stiff smile. "Can I help you with something, Mr. Kennison?"

Mercedes jumped up, taking Alec's arm. "We were just chatting, my love. We should be on our way." She turned to David as she pulled on Alec's hand. "I'll see you later, David."

Alec didn't let his gaze stray from David's until they were nearly to the door. Alec turned for one last glare at David.

"Stop that," Mercedes hissed. "You'll make it worse."

"Make what worse?" Alec growled, pulling her to his side and heading for the exit to the garden.

Mercedes led him to a corner with a high wall of hedges before she turned to him. "We have a problem."

"Aye, clearly he didn't buy our story. Damn it."

"No, he bought it." She grabbed his arm to move them away from another couple strolling in the garden. "But he's not into me."

"My arse, he isn't!"

"Shh. No, he isn't. He offered to help me leave you."

"I think you're making my point," Alec scoffed.

"He said he'd take me to a victim advocacy center in Glasgow."

Alec's mouth fell open. "Are you serious?"

"Yeah." She rubbed her eyes and took a breath. "He saw my bruises the other night. I told him I'd been in an accident. But he noticed these." She picked up his hand and showed it to him. Tinges of blue and purple colored his knuckles along with a few scabs left over from the fight with Jason. David had stared at their hands at breakfast yesterday.

"Shit."

"And last night at the fire, when I looked to you to make sure it was okay to play the guitar, he thought that was a sign of how controlling you are." There was a quiver to her voice. "Add that to the middle of the night screaming, and now he's damn near ready to call his brother. Who's a cop, by the way."

God damn it. No wonder the bastard kept glaring at him.

Mercedes paced back and forth. "Alec, what do we do? If his brother runs our names, they'll know we lied." Tears welled in her wide hazel eyes.

"Hey, hey. No. Don't cry. We're okay." Alec pulled her to him, gathering her up. She moved without resistance into his arms, fitting against him perfectly. "I'm not going to let anything happen to you, Sadie."

"Do we have to run again?" she sniffed.

"No, darling. I'll work it out."

The conversation he would be having with Gavin Kennison would be different now.

CHAPTER THIRTY-THREE

Gavin was waiting for them outside the river cottage when Alec drove his Camaro through the open gate and parked in front of the house. Alec could sense Mercedes's nerves were tightly wound. He was feeling the rush of anxiousness too. If he got this wrong, they'd be back on the road in a matter of minutes. Alec would do anything to keep that from happening. Mercedes didn't need any more disruptions.

When they stepped from the car, he wanted to take her hand, reassure her it would be okay. But they didn't need pretense anymore.

Gavin held his hand out to each of them, as he always did. His words were welcoming, but Alec could sense the change in demeanor. Far more subtle than his son, their host was discreetly surveying the two of them.

The door opened, and David Kennison stepped onto the porch. Alec saw Mercedes's shoulders tense, but her lips turned up in a soft smile.

After the exchange of pleasantries, Mr. Kennison waved them in. "Well, come on in. Let's have a look around. Don't mind the construction. David is finishing up the remodel in the bathroom."

The charm of the house couldn't be ignored. Recent refurbishments had gone a long way to modernizing it. The hardwood floors were stained deep espresso and were accompanied by a cream shag area rug and black leather sofas. A large white brick fireplace was the focal point of the living room. The kitchen was clean and contemporary. Subway tiles complimented the marble countertops and cream cabinetry. An island at the center allowed room for four tall bistro chairs.

"It's beautiful," Mercedes said. "Did you design the remodel yourself?"

"Aye. Well, my daughter Cecily worked up the design." He laughed. "We're the labor. The sunroom is new as well. Really did wonders in opening up the view of the river."

The windows of the sunroom allowed light and a stunning scenery into the space. A tall window seat with oversized pillows created a cozy nook. The doors were open to the patio, letting the cool breeze and the sound of the rushing river to sweep through. The backyard was a perfect hideaway. Hedges, at least ten feet tall, lined the sides of the grassy space. The riverbank made up the back of the property.

David's eyes trailed him. After touring the two bedrooms and bathrooms, it was time.

"Sir, I understand you used to let this as a vacation home. How much would you charge for a week?"

Gavin tilted his head. "Oh, anywhere between three and five hundred a week, depending on the season. And that was before the remodel. Now you could probably get closer to six or seven."

Alec turned to face him. "I'll pay you twenty-one hundred pounds a week to let the two of us move here for the rest of our stay."

Gavin's brows went up. David shot a look at Alec.

"Is there something wrong with the room you have now, lad?"

"Not at all, but we desire security . . . and privacy."

David shot to his father's side. "Da . . ."

His father put his hand up to silence his protest. "You'd pay three times the rent just to have privacy?" Gavin shot a look at Mercedes, clearly trying to read her thoughts.

Alec nodded, "And security." He pulled his wallet from his back pocket and handed a card to Gavin. "We haven't been entirely honest with your family. My name is Alec McKinley. I run a private security firm in London. This morning, your son approached my companion and offered to help her flee, accusing me of abusing her."

Gavin turned an eye on his son. Clearly, Mercedes had been the topic of conversation already. David grimaced but kept his eyes locked on Alec.

"The thing is, he's not wrong. Except I'm not the man who abused her."

Alec gave the Kennisons a rundown of what had occurred in the last two weeks, leaving out some specifics they didn't need to know, including their personal connection. Alec warned them of Jason's skill with technology, which was what had brought them to the estate.

Gavin listened with interest, then turned to Mercedes. "This is quite a tale."

She met his eyes. "I know. It's true, though."

"So, if his name isn't Will Cameron, can I assume you aren't Eliza Carter?" David asked.

Mercedes looked to Alec. He tilted his head at her. He'd told her it was up to her to share her personal information.

"I'm Mercedes. Most people call me Sadie. I am from San Francisco," she said to David. "I wasn't lying about that."

"Do you have any identification, lass?"

She shook her head. "No. My ex took it from me when we

arrived in the UK. He told me he was using it to get my visa in order."

"Do you have any sort of proof at all?" Gavin asked. "Anything that might help us understand what you've been through?"

Mercedes pulled up her sleeve. Mason had removed the stitches back at the safehouse, but a healing pink scar stood out against the pale skin of her forearm.

"This is the one that almost killed me. And this." She lifted the hem of her shirt, exposing the thin scar on her abdomen.

It was hard to see her delicate skin so torn. Yellowed bruising mottled her ribs.

Gavin looked with a furrowed brow. "I'm sorry you went through that, lass."

She gave a tight smile and lay her shirt down.

Gavin contemplated them both for a moment. "I won't take over four hundred a week, and you'll have to wait until tomorrow. It's not ready to be lived in."

Relief washed through Alec as he took Gavin's hand. Mercedes's shoulders relaxed.

"If you two aren't together, you might be more comfortable with a second room," David said.

"Aye. We don't have a double room, but we'd be happy to get you a second room free of charge," Gavin added. "We can move you right next door. You don't have to share."

Mercedes looked away, and Alec wondered what she thought of that. Maybe she wanted him to go, but he wasn't having it.

"Thank you, sir. But I'll not sleep away from her. We can manage for one more night."

Gavin offered them a dram of whisky, which they both accepted.

Mercedes sipped delicately and cleared her throat. "Can I take another look outside? It's such a nice day, and that yard is so pretty."

Gavin joined her. Alec watched her wander the backyard while Gavin pointed out various features of the house.

David took a seat at the table. "I'm sorry for jumping to conclusions. I only wanted to make sure she was out of harm's way."

"Aye, I know."

"So, did she hire you off the internet, or did you know her before that?" David was trying to sound casual, but it was easy to see he was digging.

"I met her at a wedding here in Scotland three years ago."

"And this guy, Jason Marsh. Was she with him then?"

"No."

"So, you and she . . . were never together?"

Alec gave him a cool smile. No way would he share anything about his relationship with Mercedes with this guy. The whisky burned as he shot the rest of it.

"Thanks for the drink." He patted David on the shoulder as he walked out of the room. Now that they had cleared the air between them, David seemed a decent bloke. But he'd be damned if he made it easy for the man to move in on Mercedes right before his eyes.

ON THE SHORT DRIVE BACK TO THE INN, ALEC EVALUATED their circumstances. Things were looking up. By this time tomorrow, they would be comfortably settled at the cottage and away from the main house. And watching how Gavin Kennison worked, Alec had no doubt he'd help keep Mercedes hidden.

Mercedes had said little since leaving the cottage. Instead, she laid her head against the headrest and looked out the window.

"Are you alright?" Alec asked.

"Yeah. Just worried. I feel like every move I make is a disaster."

"I know it's hard to trust anyone, but I think it'll be alright. Cress's background was extensive, and there's no reason for Jason to even know this place exists."

"Did she tell you?" she asked. Alec shot a glance at her. "Did she say who he is?"

It wrenched his heart to see the anxiety on her face. "No."

Her shoulders slumped.

"There's a chance he's a part of an organization that spies on corporations. There's a lot we're trying to find out."

Mercedes was quiet again, the tips of her fingers drumming on the armrest. "David asked me to have a drink with him after the fire tonight."

Fuck.

Alec's fingers clenched the steering wheel, and he forced himself to pull air into his lungs. "Did he?" He did his best to keep his tone moderate. "What did you tell him?"

"I said I didn't know." Mercedes looked to Alec. "I used to be so decisive. I knew what I wanted, and I went for it. If I fell on my ass, I bounced back without a second thought." The muscles of her jaw worked as she clenched her teeth. "Now, I can't even give a simple yes or no to a drink without second-guessing myself."

Alec swallowed hard and asked the question he dreaded most. "Do you want to go?"

She paused for way too long. "Is it okay if I do?"

His gut twisted. Was she asking if it was safe or if he cared?

Christ. Yeah, I fucking care.

But he couldn't stop her. David wasn't a threat. Alec wouldn't lie to her. She already had enough to keep her nightmares fueled.

The only way was to tell her how he felt, to clear the air and hope she felt the same. But if he threw that door open, he'd also throw out the shaky truce they'd reached yesterday. They weren't ready to rip open the wounds of the past.

The heaviness in his chest was crushing. "It should be fine. I'll be nearby if you need me."

Alec didn't know if he was strong enough to watch over her while someone else pursued her.

CHAPTER THIRTY-FOUR

The umbrella wavered precariously in Jason's hand as the wind shifted. It had been drizzling for most of the day. The bustle of the morning commute had long since died, leaving the sidewalks less congested. Londoners and tourists ignored him as they rushed by.

The scent of espresso carried to him from across the street. The memory of nuzzling Mercedes's hair after she'd gotten off her shift kept creeping up on him. The ache he'd felt since he'd lost her struck him with each assault of the breeze.

Mercedes wouldn't leave his mind.

Where is she now?

It was a question he'd asked so many times he was going mad from it. It was his own fault. Not that he'd ever admit it to anyone. Well, he'd probably say it to Mercedes. A confession of how much he had fucked up might go a long way toward winning her back.

He just needed an opportunity to tell her how much he loved her.

Of course, Alec McKinley had to die first.

Jason tightened his grip on the handle of the umbrella. He should have put a bullet in that fucker's brain three years ago.

It was Adam who had insisted they let McKinley live. Mercedes needed to be vulnerable after being dumped on her ass, not grief-stricken. If her long-distance boyfriend ended up at the bottom of the Thames, she'd never be open to meeting someone new.

Jason had to hand it to Adam. He was a manipulative motherfucker. He'd figured both of them out pretty quickly. Adam judged, given her past, that she only needed to be ignored to give up. She wouldn't chase a man who didn't want her, no matter how much it hurt.

McKinley had been trickier. He hadn't taken her silence laying down. The asshole nearly got his head blown off for it, which would have screwed everything up. Adam finally intervened, sending a series of text messages telling McKinley that Mercedes had met someone else and to piss off.

Jason thought it an especially nice touch to approach her on the romantic getaway she and McKinley had planned during her work conference in Lake Tahoe. Mercedes still had to go to Tahoe for work. All they had to do was put themselves in her way and charm the shit out of her when she felt low.

It worked perfectly for Jason.

For Adam, not so much.

Adam resembled McKinley enough with his deep blue eyes, dark hair, and chiseled body. He thought he had her in the bag. So, when he approached her at the lakeside bar, he'd been confident she'd fall all over him. Mercedes barely glanced at Adam's shirtless chest before she politely declined his offer to buy her a drink.

Jason took enormous pleasure in seeing Adam's gigantic ego knocked down a notch. When Jason was able to move in on her, Adam was forced to change course. The team had to rearrange some backstory, but they had Mercedes where they needed her.

The drizzle picked up intensity. Jason remained where he was. Although it was early afternoon, the lights from the cars were reflecting on the streets, tires splashing through the puddles. His fucked-up shoulder throbbed from shivering.

This fucking country and its god damn rain.

Checking the time on his phone, Jason got more and more annoyed. The little twit was late for work. Although no one cared he was loitering during a downpour, he couldn't wait here forever.

Finally, a car drove up to the curb, and the college girl slipped from the back seat. She ran to the door of the cafe while the car sped away.

About time. Jesus.

Jason waited ten more minutes for the other worker to leave before he crossed the street to the Cap and Vin. The smell that enveloped him when he opened the door was a shot to the gut. Collapsing his umbrella, he remembered Mercedes's smile when she'd see him come through the door.

"Welcome to Cap and Vin. What can I get you," the college girl rattled off without looking up at him.

"Corie, isn't it?" Jason said.

That caught her attention. Her pierced brow lifted at her name. Jason threw out his best smile, hoping to disarm her and distract her from what she might have been told.

Relief washed over him when she smiled. "Oh, hi. Jason, right?" She looked over his shoulder. "Is Sadie with you?"

Good, she knows nothing. "Oh no, actually. Sadie's staying with her sister in America for a few weeks. There was a chance at a job offer, so she jumped at it. It's a great opportunity, so we're keeping our fingers crossed."

"Well, I'd like to see her when she gets back."

He flashed a smile. "I'll tell her you said so."

Corie nodded, then tilted her head at him. "You okay, mate? You're looking a bit . . ." She gestured to his face. ". . .rough."

Jason touched the tender bridge of his nose, smiling sheepishly. "I joined a new gym, and my new kickboxing partner got a little enthusiastic."

The bell chimed, and Jason looked back at the customers straggling in from the wet streets. *Perfect.*

"So, what can I get you?" Corie said.

"Umm. Oh, jeez," he said, stepping back to read the black chalkboard above her head. "Sorry, I rarely ordered coffee here." Corie shifted her feet but kept a tight smile on her face. The bell chimed again. Jason turned to see a group of four coming in, shaking the water off their jackets.

That'll work. "I'll try a macchiato."

Corie smiled and punched his order into the computer. While she did that, he took his shot.

"So, Sadie said she might have left one of her scarfs here before she had to jet away. Is there any way you can see if it's here?" He grimaced apologetically. "It's one of her favorites."

"Uh." Corie's eyes flitted to the line of guests queuing up. "I can't at the moment."

"Oh, I know you're so busy. If you don't mind, I'd be happy to find it." When she looked uncertain, he added, "I've been up to Jackie's office before."

"Okay, sure," she said. "I know Sadie left a few things Jackie was hoping she'd come back for. I think they're on the bookcase."

"Thanks."

Walking past her to the staircase, Jason bounded up the steps two at a time. He did a quick sweep of the area but didn't see any other employees, nor were there any cameras in the office.

Sitting at the desk, he pulled a flash drive from his pocket and inserted it into the USB port of the computer. A few clicks later, and a full backup to the flash drive was in progress.

While Jason waited, he looked around the room, and the office phone caught his eye. Anger welled in his chest. It had taken him way too long to figure out how Mercedes had come in contact with McKinley when she was so heavily monitored. Jason's mistake had been to treat this place like the joke it was. Little did he know she'd been lying to him the whole time.

When they had figured it out, he accessed the shop's phone records. As disgusted as he was that she had been calling her sister for months without his knowledge, McKinley's number only came up twice the day before the incident. At least she hadn't been fucking around the entire time.

With any luck, she made a few other contacts out of this office.

A text box popped up showing the backup was complete. He ejected the USB and stood, walking to the bookshelf where the employees stashed a few personal items. Jason picked up a knitted scarf he'd bought for Mercedes. There was a faint scent of her on it.

Tucking it under his arm, he trudged back down the stairs. Corie was working on the last of the backlogged customers. He grabbed the to-go cup with his name on it and took a sip as he held up the scarf to Corie.

She smiled at him. "Oh good, you found it."

"I did, thanks."

"Tell Sadie I said hello and to ring me sometime."

Opening his umbrella, he stepped out onto the sidewalk. The rain had picked up. It forced Jason under the awning of a nearby hotel. Dumping his steaming drink into the nearest trash, he pulled out his phone and dialed.

Patrick answered right away. "Took you long enough."

"Yeah, the bitch was late. But I downloaded the computer, so if it's there, we'll find it."

"You better hope it's there," Patrick grumbled. "You don't have much time left."

Anger flushed up Jason's face. "Just come and get me."

Patrick sighed. "Be there in five."

Lazy asshole.

Jason ended the call and leaned against the wall to wait. Pulling the scarf from under his arm, he buried his face in it, savoring the lingering essence of the woman he'd lost. He could only hope they would find what they needed from the shop's computer. He was running out of options.

CHAPTER THIRTY-FIVE

A lec was in hell. Maybe not literal hell, but something quite close to it. It was his own damn fault. He could have spoken up, asked her not to go. But instead, he'd convinced himself to back off.

It was one drink. She's fighting for control of her life again. This is good for her. David doesn't seem like her type anyway.

All these things were true.

But sitting at a table in the rear of the lounge, watching as Mercedes was charmed by another man, made his blood simmer. Alec could have gone to the room and saved himself the torment, but he didn't think that would be any better. His imagination would make it a thousand times worse. Besides, he'd told her he'd be nearby if she needed him.

Alec turned his attention to his book, rereading the same page for the fourteenth time.

Mercedes's laugh rang out. The simmering was turned to a boil. How long was this going to go on?

Thankfully, it wasn't much longer before Mercedes stood and grabbed her sweater. Relieved, Alec closed his book and got to his feet. Slipping out of the side entrance to the bar, he strode across the lobby, stopping at the base of the stairs. She said goodnight to David, laughing at his farewell.

Alec gave her a tight smile as she approached. "Have a nice evening?" He fell into pace with her, and they climbed the staircase together.

"Yeah, it was fun."

Alec let them into their room, bolted the door, and tossed the key and his book onto the dresser. The air was chilled, so he strode to the fireplace and picked up the lighter.

Mercedes tilted her head. "Is everything okay?"

"Everything's fine. Why?" Crouching in front of the fireplace, he clicked the lighter a few times before it caught. The fire flared to life, a wave of warmth heating his face.

"You seem pissed. Did I do something wrong?"

Alec grimaced. His heart was too much on his sleeve, and she was feeling it. Determined to get his emotions in check, Alec turned to meet her anxious eyes. "No, Sadie, you didn't do anything wrong."

She sighed, clearly not believing him. "I'm going to shower then."

Gathering her clothes, she disappeared into the bathroom, the door closing with a click.

Alec stood behind the couch, staring into the fire. He burned to tell her the truth. But where would that leave him? What kind of future could they have together? When this was all over, Mercedes would likely return to the States. If she couldn't wait for him the first time, what made him think she would now?

The sound of the shower cut off, and a few minutes later, Mercedes emerged from the bathroom. Alec shot a glance at her, and his mouth went dry. The gray T-shirt and shorts she'd changed into were snug against her, amplifying the curves of her body. She'd put her thick hair into a bun on top of her head. Giving the tie a quick tug, her hair fell, cascading onto her shoulders in soft waves.

Alec turned to the fire, fully aware of each move she made behind him.

Christ.

His heart thundered in his ears. This was a losing fight.

Mercedes hung up her towel and came to stand next to him. The firelight softened her furrowed brow. She pulled her hands up, rubbing them together for warmth.

"Do you regret taking all this on?" Mercedes's voice broke through his brooding.

Alec frowned at her. "What do you mean?"

"You could have taken me to the embassy weeks ago. You didn't have to do any of this. You keep saying you're fine, but it feels like you're angry." Mercedes turned her back to the fire. "I realized you might have taken on more than you'd planned. I'm sure you don't usually go all out like this for your . . . clients."

There was an edge to the way she said the word "clients."

She had it so wrong, but his denials would all appear false. The only way to fix it was to confess everything. Alec fought to find the right words, but nothing came.

Her face fell. "I get it. It's not fair for me to ask you to give up so much. Honestly, it's okay if you want to make a new plan." Her voice trembled as she spoke and another spike of guilt rammed through him. "You can call Cress and see if I can get my ID here in Scotland. I think there's a consulate . . ."

That was enough.

"Sadie, stop," he cut her off. Her voice trailed, but she wouldn't pull her eyes from the floor. Alec took a step toward her. "I'm not angry, and I don't have regrets about being here."

"You haven't seemed like yourself today."

He had to say it, even if it made everything worse.

"Aye." His voice came out strangled. "It's because I'm jealous as fuck, and I don't know what to do about it."

Mercedes's wide eyes shot to his. Alec held her gaze, unflinching in his decision to say what was long overdue.

He swallowed hard. "When we came here, I knew what we'd have to do to keep our cover. I knew I'd get to kiss you and hold you, even though I'd have to pretend I didn't love every damn second." Alec took another step toward her. "It would at least be something."

Mercedes didn't back away as he came close enough to touch her. The look of confusion had fallen away. Now she studied him as if looking for the truth in his eyes.

"What I didn't know," he said, his voice tight, "was that I'd have to stand guard over you while some other bloke moved right the fuck in. And how much it would kill me every time you laughed at something he said. Or to watch your fingers drum on the bar because he made you nervous." Alec rubbed his hands through his hair. "Christ, Sadie, it's more than I could bear."

Mercedes looked away. A thrum of apprehension shot through Alec. The rise and fall of her chest had quickened. He braced himself for the fallout.

"So," she said, lifting her chin at him. Her eyes were laden with a dark hunger. "What do you *want* to do about it, Alec?"

Alec's pulse surged in his chest as he pulled her against him, his mouth crashing upon hers in a desperate kiss. Weeks of teasing left him greedy for her. Mercedes matched his tempo without reserve. Her hand roved under his shirt, lacing his abs and chest with fire in their wake. Tugging the hem of his shirt, she broke the kiss to pull it up and over his head. Her mouth returned to his, each swipe of her tongue making him harder.

Alec ran his hands down the length of her body and palmed her ass, picking her up. She wrapped her legs around his waist and held on as he carried her to the bed, sitting on the edge of the mattress. Mercedes straddled him, moaning as he ground his hard ridge against her. Alec moved his mouth to her throat, kissing under her jaw until she was panting.

"Alec," Mercedes whispered breathlessly, pulling away. "What does this mean?"

Searching her eyes, he could read the conflict in their depths. Alec felt it too. Torn between guarding his heart against destruction and a pure burning need to consume her. The path forward was so uncertain. But he owed her honesty.

"I don't know." Alec swept her hair from her face. "Do you want to stop?"

"No," she said, without hesitating. "Do you?"

"God, no." His voice was a rasp. "For one night, I want to stop pretending I don't need you."

Mercedes's breath hitched. "One night then?"

Alec didn't have to ask what she meant. The promise of it was written on her face.

One night.

One night where the past didn't matter and the future didn't exist, just a complete surrender to each other.

It would never be enough, but it might be all he'd get.

Swallowing hard, he nodded. "Aye, one night."

Mercedes brought her mouth down to his, scorching him with the depth of her need in each stroke of her tongue. Sliding his hands up her body, he gathered the T-shirt. Mercedes helped to pull it over her head. He brought her soft breasts to his mouth, kissing everywhere but the tender peaks. Mercedes's fingers dove into his hair, trying to steer him into giving her what she wanted. Alec denied her, enjoying the feel of her tight body squirming against him.

"Alec, please."

He relented, taking her nipple into his mouth. Mercedes threw her head back and moaned. Alec laved at one, then the other, sucking gently, her back arching for more.

"I need to see *all* of you," he rasped, turning to set her on the bed. Slipping his hands under the elastic band of her shorts, he tugged them off.

When her clothes had been stripped away, Alec drank her in. "Christ," he said. "Look at you."

Mercedes bit her lip in a shy smile, reaching for his belt. Alec's pulse thundered in his ears as she deftly maneuvered the buckle and zipper of his trousers. Once they were loosened, she brought the waistband down, freeing his length. He stepped out of them and held his breath, fists clenched at his side.

Mercedes's hands slid along his abdomen, tracing the curves of him. Her gaze followed the caresses of her fingers. Then her eyes flickered to his.

"You're so beautiful," she breathed, her fingers wrapped around him.

A pulse of energy coursed through his body, forcing a cry from his lips. Each flawless stroke left him gasping. He pushed himself into her fist, need vibrating through him.

Mercedes parted her lips to take him into her mouth. He drew away.

"Jesus, Sadie," he panted, lifting her chin. "I'll only last seconds if you do that. We only have one night."

"Fair enough." She smiled, moving onto the bed.

A feeling of surrealism hit. Alec had wanted her so much for so long. Here she was, lying naked against the pillows, dark hair spilling over the white linen. He'd fantasized about this moment so many times.

Alec covered her body with his, pulling her legs around his waist. He ground himself against her, the warmth of her skin on his making him crazy. Their kiss was deep, tongues moving together in a steady rhythm. He was desperate for more of her. For all of her.

Sliding his hand between their bodies, he kneaded the soft heat between her thighs. She broke away from the kiss, letting out a groan.

Alec watched her, mesmerized by the beauty of her face as he enticed whimpers from her. A craving for more burned in him. Shifting his weight to the side, he dipped two fingers inside her, his thumb searching for the slippery edge of her clit. Mercedes closed her eyes, gasping as he sank deeper into her. Increasing the pressure, he worked her, letting her every response guide his movements. When her hips bucked, he gave her more.

"Alec," she breathed. "God, Alec, yes."

She was everything he'd ever imagined she'd be and more.

The hum of electricity radiating from her body as he pleasured her was intoxicating.

And he wanted to be drunk on her.

So fucking wasted he couldn't think straight.

Mercedes's hand grabbed his hard shaft, stroking him. Alec moaned, the thrill of her tight fist around him spurring him even more. He fingered deep into her until she alternated between moaning and holding her breath.

Alec moved to her breasts, pulling her nipple into his mouth. He sucked her gently in time with his fingers. When he felt her hit the edge of her orgasm, he returned to her mouth.

"Tonight, you're mine, Sadie. I want to feel you come," Alec coaxed. "Come for me."

She did, writhing and crying out as each wave struck her. Alec kissed her until the last pulse tightened around his fingers. Her chest heaved as she came down. She looked at him, the fog of her orgasm soft in her eyes.

"That was the most incredible thing I've ever seen."

"It was the most incredible thing I've ever *felt,*" Mercedes responded. "So far. I'm not done with you yet."

Alec laughed, letting her push him back against the bed. "Oh, aye?"

Mercedes wet the palm of her hand with her tongue and

took hold of his shaft, stroking him in slick, tight movements. "Aye," she whispered. "Tonight, you're mine, Alec."

A rush of heat ran through his body. Mercedes smiled and took control, caressing him in a tight cadence. "Holy shit, you're amazing," he gasped.

Alec's release built, his mind lost in the electricity of her hands. He clutched the bed, trying to hold himself together.

She stilled, just as he was reaching the fevered edge. "I need to feel you inside me," Mercedes murmured, her lips brushing his.

Blood raced through his veins. Sitting up, he reached for his wallet, a sudden realization crashing over him.

Fuck.

He closed his eyes, not believing his shitty luck. "We can't."

Mercedes sat up. "What? Why?" Her voice was filled with apprehension. She was clearly thinking he'd changed his mind.

"God, Sadie, I want you so much. But I don't have a condom." Alec cursed at his shortsightedness. He'd kept one handy since he was a lad, and the one time he wanted someone more than air, he was unprepared.

"Oh," she said, relief in her tone. "I think we're okay then."

"No, I won't risk it," Alec said. "You're going through enough. I won't be the reason you have another thing to worry about."

Mercedes's face softened. "Always protecting me," she said, tracing her fingers over his cheek.

Alec would rip the world apart to keep her safe, even from himself.

"You don't have to this time," she said. "I have something for birth control, and I was tested recently. So, unless there's something you need to share with me, I'm comfortable going without."

Alec's breath caught in his throat. "No, I'm good. Are you sure?"

Mercedes nodded. "I've never been more sure. I trust you."

An ache shot straight through his heart. There had never been anyone who could make him feel the way Mercedes did. He could search for a hundred years and never find it again.

Kissing her, he took his time. She lay back on the pillow, drawing her knees up to each side of his hips.

Alec groaned as he eased inside her, taking her in small tastes. He pulled each gentle thrust back, only to sink into her on the return. Her soft moans filled his senses, heightening his arousal. She was tight and perfect. When she'd taken his entire length, he took a shuddering breath.

"God, you're incredible," he said.

They moved together, slowly at first. Alec's heart thundered in his chest. Mercedes met each thrust with an increasing urgency. She wanted more. Alec pumped into her harder, plunging deeper, holding her hips. As his need grew, he quickened his pace. His thrusts became fiercer. She held steady with him, her breathing erratic.

Alec couldn't believe this moment was actually happening. His wildest imagination couldn't have matched reality.

"Oh my god, Alec," Mercedes whimpered, tightening around him. "Please, don't stop."

He grunted, fighting his own release, wanting to feel her lose herself on his cock.

"Oh, god. I'm so close," she cried. "Alec, please make me come."

Her walls clenched around him, gripping him as she came. The sound of his name on her lips, mixed with the tightening of her climax, made his own release inescapable.

Alec cried out as his orgasm struck him, the intensity blinding him. He spilled himself into her convulsing body, shuddering deep inside her.

The room came into focus, the sound of the fire crackling and their trembling breaths calling him to reality. He gathered Mercedes in closer, and her arms wrapped tight around his back as she sighed into his chest.

"You're perfection," he murmured.

One night.

He'd agreed. Now he was going to have to feel the consequences. Not of the night they'd shared, but of letting her go. He didn't want to fucking do it.

Reluctantly, he pulled out of her and lay to her side. Her chest rose and fell with a little tremor as she exhaled. Mercedes shot a look at him, a hint of uncertainty in her expression.

Alec opened his arm out to her. "Come here?" It was more of a question than a command. Thankfully, she didn't make him wait, scooting herself closer to him.

"Oh." Her gaze landed on his knife wound. "I didn't hurt you, did I?"

Alec tucked his chin down to look at the wound and the smattering of bruises. "Nah. I completely forgot they were there. What about you? I wasn't too rough?" He ran his hand down her cheek.

"Not at all," Mercedes sighed and snuggled against his chest. He pulled the blanket over them, and they settled in together.

A thread of nerves unraveled. Kissing the top of her head, he braced himself for what he had to ask.

"Regrets?"

Mercedes lifted her head to look at him. "God, no. You?"

Relief washed over him, and he shook his head. "Never."

She smiled and laid her head against him.

A wave of drowsiness hit. Not a surprise after a session of mind-blowing sex, but Alec hated missing any part of this. He wanted to stay awake all night and not waste a second of his time with her. The dawn was approaching faster than he wanted.

A delicate tickle on his chest caught his attention. Her light fingers were strumming against him. He smiled.

Capturing her hand in his, he brought it to his lips, brushing a kiss over her knuckles. "What are you playing tonight? Something amazing, I hope."

"It was," she said after a pause. Lifting her head, she gave him a shy grin. "It was your heartbeat."

The smile dropped from his face. The ache returned, only this time, it slammed so hard into him, he lost his breath. Mercedes curled up against him, unaware of the chaos she'd ignited.

He was in love with her. He always had been.

One night.

CHAPTER THIRTY-SIX

Mercedes awoke entangled, not only in blankets but with a delightfully naked man. Powerful arms held her tight, her cheek pressed against his chest as he slept. Memories of the night before flooded her mind and made her pulse sing.

Alec.

After all these years, they'd finally gotten a taste of what distance had denied them for far too long. Moving back, she studied his face, a smile pulling on her lips.

Good lord, he's gorgeous.

What might it have been like if they'd stuck it out? Maybe if they'd experienced this mind-blowing intimacy, he'd have fought to keep her.

Last night might complicate things between them, but it didn't matter. She wouldn't regret any of it. For once, she wasn't stranded in survival mode. She'd made a choice, and it felt damn good to make it.

Alec shifted in his sleep. He'd be awake soon. Apprehension shot through her.

He'd said he didn't have regrets, but he might feel differently now morning had come.

When his eyes fluttered open, his brow furrowed. Mercedes smiled tentatively, steeling herself against the possibility he might make a run for it.

Instead, his blue eyes softened, his lips curling into a gentle smile. "Good morning, my darling."

Mercedes let out a soft exhale, her heart leaping at his tender tone. "Morning. Sleep well?"

"Aye," he said with a yawn.

She nestled against him, the warmth of his hand moving up and down her back, lacing a current of electricity through her.

"Alec," she said. "There's something I need to tell you."

His hand froze. Mercedes pulled back to look into his eyes, biting back a smile. "You are, and I mean this literally, the biggest bed hog I've *ever* seen."

Alec snorted, a grin forming on his lips. "Am I now?"

"You are. It's worse than sharing a bed with Charlotte when she was six." She snickered at his injured expression, the spark of humor playing in his eyes. "It's a real problem. You should seek help."

"Maybe I like to snuggle."

"Is that what you call it?" she teased. "I'm hanging off the bed."

Without warning, Alec tipped Mercedes back as if he might dump her off the edge. Mercedes squealed and clutched at him, laughing as he drew her back to him.

"Oh, my god! You're an ass," she giggled, dabbing at a tear in her eye. His chest shook with laughter.

Alec's fingers slid under her chin, turning her face up. His crooked grin faded as his eyes searched hers.

"I love hearing you laugh." He tilted his head and kissed her, soft at first, every gentle lash of his tongue sending warmth straight to her aching core. She deepened the kiss, running her hands through his thick hair. Alec groaned into her mouth, and the ache turned to a throb.

There were so many reasons to stop, but none of them seemed important.

Just once more.

Pushing him back against the pillow, she moved on top of him, her knees on either side of him. She rubbed the source of her ache against his hard length.

Alec gasped, clutching her hips.

"What are you doing, Sadie?" His husky tone told her he knew precisely what she was doing.

"Amending our verbal contract," she murmured. Mercedes buried her head against his neck, trailing kisses along his throat. Alec groaned, grinding his arousal against her, sparking the most delicious sensation. She was slick with need.

"Oh, aye? And what are the new terms, counselor?"

Forever. Can forever be on the table?

Fear of ruining this moment kept her from saying it. Instead, Mercedes glanced at the clock. "Half an hour. Then I'll be a good girl and keep my hands to myself."

Alec's smile didn't quite reach his eyes. "Half an hour?"

There was something he wasn't saying. Mercedes's breath stuck in her throat.

"I'll take it," he whispered.

Alec pulled her into a kiss, the play of his tongue searing her. Mercedes slid onto him, her breath shuddering as she took him inside her. Alec moaned as she sat back on her knees and arched her back. Mercedes thrust her hips, riding him, waves of pleasure licking through her with each stroke.

Alec's eyes roved her body, panting as she moved on him. "Christ, Sadie. You're incredible."

He grasped her hips, thrusting deeper and faster, his cadence hitting just the right spot.

"Oh my god, Alec. I'm so close," she whimpered.

Alec moved his hand, his thumb finding the slick nub of her clit. Mercedes threw her head back and cried out, the heated touch shattering her. She came hard, convulsing around him until the last spasm of pleasure waned.

In a flash, she found herself on her back, Alec plunging hard into her. She arched against him, matching his thrusts.

Alec's moans became fevered. He was getting closer.

"Come, Alec," she coaxed. "I want to hear you come. Please."

"Jesus, Sadie," he rasped.

Alec clutched her hips and roared, pulsing inside her. The muscles of his body jerked with every wave of his orgasm. Mercedes trembled under him, wanting him to stay with her.

When he drew back, there was a reluctance on his face.

This was it. Their last moment. They both knew it.

Alec settled in next to her and tugged her into his arms. She didn't resist. Resting her head on his chest, she listened for the steady rhythm of his heartbeat.

A sadness fell over Mercedes. There was an invisible thread that always pulled her heart toward Alec. She'd resisted it as long as she could, knowing it would end with the ache of grief. It tugged on her now, telling her she'd made a mistake.

But she hadn't. This would never be a moment she'd hate herself for. Even though it would hurt to let him go, it had been worth it.

"What time are we meeting the Kennisons?" she asked, wondering how long she might put off leaving the bed.

"Nine o'clock," Alec said. Mercedes didn't miss his shoulders tightening.

Damn. She hadn't meant to break the moment with a reminder of how it started.

"About last night . . . and David. I just . . ."

"No, you don't need to tell me anything, I shouldn't have . . ."

"He's just a friend," Mercedes cut him off. Alec's lips pursed. He didn't believe her. "It's true. I made it clear to him last night. We mainly talked about his daughter and her mother."

And you. But she left that part out.

"I'm sure you did." His mouth turned up in a smirk. "But it's obvious he wants more than that."

"I doubt it." Mercedes shook her head. "But I've been upfront with him. I'm not exactly the kind of woman who would lead on one man and sleep with another."

Something crossed behind Alec's eyes, and he looked away.

Mercedes's spirits sank. Was that how he saw her?

"Alec?" She propped her head on her elbow. "Did I say something wrong?"

"Nah, everything is fine." He shot her a tight smile and sat up. "We should get going. We'll grab breakfast before we go."

Mercedes watched him leave the bed and gather his clothes. A few moments later, the shower broke through the silence.

She'd already lost him.

It hit her like bricks falling onto her chest. She'd known it was coming, but she'd hoped she'd be more prepared.

Mercedes picked up Alec's button-up shirt from the floor and slipped it on. She set to work packing her clothes into her bag. Self-pity niggled at her. Last night was a reprieve from the emptiness she'd been living in. But like so many other moments with Alec, it was a mirage. An illusion that she'd found the security of home in his arms.

The door to the bathroom opened, and Alec stepped out. He was shirtless, a pair of khakis riding low on his hips. He stopped and stared at her, his eyes roving her body.

"Sorry, I borrowed your shirt. Do you need it back?"

"No." His voice was tight. "I was going to wash it, anyway." He crossed to the chair where his bag lay and started filling it.

Great. We've moved into the awkward post-sex phase.

After taking her own shower, Mercedes packed the rest of her meager belongings. She zipped her bag and slung it over her shoulder.

"Ready?" Alec asked.

"Yeah, I think that's everything." She followed him to the door.

Instead of reaching for the knob, Alec dropped his bag on the ground. "There's one more thing."

Without warning, he pulled her body to him, crushing his mouth against hers. She let out a gasp of surprise, then sank into him. The bag slipped off her shoulder with a thump, but they ignored it. Alec turned her, pressing her against the wall, his tongue stroking the fire of need in her. Mercedes dragged her nails on his scalp, tugging on his hair to bring him in deeper.

When he broke away, he laid his forehead against hers, his breath unsteady. "Sorry, I got greedy," he rasped.

Mercedes's voice stuck in her throat. So she nodded at him.

Alec shot her a smile and picked up both their bags. He opened the door and stepped into the hall.

Mercedes leaned against the wall, her heart pounding. Taking a deep breath, she peeled herself away.

Oh god.

If he kissed her like that again, she'd be lost.

CHAPTER THIRTY-SEVEN

Jason ran through the system one more time, needing to catch a god damn break. Something, anything that could give them what they needed. The urge to slam the computer into the wall was growing.

Where the hell was she?

This was a stupid waste of time.

Jason had combed Cap and Vin's hard drive a hundred damned times. Nothing else belonged to Mercedes. It was filled with the shop's financial software and employee schedules, but little that looked unusual for a small business. Jason studied every number, making sure there weren't any hidden meanings.

Nothing.

The only thing that held any promise was a single email address. He'd figured out how to get into it, but it looked to be a throwaway account. The one she gave when she wanted someone to get off her ass.

Home decor. Holiday crafts. Summer table arrangements. Stupid shit.

The whole damn inbox was filled with advertisements from places Mercedes had nothing to do with. Fucking Williams Sonoma? She wouldn't know what to do with an air fryer if she was hit upside the head with it. There was no way she had signed up for some of these lists.

There was a newsletter from the San Francisco Orchestra. She'd been a big donor to some Bay Area Youth Symphony programs. Of course, that was before he'd gotten his hands on her money. Convincing her to invest her cash in a business he'd chosen had been efficient. It was a legit company, and he'd made her a lot of money, but she was quite short on cash in the meantime.

On page six of the inbox, a little arrow showing a reply to an email caught his eye. It was one of the few replies she had given, so he clicked on it.

Jason's pulse soared. This was different. Mercedes had been here.

Reading through the site, Jason recognized it was more than a commercial site looking to entice clicks from the email recipients. Doing a quick search, he found other emails from the same address, each with a reply from Mercedes. No message, just an attached flyer for the coffee shop.

Fucking hell. There it was, hidden in plain sight.

Picking up his phone and dialing, he studied the image on his screen.

"Yeah," Adam answered.

"I think I found the target."

"Where?"

"Out in the middle of bum-fuck nowhere. A small town up north. I'm almost sure it's her."

"How do you know?"

He didn't. This was purely a hunch. But he had to sell it to Adam. "Because I know Sadie. She had safeguards hidden everywhere, and I found one."

"You don't know shit about her, but cool. Send me what you have. I'll look it over and see if it's what we need."

Fuck you, motherfucker.

Jason's jaw clenched tight, his words strained. "I know what I'm doing."

"Sure you do," Adam sighed. "If this is what we've been waiting for, the boss will be thrilled as fuck. But if not . . ." The unspoken threat registered loud and clear.

Jason's heart raced. "It is. Get ready. We'll want to move as soon as possible."

"It'll be you and me," Adam said. "I'm not bringing the others in until I know it's her."

"We'll need more than the two of us. If we fuck up, I don't think I can get us another shot."

"Then don't fuck up."

The phone beeped in his ear. Adam had hung up. Jason slammed the phone on the table. He allowed a moment for the rage to course through him. Then, he moved the inbox to the side and started his research.

He needed to be ready.

CHAPTER THIRTY-EIGHT

A lec wrapped his palms around his teacup, letting the warmth soothe the nerves needling through his fingers. It had been three days since he and Mercedes had moved to the river house.

Three days without the air he needed to breathe.

He was so fucking lost in love with her.

Every hour since that night tore at his resolve to keep it to himself. She'd become his everything and his kryptonite all at once.

Alec had almost told her earlier this morning. She'd looked so damn beautiful, curled up on the window seat in the sunroom, the light pulling a touch of auburn from her hair. A smile of contentment played on her lips. Knowing he had finally given her an ounce of peace was enough to make him hold his tongue.

Why should he put either of them through the heartache? Mercedes was going to leave anyway. She hadn't verbalized her decision, but the dread in his gut told him it was coming.

So the truth had been silenced once again.

A gentle gust swept through the house, the notes of a violin spiraling along with it. In the afternoon, Mercedes liked to take it out to the riverbank to play. Alec wasn't versed enough in classical music to know what pieces sang out from the instrument. He only knew the way it relaxed her shoulders, easing the tension she'd had since he'd first seen her in the coffee shop.

There was little doubt she was putting some distance between the two of them. The night they shared was a topic neither of them was willing to dive into. But the energy that arced between them was still there, sizzling below the surface. They ignored it, choosing instead to adopt the appearance of friendly flatmates.

Alec shot a glance out the window to where she was pacing circles in the grass. The violin was at her chin, her brow furrowed in concentration. Clearly, she was working something out, and it was frustrating her. He smiled, loving the way she scrunched up her face when she was deep in thought.

That was until she sucked in her lower lip.

Memories assaulted his senses.

His entire body clenched in unexpected arousal.

The smell of her hair. The feel of her body under his. How she cried his name as he lost himself inside her.

Bloody fucking hell.

Alec knew he was a stupid man.

A week ago, he'd thought—like an idiot—that maybe if he slept with Mercedes, it would make it easier. That somehow, it would shatter the mysterious allure surrounding her. Then he'd be able to go about his life with that crazed hunger for her satisfied.

He'd never been so wrong in his whole fucking life.

Mercedes was consuming him.

Nighttime was the worst. More than once, Alec had paused at the bottom of the steps, wondering what she'd do if he climbed them and knocked on her door.

"You doing alright?" Her voice broke through his spinning thoughts.

Mercedes was standing in the open doorway, the neck of the violin held in her grasp. When he didn't answer, she tilted her head and frowned. "Alec?"

He cleared his throat. "Aye, I'm good. Just thinking about work."

Did he really say that?

Mercedes seemed to accept his answer. She gestured to a file folder sitting in front of him. "Is that for work?"

Alec slid it across the counter to her. "Take a look. Actually, I wouldn't mind your opinion on it."

Mercedes smiled and flipped the folder open. "A property report for this house?" Her eyes shot to him. "I was only kidding the other day. I didn't think you'd seriously consider buying it."

"Maybe. It's a beautiful place. I'd like it to be closer to London, but some clients wouldn't mind being out here. Especially if they're trying to get away."

She thumbed through the documents. "Would Declan want it to be that far?"

"I might make it a personal investment. That way, I use it whenever I want and rent it to the company if needed."

Mercedes scanned the papers. "I don't see anything in here that would be a red flag. You'll want a full title search, of course. They also gave you the numbers for the vacation rental for the last few years, so I can calculate the cap rate and analyze the market to make sure it's a steady investment." She flipped to the next page.

Alec bit back a smile. One second, she was playing some crazy Mozart piece; the next, she was talking about cap rates and market analysis.

Mercedes looked up and caught his gaze. Alec held it, his blood thrumming as her soft mouth turned up into a smile.

She let out an exhale, sweeping her eyes away, a faint blush staining her cheeks. Standing up, she closed the file.

"I, um, should get ready to go." She brushed past him on her way to her room. The scent of coconut lingered as a reminder.

Christ.

That look was meant only for him. He could feel it. His throat tightened. He had to do something.

The danger of her situation hadn't passed, but it was time for them to work things out. He had to give her a chance to explain why she hadn't waited for him. Maybe it was wrong to want a woman who'd stomped on his heart, but he was tired of pretending she wasn't otherwise the most perfect woman he could imagine.

Tonight, I'll say something.

The Kennisons had invited Mercedes to play with the family at tonight's fireside. After they returned, he'd lay it all on the line. Ask for answers, willing himself to listen without judgement.

Did the past even matter anymore?

THE FIRE CRACKLED AND POPPED, THE AIR TINGED WITH woodsmoke. The handful of guests were cuddled together under blankets to keep out the cool breeze. Rain clouds threatened, but the fire made the night comfortable.

Alec sat alone, undisturbed by the chill in the air. His attention was on Mercedes. Her eyes sparkled with the magic of playing for others. She was grinning at something the youngest Kennison said. When Gavin began his tale of the selkie girl, Mercedes accompanied the story with her music.

A sudden prickling at the back of Alec's neck made him pause.

Someone was watching him.

What the fuck?

Out of his peripherals, he spotted the figure. Darkness shrouded him, but he was definitely a man, solidly built. The man wasn't interested in storytelling. He was watching them. Both of them.

Alec's pulse rose as he leaned forward, finding the hilt of his gun. He held steady, muscles tense with anticipation.

The figure stepped forward, his stance casual. The firelight illuminated his face, and the dancing blue eyes, so much like his own, came into view.

Breathing out in relief, Alec shook his head.

Declan sent him a crooked smile, clearly amused with himself.

A deep uneasiness settled in Alec's stomach. *What the hell is he doing here?*

Alec got to his feet, asking the pardon of the other guests as he made his way to join his cousin. They stood together, shoulder to shoulder, watching the show in front of them.

"Look at her," Declan murmured. "Like nothing ever happened."

Alec frowned. "Almost, but not quite."

"How are things working out with you two? Any progress?"

"Not enough."

Declan was quiet for a moment. Then he sighed. "You're a moron, you know that?"

"Aye, I know," Alec grumbled.

"Whoa, listen to that," an enthusiastic voice said from behind. He turned to find Shake, his big brown eyes bright as he took in the scene. "She's something, huh?"

Alec patted his shoulder and looked around them. "Where's Cress?"

Shake's gaze jumped to Declan, then he rolled his eyes and looked away.

Alec gave Declan a dark stare. Declan grimaced. "She drove her own car."

Annoyance flashed in Alec. "You were supposed to stay with her. Keep her safe, remember?"

"She *is* safe." Declan had the nerve to sound offended. "Mason's with her. They were right behind us."

Alec decided it was better to drop it for now. He probably didn't want to know what happened anyway.

"You came a long way. Must be important since you didn't call."

"Aye." Declan's face was grim, and he turned his gaze once again toward Mercedes, who was playing the final chord. "It's a game-changer, mate."

Ice formed in Alec's gut. Even Shake's usually playful eyes were somber.

The storytellers paused for a quick break. Mercedes, having caught sight of the new arrivals, came bounding up, her eyes shining.

"I thought that was you!" she exclaimed.

Declan grinned and enveloped her in a hug. "Hey lass, damn good to see you."

"You too. Now, why are you here?" Mercedes studied Declan's face. The same apprehension in her eyes was churning through Alec's veins.

Declan's smile faltered, and he seemed to be doing his best to keep casual. "I missed this git so much I had to drive all the way here."

"Uh-huh." Mercedes's lips quirked up in disbelief. She gave Shake a quick kiss on the cheek. "Makes sense to drive for hours just to say hello."

Alec cleared his throat. "Dec and I are going to take a little walk. Shake will be here if you need anything."

Mercedes's eyes shot to his, and she opened her mouth as if to protest, but Alec stopped her. "It'll be quick. Trust me."

She pursed her lips. "Alright, then. Come on, Shake, let's get you a seat."

Alec turned and headed up the path to the walled garden. Declan fell into step with him, not saying anything until they found a secluded corner.

Alec sat on the stone bench and looked to his cousin. "Okay, what did you find?"

"It's what we feared. Sadie was the mark."

"Her work?"

"Aye."

Alec closed his eyes. He'd known it. Men like Jason didn't use corporate attorneys as a cover for their crimes. But the confirmation of it burned through him.

"There's a wee bit more," Declan said.

Alec waited.

"You were part of the collateral damage."

Alec's heart shuddered to a stop. "Me?"

Twenty minutes later, Alec was rooted in his seat. When Declan had said it was a game-changer, he wasn't exaggerating. Every single thing they thought they knew had been spun on its head.

Everything had been a lie.

He folded his hands against his forehead and tried to focus his breathing to slow his racing heart. Declan was silent, watching him, a powder keg ready to spark.

"You've verified it?" Alec said, his voice thick with rage.

"Aye, Cress has all of it."

Alec stood, his limbs heavy. "We should get back before she worries."

"You alright?"

"No." The tightness in Alec's throat made it come out as a growl. "Fuck them."

"Aye."

"Christ, Dec. Just this morning, I watched her, thinking how at peace she was here. How ready she was to move on with her life." His gaze met Declan's, and he shook his head. "That's not going to happen, is it? There is no normal life for her."

The reality of her situation was becoming frighteningly clear.

"That fucking bastard is going to destroy her world again."

CHAPTER THIRTY-NINE

Relief washed over Mercedes when Alec and Declan walked out of the shadows. That was until she caught the look on Alec's face. The expression in his eyes was that of someone who had learned a beloved family member had died.

It terrified her.

When the last tale had been told, Mercedes rushed to put her violin in its case. Her hands shook as she secured the bow under its clip. By the time she returned to him, Alec was alone, his expression stoic as he stared at the ground.

He stood as she approached, giving her a smile that didn't reach his eyes. "Ready?" he said.

"I am. Where are the others? I thought I saw Mason and Cress. Are they here too?"

"Aye, they are. I gave them the keys to the cottage. They had a few things to set up."

Neither of them moved. Mercedes searched his face. "It's that bad, huh?"

Alec looked away, his jaw clenched tight. Anger and pain were fighting for dominance on his features. His blue eyes were hard when he returned his gaze to her.

"Aye," he said gruffly. "We should go."

The drive back to the cottage was quiet, Mercedes's mind spiraling. Since finding out Jason wasn't who he said he was, her thoughts had made up all sorts of scenarios he could be involved in. It turned her stomach to think he might have been trafficking children or running drugs while he slept next to her each night. That he might have used her to cover his crimes.

Alec pulled the car into the drive at the river house, parking next to two other cars. Mercedes got out and walked to the door.

"Sadie, wait." Alec took her hand, and she looked up at him in surprise. In the dim light, she could see his pained expression. "No matter what happens, I'm going to be here. Whatever you need." He paused, the next part coming out strained. "And I would have been there for you before . . . if I had known."

Mercedes frowned up at him. "I don't understand."

"You will. Just remember, okay?" He pushed the door open.

She shivered. "Okay."

Mercedes wasn't sure what she expected, but the chorus of greetings that came when they entered was a surprise.

"Hey, beautiful lady," Cressida said, wrapping her in a warm hug. Taking a step back, she looked Mercedes over. "Jesus, look at you. You look amazing!"

"Well, the last time you saw me set the bar pretty low."

Cressida snickered. "You have a point."

Mason was the last to greet her, handing her a glass of whisky as he released her from his embrace. "You'll want this."

"Doctor's orders?" she said, taking the crystal glass in her hand.

"Something like that." Mason flashed a smile at her. "It may not make things better, but it'll take a little of the sting away."

She clinked her glass on his and walked to the loveseat. Alec had taken up a spot on one of the other sofas.

"Alright. Let's do this. Who wants to start?" She strummed her fingers along the indentions of the crystal glass.

Declan cleared his throat. "We want to confirm a few things first if that's okay. I have a few questions that might be a little uncomfortable."

Mercedes nodded. At this point, she didn't think she had many secrets from these people. Nevertheless, the next words from his mouth couldn't have surprised her more.

"After Luke and Charlotte's wedding, you and Alec carried on a long-distance relationship. Is that right?"

"What? What does that have to do with anything?"

"Bear with me, lass." Declan looked like this was the last thing he wanted to be discussing. "The two of you were talking a few times a day? There was talk of him coming to the States for a visit?"

"Yeah." Her pulse rang in her ears.

"Can you tell me what ended things between you?"

A flush crept up her face, and she shot a glance at Alec. His gaze was boring into the glass in his hand. He obviously didn't like these questions either.

Mercedes hedged. "I don't know how this matters."

"Lass, we all have a good idea what you might say. But I want to hear your side of things."

She took a large, burning swallow of her whisky. Mason was wrong. It wasn't doing anything for the sting.

"He stopped returning my calls. My texts went unanswered for a week or two. Eventually, I took the hint and stopped trying." She shrugged. "I figured the long-distance got to be too much."

Declan's head bobbed in confirmation. "Do you remember the last time you talked to him?"

"Um, yeah. It was the morning of my birthday. I was

going to go to dinner with my sister and Luke, so I told him I'd try to call him when I got home that night."

"And did you?"

"I did. He didn't answer, so I left a message. I figured he was sleeping. It would have been around five in the morning for him. He always called when he got up."

"But he didn't call back?"

She shrugged. "I never heard from him again."

"And you didn't block his number or make any changes to yours?"

Mercedes frowned. "No."

Declan looked at Alec like he was asking for permission. Alec gave a single nod, his body tense.

Declan grimaced in a silent apology. "So, you didn't fall for another man and break it off with Alec?"

Her mouth dropped open. "What? No! What the hell's going on?"

Alec abruptly got up from his seat and paced into the kitchen, his body tense and angry.

Mercedes's eyes followed him. "You think I cheated on you? Why would you think that?"

"Because you told me so," Alec ground out. "At least, I thought it was you."

Mercedes was at a loss for words.

"Back at the safehouse, you said something about Alec not even sending you a text to break it off," Declan said. "I was there, and I know Alec was quite upset when *you* stopped talking to *him*. About a week later, you sent him a text message, ending it."

"I don't understand . . ." Mercedes tried to wrap her mind around Declan's words.

"It's true." Alec's voice was pained. His stormy eyes were caught between anger and regret. "I never stopped calling. At least not until you were good and done with me."

Done with him?

The realization of what this meant hit her. The oxygen seemed sucked from the room. Mercedes's chest heaved as she tried to pull in enough air.

"We were able to hack the phone system they were using and found messages," Declan said. "Neither of you have heard these, so . . ."

Cressida, who was sitting at the counter with a computer in front of her, pressed a key. Mercedes's voice rang through the air, carefree and joyful. Alec's shoulders tensed.

Hey Alec. Just got home from dinner. Charlie sends her love, Luke said to tell you that you're an asshole. I disagree, of course. Call me when you wake up.

Why were they playing this? She told them she'd called him after she got home that night.

Another message played. At the sound of his voice, the blood left her face.

Good morning, darling. I hope you had a lovely birthday dinner. Hopefully, you're not too hungover on that piss my cousin calls whisky. I have a meeting at two o'clock my time. Call me when you can.

Her voice played again. She remembered the messages she'd left like they were yesterday.

Hey you. Where'd you go? I secured a house on the lake. So excited. I need a break from this case, and I can't wait to see you. Anyway, I sent the listing. Let me know what you think.

Message after message played. Mercedes's calls tapered off, but his kept coming. By the time he threatened to change his ticket and fly to San Francisco, she was no longer even trying.

He kept trying.

Hey Sadie, It's Alec. I got your text, and I'm . . . well, I'm confused. I thought everything was going well. So . . . um. Please, call me? I think we can work it out if you'll just talk to me.

Alec's last message stabbed her heart. His voice was strained but strong.

It's Alec. I need to make this my last call. I'd hoped we could work it out. He cleared his throat as if speaking was painful. *Clearly not. I just . . . I wish I could understand how everything came apart. But it's time for me to move on. Best of luck to you . . . my darling. You're an amazing person and deserve to be happy.*

Tears flowed down her cheeks as she tried to make sense of everything. Mason brought her a box of tissues, and she took a handful. Her hands needed to stay busy.

"How did this happen?" The dagger in her throat made it come out more like a half-whisper.

It was Shake who answered. "Someone went into your accounts and manipulated the inbound calls and texts to a third-party number. Basically, whenever you called Alec, it was forwarded to the number. And the same for his calls to you. A voicemail captured the messages from both of you."

"Who?" She was trying to keep her breathing under control. "And *why?*"

"Jason." A steel edge had taken over Alec's voice.

Mercedes gaped at him. "There's no way he could have done that. I didn't even know him."

Alec strode across the room and sat on the coffee table in front of her. His warm hands wrapped around hers. "He's a corporate spy. He's paid to dig up information his employer deems valuable. There's little he wouldn't do for that information."

"Why would a corporate spy want to manipulate our relationship?"

"To get me out of the way."

"That's an enormous hassle. There are hundreds of single lawyers in the Bay Area he could have used to cover his work."

"Darling." Alec shook his head, his blue eyes softening. "You *were* his work."

The thundering in her ears made it hard to hear. "That can't be," she whispered.

"Think about what you were working on. Now, think about what I do for a living. I'm not a regular bloke, so to speak. I've spent my career being trained by MI6 as an intelligence officer, and now, I own a private security firm." He gently cupped her cheek. "What do you think I would have done for *you* if I'd been there when your world fell apart?"

"You would have looked for answers."

Alec's eyes were filled with pain. "They had to make sure we *never* spoke again."

Mercedes's mind worked to process it all. Jason had removed Alec from the picture and then took that place for himself. Full access to everything she had.

Think about what you were working on.

It hit her like a brick to the gut. The biggest case of her career, her advancement into the junior associate position. Billions of dollars at stake. Jason was there through it all.

"Oh, my god. Seth?"

Alec didn't have to say anything. His eyes held all the confirmation she needed.

The room narrowed and spun.

Her mind flashed to the small conference room, the detective greeting her with a grim handshake. He had news Seth's body had been found, but instead of telling her where Seth was, he showed her. Seth's bloated, purple corpse floating in the shallow rocks of Richmond Bay.

Jason did that.

He said he loved her, then he destroyed her life.

"I can't breathe." Mercedes jumped up and paced the

room, the others watching her. They couldn't help her now. She was losing her fucking mind.

Desperate to regain her breath, she hurried to the back door, wrenching it open. The clouds had opened up, and a soft rain pattered all around. Mercedes didn't care. She gulped the cool air.

At least this time, she recognized the panic attack for what it was. She leaned against a tree and tried to get control, focusing on the sound of the rapids crashing against the nearby rocks.

It was too much.

She'd been screwing Seth's murderer. More than that, she had given him access to end Seth's life.

Bile rose in her stomach.

Quiet footfalls on the grass made her look up. The darkness only revealed his tall silhouette. He wrapped a thick sweater around her shoulders. Warmth enveloped her, and she shivered against it.

"Come sit with me?" Alec took her hand and led her to a covered swing at the bank of the river. Mercedes sat and pulled her knees up. Alec sat next to her, and she put her head on his shoulder, willing herself to stop trembling.

"I don't know what to do. I feel . . . paralyzed," she choked out. "How could this have happened? He took everything from me. Why?"

"There are a lot of questions I don't have answers to. But I'm going to do everything I know to get it all back for you."

And I would have been there for you before . . . if I had known.

A sob escaped her, and she tried to hold it back, but the tears kept silently coming. Alec slipped his arm around her and pulled her tight against him.

"It's alright, darling. Let it go. When you're done, we'll make plans."

The fight went out of her. She broke against him, clinging to his warmth.

Jason had robbed her of everything she was. She could name them, the things he'd systematically ripped from her. Charlotte, friends, her career, music, self-worth.

Alec.

All ripped away with little protest from her. The raw wound that had been her life for three years was laid bare.

Eventually, the tears subsided, and fatigue set in. A heavy ache in her chest crushed her, pulling her down. Alec anchored her, but nothing could keep her heart from thrashing in the currents.

The night chill was breaking through, and Alec shivered beside her. She couldn't keep him outside all night. Whether she wanted to or not, she had to face the way things were.

Taking a long, cleansing breath of fresh air, Mercedes sat up.

"I think I'm ready."

CHAPTER FORTY

The slump of Mercedes's shoulders was enough to gut Alec. She was a hell of a strong woman, but there was only so much a person could take.

Someone had to be held responsible for the shit that went down. He wanted to believe that Jason Marsh, or whoever the fuck he was, was the only one he'd have to kill, but it was looking like an entire team would need to be neutralized.

Cressida met them at the door and pulled Mercedes into a hug. "We're going to get these fuckers."

Mercedes gave a tearful smile. She had the look of someone walking through the fog, lost in the mist. Hanging up the jacket he'd given her, she walked to the couch and sat. Her fingers tapped on her knee.

"What's his name?" The question broke through the silence like a cannon.

"Edward," Cressida said. "Edward Jason Hollis."

"Edward Jason Hollis," Mercedes repeated slowly, her empty stare aimed at the floor. "He doesn't look like an Edward."

Alec's heart wrenched to see her so defeated. The blaze he had seen in her hours ago had dimmed.

Mercedes rubbed her eyes. "Alright. You need information. Where do I begin?"

"The case you were working on. If I remember correctly, it was a lawsuit between two pharmaceutical companies, right?" Alec probed. "Why don't you start there?"

"Our client was a small pharmaceutical company called Henley Medical. They'd created a new painkiller called Cannativa, one of the first derived from the cannabis plant. If it did everything it was expected to do, patients would have access to long-term pain relief without the addiction that comes with opioids.

"For the American Food and Drug Administration to approve a drug, it goes through four phases of human trials. Henley completed the first two, but the next two are extremely expensive. Often, small companies can't complete them alone, so they sell their formula to larger research labs. Henley sold the Cannativa formula to Cooper Pharmaceuticals for eighty-six million dollars."

"Holy shit!" Shake exclaimed. "Eighty-six million dollars? That's insane. Did they not get the money then?"

"Oh, they got the eighty-six million up front."

"Well hell, I'd have taken the money and ran for it. Why did they sue?"

"Because the contract stipulated that for each milestone the drug hits in phases three and four, Cooper would pay an additional dividend to Henley, with the largest payout to be when it received the final FDA approval. Once it was on the market, they'd receive a percentage of the sales."

"So how much would it be when it got the approval?" Declan asked.

"In total, just over a billion dollars, not including the sales. With sales, it would be upwards of three to five billion in the next three years."

"Fuck me. That's the type of cases you were working on?" Shake blurted.

"You knew she was a lawyer." Cressida rolled her eyes at her brother.

"Well sure, but I thought it was the 'sue your crazy neighbor' kind or something." Shake shrugged in disbelief.

Alec cleared his throat. "So, what happened in phase three then?"

"There was no phase three. That's why Henley hired us. For months, they waited for word the trial had started, but Cooper gave them the runaround. So, we filed a complaint for breach of contract, which forced a response. Cooper Pharma claimed Henley's trial data in phases one and two were flawed, and they would need to restart the entire process. Years' worth of research and study were lost. And because Cooper claimed they were unprepared for phase one, they would need at least two years to get started."

"So, on hold indefinitely," Alec said.

"Essentially, yeah. We were looking at years of litigation with little proof they were lying. But our team caught a breakthrough."

Mercedes's team had discovered a conflict of interest. Marcus Cooper, the CEO and president of Cooper Pharma had created another drug, Sutanyl.

"It's a derivative of Fentanyl, one of the most dangerous opioids on the market. The drugmaker claimed they somehow removed the habit-forming side effects. It's incredibly popular as pain management, even today."

"They offered it to you in the hospital, and you refused it," Mason said. "I couldn't understand why you would want to go without."

"That's right. You should never take that shit."

"Why would Cooper's stake in this other drug matter? Wouldn't he make more money from the new drug?" Shake asked.

"No, it was a catch-and-kill scheme," Mercedes explained. "Cannativa would have been a direct competitor of Sutanyl.

Even though he's not directly named on the company, Marcus Cooper receives sizable dividends from Sutanyl sales. And it's *a lot* of money."

"Why wasn't this conflict discovered prior to the sale?" Cressida asked.

"Cooper didn't make it easy to find the link. There were name changes and hidden corporations changing hands several times. We were running out of avenues when a whistle-blower stepped forward."

Mercedes stopped, her voice tightening with emotion. "Seth Collins was a chemist who worked directly under Marcus Cooper. His sister overdosed on opioids when she was nineteen. He was committed to ending the opioid crisis."

"When Marcus Cooper directed him to kill the trials and falsify his data, he came to us. We built a solid case against Cooper and were days away from presenting everything to the feds. The case would've exploded, with worldwide consequences."

Her voice broke. "And then . . . I made a mistake." Tears came to her eyes, but she cleared her throat and pushed on. "I attended a retirement party for one of my colleagues at this high-end restaurant. I drank too much, and the next morning my laptop was missing. Sometime that night, my account was used to locate all the files. The most damning documents Seth provided were gone. Deleted and unrecoverable. The same night, our office was broken into, and they took the hard copies. By that afternoon, the police informed us Seth was missing. Without his evidence, we had to drop the suit."

"How much did you drink?" Declan said.

"Honestly, I don't know. They had bottles of wine on the tables. Jason kept topping my glass off. Next thing I knew, I was waking up at home to twenty missed calls and hell breaking loose."

Those absolute fuckers.

Mercedes looked between Alec and Declan. "I was

drugged, wasn't I?"

Alec met her eyes. "It looks that way."

Silence filled the room as everyone took in the information.

"There's something I don't understand," Cressida said. "If Jas—Edward, whatever the hell his name is, was just a plant to get information, then why did he put Mercedes in the hospital?"

"It's two separate things," Alec said. "The mission was to keep her isolated and reliant on him, so he'd have access to what they needed. The physical abuse was all him. He's like any other dirtbag who beats women. Control issues, raging narcissism, an insane amount of jealousy."

Shake piped up. "But they got what they wanted from her —whistle-blower's dead. The case was dropped. Should've been a done deal in San Francisco, right?"

"Should have been," Alec agreed. Shake was putting to words what he'd already been thinking.

"So why drag her all the way here? Why didn't he piss off back to wherever?"

"Crazy obsession?" Mason offered.

Shake shook his head. "Nah, mate. Sadie had twenty-four-hour surveillance the entire time she was in hospital, and none of it was by him."

Cressida finished her brother's thought. "So, what did they have to gain from it?"

Mercedes got up from her chair and walked contemplatively to the kitchen, arms tightly crossed. Alec could read her face. Fear etched with understanding.

"They still want something from her."

She closed her eyes.

Christ, she knows why.

When her gaze landed on Alec's, he knew she'd had enough. "I think Sadie needs a break and a little time to process. Let's regroup tomorrow."

Mercedes shot him a wary smile.

One of the worst parts of all this was watching the light go out in her eyes.

The team packed their equipment and headed to their cars. They would stay the night at the inn. Alec followed them out to the driveway.

Shake and Mason took one car back, but Cressida and Declan stayed behind.

"She knows what they want, doesn't she?" Declan asked.

"Aye, I think so."

Declan sighed. "We're going to need that information if we have even a chance of helping her out of this."

"I know. What about what she gave us tonight? Will we be able to use it?"

"It's doubtful," Cressida said. "We can prove someone interfered with your relationship three years ago, and that's it."

"What about working on the Cooper Pharma part of it? He has to have a role in this. Otherwise, who's paying them for their work?"

"We'll dig and see what we find. But without the whistle-blower, we'd be in the same spot her firm was."

Cressida gave him a pat on the shoulder and got into her car, but Declan stayed where he was.

"About the past," Declan said. "I don't know what you're planning for the rest of the evening, but if it doesn't include sweeping that woman off her fucking feet, you're a god damn moron."

Alec scoffed at his cousin's bluntness. "Thanks for the tip."

"I'm serious, Alec," Declan said. "Three years ago, she messed you up pretty bad. Now you have the truth of it. If you won't fight for her now, you don't deserve her."

Alec swallowed hard, his chest aching.

"Who said I wasn't going to fight for her?"

CHAPTER FORTY-ONE

Mercedes sat on the sunroom's window seat, her bare feet resting on the cushion, knees held against her chest. The rhythm of the rain on the glass cut through the quiet of the house. A hollowness radiated from her heart, spreading throughout her limbs.

She replayed the last few years in her head, connecting events to her new reality. In a way, it was a relief to have an explanation for everything. What angered her the most was how easily she'd been manipulated. It had taken little effort to remove and replace Alec in her life. His sudden silence tore right into her insecurities. Wounded and lonely as hell, she'd been a soft target for a charming man to take her mind off of it all.

If only she'd been stronger, she'd have pushed harder to know where Alec went.

They must have listened to her calls with Alec. How else would they have known how important he was to her? Mercedes flushed thinking about someone listening in on the conversations she and Alec had shared, some of them quite intimate.

A familiar sense of violation returned, turning her stomach, but it was quickly replaced with anger.

Fuck them.

She and Alec had done nothing wrong. She'd be damned if she let them taint those memories. They were hers.

And all this time, Alec thought she'd met someone else. That *she* was the one who'd wrecked what they had.

God, he must have hated her.

Looking back, she'd seen it in his eyes. The conflict when he kissed her. His excuse that he had to focus on the job. The way his expression shifted when she joked she'd never lead one man on and sleep with another. He'd practically ran from her bed that morning.

She sighed, thinking of that night. Alec had brought her a few hours of the peace she'd craved. There were other things she should be consumed with right now, but damn if she didn't want to lose herself in him again. It wasn't only her body that ached for him; it was also her soul. He'd always meant more to her than she'd ever had the courage to tell him.

Nerves shot up her spine at the sound of the door opening. The scent of rain-soaked air and wood fires followed him in. He caught her eyes, his lips curving up. Hanging up his damp jacket, he strode to the bar and uncorked the bottle of whisky.

She saw his every movement in a new light. This wasn't the man who had casually tossed her aside, shattering her soul.

He'd fought for her. He'd wanted her.

Did he still?

His last message to her reverberated through her mind.

It's time for me to move on . . . Best of luck to you . . . my darling. You're an amazing person and deserve to be happy.

The pain in his voice had pierced her.

How do we even begin to repair this?

Alec offered her a glass of whisky, and she took it, letting her fingers brush his. She took a sip of the amber liquid, its warmth flowing through her.

He cleared his throat. "So. Are you going to tell me why he brought you here?"

Mercedes closed her eyes, her stomach dropping. She wasn't ready. Her mind was scattered in fifty different directions.

When she spoke of the secrets she kept, she had to be sure she knew what she was doing.

"Tomorrow. I don't want to talk about him anymore tonight."

Alec sat next to her on the window seat. "Fair enough. I don't either."

The current rushing between them swirled in her veins. They'd avoided their past for far too long.

Mercedes steeled herself. "Why did you agree to meet with me at the shop?"

The corner of his mouth pulled up. "I think you know why, Sadie," he said, blue eyes saying what his words didn't.

"You thought I cheated on you," she said. Alec winced, a flash of pain behind his eyes. "Why would you want anything to do with me if that's who you thought I was?"

"Honestly, I didn't think I had a right to see it as cheating."

Mercedes tilted her head. "What do you mean?"

Alec ran his fingers through his hair. "When you and I met, we spent a total of eight days together. Most of that time was in the presence of my *entire* family. I really liked you, but I didn't plan on it becoming serious. I don't think you did either." Alec shifted his weight, setting his elbows on his knees. "Then I called you, just to make sure you got home safely, and I didn't want to hang up. Before I knew it, I changed my schedule to pour my life out to you when you'd call. I've told you things I've never even told Dec."

"And yet you didn't think me sleeping with another man

was cheating?" She stood, setting her glass on a shelf. Turning to face him, she crossed her arms in front of her.

Alec shook his head. "It ripped me apart to think about you with someone else. But I didn't feel you were mine yet. We'd never talked about it being just you and me. We hadn't even slept together. It felt wrong to ask for that kind of commitment when we were half a world apart."

Mercedes's heart sank. "Does that mean you were with other women?"

Alec stood and crossed to her. "Christ, no, Sadie. I swear, there was never anyone else. I only saw you."

"I only saw you too," she sighed.

The restraint she'd seen in his eyes cleared. His fingers intertwined with hers, and sparks sizzled up her arm, warming her entire body. Alec's breath caught, and she knew he could feel it too.

He stepped closer to her. "The trip we'd planned would have changed everything. I was going to tell you what I felt for you. Everything I wanted. All the things I couldn't say on the phone. I never got the chance."

"Tell me now," she whispered.

Alec leaned down. Mercedes sucked in her breath when he kissed her neck. "I'd have told you that you were the most incredible person I'd ever met. And you made every day of my life better."

Mercedes closed her eyes, tilting her chin into him.

"But it wasn't enough," he murmured.

"It wasn't?" Her words sounded distant.

"No, I wanted you with me. Not on weekend video chats, but in my bed every night." His lips were getting closer to her mouth. "I had a plan to make it happen."

"What kind of plan?" she murmured.

"The kind where I expand my company into California."

Her eyes flashed open. "What?" She put her hand on his

chest, pushing him back to meet his gaze. "You were going to move for me?"

"Aye, if you'd wanted me to."

Alec's warm hand slid down her back and pulled her to him. The searing heat of his body made her dizzy.

"Why would you've done that?"

Alec let out a shaky breath. "Because I was in love with you."

Her pulse roared in her ears.

"You were?"

His lips turned up into a crooked smile. "I'm still in love with you."

"Alec . . ."

His mouth crashed onto hers, cutting off the words. His kiss was hungry and sinfully hot. Mercedes wanted him, *all* of him, to be hers. She'd lived far too long without his light. Desperate to tell him, she pulled away.

"I love you too." Her voice trembled. "I've loved you for so long."

"Christ, Sadie." Alec gave a sharp exhale, leaning his forehead against hers. "I've waited years to hear you say that."

Alec's mouth was on hers again, need radiating off of him. His tongue lashed hers, sending desire surging down to her core. Mercedes clawed at his shirt, aching to feel his skin. Alec whipped the shirt up and over his head, then pulled hers off too. Mercedes brought her mouth to his throat, savoring the taste of him.

He moaned, tilting his head. "Do you know how hard it's been to be near you and not touch you? God, I want you all the time."

"I know exactly how that feels," she rasped.

Alec walked her backward until her legs pressed against the window seat. He tugged on the waistband of her pants, and Mercedes sat while he slipped them off her. The chill hit her heated skin, making her shiver.

Alec knelt and pulled her knees on either side of him. Groaning, he tugged down the top of her bra, freeing her nipple from under the lace. Leaning in, he drew the sensitive peak into his mouth, teasing her until she was panting. He unhooked her bra and slid it off her arms to turn his attention to her other breast.

Holy hell, his mouth is amazing.

Alec tugged the edge of her panties, and Mercedes lifted her hips as he slipped them off. When his fingers found her, she moaned, pressing herself into his hand to relieve the ache he'd created.

"Oh god, Sadie. You're soaking," he murmured.

She pulled his chin up to look at her. "See what you do to me?"

Alec paused for a beat. Then he growled and jerked her head down, kissing her hard. His thumb massaged her swollen clit. Mercedes whimpered, her need for release becoming painful.

He broke his kiss away. "I've wanted to do this for a long time,"

She gazed at him through hooded lids. "Do what?"

In a swift movement, he hooked her legs over his shoulders and tugged her to the edge of the seat. Dipping his head between her thighs, he replaced his thumb with his mouth.

Mercedes gasped, tangling her hand in his hair. Alec laved at her clit, swirling and sucking, each burning stroke tormenting her. The world fell away. All she knew was him.

The sheer bliss built her orgasm quickly. Alec's rhythm increased, matching her hips as she ground against him. He sucked in, his tongue lashing in the same beat.

"Holy shit, Alec," she heard herself say. "Oh my god, please don't stop."

Alec made her body tighten until it shattered. The climax pulsed through her, the heat of his mouth staying with her as her body shuddered through each wave.

Reality slowly returned. Rain pelted the windows. Alec was still between her thighs, his tongue moving languidly on her. His gaze caught hers, desire blazing in the blue depths.

Mercedes slipped her leg off his shoulder and sat up, crushing her lips to his, tasting herself on him.

"Stand up," she said huskily. She slipped to her knees in front of him. Her hands shook as she wrestled with his buckle and zipper. The second his thick length was free, her mouth was on him. She sucked him slowly at first, her tongue swirling on his tip before pulling him in deep. Alec groaned, wrapping his fingers in her hair.

"God, you make me crazy," Alec gasped.

Mercedes bobbed on him, quickening her pace. Each moan spurred her to give him more. She loved the sounds he made.

Alec stopped her. "I need to be inside you so fucking bad."

Mercedes's heart thundered. "Couch or bed?"

He pulled her to her feet. "Bed. Now."

Alec led her through the house to the stairs. They tumbled into the room, pulling off the rest of his clothes. Once they hit the bed, Alec was on her, aligning himself with her core.

"Look at me," he rasped. He guided her chin to meet his gaze. "Tell me again."

Mercedes's breath caught. "I love you, Alec."

He groaned, thrusting deep inside her. The fullness of him scorched through her. They moved together, her nails pulling down his back. Alec hissed and pumped harder into her. The next climax worked its way through her, tightening her walls around him.

"Sadie, I can't . . ." His breath was ragged.

"Don't hold back," she coaxed. "Come inside me."

"Oh god," he moaned as his release took hold. "Jesus, Sadie."

The spasms of his pleasure coursed through them. He didn't stop at his own climax, driving into her just where she needed it. As her orgasm crested, Alec whispered. "I love you." It hit her hard, her walls clenching around him. Mercedes cried out, riding out each wave until she lay panting under him.

Without warning, Mercedes's throat tightened and tears sprang to her eyes. Hope and relief crashed over her. Alec loved her. She didn't deserve him, but he loved her anyway. She buried her head in his chest, his heartbeat dancing in her ear. A little sniff escaped her.

Alec pulled himself to his elbows, searching her face. "Christ, Sadie." Alarm rang in his voice. "Did I hurt you?"

She laughed, feeling silly as she dabbed at her eyes. "No, you're amazing."

The furrow in his brow deepened. "Then why?"

"It's just," she said through a sob, "I've missed you so much."

"I missed you too." Alec's voice was tight with emotion. He slipped to her side, gathering her into his arms. "Darling, don't cry," he soothed. "We're alright. Everything is going to be alright."

The crying fit was thankfully brief, and Mercedes relaxed into his warmth. The rain tapped against the window, lulling her. She was about to doze off when Alec broke the silence.

"I don't want you to go back."

Mercedes raised her head and frowned. "Mm? Go back where?"

"To California." Alec's brows creased in confession. "At least not permanently."

Mercedes hadn't decided what she'd do, but clearly, Alec had thought about it.

"I'd love for you to live with me, but I'd understand if you wanted your own place for a bit. I . . ." He swallowed hard. "I don't think I can watch you leave again."

Her chest ached. She'd never seen him so vulnerable. "Then I won't leave."

He let out a breath of relief and kissed her. Mercedes never wanted to be away from his touch again.

Alec was her home now.

PART III

CHAPTER FORTY-TWO

The rain had finally let up when Jason guided the sedan into a parking space along the busy street. Adam sat sullenly beside him. His pissy demeanor was a source of entertainment for Jason. Fucker hadn't believed him when he said he knew Mercedes.

Of course, he knew her. She belonged to him.

Even Adam and his shitty deduction skills couldn't deny they were onto something. After running it by the boss, Adam had no choice. Jason gloated every chance he got.

Stepping out of the car, he pulled in a deep breath of night air. For the first time in forever, the atmosphere wasn't scented with bus exhaust and piss—a vast improvement over the city. Decorative streetlights reflected off the cobblestone sidewalks. Narrow alleyways mazed through the ancient buildings. It was a quaint little hamlet.

Mercedes would love it here.

Jason fell into step with Adam, his hands in his pockets. A group of college-aged girls, dressed in nightclub tramp gear, shot coy glances at them as they passed by. Jason ignored them, but Adam's mouth curved into a smile, turning to watch them as they passed. They let out peals of giggles at Adam's attention.

This asshole must get laid a lot.

They worked their way to the village center. Shops were shuttering for the night while the restaurants and clubs that skirted the square were filling up. It was a vibrant tourist trap.

Adam nodded to Jason, and they split apart, Adam disappearing down an alleyway. The shop from Mercedes's email loomed ahead. The window display held a variety of books and vintage gifts. Jason found a wall to lean against and waited. The longer it took, the harder his pulse hammered. He couldn't afford to be wrong. If he was wrong, and she wasn't here, he was a dead man. Adam might take him out right now.

The lights went out, and the door to the shop opened. A woman stepped out, bundled in a cardigan and colorful knit hat. She turned to lock the door, her face obscured by shoulder-length blonde hair.

The hair color was right, but Jason couldn't tell if it was her.

Fuck.

Then she turned.

Her blue-gray eyes caught his, and she froze.

A wide smile spread across his face as he held her eyes. They had only met once, but recognition filled her eyes.

I knew *it.*

She took a few steps back, trying to act like she didn't know who he was or what he was doing there.

She knew.

Jason followed her, keeping a natural pace. She only had one possible route. Her phone was in her hand, and she was typing on it as she scurried along. Probably calling the police. Not that it would do any good. They'd never get to her in time.

The end of the alleyway opened to the stone river walk.

Her head was turned to watch Jason when she ran smack into Adam.

Adam's hand snaked out, grasping her by the arm. "Hello, Mara. Been a while, hasn't it?"

Terror lit her face. She tried to wrestle free, but Adam held her tight.

"Stop fighting me," Adam growled. "We're going to take a little walk. Don't make a scene, or we'll make sure it hurts."

"Fuck you and fuck Marcus. I'm not going anywhere with you," she hissed. She struggled again, this time screaming, "Help me! Please, my ex is going to kill me!"

Ah shit.

It caught the attention of the milling crowd.

"Hey mate, you got a problem with the lady?" a man hollered at Adam, stepping in his way. Wrenching her hand from Adam's grasp, Mara turned and bolted along the river.

Jason slipped past them, breaking into a run after her. Pain from the wound on his leg burned through him, but he ignored it.

The phone was clutched in both hands again, her fingers moving on the screen. A sinking feeling hit him.

Fuck.

He needed that fucking phone.

Jason couldn't get to her fast enough with the crowds blocking his way.

She skidded to a halt at the stone embankment of the river and shot a look at Jason, the honey-blonde sticking out of her cap and blowing across her face. Her hand came down, smashing the phone on the stone barrier, and then she threw it into the water, where it landed with a plop.

Bitch.

Jason was inches from her when she bounded up to the top of the embankment and launched herself off, falling to the icy waters below. The splash from impact reverberated, and a passerby cried out. Concerned citizens flocked to the wall, looking for where she might surface. It was a survivable fall, but the water would be cold as hell. She'd need to get out soon.

But without support, they had little chance of tracking her.

Adam came up next to him, his jaw set. The evening light had faded enough so that the only thing they could see was the knitted cap she'd worn, floating on the water.

"Would've had her if we'd had backup."

Adam glowered. "Shut the fuck up."

CHAPTER FORTY-THREE

Alec awoke in a different bedroom. In Mercedes's bed. The events of the night before flashed in his mind, and he smiled, contentment running through him.

She loved him. *Holy shit.*

As unreal as it all seemed, he'd never been so happy in his life. He wasn't letting her get away ever again.

Finding his trousers on the floor, he shimmied into them and opened the door. The scent of coffee wafted through the house. He went down the stairs, and his heart stopped.

Mercedes was wearing his shirt again. She poured cream into two mugs and hummed a song only she knew. Her hair was tossed up in a crazy bun. So damn beautiful.

And she was his.

Mercedes turned to him, two coffees in hand. "Oh, you're up." A smile lit her face. "I was about to bring you breakfast in bed." She handed him a steaming drink.

Alec laughed. "Coffee for breakfast?"

"Uh, yeah." Her eyes sparkled behind her cup. "I don't like the idea of killing you with my cooking. But I make amazing coffee now. So, *bon appétit.*"

Alec took a sip and set it on the counter. He pulled her into his arms and kissed her. Her body molded against him so perfectly, and a soft moan escaped her. Heat rushed through his spine, making him hard.

"Do we have time?" she asked, her chest heaving.

"Aye. I told Declan not to be here before ten."

Mercedes slid her hand between them, cupping his hardness. Her touch had him in flames.

"Perfect. Why don't you move your things into my room and meet me in the shower?"

God, she's going to kill me.

Shower sex was an amazing way to start the day, but reality was about to break through their blissful morning. The closer they got to ten o'clock, the quieter she got. Alec could feel the nerves coming off of her. Her fingers were dancing by the time the knock at the door came.

The exuberant greetings of the team broke the solace. Mercedes offered them coffee and tea while they set up in the living room. Cressida and Shake were arguing over a seat at the table. Mason laughed at something Declan said.

While they set up, Alec wrapped his arm around Mercedes's waist. "You okay?"

"I'm scared. I've never told anyone about this."

Alec brushed his lips over hers. "I'm right here. Everything will be okay."

"Aww, you guys." Shake's big brown eyes were wide, and his lips pursed, his hand on his chest. "Oh, my heart."

"Bout bloody time," Declan grumbled, but he caught Alec's eye and gave him a little shrug that said, 'I guess you're not a moron after all.' A lovely blush crept up Mercedes's cheeks as she took a seat on the couch. Alec sat next to her, pulling her hand into his.

Cressida cleared her throat. "Okay, love. Let's do this. Why did that asshole separate you from Alec and drag you across the pond?"

Mercedes swept her hair back. "They brought me here because there wasn't one whistle-blower. There were two."

Ah, shit.

"Her name is Mara Donovan. I'm likely the only person who knows where she is."

Alec's heart sank. "How much does she know?"

"Everything." Mercedes's fingers tapped on her knee.

"Everything Seth Collins knew?"

"Way more. Seth gave us the data proving Cooper killed the Cannativa trials. Mara gave us evidence not only that Cooper's cash cow Sutanyl was addictive, but also that they had bribed their way to an FDA approval."

"Holy shit," Mason said.

"She told you this verbally?" Alec said.

"No, she has solid evidence. Lists of names, how much each bribe was and who received it, what they gave to Cooper in return for the money. Even the financial records showing the payouts leaving one bank and being deposited in the other."

"How did she get them?"

"It was her job to keep track of it all. Mara was an insider to Cooper's empire, a bookkeeper of sorts. Only the books were filled with favors that could be called in."

"So, what happened to her?" Alec asked.

"I was vetting her evidence when Seth died. She freaked out and ran for it, taking everything with her. She said she wanted to keep it as an insurance policy. I took what I had to the partners at my firm, but my reputation was in tatters. They told me to pack my desk."

"But why move you to London? Why not keep you in San Francisco?"

"Well . . ." Mercedes took a deep breath. "Because Mara's

here in the UK. She's a British citizen. I've kept in touch since she ran, trying to convince her to come forward. She refuses, but she wanted a contact who would know what to do with the information if something happened to her. Maybe they wanted me to draw her out. But my communications with her are so limited I don't think they know I talk to her."

"How do you communicate?"

"Our first meeting after I moved to London was face to face. Since then, it's been through a monthly junk email. I receive an advertisement from her, and in return, I respond with a newsletter from the shop." She shrugged. "It was rudimentary, but it worked for us."

"Is it possible they know of your secret check-ins and are narrowing the whistle-blower's identity down that way?" Cressida asked.

Mercedes shook her head. "Her identity has to be known. She was Cooper's executive assistant for ten years and his mistress for at least five of them. He'd be looking for her."

"So, we find Mara Donovan and offer her protection," Declan said. "Then we hand the evidence over to the FBI. We have some contacts within the bureau, and they'll be able to help,"

"I doubt Mara would want to have anything to do with us. She trusts no one. Not even me. And when she finds out I told you about her, she's going to run for it." Mercedes shook her head. "Honestly, I'd rather leave her alone. I messed up before, and someone died. I can't make another mistake."

"I know you're scared, and you have a good reason," Alec murmured in her ear. "But if we're ever going to have a real life again, we have to do something."

"How about this?" Cressida said. "Let's get you a secure internet portal and see if she's checked in."

It only took Cressida a few minutes to access a secure network. Alec stood over Mercedes's shoulder as she waded through the trove of Pottery Barn and Amazon messages. A moment later, her fingers stopped over the keys.

"What is it?" Alec said.

She turned her eyes up to him. "Someone's been reading my messages."

CHAPTER FORTY-FOUR

Mercedes pushed her pasta around her plate. It was delicious, but she wasn't hungry. The inn's dining room was bustling with weekend travelers, so the six of them were packed tight around a table.

They had spent most of the day running through scenarios. Cressida and Shake researched the village, the bookshop, the layout of the streets, every piece of information that could be used to find Mara Donovan and offer her protection.

Mercedes could feel Alec's concerned glances throughout dinner.

"Sadie," Alec murmured.

"I'm okay, Alec, I swear."

"That's good, darling. But David's on his way to our table."

Mercedes broke from her reverie to find Alec was right. David was nearly to them, his eyes lit in greeting. She lifted her hand to wave at him.

"Is he going to be a problem?" Alec murmured.

"Not at all." Mercedes laced her fingers through his. "He already knows about you, my love," she whispered.

"Hello all and welcome." David's eyes swept around the table. "I hope you're enjoying your meal."

Various sounds of approval came from their group.

"That's good, so glad to hear." David's eyes landed on Mercedes's hand, intertwined with Alec's. He stopped and gave her a questioning look. Mercedes's smile lit up her face.

"Well, now. That's damn fine, lass." The welcoming grin widened, and he turned his gaze to Alec. "I see you've finally come to your senses. Well done."

"Thank you."

Mercedes leaned toward him. "I told you he was just a friend."

A quick tug on her arm pulled Mercedes's attention away. Cressida gave Mercedes a look that screamed for an introduction.

"Oh, David, this is the woman I told you about the other day, Cressida Bennett."

Cressida extended her hand to him. "David, it's nice to meet you." Interest blazed in her eyes.

Mercedes blinked in surprise.

Cressida was a chameleon. Sweet Girl Scout one minute, seductive temptress the next. It was impressive to see.

"I saw you play last night. It was beautiful." Cressida leaned forward on the table, stroking her neck with the tips of her fingers. "I'd love to hear more."

David flushed. Cressida's attention was clearly working. "Aye, we'll be starting in about an hour. I'd love to see you there."

"I can't wait." Cressida's dimples were on full display.

David cleared his throat and turned back to Mercedes. "Are you coming tonight as well? We always love having you play."

"Not tonight, I'm afraid. Alec and I are having a night in."

"We are?" Alec quirked an eyebrow.

"Yep." She held his gaze. His expression turned positively sinful.

Mercedes had used the inn's evening entertainment to avoid being alone with Alec. Now she was eager to get him on his own again.

After David said farewell, Cressida's eyes followed him, a smile playing at her lips. "Ooh, he's yummy. I owe you, Sadie. I'm partial to dark-haired Scotsmen."

A snort came from Alec, which he covered with a cough. Declan's expression had darkened, his normally laid-back manner tense.

"Now might not be the time for going out on a date." Declan's voice was tight.

Cressida shrugged. "Why not? What else is there to do?"

"I don't know, maybe you could get some work done?"

Cressida scoffed. "Bloody hell, Dec. I've worked all day. And you heard Sadie. She and Alec are going to go get theirs. Why shouldn't I get mine?"

Declan stiffened. "Jesus, Cress . . ."

"You know, last time I checked, I only had one brother sitting around this table." She turned to her twin. "Lysander, darling, do you care if I get a little action tonight?"

Shake scoffed, amusement sparkling in his eyes. "Nope."

"Good. We settled then?" Cressida's eyes clashed with Declan's hard stare, the muscles in his jaw working.

What the hell's going on?

Alec sighed and stood, breaking the sudden tension. "Catch the bill on your room, would you Dec? Sadie and I are going home."

He held his hand out to her as warmth rushed through her.

Home.

It was hard to remember what having a home felt like.

Declan grunted his response, and Alec took her hand.

"What was that all about?" she murmured.

Alec scoffed. "I don't know. They normally get on well. He's been acting strange since they arrived."

"Huh," Mercedes said, noncommittally. Declan's problem seemed pretty clear to her, but she didn't think Alec wanted to talk about that tonight.

Alec pulled the car up to the gate, pausing for it to open. Mercedes's heart fluttered in anticipation. She had Alec all to herself with nowhere else to be. She planned to take full advantage of every moment until morning.

SOMEWHERE IN THE DISTANCE, A PHONE WAS VIBRATING. Mercedes ignored it. Only one thing mattered.

Alec.

His beautiful mouth found her right nipple and pulled it in, sucking deeply. He licked at her, each stroke making her hotter.

Mercedes thrust her hips, whimpering in need. She hadn't stopped thinking about the way his tongue felt when he tasted her the night before.

The vibration at the bedside table broke through again.

Damn it.

"Alec," Mercedes breathed. He didn't stop his attentions. "Alec." This time pushing on his shoulders and sitting up.

"No, they'll go away." As if on cue, the buzzing stopped. "See," he said, a smug smile on his face. He launched a new assault on her neck, nipping at her.

Mercedes moaned. "It has to be important. They wouldn't call so late if it weren't."

"It's fine. They can wait." Alec pushed her back, his firm body covering hers.

Mercedes lost herself in his touch.

The phone buzzed again.

Alec groaned against her throat. Snatching up the phone,

he answered it out of breath. "Christ, Declan, this had better be important."

There was a tense pause. "You're sure?"

Mercedes sat up and looked at the clock. It wasn't as late as she thought.

"We don't have a computer here yet. Right now? Aye." Alec sighed and hung up. "Declan and Cress are on their way over."

"Now?"

"Yeah, we need to get dressed. Something's happened."

Ten minutes later, Mercedes was adding water to the kettle when the knock on the door came. Declan and Cressida walked in, each with a computer bag.

"So sorry to bust in on you like this." Cressida tilted her head in apology. "I know you wanted some alone time."

Mercedes waved it off. "How did it go with David? He's sweet, isn't he?"

"Very, but I didn't get to talk to him for long. Dec brought this to me, and I had to leave early."

A tone sounded from the computer. Cressida tossed her head back. "Network's ready, Dec."

Declan joined them at the table. "So, this afternoon, we set up news alerts for anything related to Mara Donovan. News broke of an incident in the town square where the shop is located. This happened last night, but the police released this footage tonight. Take a look."

Mercedes and Alec both leaned in. Mercedes wasn't sure what she was looking for. When Jason appeared in the frame, she gasped. He wore a ball cap and walked with a limp, but there was no doubt it was him.

When Mara Donovan came on the screen, Mercedes's gut churned. "Oh, god."

Alec put his hand on her back. "That's her?"

Mercedes nodded. She'd failed again. Jason and Adam had found Mara Donovan, and now she was likely dead.

"I feel sick," Mercedes whispered.

Alec squinted at the screen. "What is she doing? Is she texting?"

Mercedes leaned in just as Mara broke her phone over the stone barrier, then launched herself off the side.

The blood left her face.

"Cress, I need to check my email."

Cressida brought it up and scooted the computer to Mercedes. Mercedes's hand trembled as she skimmed through the onslaught of messages. Her eyes landed on the one she hadn't thought she'd ever see. There it was between ads for kitchen supplies and a furniture store in Berkeley.

"Holy shit," she whispered. "She sent it to me."

"Sent what? I see adverts," Cressida said.

Mercedes clicked on the message from an online hand-crafted jewelry store. Scrolling through various glass pendants, she landed on one called The Mercedes Mirror.

"The other links probably don't work, but this one will. It looks like a necklace, but it'll open a PDF file." Mercedes added the pendant to the shopping cart and clicked to check out. Instead of adding a credit card, she clicked on the discount code and typed in the code Mara gave her.

As soon as she hit enter, the file downloaded and opened. Mercedes let out a breath. Mara would never have sent this file unless she thought she was going to die.

> *Mercedes,*
> *If you are reading this, they found me. I leave this in*
>   *your hands. I wasn't strong enough to take them on.*
>   *Maybe you will be.*
> *Mara*
> *Knightsbridge Security Boxes*
> *#18759*
> *Code: UvxRG3*

Mercedes's mouth went dry. Everything she needed to take down Marcus Cooper, his company, and every person he'd ever paid off was waiting for her in a safe deposit box in London.

They spent the next hour deciding what to do with this information. Alec and Declan discussed their connections, who might be the best agency to hand the documents to.

"It should be Nick," Alec said. "This started in America, and it's where the crimes were committed."

Special Agent Nick Kessler was a seasoned FBI agent and an old friend. Alec assured her he had full trust Nick would get the information to the right place. Alec left his friend a message to call him.

"Should we go to London tomorrow and get the documents?" Mercedes asked.

"Let me talk to Nick first. I want a secure place to take them before we open that box."

It was after midnight when Cressida and Declan packed up and left.

"Once we turn this over to the FBI, do you think I'll be free of this?" Mercedes asked. "I don't know where Mara is, and the evidence will be out of my hands."

Alec's shoulders tensed, but he smiled at her. "I don't know. Cooper's men might not need you, but I doubt Jason will be that easy to put off. He has different reasons for searching for you."

Mercedes wanted Alec to be wrong. It would be easier to sleep at night if he wasn't trying to track her down.

But somehow, she doubted her life would ever be the same again.

CHAPTER FORTY-FIVE

Alec and Declan got through to Special Agent Nick Kessler the next morning.

"I don't know, Alec," Nick said. "It's awfully hard to agree to this kind of meeting without knowing what we're getting into. I need a little more to go off."

Alec grimaced. His line was secure, but he didn't want to go into too much over the phone. "You've heard of Cooper Pharmaceutical, aye?"

There was a pause. "I have."

Alec paced the floor of the kitchen. "I may soon receive some documents you may find interesting."

"Is that so? What did you say your client's name was?"

"I didn't. Her last name is Elliott."

Another pause came on the line. "Mercedes Elliott?"

Alec froze and shot a look at Declan. "How did you know that?"

"Yeah, we're going to want to talk to her. I'm in Washington, so I can't meet her personally. But one of our agents, Doug Michaelson, has been in your part of the world. I'll see if he can interview her. Can you have her in London tomorrow?"

The swift change in direction made Alec's heart thunder in his chest.

"Aye. But I want to make it clear I'll be staying with her the whole time."

"Shouldn't be a problem unless they have to transport her home. You could follow on your own dime if you wanted."

"She doesn't have a passport."

"I'll see if we can get a spot at the embassy then. She can get her paperwork in order while she's there. I'm going to warn you now; there's a good chance she'll be on the flight with Doug."

Unease settled in his gut when they ended the call.

"Jesus, how deep into this case are they already?" Declan said.

"Hard to say."

There were so many unknowns. Would the evidence in the security box show the corruption Mercedes hoped it would? Would it even be there?

A peal of laughter broke through his brooding thoughts. Mercedes and Shake were in the backyard, sitting across from one another at the patio table. He was telling her a story with his usual animation. Shake had a way of distracting people with humor when they needed it most.

Mercedes deserved this life. One surrounded by love and friends. Alec wanted so much to give it to her, to erase every trauma she'd endured.

Declan came to his side, watching Mercedes tease Shake, a giggle rippling through the air.

"Thank you," Alec said.

"For what?"

"You brought her back to me," Alec's voice tight with emotion. "I don't know if I can ever repay you for that."

"Eh, she was going to come back to you on her own."

Alec laughed. "Maybe."

They would never know. Not that it mattered. She was his.

"I'm happy for you, Allie," Declan said. A warmth coursed through Alec at the sound of his childhood nickname. "She's going to make you a better man."

Alec's lip curled into a grin. "She already has."

WATCHING MERCEDES SAY GOODBYE TO THE KENNISON family hurt more than he thought it would. She assured them all she'd come back as soon as the river house purchase was final. Alec wanted nothing more than for that to be the truth.

They would leave in the morning for London. The plan was to pick up the box and catch the meeting with Nick's colleague in the afternoon. The others had already left, wanting to get a head start on surveilling Knightsbridge Security Boxes. He wouldn't take Mercedes there without knowing it was clear.

They walked along the river as the sun slipped below the horizon. Mercedes seemed to take her time, enjoying the trail they'd taken so many times. When they returned to the house, Alec lit a fire to cast away the chill. Mercedes stared into the flames, her fingertips tapping against her lips.

"What are you thinking?" Alec sat next to her.

She snuggled up with him, her body cold from the walk. "I'm second-guessing every decision we're making."

"Aye, I am too. I think this is our only real option."

"I used to be so good at making my own choices. But now . . . How can I trust myself? The decisions I've made have gotten people killed."

He kissed the top of her head. "You were fighting an enemy you didn't know existed. Now you know who they are. You'll know what to do."

Alec lifted her chin and kissed her, her tongue soft against his. She slipped her hands under his shirt.

"Ah!" he yelped. "Christ, woman. What's wrong with your hands?"

"Oh. Are they cold?" she asked innocently, sliding them down his stomach and under his waistband. Her fingers wrapped around him, stroking him slowly in icy bliss.

Alec stiffened and gasped. Her touch was like a glacier on his bare skin.

"Ooh, I like that sound," Mercedes purred.

Alec moaned, laying his head back on the sofa. She leaned over and kissed his neck, her tongue swirling on his skin. Alec's heart beat hard in his chest. He pushed his hips up, panting as she worked him.

"We should go to bed," Alec whispered.

Mercedes chuckled. "It's only five-thirty."

Need for her pulsed through his body. "Aye, we should go to bed."

They took their time, savoring each other, Mercedes's cries of pleasure searing into his mind. No matter what happened in the next few days, she'd always be his.

CHAPTER FORTY-SIX

A lec was struggling. Handing her over to someone else, someone who didn't need her the way he did, was ripping his nerves to shreds. They sat together in the American embassy, awaiting their appointment. His gut churning with anticipation.

"Ms. Elliott," a voice cut through the air. A young man in a suit and tie came to stand before them. "I'm Jared Silva. I'll be taking care of your travel documents, and I understand you have a meeting with Special Agent Michaelson as well."

"That's right," Mercedes said, standing to follow the man.

"He's not here yet, but I can get you started."

They were nearly through processing when a knock came on the door. A distinguished white man with salt-and-pepper hair stepped into the room.

"Hello, I'm Doug Michaelson. I'm sorry to keep you waiting." He pulled a chair to the desk and pulled out his leatherbound notebook. "I understand you have some documents to deliver to Special Agent Kessler. Mind if I look?"

Alec studied the man. "I do. Can I see some ID?"

The agent's thick brows shot up. "Oh, of course. I'm so

sorry." He pulled his badge from his coat jacket and handed it to Alec.

Alec looked to Jared Silva. "Can we have the room, please?"

"Of course. I'm nearly finished with my part. I'll be back to check on you." Jared Silva left the room.

Agent Michaelson took his phone out. "If it's okay with you, Ms. Elliott, I'd like to conference Special Agent Kessler into our discussion today. I know he'd be interested in talking directly to you."

"Of course."

They waited for the call to be set up. Once Nick was on the call, Michaelson turned to Mercedes.

"Alright, Ms. Elliott, you have our attention."

Mercedes told them everything, beginning with her assignment to the case and ending with Mara Donovan sending her access to the safe deposit box. Michaelson took careful notes, both he and Nick asking questions as she laid it all out.

When they finished up their questioning, Michaelson stepped into the hall to confer with Nick in private. When he returned, he wore a pleasant smile.

"Well, Ms. Elliott, we've been in contact with our superiors, and they would like to meet with you in person tomorrow. I've asked that your passport be expedited so we can get you on the flight."

"Wait. A flight to where?" A tinge of panic coated her words.

"To Washington D.C. I know it's sudden, but they don't want to wait. I was already set to fly out tonight. They've asked me to escort you there. Tomorrow, you'll be debriefed, and our analysts will look over the documents you've brought with you."

"Why are they moving on this so quickly?" Alec said. The cogs of government were notoriously slow.

"I can't reveal too much, but I can say Cooper Pharmaceuticals has been under investigation for some time now. A team of agents has hunted for leads for years. If what you say you is true, they want the evidence right away."

"That will be hard for them to do considering they won't have access to the documents."

Michaelson's head snapped up. "What? I thought you had it on you today?" His eyes shot to Mercedes's bag on the floor.

"I may have . . . misplaced it." Alec shrugged, his mouth twitching. "I might find it again if I happen to be on that flight to Washington."

Michaelson's mouth curled up, and he sat back in his chair. "Nick told me to expect a little pushback from you. I'm sorry, I really am. But I'm not authorized to take a British citizen on an American transport. However, I may tell you where she'll be housed and how to get access to her accommodations."

Alec didn't like being separated from her, but there was little chance they would get a more secure transportation. Mercedes would be safer on this flight than on a commercial one.

"Very well. I look forward to handing the documents to you when I'm standing by her side in Washington."

The documents in question were being evaluated by Cressida and Declan as they spoke. This would give them time to review them before he turned the originals over.

Michaelson balked halfheartedly but eventually relented. There was no way to force Alec to give him anything.

"Jared Silva will come for you soon to complete your paperwork. Once it's all set, we'll be on our way." He looked between them. "I'll give you two a minute."

Now for the hard part. Tears welled in her wide hazel eyes. The fear in them pulled his heart apart. He opened his arms and she settled into him, her fist curling around his shirt.

"Hey, it's only a few hours really, one day tops. I'll be right behind you."

"I know. I wasn't ready for them to separate us so soon. I thought we'd have one more night."

"I did too. But maybe it's better this way. We'll get it over with and be back together before you know it."

A tear escaped down her cheek. "I love you."

Alec's heart swelled. He'd never tire of hearing her say it. "I love you too. Don't forget that, aye?"

He kissed her, wanting to keep her with him forever. But he had to let her go. This time, she'd come back to him.

CHAPTER FORTY-SEVEN

A knock came, and Jared Silva peeked in. "Agent Michaelson asked me to come get you and bring you upstairs. Right this way, Ms. Elliott."

Silva had the good grace to step into the hall and avert his eyes politely as Alec pulled her into his arms and kissed her. Mercedes's heart was saturated with fear and resentment. If she had a choice, she'd never leave him again.

She stepped away, the taste of him lingering on her lips. Shooting Alec one last look, she picked up her bag and joined Mr. Silva in the hall.

Mercedes was grateful he didn't try to make small talk. She wasn't in the mood to listen to comments about the weather.

Mr. Silva led her to an office several floors up. "Make yourself at home." He gestured to the chairs. "It'll be a little while before your documents are ready. Can I offer you a beverage? Water? Tea?"

"Water would be great, thank you."

He bobbed his head and hurried from the room.

Alone, a sinking feeling came over her. The white noise of the wind and the traffic below was eerie.

Mercedes crossed to the window and looked out at the London skyline. She loved this city. It was too bad she hadn't taken the time to enjoy it. That would change when she came back. She'd make Alec play the tourist with her. They'd take in a West End play or visit Tower Hill. It gave her something to look forward to.

The door to the office opened and softly shut with a click.

Then, the quiet voice of her nightmares cut through the silence. "Hey, beautiful. I brought you water."

She could see the figure behind her in the window's reflection. Mercedes's gut turned to ice. All the work they'd done to keep her safe hadn't mattered.

Jason had found her anyway.

CHAPTER FORTY-EIGHT

Jason saw her shoulders stiffen and pushed away a flash of anger. When Mercedes turned, her hauntingly beautiful eyes struck him. They were mostly green today, with a touch of gold flecks.

He walked toward her and held out the bottle of water. A peace offering of sorts. She didn't move. He lowered his arm and put the water on the table.

"You look good." The catch in his throat surprised him.

"No thanks to you."

Regret churned in him. Her expression filled with pain. He'd done that.

She didn't have a reason to trust him, but she was going to have to.

"Sadie." Jason took a step toward her. Remorse filled him when she backed toward the window. "I'm sorry for what happened. I swear I didn't . . ."

She cut him off. "How did you find me?"

"We have our ways." Jason hardened himself against the look of disgust on her face. "You need to come with me."

"I don't think I need to go anywhere with you, *Edward*."

It was like a punch to the gut.

Fuck.

"Don't call me that," he ground out.

"Why not? It's your name, isn't it?"

"No." He took a step toward her. "Let's go."

"I'm not going with you." Her voice trembled. "There are Marines everywhere. I'll stir up so much shit we won't make it to the elevator."

He inhaled, reining the anger in. She knew how to push his buttons. It would do him no good to allow her willfulness to goad his temper.

Instead, he pulled his phone from his pocket, dialed, and put it to his ear.

"What's the twenty?"

"Right where we want him," the voice on the other line said.

Jason smiled and tucked the phone in his pocket. "Beautiful view, isn't it?" he said brightly, and as if nothing were amiss, he strode to the window beside her. Mercedes backed away but had run out of places to go.

He wanted her off balance, and the change of tone had the intended result. Mercedes's brow furrowed as he got close to her. He snaked his hand out, capturing her arm and wrenching it behind her back. Spinning her, he slammed her face into the glass. She gave a satisfying cry with the impact.

"Shh, shh. I know that hurt. Just wait," he murmured in her ear.

Jason couldn't help but press against her. He'd missed her tight body so fucking much. He grasped her chin, guiding it down so her eyes were on the street below.

"Look down there, love. Can you see what I see?"

She stiffened.

"Yeah, you see him, don't you?"

Alec McKinley was moving at a quick pace. His head was down, but he easily stood out amongst all the other pedestrians.

"Now look up there." Jason jerked her jaw toward the brick building on the opposite side of the street. His man's form was clear on the roof of the building. As expected, he was already in position, on his knees, eye to the scope of a rifle resting on a tripod, his target sighted.

"I can make it happen. Right now." His grasp tightened. "There's nothing I'd rather see more than that piece of shit's brains painting the pavement. Or to see him take a gut shot, gasping for breath as he dies, slowly, painfully. Will you give me a reason to give that order? Hmm?"

When she didn't answer, he relaxed his grip on her chin and allowed his fingers to caress the smooth curve of her cheek. The scent of her was intoxicating. He breathed her in.

She had been away from him for far too long.

"We need to talk, you and I. There's a lot to be said." He took a steadying breath. "But right now, we have to go."

He stepped away from her reluctantly. She stayed at the window, watching as McKinley made his way along the sidewalk.

"There are several people following him. If he slips away, we have backups. Think about all the people you love."

Mercedes turned to him, the heartbreak in her eyes tearing at his heart.

This was why he loved her. She made him feel. It reminded him he was still human. He stepped to her and took her hand gently. "I know you have no reason to trust me, but I need you to listen to what I say and do what I tell you. Or they will kill you."

The door to the office opened, and the embassy representative walked in. He halted at the door. His pleasant smile shifted to wariness.

"Can I help you, sir?"

"I'm Jason Hollis. I'll be taking Ms. Elliott off your hands now."

The young man shut the door quickly behind him. "It

wasn't in the plan to do this here," he hissed. "You're supposed to take her at the airport."

Stupid little fuck.

Jason didn't try to mask his annoyance. "We got eager. I'll be taking her now. And she's going to be a good girl, aren't you, Sadie?"

Mercedes said nothing, but her face was filled with submission. There was nothing she could do here. The only thing keeping McKinley alive was her compliance.

Jason put his hand on the small of her back and guided her past Jared Silva. "Why don't you escort us to the car?"

Mercedes stiffened as she passed an armed guard. Jason tightened his grasp on her arm. Once they entered the car park, he released her.

"You did well," he said. "Keep it up, and McKinley might see tomorrow."

Jared Silva walked ahead of them, leading them to a black car parked in the back corner of the garage. "The cameras are off back here, as was requested."

Adam was there, rifling through the car. "God damn it."

"What?" Jason cast his eyes around the garage, hoping Adam wouldn't bring them any heat.

"It's not here." Adam picked up a bag and dumped it on the ground.

"Are you serious?" Jason said. He turned on Jared Silva. "You told us they brought the package with them."

"I thought they gave it to the agent."

Jason whirled on Mercedes. "Where the fuck is it?"

"I don't know what you're talking about."

Adam moved, latching onto Mercedes by her hair and pulling her around the car.

"Oh my god," she screamed, trying to break away from Adam's grip. Jason peered over the side. Special Agent Doug Michaelson lay in a pool of his own blood, a gruesome tear opening his throat.

"Stop it. Mercedes, that's enough," Adam barked. "We aren't fucking around anymore. Where's the package Mara Donovan gave you?"

Jason's heart was thundering. Watching Adam rip at Mercedes's hair was enough to make him blow his lid. But the timing was all wrong. And Adam needed answers.

Tears flowed down her face, and she looked up at Adam. "I don't know. Alec gave it to him. He said he was going to take it to a secure facility in Washington."

Jared Silva piped up. "You need to leave. The ambassador gave you the green light to take the woman. Not to kill an FBI agent."

Adam's eyes met Jason's. Mercedes gasped, her mouth hanging open at what Jared Silva had exposed to her.

Stupid motherfucker.

Adam shook his head and pushed Mercedes. She landed in Jason's arms. With a quick turn, Adam's knife plunged into Jared Silva's neck. Gore poured from the wound. The wet slurp of the blade being pulled out cut through the quiet. Adam dragged Silva's body next to the agent's, ignoring the gurgling sounds coming from the dying man. He wiped the knife off on Silva's suit and tucked the blade away.

Mercedes was taking gulping breaths, trembling. Adam stalked toward her. She shrunk away. Jason tightened his hold, but he didn't like the way Adam was glaring at her.

"Where the fuck are the documents?" Adam growled.

"I told you. I don't know." Fear tinged her words. "Alec gave them to the agent."

"Hold her." Adam ran his hands down her body, fingers grabbing at her breasts and moving to her crotch.

"What the fuck, man?" Jason shoved Adam's hand away.

"Making sure she isn't hiding a flash drive."

"Get your hands off her. I'll do it."

Mercedes flinched but let him run his hand over her body. Nothing.

"Shit. McKinley must have kept it," Adam said. "Get her in the car. We need to get the hell out of here."

Jason clamped his hand on her arm and led her to their car. Mercedes didn't fight him, which was good. Adam was at the end of his rope and would likely kill her if she didn't do as she was told.

Jason would need to keep her quiet and cooperative if he was going to keep her alive.

CHAPTER FORTY-NINE

Mercedes could make the lights from the streets below turn into long glowing stars when she squinted her eyes. Traffic on the motorway was slowing up, elongating the distance between the white and red lights snaking through the city.

She'd been confined to this room since they'd left the embassy the night before. It was comfortable enough. A small but well-furnished guest room with an attached bathroom. Mostly, they left her alone, although Jason had attempted to talk to her several times.

The dichotomy between Jason and Adam had thrown Mercedes. She'd always thought Jason was the one calling the shots, but there was a tension between the men. No one looked to Jason for direction or even seemed to take him seriously.

And they kept him from seeing her. Mercedes was grateful for that. She'd envisioned the horrors Jason was plotting to unleash on her. Punishment for running from him. For running to Alec.

Mercedes had done her best to push thoughts of Alec aside since they had taken her hostage. She could make herself panic thinking of him. Was he safe? Did he know she was missing yet?

Raised male voices punctured the quiet of her prison. Fear shot through her when she recognized one of them as Jason's. He was coming close to her door.

"I want to ask her a few questions, that's all." His tone had taken on a manipulative quality. For once, it didn't work.

"Why the hell would I do that?" Although she had seldom heard him speak, Patrick's voice was unmistakable.

"It's just a couple of questions. What's the big deal?"

"Like all those other times you wanted to *question* her, and she ended up in the ER? Then I gotta sit my happy ass in a hospital waiting room for a week, watching Judge Judy reruns and explaining to the boss how I let it happen? No fucking thanks."

She couldn't hear Jason's response, but Patrick cut him off. "Look, I'm under strict orders. You're not going in there. Period. You want another go at her, you need to clear it with the boss."

The sound of a door slamming made her jump. For a moment, she thought Jason had left. But a cacophony of greetings told her new people had joined them. A feminine voice cut through the noise and Mercedes's muscles tensed.

Mariah was here.

Of course she was. For a time, she'd forgotten the bitch existed. The sound of her shrill voice slicing through the air grated on her nerves.

Sudden footsteps and a key being roughly jiggled in the knob made her sit up. Patrick swung the door open and beckoned her to join him. Nerves pulsed through her.

Mercedes stood and put one cautious foot in front of the other. The room had a modern feel. Ivory furniture with gray accents was everywhere. The large balcony windows opened to a view of the Tower Bridge. A view worth millions.

Instrumental jazz music played in the background, giving

off a false sense of tranquility, as if she were a guest for a dinner party. Adam and Mariah sat at a marble countertop. Adam's expression was one of boredom, but Mariah had a catty smirk on her face.

Mercedes ignored her. Nothing could be gained by engaging that bitch.

The tinkling of glass drew her eye to the large bar near the balcony door. Someone was shuffling through the bottles.

Mumbled swearing came from under the bar. "You would think with what I pay the staff, the bar would always be fully stocked."

Mercedes gasped when the man finally emerged with a bottle held triumphantly in his hand.

"Found it," he announced, as if the entire room had been concerned their host might be out of gin. Marcus Cooper looked up at Mercedes with a friendly smile, pouring a generous amount of the clear liquid into a shaker.

"Gin martini alright with you, Ms. Elliott?"

Mercedes's voice didn't work, so she nodded. He smiled and popped the lid on and shook it a handful of times.

Ruggedly handsome, with tanned skin and a fit body, Marcus Cooper was the model of wealth and excess. Cooper was known all over the world for his philanthropic ventures as well as his social prowess. A handful of well-timed scandals had rocketed him into the public view. Mercedes had little doubt he'd soaked up the attention.

A delicate glass pick with two olives garnished the chilled glasses, and he bought the cocktails around the counter.

"May I call you Mercedes?" He extended the martini to her with expert grace.

"Sure." She took the glass and held it to her lips, careful not to drink any of it. She might be a little disoriented by his friendly demeanor, but she couldn't forget where she was.

Marcus Cooper held his hand out for her to sit on the

cream and gray sofa. He sat across from her. She placed her untouched drink on the coffee table.

"I'm Marcus Cooper. Of course, you probably knew that. I apologize for not being here to greet you before today. I flew in as soon as I heard you were my guest. Thank you so much for joining us." At her quirked brow, he added, "I mean, I know you didn't have a lot of choice in the matter. My men can be quite determined when I ask them to get something for me." He sipped his drink delicately and said as if confiding a secret to her, "I rarely ask how they do it, but . . ." He turned to the others. "How did you persuade Mercedes to join us?"

"We threatened to open up her boyfriend's skull on the sidewalk." Adam stared at Mercedes in warning. A shiver ran through her. He was hitting his mark.

"Oh, my!" Cooper hooted as if Adam had told a board room joke and not threatened to murder someone on the street. "That is *really* effective. So violent." He shook his head as he took another sip of his drink.

Jason, who had been watching quietly from the corner, stiffened and walked to the window, but not before Mercedes saw the anger flash in his eyes.

Cooper sensed this as well. "Ah, now. Our Mr. Hollis doesn't enjoy being reminded of your new beau." He gave Mercedes a conspiratorial wink.

Jason said nothing, his fists curling against his thighs, his shoulders squared in rage.

Cooper's voice shifted to one laced with warning. "Perhaps Mr. Hollis needs to be reminded not to let his jealousy get away from him."

Mercedes's eyes shot to Jason's tightly wound silhouette. He seemed to contemplate this.

With another delicate sip, Cooper leaned forward. "You see, Mercedes, I don't give a shit who you fuck."

A chill ran up her spine. The contrast of his friendly tone

and the coarseness of his words were unsettling. This was intentional. He was trying to bait her.

Mercedes smiled. "That's good. I wasn't planning on discussing my latest fuck with you."

A pause charged the room. Cooper burst into laughter.

"Oh, I like that response, Mercedes. Well done." Cooper's eyes shifted back to the window. "What do you think, Mr. Hollis? Do you think she means you?"

Jason's hadn't left the window, but his arms tensed at his sides.

"So, here's the thing." Cooper was suddenly serious. "There was some damaging information collected by someone who was once close to me. I'm sure you know what sort of information I mean." She said nothing, so he went on. "I know your meeting at the embassy was meant to turn everything over to the FBI. Obviously, we couldn't let that happen."

Cooper stood and walked to the bar, grabbing the bottle of gin. "It's a shame about that agent we had to eliminate. That's going to be quite the mess to clean up. But we couldn't have anyone running around with your story in a notebook, could we?" Cooper had finished his martini and now mixed another, the ice on metal rattling her nerves.

He walked back to the sofa and smiled. "I will get the original documents back. Even if I have to destroy everything and everyone in your life." The false joviality was gone, replaced with a cold directness. "Where are the files?"

"I don't have them."

"Well, of course, you don't have them *now*." The base of the martini glass left a circle against the leg of his tan slacks. "But you know where they are."

It wasn't a question.

"I actually don't."

"Mm-hmm." He took a long drink of his martini, his eyes not leaving hers. "Where is Mara Donovan?"

"I have no idea. Last time I saw her, she was running for her life on the news."

"How did she get you the files?"

Mercedes stared at him.

"You are going to make this tough for us." Cooper sat back with a sigh. "Well, that's unfortunate."

Cooper stood, polishing off his drink. "If you can't help us, we'll appeal to the ones who know more." He turned to Adam. "Send a message. Just don't be too rough. She's not useful to us if she's damaged."

Adam said nothing but looked at Jason. Fear ran down Mercedes's spine.

Cooper offered her a smirk. "I'm afraid I'll be stepping out for this part. I do hope you'll remember something soon. I'd hate for Mr. Hollis to ruin that pretty face of yours." Cooper swept Mercedes's martini away as he left, leaving her alone with her nightmares.

Jason stalked closer to her, his jaw set. The anger burned in his eyes. She whimpered and scurried backward, trying to stay out of his reach.

The first blow hit her cheek. Mercedes fell back against the couch, her elbows trying to protect her face. Jason was on her, the weight of him pressing on her hips. She took his fist two more times to the face. Her nose broke open. The metallic smell filled her senses, blood staining the fresh cream cushions.

"Alright, that's plenty," Adam said.

Jason pulled away, his weight leaving her. Mercedes bolted for the door, but Mariah got to her first, tackling her with a grunt. Mercedes screamed, squirming to get away from Mariah's iron grip. Blood smeared on the ivory marble tile. Mercedes kicked, connecting with Mariah's face.

Jason suddenly loomed over her. He punched her hard, making her head bounce off the floor. Stars swam in her eyes, nausea building in her gut. He pulled her to her feet, his arm wrapped around her waist.

He nuzzled her ear and murmured. "Stop fighting. You're making this worse."

Jason was enjoying this. She could feel his erection pressing against her ass. Her vision wavered. His fingers tightened, taking an even firmer grip.

"Patrick, get the camera ready. Bring her in here."

Mercedes leaned against the wall, trying to contain the flow of blood between her fingers. She stopped and let it drip. Perhaps some intrepid crime scene unit would collect it as evidence after these assholes killed her.

Patrick returned from the hallway carrying a tripod with a small camera attached to the top.

The room shifted. She held back vomit.

"Ready when you are," Patrick said.

Mercedes watched warily as Jason approached her and the camera.

"Hello there, Mr. McKinley." He sneered into the camera. "As you may be aware, the lovely Mercedes Elliott is not where you last put her. In fact, for the last twenty-four hours, she's been a guest of mine. I've enjoyed my time with her immensely." The innuendo in his voice was unmistakable. A calculated lie designed to create maximum pain. "You need proof, though, of course." Lunging at Mercedes, Jason pulled her to stand in front of him and forced her to look at the camera. She tried to pry his hand away, but he only held on tighter.

"You have something we need, Mr. McKinley. I believe we can work out a deal. You produce the files, and I'll consider giving her back to you in one piece." His hand slid down the length of her body, pulling her into him suggestively. "Mostly." The taunt in his voice turned Mercedes's stomach. "But if you even dream of going to the police or the FBI, I'll send her to you in pieces."

Jason held her upright while they reviewed the playback.

"It'll work. Send it to McKinley now," Adam barked,

grabbing Mercedes by the arm. She teetered as he dragged her down the hall and shoved her inside her bedroom.

"Clean yourself up." The door slammed behind him.

Mercedes tripped on her way to the bathroom but got there in time to throw up in the toilet rather than all over the cream carpet. Unable to get off the floor, she leaned against the wall. She took large breaths and hoped the room would stop spinning.

There was no way she would survive this. Even if Alec handed everything over, they were going to kill her. Her heart raced in fear. Fear for herself. Fear for Alec and the others.

None of them were safe as long as she and Mara Donovan were out here.

CHAPTER FIFTY

"The bodies of two men, both believed to be American, were found in the car park of the United States Embassy. Local investigators are working with the American authorities to identify the victims and determine the cause of death. The US ambassador has issued a statement . . ."

Alec tuned out the rest of the news report. His mind was reeling. Pacing the length of the conference room, his stomach lurched with each step. The news reports had been breaking all afternoon.

They fucking had her.

"How the fuck did this happen?" he yelled, not for the first time. "I thought the United States embassy would be crawling with security."

"They had to have had someone inside," Mason said. "Nick said Jason waltzed right in there with a security card. It might have been Jared Silva, the rep that was found with Michaelson. He walked them to the car."

Alec tried to sit but couldn't make his muscles cooperate. He hadn't been able to stop moving since Nick Kessler called, letting him know his agent was down and Mercedes was gone.

"Do you think she's already dead?" The words were poison in his mouth.

"No," Declan said. Alec searched Declan's face, trying to find a spark of hope. "They'll let her live until they have the files. They gotta make sure they contain any sort of damage these two women have done."

"Except we have the files." Alec let out a breath.

"And Nick's expecting them," Mason said.

"He's going to have to wait. Or better yet, he can help us find her. But those files stay with us until she's found. After that, I don't give a shit who has them."

"I think Sadie would disagree," Cressida said, looking up from her computer. "Sadie's whole life has been a wreck for the last three years because of this. She's going to want to clear the ledger."

"I just want her alive and back with me."

"Aye, one step at a time, mate. We'll find her." Declan said.

"Oh, shit," Cressida burst out. "Alec, we got a message."

She met Alec's eyes. His heart shuddered in his chest. Coming around the table, he could see the image on her screen. It was a thumbnail image of Jason Hollis. Cressida clicked the mouse, bringing the video to life.

Breathing became difficult as he listened to the message. Jason pulled Mercedes into him, displaying her broken face. Blood coursed down her small hands. Spots filled Alec's vision. He backed away from the computer.

What had he done to her when the camera wasn't on?

Alec leaned against the wall, forcing his mind to focus. All that mattered was getting her back.

He stalked back to the desk.

"Play it again."

It wasn't any easier the second time, but he could analyze it. Mason and Declan stood next to him, doing the same. There wasn't much to go off of. Gray wall in the background, no sound, nothing that cast a reflection. They had nothing.

Alec's phone vibrated in his pocket. He pulled it out and checked the screen. An unknown number. He read the words and froze.

Did you like my message?

It took all Alec's restraint not to break his phone into pieces. Instead, he responded.

Proof of life. Then we'll talk.

The room was silent as they waited for a response. Holy god, what if he couldn't provide it?

Then the phone rang.

CHAPTER FIFTY-ONE

Mercedes hadn't left the floor of the bathroom. Blood crusted in her hair, but she was beyond caring. It felt like a power saw was grinding into her skull. The plush bathmat seemed a suitable place to lie for a while.

Footsteps alerted her someone was coming, but she didn't have the energy to move. Jason burst into the bedroom and found Mercedes lying on the floor.

"Come on, babe." He crouched beside her. "You need to say hi to someone, okay?" He sat her up. Bile rose in her throat, but she kept it down.

Jason took out his phone, dialed, and held it to his ear. It only took a second for the call to be answered.

"Tsk, tsk . . . you don't trust me?" The taunting in Jason's voice made her skin crawl. "Oh, well. I don't blame you. Here you are."

Jason held the phone to Mercedes's ear. "Say hello, beautiful."

God, what is this now?

She whimpered in pain. "Hello?"

"Sadie?" Alec's voice broke through the line. "Christ, are you okay?" The fear in his voice tore at her heart.

"Alec," she whispered. Tears welled up in her eyes. "I'm okay, just a little banged up."

"Stay strong, aye? I'm coming for you. I'll see you soon."

Jason snatched the phone away from her and put it to his ear.

"I'm going to text you an address. I expect you to be there tonight at three a.m. sharp. You bring anyone with you, or leave anything out of the package, and she's dead. And I'll make sure it hurts. I'm not fucking around with you."

Jason towered over her. He ended the call and handed the phone to Mariah, who had been waiting outside the door.

"Send him the address to the drop site and tell everyone to be in place by two."

Mariah snatched the phone, paused, and looked at Jason. "You're not supposed to be in here with her." Her gaze landed on Mercedes and she touched the bridge of her nose, which was just starting to swell. "Good thing Adam left with Cooper, huh?" A malicious smile spread across her face as she backed away to the door. "Have fun, Sadie."

Fear crawled up her spine. Jason seemed calm right now, but his temper was a powder keg, waiting for her to set him off.

Jason moved to the sink and wet a towel with warm water. He kneeled on the floor next to her. Mercedes flinched away from his touch.

"Shh, you have blood on you," he soothed, his hands gentle. The heat from the towel relieved the ache in her temple.

Mercedes regarded him warily. "You've never helped me clean up before."

Jason grimaced. His gaze shot to the door and back to her. "I didn't want to do this. I don't want to do any of this." His hand brushed a stray hair from her cheek.

"You sounded pretty committed on the phone."

"Well, I was talking to Alec. He has something they want,

and if I don't get it, they'll kill you." He wore a mask of shame so well. "I've never wanted to hurt you, Sadie."

Mercedes tilted her head, her eyes narrow. "That doesn't seem like an accurate statement, Edward."

He flinched at the sound of his name. "I've always gone by Jason. Edward was my father. He was a piece of shit." His fingers dabbed her chin, angling it to clean the remnants of his work off her face. "I knew you'd figure it out, eventually. Especially after he took you from me."

"He didn't *take* me from you. I went with him on my own."

Jason's eyes were like ice. "Did you sleep with him?"

A fresh wave of terror shivered up her spine. Nothing good would come from this line of questioning. Pulling what she hoped was an impassive face, she said nothing.

Jason's eyes welled with tears. "Do you love him?"

"I'm not going to talk to you about him."

Jason's pained look was one he had when he was filled with regret. The one that could suck her back into his orbit. It had no effect this time. He might feel a moment of remorse, but it wouldn't stop him from destroying her again.

He wiped his eyes. "I know I messed up a lot with you. I'm sorry for that."

"Sorry?" She stared at him, her mouth hanging open. "I don't even know who you are. You've nearly killed me multiple times. You murdered Seth and destroyed my career all at once."

His head jerked up. "I didn't kill Seth. That was Adam."

She smirked at him. "Really?"

"Yeah, really. I was supposed to be there, but I stayed at your house and protected you."

"What?" Mercedes frowned at him in disbelief.

Jason shifted, sitting next to her, his back against the wall. "You were supposed to be floating in the bay with the Collins kid that night. That was the plan. Burn everything to the ground and kill the witnesses. I kept you valuable. They had no idea you had a second source. So, I hid her existence until they were ready to take you out. Then I popped up with it and suddenly keeping you alive was all they wanted. It's a good thing you went for me and not Adam. Otherwise, you'd be dead."

Mercedes frowned. "Adam?"

"Yeah, he hit on you first. At the bar in Tahoe?"

He did? She had no recollection of meeting Adam until Jason introduced him.

Jason shrugged. "Adam looks like McKinley, so they thought you'd go for his type."

Mercedes scoffed. "He looks nothing like Alec."

Jason frowned. "A big fucker with blue eyes and black hair? Pretty much the same."

"Adam has dead eyes."

"And I don't?"

Mercedes held his gaze. "Sometimes there's a spark of humanity in there."

"I love you. Does that make me human?" His crystal blue eyes welled with tears again. This was the man she'd cared for, maybe even loved. Vulnerable and broken.

A complete liar.

Mercedes didn't answer or acknowledge his lie. Instead, she grabbed the edge of the counter and pulled herself to a stand. "It sounds like I'm going to die tonight anyway, so thanks for the last six months, I guess."

Jason moved to her side and helped her up. As much as she hated his touch, dizziness made it hard to walk on her own. He walked her to the bed, where she collapsed on the fluffy pillows. It was early, but she wanted sleep.

Jason leaned down and kissed her, his lips soft on hers. Mercedes's heart plummeted.

She was in no shape to fight him off. Revulsion moved

through her, but she kept herself still. He broke away and nuzzled against her cheek. When he whispered in her ear, her heart nearly stopped altogether.

"I won't let them hurt you. But you must do what I say if you want to stay alive."

CHAPTER FIFTY-TWO

A shaking on her shoulder brought her out of her fitful sleep. Mercedes opened her eyes to a dark figure silhouetted against the city lights.

"Wake up," he hissed. "Wake up, babe. We have to go."

The light on the bedside table clicked on, blinding her. "Jason? What are you doing?"

He knelt on the side of her bed, his eyes filled with panic and desperation. "I want you to choose me."

"What?" She sat up, her head throbbing. At least her stomach had settled.

"I want you to choose me," he said again. "I'm so sorry for everything I did to you. For the lies. For hitting you. For all of it, I know I fucked up."

The room spun. Honeyed promises could never erase the damage he'd caused her. "Jason . . ."

He shook his head to silence her. "Let me show you. I'll change. I'm willing to get you out of here. Right now."

"What about Cooper? He's not going to let us go."

"Fuck him. He got his money's worth from me. I'm done." Jason took her hand, breathless. "Cooper's already given the order to Adam. You're going to die tonight."

Mercedes's pulse raced in her ears. What was worse? Going on the run with Jason, or staying in this prison to take her chances with Adam and his orders? At least on the run, she might escape and get back to Alec.

A door closed in another room, and Jason tensed, his eyes flitting to the door. "I need you to decide right now. Or it'll be too late."

"Alright," she whispered, knowing she was making a deal with the devil. "I'll go with you."

Jason pulled her into a kiss. Mercedes did her best not to recoil when his tongue flicked over her lips. It was thankfully quick, his body primed to run.

"Mariah left, so it's only Patrick out there." He handed over her shoes and waited while she slipped them on. "Ready?"

Her heart was ready to explode. "I . . . I think so."

At the door, Jason paused. "I'm sorry for what you're about to see." He opened the door, and Mercedes stepped into the hall behind him.

Patrick's voice rang out down the marble hallway. "What the fuck, Jason? You aren't supposed to be in there with . . ."

Jason raised his arm. The gunshot split the night, cutting off Patrick's words. Blood and brain matter spattered the fine ivory tiles.

Mercedes shrieked. Her vision tunneled, a whooshing sound filling her ears.

This isn't happening. This can't be real.

"Sadie, look at me. Fucking look at me." Mercedes was dimly aware of Jason's words. She glanced up into his face, barely able to pull her eyes away from the gore. "We have to run. Now."

CHAPTER FIFTY-THREE

*S*he doesn't love me now, but she will.

Jason held Mercedes by the waist as they hurried down the service hall to the wide elevators designed to bring up furniture. Mercedes was unsteady after the hit she'd taken earlier. He should have pulled his punches, but he had to admit it felt good to unload on her.

Now he was feeling a tide of remorse, which pissed him off.

Fuck Cooper for making me hurt her. If the man didn't have more power than God, he'd put a bullet in his brain too.

Jason jabbed the button, impatient for the door to slide open. Once they stepped onto the lift, he wrapped his arm around her, wanting to feel that magnetic warmth she always brought to his world. Instead, she stood straight and cold, her arms crossed in front of her.

She needed to remember what they meant to each other.

They would have time. Jason had been planning this for a while. By tomorrow afternoon, they would be soaking in the sun on the beach in southern France. Mercedes would look incredible in the little bikini he'd picked out for her. He was going to shower her in the luxury she deserved—the luxury he'd wanted to give her when they came here.

In another hour, she'd have no other reason not to love him completely.

"Why are you doing this?" Her voice was distant and strained.

A wave of guilt swept through him, making his heart race. He hated feeling guilty. Why couldn't she understand?

"I love you, Sadie. I'm the only one who has ever loved you like this."

The doors slid open, and they stepped out. The car was only feet from the entrance, ready for them. Mercedes didn't resist when he pulled open the passenger door and pushed her in. They were pulling out of the garage when a police car pulled up to the curb.

Shit.

A neighbor must have called it in. Jason thought he'd have more time before they discovered the body. Once they found Patrick's rotting carcass and their prize captive missing, they'd know exactly what he'd done. This was going to fuck with his whole timetable. Adjustments would have to be made.

Jason drove for a while, making sure they weren't followed. He found a parking space in a quiet residential neighborhood. Mercedes didn't move. She wasn't going to run for it. He'd catch her easily.

Jason pulled the phone from his pocket and dialed. He could feel her eyes on him as the ringing filled the car.

"This is Alec." The short greeting came on the line. God, he hated that fucking voice.

Mercedes gasped. Jason shot her warning glance.

"Wakey, wakey asshole. There's been a change of plans."

"Jason, what are you doing?" Mercedes cried.

"Shut up," he growled.

"Sadie?" Anxiety laced McKinley's voice. "What the fuck, Hollis? We had a deal."

Such a fucking Boy Scout.

"Well, we did. But now I'm going out on my own. You happen to have a little piece of insurance I need to stay alive. I figure my girl here can convince you to give it to me with little hassle, so I've come up with a new arrangement."

"She's not your girl," McKinley hissed. "And you're taking a risk meeting me without your crew."

Jason's blood boiled. Not because McKinley was underestimating his skill, but because he was right. Jason could handle himself, but he'd never taken on someone like McKinley on his own. He'd always operated with a troupe of experts.

Fuck him.

He pulled his gun and cocked a round in the chamber, making sure it was right next to the microphone. Then he took aim, right at Mercedes's head.

"Jace, no!" she shrieked, cowering toward the door.

"Should I just end her now?" Jason shouted.

This had the desired effect. "No! What do you want?" McKinley yelled through the line.

A smile coiled on his lips. "Same location in ten minutes. Come alone and unarmed. Nothing missing from the package, or she's dead."

"Wait! I can't get there in ten minutes."

Jason smiled, liking the sound of panic in the bastard's tone. "Yeah, neither can anyone else. That way, I know you're alone."

"Fuck! Fine," Alec conceded. "I need fifteen minutes. She'd better be unharmed, or I swear I'll gut you."

Jason scoffed. "Sure you will, pretty boy. See you in fifteen."

He ended the call, putting the gun away.

Mercedes leaned on the door, her chin quivering.

Shit.

"Hey, babe. You know I was never going to hurt you, right? I had to say that. Otherwise, he wouldn't come." Jason's heart ached to see her so distressed. "We can't start over while he's standing between us."

Mercedes lifted her head, tears streaming down her face. "You don't care about the files, do you?"

He shook his head and smiled. "Not even a little."

Mercedes covered her face with her hands, letting out a sob. Jason reached for her hand, but she shrank away. A flash of anger pulsed in him. He was saving her life, and she was being a little bitch about it.

He started the car, steering away from the residential street.

God damn it. It was one more thing he was going to have to make up for when they got to France.

CHAPTER FIFTY-FOUR

A lec threw the phone into the cupholder, his hand slamming the steering wheel in frustration. Every nerve in his body thrummed with anxious energy.

"Well, at least we don't have to wait for hours," Declan said, the glow of his night vision glasses casting a green light around his face.

The address they'd been given was for an open construction site early in its development. The ground had been cleared, the skeleton of walls surrounded by scaffolding. The team had been in place as soon as it grew dark.

"Artemis, did you copy all that?" Alec said into his earpiece.

"Copy," Cressida responded. "In position."

"Apollo, get the bird up. Give me a signal when you see movement."

"What the hell is he up to?" Declan asked.

Alec shook his head. He was clearly setting a trap. Jason wasn't going to give Mercedes up. The man was obsessed with her. He was also an erratic mess. There was no telling what he had planned.

Declan looked at Alec. "Be careful, mate."

"Aye. Good luck."

Declan pushed the door open and disappeared into the night. Alec only had to wait another five minutes.

"Car approaching from the east," Shake said. "Only two people in it. No one in the surrounding area."

Alec started the car and drove to the dirt lot next to the construction site. When he pulled around, Jason got out of a car ahead and went to the passenger side. Alec's pulse crashed in his ears to see Jason's hand gripping her arm. Mercedes was leaning into him, her walk unsteady.

Alec grabbed the bag containing the prized documents and got out of the car. He put his hands up.

"I'm alone and unarmed," Alec called.

The lights from the car lit up Mercedes's face. A bruise had formed on her cheek, and her face was red and tearstained. "Are you okay?"

"I'm fine." Mercedes's eyes fell to the bag and back to him. She gave a little shake of her head. The tears that filled her eyes told him all he needed to see.

Jason hadn't come for the files. He'd come for Alec.

Alec tossed the bag on the ground and held his hand out to Mercedes. "Sadie, walk to me. You'll be alright."

She only took a step before Jason stopped her. "No, that's not how we're doing this." A sneer broke out on his face. "She's going to choose. Right now."

"What?" Mercedes's eyes flicked between the two.

Dread filled Alec's gut. No way the bastard would let her choose Alec. The confirmation came when Jason pulled the gun and aimed it at Mercedes's head. She tried to squirm away, but Jason's grip tightened on her.

"Hey, hey, wait. I held up my end." Alec put his hands up, fingers widespread.

"I don't give a shit about what's in that bag. Cooper can take a dick," Jason hissed. "Mercedes is going to tell you right now what she told me earlier. That she loves me and wants to be with me. Then I'll put a bullet in your head, and we'll be on our way."

Alec kept his hands up. "So, what if you're wrong and she chooses me?"

"Then she's no good to me, is she?"

Mercedes let out a whimper as the barrel pressed into her temple.

"Don't worry, I'll let you live," Jason said. "After I kill her, I'm going to eat the next bullet myself. That way, you get to live with seeing what's left of us." He turned Mercedes's face to him. "What's it going to be, babe? Alec or you and me?"

Fucking lunatic.

Mercedes jerked her head away and looked at Alec, her eyes wild. He needed Jason to take his fucking gun off her for a second.

"Sadie, it's okay. You can choose him." Alec held her eyes, silently sending her a message to trust him. She frowned, giving a slight shake of her head in resistance.

He narrowed his eyes at her. *Say it.*

She blinked and took a trembling breath. "Okay, okay, Jason. Let's just go."

"Say it," Jason growled. "Say you love me."

Her eyes flashed to Alec. His nod was so slight, he wasn't sure she saw it. "I do. I love you, Jason. Take me out of here."

Jason's eyes lit up. A smile broke out on his face.

The second the gun shifted away from Mercedes, Alec lifted his arm and closed his fist.

Two shots came from the night.

The impacts jerked through Jason's chest. His grin twisted into confusion. The gun dropped from his hand. Alec closed the distance, taking him to the dirt, and pummeled him with a fist. Jason's face broke open. The smell of blood hit the air.

Two bullet wounds in his body, and Jason wouldn't relent. He twisted and bucked, trying to free himself of Alec's weight. Alec grasped his throat and squeezed. Jason gagged and kicked, clawing at Alec's face, nearly catching his eye.

Fucker.

Alec jabbed two fingers into an entry wound, digging into raw, open flesh. Jason spasmed in a choking cry, his face turning red. Alec dug in harder, the walls of the injury tearing. Jason fell limp under him, but he didn't let up. Thick blood pumped from the wound.

"Alec. Alec!" A distant voice pulled him back. "You have to stop. We got him."

The world snapped back. Jason wasn't moving. Declan's knee came down on Jason's chest while Mason worked to secure him. The second they had him, Alec jumped up and ran to Mercedes. He nearly knocked her off her feet, clutching her to him.

"I thought it was you." Her voice was shrill. "I heard the gunshots and thought he got you. I don't know what I would have done."

"Shhh," he soothed. "I know, my love. I've got you."

Alec held her close, relief washing over him. His gaze shot to where Declan and Mason were bent over Jason's limp form. With any luck, the bastard was already dead.

Alec stepped back, taking stock of her injuries.

"Let me see you. Are you sure you're okay?"

A cracking came through his earpiece. "—movement to the north of you." Shake's voice broke through. "Do you copy? Ren? Matrix? Do you copy? Shit."

A beam of red light flashed from the scaffold above. Its endpoint was Mercedes's heart.

"Sniper!" he shouted, throwing himself on Mercedes's body.

It hit him like a sledgehammer. Pain screamed through his abdomen. Alec dragged Mercedes behind a piece of construction equipment and fell on top of her, her head tucked into his arms. Gunfire erupted, the sound of bullets pelting around them. It stopped as quickly as it started.

The sirens were close now, lights flashing on the skeletal walls.

New voices shouted commands.

The whooshing sounds in his ears grew louder, drowning out Mercedes's screams for Mason to help. Strong arms pulled him off Mercedes. His head slumped, seeming to weigh fifty pounds. Mason tore his shirt open. Agony dulled to a bone-deep ache.

Mercedes's tearstained face was nearby, talking to him in calm tones.

"I love you, Sadie," he said before the world disappeared.

CHAPTER FIFTY-FIVE

The damn beeping was back.

Mercedes lay in a bed, a curtain blocking her view of the world around her. Her mind and body were completely numb, listless with pain and grief. The nurses had given her a sedative. She welcomed its dullness. The pain she could feel was enough to bear.

If he wasn't already gone, he would be soon.

We need to be ready, Declan had said.

Never. She'd never be ready.

The incessant beeping. If she could move, she'd throw the damn thing into the hall. But she couldn't move. So she lay on her side, her eyes focused on the ugly curtain, waiting for the words she knew were coming. The words that would utterly destroy her.

When the curtain moved, Declan peeked around it. His eyes were red-rimmed, but he smiled at her. Pulling a chair to the side of her bed, he took her hand and swept a lock of hair off her cheek.

Tears pooled in her eyes. "He's dead. Isn't he?"

"Nah, lass. He's still fighting." Declan exhaled sharply, keeping his own emotions at bay.

She frowned at him, the words not making sense in the fog.

"They've finished up surgery now and moved him to the ICU. He'll need time to heal."

"He's going to be okay?"

Declan nodded. "Aye. They feel pretty good about him pulling through."

Once the tears started, they wouldn't stop. Declan gathered her up in his arms, her body wracked with sobs. His sniffs matched hers. They probably looked a mess.

"We can't see him tonight. It's well after midnight, and they're getting him settled." Declan pulled away. "They aren't admitting you, so you're free to go. C'mon, I'll take you home."

"I don't have a home."

"Well, you have one for now. You need a shower and proper sleep. We'll be back first thing."

Declan decided to take her to Alec's apartment. Not only because it was closer to the hospital, but because she might rest better around Alec's things.

Mercedes had never seen Alec's home. At least not outside of a video screen.

This is his space. She could feel him here.

Alec's bedroom was warm yet subdued in its decor. A double bed took up most of the room, with a small dresser in the corner. A fluffy dark blue duvet covered a goose down comforter with blue and white pillows. A single chest of drawers matched the simple bed frame.

A few pictures dotted the room. One caught her eye. It was a picture of the two of them at Charlotte and Luke's wedding.

They made quite a couple. The best man and the maid of honor. They had danced together for the couple's first dance, and she'd had just enough whisky to lower her inhibitions. His blue eyes were vivid, his smile mischievous.

"I used to have this picture," she said. "I gave it to Charlie after Jason came along."

Declan came up next to her. "He was pretty far gone on you before you even stepped on the plane home. He didn't think it was possible to connect with someone the way he did with you."

That makes two of us.

After her shower, she pulled back the covers and snuggled into the nest of downy fluff. The scent of Alec was everywhere, lulling her to sleep. She dreamed of the laughing photograph and wished beyond anything she could be there with him again.

CHAPTER FIFTY-SIX

Mercedes and Declan returned to the hospital as early as the nurses would allow. As much as she'd tried to prepare herself, it was a shock to see Alec. The black of his hair contrasted sharply with the pallor of his skin. Anxiety tore through Mercedes. She didn't want false hope that he'd be okay.

She only left the room when the police or FBI agents wanted to talk to her. Declan stayed by her side through the interviews. Even after they assigned a security detail to her, she relied on Declan to make sure she was safe.

Alec's family arrived the following morning. They were the sweetest of people, but Mercedes knew nothing about being in a real family.

"Hey Auntie, Katie," Declan led Mercedes to where they waited outside the room. "You remember Sadie Elliott, Charlotte's sister?"

It was clear they knew exactly who she was. Mercedes's heart thundered in her chest as she tried to pull a smile on her lips.

They have to hate me. It was her fault Alec was in this condition.

"Oh, aye." Moira McKinley studied Mercedes's face, her green eyes skimming over the bruises on her cheek. "You poor thing. It's so good to see you again, lass." She pulled Mercedes into a warm hug. Tears pricked the back of Mercedes's eyes. She'd never been with a man who had a loving mother.

Katie, Alec's younger sister, watched Mercedes with interest. Katie was gorgeous, with long black hair and deep blue eyes like her brother's. She was quite shy, her face drawn with the stress of her brother's condition.

Alec was kept sedated to help him heal. Since space was limited in his room, Mercedes spent most of the day in the waiting room. She didn't mind, as long as Alec wasn't alone.

Mercedes used her time to plan her next steps. First, she'd get her money out of the investments she had made with Jason. It might take a little time, but she'd have a good deal of money to set up her new life in London.

That afternoon, while she and Declan sat in the waiting room, a slender Black man in a business suit made his way to them.

"I thought nothing could get you to come back to London." Declan stood. "Sadie, this is Nick Kessler, with the FBI. We go way back."

Mercedes shook his hand. "I'm sorry for the loss of your agent. He seemed like a good man."

"Thank you. And I'm sorry for all that's happened. I was hoping you wouldn't mind sitting down with me so we can go over a few things."

"Am I going to need my lawyer?" It wasn't the first time she'd asked that.

"I don't think so, but I'd like to talk in a more secure setting. The hospital's letting us use their conference room if you wouldn't mind coming this way."

Mercedes traded a glance with Declan. There wasn't much more to say. But she wanted to cooperate, so they followed him.

Nick sat across from her, his expression apologetic. "I'm not sure if anyone conveyed this to you, but Jason Hollis survived surgery and is currently recovering in the ICU."

A shiver ran down Mercedes's spine. "Thank you, yes. They've been updating me." It turned her stomach to think of Jason recovering on the same floor as Alec.

"We want to thank you for delivering the documents to us. We've briefly gone through them, and I gotta say, they're incredibly damning. Unfortunately, we have a problem."

She shared a look with Declan. "What kind of problem? I gave you everything I had."

"You did. But the more we look at this, the more we think you need to be in the WITSEC program."

Her heart bottomed out. *Oh god, no.*

"The Witness Protection Program?" Panic welled in her chest. "That's a massive overreaction, don't you think?"

"This is a pretty fluid situation, Ms. Elliott. This case is . . . complex. But we don't think this is an overreaction."

She tapped on the table, trying to calm her nerves. "You have Jason in custody. Right? Can't that be enough?"

"He is, and no doubt Jason was a major threat to you." Nick leaned toward her, speaking quietly. "But we know it was never Jason Hollis in charge, but Marcus Cooper himself. And his reach is extensive. Just look at how he compromised our embassy. They knew our plans, killed our agent, and removed a witness without even breaking a sweat."

"But I have nothing of actual value to offer about Cooper."

Nick's brow furrowed. "You're not a criminal attorney, but you know that isn't true."

He was right. Mara Donovan was presumed alive but hadn't been located. Without her, Mercedes became the key witness. Cooper hadn't hidden his part in it all because he thought she'd be dead by now. That red laser had been aimed at her, not Alec.

Mercedes shook her head. "When the time comes, I'll return to the US to testify. But I am *not* leaving Alec. I just got him back." Mercedes stood and gathered her things. Declan joined her, silent in his support.

"Mercedes, please think this through. Alec can no longer protect you. Cooper has too much to lose here. It is only a matter of time before they come for you." Nick stood as well, looking between Mercedes and Declan. "You have a few days to decide."

"I already decided. I'll make myself available for depositions and whatever else is needed. But I'm staying in London."

CHAPTER FIFTY-SEVEN

Space was limited next to Alec's bed, so Mercedes waited in the hall, her fingers tapping on the armrest. The doctors were confident he'd make a full recovery, but it wouldn't be real to her until she talked to him. The nurses warned them he'd be disoriented when they pulled him from the drugs. That was fine, as long as Alec was in there.

Declan sat next to her. He rarely left her side. He did it for Alec, and she loved him for it.

"Mercedes?" Katie's soft voice came out of the room. Her eyes were rimmed with red, but she was smiling. "He's awake. He wants to see you."

The breath rushed from Mercedes's lungs as she hurried into the room.

Although his eyes were closed, the frown on Alec's face deepened. His hand raised up weakly, only to fall back to the bed with a soft thud. Mercedes took his hand in hers, squeezing it in reassurance.

"Shh, I'm right here, shh," she soothed, brushing the backs of her fingers over his cheek. His chest eased, and his breathing slowed. He squeezed her hand weakly. Tears sprang to her eyes. It was his first real response to her voice in days.

"Okay?" he rasped, his voice barely loud enough for her to hear him.

"Yeah. Just a little banged up. Everyone else is okay too. You're the one we're worried about." She stroked his forehead. A bead of sweat had formed on his brow.

"Jason?" he whispered.

"He's alive. The Americans and Brits are fighting over who gets him first."

"Damn, hoped we'd killed him."

"Afraid not."

A faint smile played over his lips. He nodded an acknowledgment.

Mercedes didn't want to let him go, but one look at Moira McKinley made her relent.

"I want to spend every moment with you, but your mom needs to love on you for a while. I'll be close by, I promise. And Dec's with me. Okay?"

Alec smiled again. "I love you," she whispered, giving him a lingering kiss on his forehead. Moira shot Mercedes a look of gratitude before she bent over her son, murmuring to him.

Mercedes rejoined Declan in the doorway, watching Alec's family. The familiarity with which they touched him made her ache for a family like theirs.

CHAPTER FIFTY-EIGHT

Alec had moments when he felt like a truck had hit him. It was mostly in the evenings after his family had been to see him. Mercedes was so patient, but Alec could tell she was struggling. He loved his family, but he craved time with her. He didn't want her to go through it on her own.

This evening, Mercedes had run to the cafeteria to grab something to eat. He lay back in bed, hoping to catch a little rest while she was out.

A knock at the door roused him. Nick Kessler peeked into the room. Alec waved him in, sitting up. He had a feeling he knew why Nick was there.

"How are you feeling, man?" Nick's warm brown eyes were sympathetic.

"Getting better every day." Alec smiled back at his friend, extending his hand to shake Nick's.

"That's good. We were sure worried about you for a time." Nick cleared his throat. "I'm here about Mercedes." When Alec didn't comment, Nick continued, "She isn't safe, Alec. At all. Every day that she's out in public, she's at risk."

"And you want to put her in your Witness Protection Program?" Alec responded.

Nick didn't seem surprised Alec already knew. "We don't want to. We need to if she's going to survive."

"Why is she so valuable to Cooper?"

"I don't know how much she's shared with you about her time in their custody, but Cooper met with her directly. He asked for the stolen data and admitted it was damaging. He ordered his men to assault her and send the video to you." Nick paused. "Her testimony and the evidence she gave us can *literally* take down a multi-billion-dollar pharmaceutical company. And we haven't even started on the list of corrupt officials involved."

Damn.

"Does she know this?"

"Of course, she does. She's a damn good lawyer. It's not a question of if, but rather when."

"So, you're talking to me about this because . . ."

"She's refusing to go. My guess is you have something to do with that."

Alec wasn't going to pretend not to understand Nick. "You want me to convince her to go."

"Yeah, and quickly."

Alec's heart rate picked up. "How quickly?"

"I have to be on a plane back to the States late tomorrow night. If she's going to take the offer, she needs to be on the flight with me."

Tomorrow? The pit in his stomach grew, and he closed his eyes.

Nick winced. "I know. It's not an easy thing. But my boss is eager to get her hidden. She's incredibly exposed here."

"How long would she be in the program?"

"Depends on how long until the trial. Could be as long as a year and a half."

Unacceptable. "Can I go with her?"

"Not unless you get married, but in your condition, you'd be a liability."

Alec would marry Mercedes in a heartbeat, but Nick was right. He could barely stand, much less fight off an attack. And he was going to need a lot of therapy to get his body functional.

Nick walked to the door. "Please think about it. I know you want what's best for her. That's what I want too."

Alec sat in his quiet room, heaviness pushing him down. When Mercedes breezed in carrying takeout containers, he smiled at the brightness of her eyes and the flush in her cheeks. She was so beautiful. He ached to touch her, to be with her for every painful moment. But he had to do what was best for her.

"Hey, you." Sitting on the bed next to him, Mercedes leaned in for a kiss. Alec pulled her to him, letting the kiss linger. She snuggled up to him, careful not to jar the bed too much.

Something must have looked off in his face because she paused and frowned.

"Everything okay?" She pressed her hand to his forehead. "Are you getting chills?"

"Darling, I'm alright." Alec took her hand and kissed it. "Nick came by."

"Did he?" Her tone darkened as she read his face. "And what did you two decide?"

"Sadie . . ." She pulled her hand away from his and looked away. "I can't decide anything for you." He cupped her face, guiding her to look at him. "But I also can't protect you. I don't know what I'd do if something happened to you because I was too laid up to stop it."

"So, you want me to leave then?" Mercedes blinked away unshed tears.

Alec thought his heart would break. "I don't want you to leave. God, it hurts to even think about it. But I think you have to. Cooper isn't going to let it go."

"I can't," she whispered, her hazel eyes wide with pain.

"You can." Alec pulled her to him. "You've been through so much. Asking you to do it isn't fair. But you *can* do this."

Mercedes sniffed, burrowing against his shoulder.

"Will you think on it tonight? You'd have to leave tomorrow night." His voice broke.

She shot up. "*Tomorrow?*"

Alec's throat tightened. "Aye."

"I'm not leaving you tomorrow."

"Sadie, I'll be okay, but I have a long road to recover from this. If I can't keep you safe, I have to give you to someone who can."

Mercedes lay against his chest. "Can't we go back to Scotland?"

"I wish we could." There was nothing he wanted more. But they had to face reality. There was no other option but to put their lives on hold for a little longer.

CHAPTER FIFTY-NINE

It was the end. Mercedes had denied it as long as she could, but the truth was clear. She'd have to go.

Mercedes stood in Alec's bedroom, her heart weighed down, knowing it would be months, maybe years, before they shared a bed again. The hollowness was more than she'd expected.

In her hand, she held the neck of her violin. It seemed heavier than usual. There would be a lot of goodbyes today.

Last night, after she left the hospital, she spoke to Nick and two federal marshals who would escort her to her new life. The rules were explained. Her cage was primed. She only had to step into it.

Mercedes Elliott would be scrubbed away. Music, in general, would be kept to a minimum. The violin was not to be used at all. Too identifiable.

She placed the instrument against Alec's pillow. If she couldn't be herself wherever she was going, she might as well leave that piece of her here. Alec would take good care of it.

Once she'd made the decision, everything moved quickly. She was grateful for Declan's quiet presence as she processed how much was changing overnight. Again.

When they arrived at the hospital corridor, Declan stopped and turned to her. "I arranged for the family to be away, so you'll have him all to yourself. Nick and the marshals will be here soon to take you to the airport."

It wasn't enough time. The anticipation of it was nearly as hard as the thought of getting on that plane.

She gave Declan a hug. "Thank you for everything you've done," Mercedes whispered into his shoulder. "You'll take good care of him?"

"Always, lass."

Alec was reading when she came into the room. "Ah, there you are." He grinned at her from over his book. "I thought you'd decided not to come back to say goodbye. Glad I was wrong."

Mercedes bit her lip, tears tingling in her eyes. They had this one final moment before their worlds shifted apart again.

Alec's smile faded, and he reached his hand out to her. Gently, she snuggled next to him, his arms wrapped tight around her. "If you could go anywhere in the world, where would you want to go?" Alec said.

"Are you coming with me?"

"Of course."

"Mmm…I don't know. There's this lovely little river house in Scotland I know about." Mercedes tilted her head up to look at him. A smile played on his lips as he considered this choice.

"I'm pretty partial to that particular place as well." His eyes lost in a thought.

"What about you? Where would you want to take me if you could pick anywhere in the world?"

Alec's smile became wistful. "I'd want to go to see where you grew up."

"San Francisco?"

"Aye, I missed out on that trip. I've always wanted to be there with you. To see where wee Sadie Elliott played violin in the park. Visit all your favorite places. It would be like a little look into you."

"That sounds amazing."

When he spoke again, his voice no longer held the mirth it had before. "I didn't think this would be so hard."

Mercedes sat up on her elbow facing him, her fingers laced in his. "We should probably talk."

Alec's eyes shifted to wariness. "About what?"

Mercedes took in a breath and hoped it was enough to give her the courage she'd need for what came next.

"A case like this can drag on for at least a year, if not two. I won't be able to call or even write a letter. You and I wouldn't have a real relationship." She took a shuddering breath. "I think we should end this now."

"Is that what you want?" Alec's voice had grown husky.

"God, no." A tear left a trail on her cheek.

His brow furrowed. "Then why?"

"Because what I want doesn't matter. If someone else came into your life. Someone you wanted to be with…" Her throat tightened. "It'd be selfish of me to ask you to wait."

Alec's gaze fell to their hands. "Alright," he agreed.

The finality of it cracked Mercedes's heart into a thousand pieces.

"Okay." She shifted, ready to let him go, but Alec tightened his hold, keeping her close.

"Then I'll be the selfish one," he said, his voice thick with emotion. "Stay in love with me. Tell me you'll be mine through it all. And when it's over, come home." The anguish in his cobalt eyes was more than she could bear.

Tears blurred her vision. "Alec…"

"I won't want anyone else." His lips brushed hers. "I love you, Sadie."

"I love you." She held back a sob. "So much."

"Then I'll wait forever, aye?"

At her nod, Alec exhaled sharply, and he kissed her, slowly

at first. Heat ignited through her body. He groaned and deepened it, stroking her tongue with gentle lashes.

He pulled away, his breathing rough. "I have to stop. Otherwise, I'm afraid we'll scandalize the nurses."

Mercedes laughed and curled up against his chest, careful not to jostle him.

A soft knock at the door dropped out her heart. Alec's arm tightened around her. Nick Kessler opened the door and peeked his head in.

"I'm sorry, guys, but we need to be going." Mercedes felt Alec nod, and the door clicked closed. She was slow to move away, wanting each touch to last.

Alec's blue eyes were glossy with tears. "You've been through so much, but you are stronger than you know. We're going to get through this."

Mercedes kissed him one last time, memorizing the feel of him. Then she sat up and slipped off the bed. She looked back at him, still paler than she'd like to see him, but beautiful. Strong. Alive.

"I love you."

Alec's smile broke. "I love you too."

Mercedes turned and walked out the door, leaving a piece of her behind. The click of the latch rang out, snipping the final thread to her old life.

MERCEDES AND ALEC WILL RETURN
IN "THE LIES THAT SHATTER"
AUTUMN 2021

Pre-order the ebook of *The Lies That Shatter* on Amazon, or look for paperbacks and hardbacks at your favorite retailer.

ACKNOWLEDGMENTS

What a crazy ride this has been!

Back in the summer of 2019, I finally broke down and started writing one of the stories in my head. For some reason, Alec and Sadie would not stop nagging me!

One on-going pandemic later (suck it 2020) and I'm finally taking the huge step of putting my book baby into the world. Eeek!

There are so many people to thank for helping me along the way. It's hard to know where to start.

I think I'll start with my amazing Alpha readers. Without you, I never would have braved letting anyone read my work. Like, ever. Your encouragement meant everything to me and I can't thank you enough for wading through all the rookie mistakes and plot holes.

My angel Alphas are; Greer, Garnet, Renee, and Hope. I love you ladies so much!

Then there are my lovely Beta readers. I can't thank you enough for volunteering your time to read a new author's work and provide feedback on it. I am so grateful for your amazing words. Some of you legitimately made me cry.

I want to send a special shout out to my British beta readers, without whom, Alec would have talked about jello and had a garbage disposal.

My beautiful Betas were; Emily, Jessica, Dixie, Mary, Maxine, Ashlyn, Charlotte, Crystal, Natalie, Chantice, Sara H., Colette, Nerys, and Sarah R. I can never thank you all enough!

Thank you to my editors, Stefanie and April at Salt and Sage. I appreciate your attention to detail. Especially since I am so bad at using commas properly.

Thank you to Robynne and Damon at Damonza for the beautiful cover. It's a perfect blend of romance and suspense. I love it!

To my kiddos- Thank you for not laughing too hard when you'd find me snoozing at my desk in the middle of the night and for just being amazing all the time. This year has been really hard and I love you all for your strength.

To my husband Dominic for encouraging me to pursue this crazy path. I honestly don't know what I would do without you. I love you.

And to the readers- Thank you for taking the time to read this labor of love. I truly hope you enjoyed it. I can't wait to share more of this story with you all soon!

ABOUT THE AUTHOR

American writer AV Asher (Avie) was one of those kids always who got in trouble for reading in class. She has been creating stories since childhood, but only recently began writing them down. *The Truth Keeps Silent* is Avie's debut novel. The second book in the duet, *The Lies That Shatter*, is expected to be released in the Autumn of 2021. Avie lives in Northern Nevada with her husband and three children.

amazon.com/~/e/B08Y64CX66

facebook.com/av.asher.author

twitter.com/av_asher_author

instagram.com/av.asher.author

WHERE TO FIND ME!

Want exclusive updates? Sign up for my newsletter at
www.avasher.com.

Instagram: @av.asher.author
Facebook: @av.asher.author
Twitter: @av_asher_author

Be sure to add Truth and Lies to your TBR list!

Printed in Great Britain
by Amazon